The Lightbringer's Sigil

The EarthZero Evolution, Volume 1

Dave Newton and Todd King

Published by Anshadar, LLC, 2019.

THE LIGHTBRINGER'S SIGIL

First edition. March 13, 2019.

Copyright © 2019 Dave Newton and Todd King.

ISBN: 978-1732980280

Written by Dave Newton and Todd King.

PROLOGUE

eVo.143.999.mOd.112.sCe.11235812 | EARTH | THE END OF ALL THINGS

THERE WAS A TEARING noise, out of proportion with anything natural: a rending and ripping that could have been the sound of massively amplified guitars stroked with jagged nails in ecstatic abandon, except this sound was far too loud for any earthly venue, and it was accompanied by a crack in the sky fifty miles long. Blackness rent the cloudless blue Southern California sky as the interdimensional crack ripped like lightning, never fading, but growing by the moment. An airplane, unable to change its flightpath in time, flew into the massive gap of nothing and was no more.

The tearing evolved into a preternatural shriek that shattered windshields and plate glass from one end of Los Angeles to the other. Freeways full of commuters buckled, buildings of steel and glass toppled from Orange County to Ventura, and the resulting megaquake, a product of the shriek's hateful resonance, sheared away the Palos Verdes peninsula. As it sank into the Pacific, the ensuing tsunami sent destruction from Long Beach to Disneyland.

From the widening maw in the sky issued a moan, heard and felt all the way to Death Valley, where it joined with that from the crack over Las Vegas. The sounds formed an acoustic resonance that built upon itself until the shrieking, ripping moan shook the ground all the way to the Gulf of California. And then *they* came.

They fell from the crack with spread wings and gaping jaws, the legions of death came. The size of the creatures was not apparent until they reached the ground, crushing houses, and roaring in fury as they devoured every living thing in their path. Millions upon millions of the creatures swarmed the sky and land, feeding not only on flesh and blood, but also the screams and psychic energy of all the inhabitants within the region. Vegetation withered, and waterways filled with dust, blood, and offal from the onslaught.

As fear, pain, and death spread through Southern California, the cries of the victims joined with the screams of the predators and the moaning sky to form a discordant cacophony marking the beginning of the end.

By the time any meaningful military response could be brought to bear, the number of Death Horde warriors already through the interdimensional rifts made short work of any jets, missiles, or tactical armaments that the defenders could muster. What technology the Earth had to offer in defense was easily overwhelmed by the savage forces from the sky.

All around the globe, the same pattern of destruction reduced civilization and humanity to ashes and ruin. In a matter of hours, the Earth was a shattered husk, devoid of life and left adrift in the shadow of a blood red moon.

...

zEt.0 | THE ZEROTIME | THE UNION OF SOULS

IN CRUCIFORM REPOSE, his nine chakras seamlessly woven into those of the cosmos itself, Helel the Shining One dispassionately observed the final fate of his $143{,}999^{th}$ Celestial Shaping.

The Death Horde – the Vanth'Vash'Var, the Sentinels of the Anti-Life, the Lords of the Void – had despoiled the simulation, its prime Earth falling victim for the $143{,}999^{th}$ time to the Horde's superior technology, superior aggression, and superior puissance in the ways of war.

Again, Helel thought as his virtual presence in the simulation shifted to that of a meta-view, enabling him to perceive the entire universe. *Always, each and every time, the same ending.*

And thus it was, as the End Game routines fired, initiating cosmic Armageddon via an ultra-massive array of galactic-scale singularities; a cross-hatched nightmare of black holes appearing abruptly, absurdly, on all possible grid points in the universe. He watched, jaded, as the singularities, pulsing as one, emitted symmetrical, antipodal jets of white light, the data-rich jets gradually evaporating until nothing but darkness remained, officially terminating the scenario.

Now, in the place of light without heat, far above the Source, far beyond the Void, Helel was back in the ZeroTime, the home of the Children of the Light. Here, in the massive Union of Souls, he was once more physically among his peers, one among many millions of realized, immortal souls-made-flesh currently extant and officially recognized in the noosphere of the ZeroTime. This was the place of Metacosmic Instantiation, where Celestial Shapers, like Helel, worked ceaselessly on their divinely appointed task: the infinite and omnipresent celestial shaping of the Ontopoietic Cosmogenesis Simulation.

A virtually innumerable count of cosmic simulations had been performed. Never yet had any simulation made it past the critical End Game point. Not just his simulations, which were over one hundred thousand in number, but all simulations from all of the Celestial Shapers throughout all 144,000 of the concentric, circular tiers of the Union of Souls; the tiers having room for 14,400 Shapers each, and always the tiers being filled to capacity. So many simulations, so many deaths. So many uncounted, wasted souls.

The silvery sheen of his personally incorporated Zen-Sidhe warped and billowed for a moment around Helel's form like a giant soap bubble in a gentle breeze. Their communion severed, the Zen-Sidhe neatly reduced its diameter until it was approximately the size of his eye, then phased into the middle of his forehead, returning to rest within his eighth chakra.

Helel gazed around at the thousands upon thousands of silver Zen-Sidhe that rested in the concentric, circular tiers which rose from the electric blue vector grid of the virtual floor to the top of the perfectly reflexive vault of the great spheroidal construct. He certainly could appreciate the inherent aesthetics, the elegant yet exacting design within designs, the pure fractals and brilliant holographic bindings.

Everything was of course beautiful, efficient, and, unfortunately, entirely predictable.

Ontopoiesis, especially at the cosmic level, required more rigor than this, he thought, and the sophomoric cosmogenic scenarios, even collectively in their trillions upon trillions, contributed nothing more than an occasional statistical tick to the probability of anyone actually moving past the dread End Game state. Trillions of distinct universes, nurtured from birth to empower a specific generation of descendants to succeed in but a single task, yet still, failure.

But not this time. For Helel's next run, the $144,000^{th}$, would not be yet another cosmos aborted before it ever was born, he thought ruefully. A cold smile froze on his serene face as he willed the now recharged Zen-Sidhe to life once more, summoning it from his eighth chakra. This time, he would seed the proverbial cosmic womb with his own carefully min/maxed players and game pieces, the ones which he was convinced could be used to hack the winning conditions of the great cosmic game. He would break the rules in order to make them truly immortal. Powerful, their chakras would transcend the mortal boundary of a mere seven. There would be true Hekatek, the hybrid of magick and technomagick. There would be both Null and Void, the physically incarnate Omega variants of each. Two unique souls, who would catalyze the other players and pieces on the cosmic chessboard of the First Cause itself, guiding them to transcendence, and, ultimately, to victory. Finally, the One Above would lose.

So, Helel began again, his destiny to fulfill as he struggled to do the impossible: Defeat God.

The Lightbringer's Sigil

Part 1

13.8 Billion Years Later

eVo.144.000.mOd.0.sCe.0 | EARTH | UNITED STATES | CALIFORNIA | MOUNTAIN VIEW | SETI

JANICE PULLED INTO the parking lot at 5:45 AM and parked her aging Subaru in the closest space near the front door. Grabbing her briefcase, she slid out of her seat and walked hurriedly across the lot and past the large SETI Institute sign. Fumbling her keys in the predawn light, she let herself in, locking the door behind her.

"Goddamn VOEvents," she muttered for the hundredth time. She resolved to have a talk with the programmers about the system that sent out automated texts every time a transient phenomenon was noticed. She was beyond pissed this morning; her phone had started going off at around 2:30 AM and hadn't stopped since. Janice had logged in to the VPN and checked the data, comparing it to the other messages as they came in, with the same result.

Due to budget cuts, she couldn't even pass off this stupid task to someone else. *I mean who even bothers with radio signals now, when there were so many other, more reasonable ways to gather useful data?* That science-denying assclown in Washington and his filthy carpetbaggers had cut so much from the Institute, Janice was surprised that anything worthwhile was being done at SETI. The radio astronomy group was reduced to a skeleton crew, and the Allen Telescope Array up in Hat Creek had unresolved technical problems with not enough engineers to fix them all.

Moving through the break room, Janice turned on the lights and turned on the Keurig, even as her phone chimed to indicate another text. While the coffee brewed, she sent yet another message to Randy the SysAdmin, but knew the lazy bastard was probably ignoring her while he got one last go at his boyfriend. She wouldn't see him for a few hours, and by then, it would be moot.

She took her coffee into her office, woke up her PC, and started the download processor. Fucking seventeen texts, seventeen anomalies. The mainframe algorithm must have glitched and re-sent the same message.

"Probably another squirrel on the transformer, blew the power and bounced the process." Janice grimaced as the data came streaming in, screens and screens full of XML. She rubbed her eyes and examined the source data. And noticed that the timestamps were not the same. In fact, the data each had similar, but not exact checksums.

"Holy..."

Janice stood, knocking her coffee cup off the desk, sending shards of porcelain and rivers of coffee across the tile floor. She picked up the handset of her desk phone and rapidly dialed a number, even as her cell phone pinged again.

"Molongo, this is Jake," came the heavy accented Australian voice.

"Yeah, Jake, this is Janice Murphy at SETI. I need you to check something for me. I'm going to give you some coordinates and I'd like you to see if you are getting the same thing I am. Ready?"

"Oh, g'day, Janice! Haven't heard from you in forever. How are—"

"Look Jake, I don't have time to chit-chat. I've been getting a series of VOEvents, and I need to make sure these are legit. Can you just check this for me? Should be on your horizon by now."

"Sure, sure, Janice. Pass them over."

Later, as the morning sun began stretching through the blinds and across the wall, a shocked Janice hung up and dialed another number, one reserved for only specific occasions.

"Sir, I have a confirmation. We have a repeating signal, verified by Molongo Observatory. Something is sending us a message. Yes sir. I understand, sir."

Once the man on the other end had hung up, Janice sat heavily in her chair and exhaled a long, shuddering breath. Of course they would continue to monitor the message from space. Because the world had just changed. *Everything* had changed.

Aliens were calling.

eVo.144.000.mOd.0.sCe.1 | EARTH | UNITED STATES | ALABAMA | HUNTSVILLE

CORY CHRISTOPHER TATE was rudely roused from his dreamless slumber by an insistent *meow-meow!* pinging from his Samsung smartphone. The sound from his phone aurally flogged him with its digitally sampled, sickeningly sweet kitten calls until, finally, mercifully, the *meow-meow!* stopped and went to voice mail.

"Not in right now," he heard himself say, ruing the day he had installed the "Out Loud" app which forced the phone's normally silent answering mode to play – *whaddya know?* – out loud. "Name and number after the tone, and I'll get back to you soon as I can."

Cory forgave himself the fact that, indeed, the "tone" had been yet another *meow-meow!* once he heard Jennie Torres' voice. "Cory, it's me, Jennie. Check the online repository. Special package. Need your attention ASAP. Sorry to bother you so early, but it's—"

He quickly picked up the phone. "Jennie! Wait, don't hang up."

"Wasn't planning on it, Cory. You know I love to talk to you."

"Same here, Jennie," he said, snagging his Apple MacBook 4K from the empty side of his bed. "Gimme a sec, getting my laptop ready," he told her. A few seconds later, after establishing connection to the Deep Oracle Extra-Set Repository, one of Cory's customized scripts evaluated the files in the repository, then automatically updated the file. Noting that the new file did not download almost immediately, he scanned the incoming data bar on the browser. "It's a few terabytes. What the heck?"

"It's a good bit of data. Just need you to check it and confirm it."

Cory noticed the tone in her voice. He was always quick to pick up on such things. "Jennie, what's wrong? Don't tell me we got de-funded and you're doing a source dump on me."

She laughed nervously. "Not yet. And no dump. They keep trying, but we keep clinging to the edge of the cliff. While they keep stomping on our fingers."

"I know, I know," Cory sympathized with her, marveling at the massive incoming XML and binary streams spewing onto the newly created "Daily Dump" folder. From there, most of the processing would remain hidden, as Cory seldom used programmatic UIs himself. The end result would be nothing more than a glorified popup screen with a few figures and numbers on it. A proper programmatic UI awaited him if he wished to continue from that point, which, usually, he did not, though this particular data set might be an exception. "I think MorthonTech does that as a matter of rote, because they're corporate ass hats, and that's how they think they have to get the job done. At least it's not purely NASA. Or DoD." An exciting chill ran up his spine. This much data, combined with what he'd been hearing today on the rumor mill ...*No way, no way, no way!*

Cory shifted the phone to speaker, and set it down next to his laptop, which sat atop his covered legs. "Switching to speaker," he told her. "Give me a second, and I can get this done and returned to you in just a few minutes."

"Really? Holy shit, Cory," she laughed. "Even Deep Oracle can't run it that fast."

"How long did its primary run take?" he asked.

"Most of the day today. I mean, yesterday, now. I've been up all night doing more primary runs and filtered/gated runs for comps and diffs. So however long ago that was."

"Did you get this data set straight from VOEvent through Deep Oracle, or through Janice's filters?"

"Erm, at least one of those?" They were way beyond proprietary information and non-disclosures, but Jennie didn't want to come right out and say it. Even though she was sure that Cory already knew. He had the quickest mind she had ever encountered, and she had rubbed elbows with the best and brightest at both NASA and in Silicon Valley. She always had thought that it was just terrible that he was such an introvert. Maybe even more than that, she had to admit, knowing that getting information out of Cory about Cory was about like getting a pearl from an oyster with advanced lockjaw. She knew he could have done so much more with his life and could have been very happy and personally satisfied doing it, were it not for his antisocial tendencies. What a waste.

"Okay," Cory laughed back. "I won't pry. I'll just mention that my sources say that, sometime very recently, we got a series of fast repeaters that look pretty interesting."

"Understatement of the year," she said under breath. "And frag your sources, you hacker," she said, her voice a bit louder. "You're neck deep in the astro community anyway, and you've got access to the same online sources that we do. You've probably got all the VOEvent stuff already parsed, and you're just yanking my chain. All that bullshit you push! You're lucky I knew you from school. And how come you're able to go through this data faster than Deep Oracle itself? That's a bloody hack if I've ever heard of one."

"Just my normal laptop," he replied, initiating several unnamed, color-coded program icons that sat among dozens of similarly unnamed ones on his laptop's desktop UI. He had them all memorized, and if they were started out of order, the 'normal' laptop would lock. "And you know I don't have access to all of your sources, normally. Besides, it's not the size of your CPU, it's the way you use your algorithms. And mine have evolved and improved over the past few years since we initiated Deep Oracle."

"Don't mean to rush, but please hurry," Jennie pleaded through bleary eyes. She gave a quick glance outside her office's window. "The office is crawling with people, even at this time of night, because of the event. And I don't recognize everyone here. I'm exhausted, and I think I'm getting paranoid, because some of them really don't look like scientists or techies."

"Hang in there. You're two hours behind me, so it's not that late. Not yet, anyway. I'll have this in a minute, Jennie, just hang on."

Cory had given Jennie the concept of Deep Oracle a few years back, thinking that she'd not really taken him seriously until, miraculously, she had informed him that MorthonTech had elected to finance the project, no strings attached, and, also miraculously, get it implemented *in situ* at Ames. Cory had suspected that either Professor Gilmour or his own friend, M. K. "Maynard" James, had hooked them up with MorthonTech, but both had denied it. Both had also, for the one millionth time, told Cory that he should finally go straight, get out from the shelter of his comfy man cave, and quite possibly get a real job, where he could put his insane computer skills to good use.

Cory's answer had been the same as it always had been: *Go fuck yourself. And I'm only good with algorithms, anyway.* Said with no aggression of course, because they were both good friends, and Maynard might be his closest friend. But still said, *because fuck you, that's why.*

Word had spread quickly through the tight-knit astrophysics and astronomy communities today that SETI had finally found a true repeater, a primary source, but, due to a host of good reasons, was not going public with it yet. And Cory had been on top of it from almost as soon as it had begun. Apparently, the news had leaked from SETI almost immediately to NASA Ames Research Center's NASA Astrobiology Institute, where Jennie Torres, PhD, Physics, served as a Principal Investigator. Her externally funded project, Deep Oracle, backed by MorthonTech's Exo-Physics department, was effectively a living meta-analysis of NASA's current extra-Terran projects. She and her small team sought to discern connections from among the multi-vectored, multi-origin data being collected by the vast array of disparate NASA remote sensing and *in situ* projects, then establish a Big Data nexus among all of the data. Then, they would use unique, custom, deep-scanning algorithms to parse out possible life-indicating signals from organics. The organics ranged from microbes and Archaea to, hypothetically, more advanced species, up to and including sentients. Thus, Jennie's team interfaced directly, and often, with the nearby SETI team. Cory reckoned it had not taken Professor Janice Murphy, one of the last remaining radio astronomers on the SETI team, more than a few minutes to reach out to Jennie for a solution to an issue for which she simply had to have a solution: Was SETI wrong?

Cory wasn't necessarily jumping to conclusions with his personal analysis of the chain of real-world events, either. That was probably the only question that could be asked by Janice, or Jennie, considering the politics in play for both of them – *for all of them now,* he corrected himself. So he reasoned that there would be no issue, and no skullduggery being worked in so clandestine a manner, if SETI-cum-NASA were in doubt of anything. No, they had to be more-than-absolutely-certain that they had finally heard "it", and, being bound by their own set of political chains, they were being forced to ask for possible negations, rather than just come right out, hold an impromptu press conference, and shout out to the world that ET was phoning home.

Technically, Janice and Jennie worked for the same team, so it was not unusual at all for them to double-check troublesome data. With the advent of Jennie's Deep Oracle project, data-crunching no longer required booking time days in advance on any of the considerable number of supercomputers in the Valley. Janice and her team could just ping Jennie, and Jennie's massive Deep Oracle supercomputer could crunch the data in mere minutes. Well, in most cases. In this case, there was a lot of data – practically everything capable of producing data for the VOEvent service and everything that NASA had in the field was picking something up; not always the same event, either. But close enough to be, possibly, the same event. If that were the case, then this was the biggest event thus far in mankind's relatively short experience in remote sensing and extra-planetary data collection.

So both Janice and Jennie probably had already arrived at the same conclusion, which probably had appeared to be a true positive. Now, after considering the heavy gravity of the politics in play – politics that included not only losing their own jobs, but also tarnishing the reputations of their respective institutions, which could cost many more jobs – they had appealed to Cory's expertise in his own algorithms to resolve the issue for them. To tell them, beyond shadow of doubt, that they were not wrong, but that they were right. And that, yes, for the first time in recorded human history, ET was calling Earth to inform us that, indeed, we were not alone.

A simple countdown timer, starting at 10, appeared front and center on Cory's laptop's screen.

"Cory? Cory!" Jennie called out, fear in her voice.

9.

"Jennie? What is it? What's going on?"

8. 7.

"Oh my god! These guys, they have guns! They're escorting everyone out of the building. Cory!"

6. 5. 4. 3.

"Jennie! Hold on, we're almost done! Try to find a place to hi– "

2. 1.

"Cory!"

0.

Glass shattered on the other end of the line, and Cory heard Jennie scream. His gaze shifted to the phone. Curiously, he felt totally calm, as he heard a husky male voice command Jennie to evacuate the building immediately, emergency protocol was in effect. Then, mercifully, the line disconnected.

If they've hurt her, I'll crucify them all... This, he promised himself, staring at the "99.98% Source Confirmation" on his computer screen.

eVo.144.000.mOd.0.sCe.2 | EARTH | UNITED STATES | ALABAMA | HUNTSVILLE

"SO, IT'S TRUE," CORY said quietly to himself. "We're not alone." He allowed himself a brief, clenched smile. His focus would not disengage from what he had just heard happen to Jennie, however. "They were aggressive, breaking the glass to get into her office. But, prior to that," he recalled, re-scanning their conversation in his mind, "she had mentioned that there were people there, people she didn't recognize. Probably security. Probably external security, which means private security, corporate security, or military security. Probably private or corporate, because she didn't say anything about soldiers. I'm not aware of any NASA or SETI security personnel, which narrows things down to, most likely, the folks who footed the bill for Deep Oracle. And that means MorthonTech. And that means, at 06:30, I'm going to be breaking my own protocol and speaking directly to Mr. Simm. In person. So, I've got a few hours remaining," he said, his fingers insistently tapping across the keyboard as he went to work, combing over the data with some highly specific filtering, meta-analysis, and meta-tangential algorithms. Just a single, quick glance at the sparse resultant data in the popup had tingled his Spidey-Sense, and he was rapidly checking out a few bizarre hunches that had abruptly bloomed in his fertile mind.

He didn't like to work in haste, but, in this case, he had no choice. First, he had to compartmentalize and tuck away for later what had transpired with Jennie. Thinking about it, even for a second, would be disastrous, and, frankly, there was nothing he could do about it right now, as she was thousands of miles away on the West Coast. Plus, there would have been no reason for them to have become violent with the project's PI, as they were, more than likely, MorthonTech security personnel. It was very likely that, taken at face value, Jennie had decided only moments prior to her call to him that she had to do something to save the precious data that, he could now see, had Deep Oracle's processing marks on it, yet, originally, those of SETI. So SETI had been the originator after all, and Janice had analyzed it first using SETI's in-house analyzers, passing it over to Jennie and Deep Oracle only after arriving at the conclusion that the data was valid, with a 99%+ probability that it was not only of organic origin, but also of sentient organic origin.

Satisfied, Cory filed all of that away, and dove completely into his work. Realizing that something was missing, he sneered aloud, "Miss No-Pants!"

"Yes, Cory?" came the reply from his massively hacked Echo. He and Maynard often joked that the new voice was so sexy, it seemed she should end every sentence with 'and take off your pants.'

"Hit me with some JINJER. Make that shit loud as fuck."

"Yes, my master," Miss No-Pants complied immediately, and "I Speak Astronomy" began to stream, loudly, giving Cory the clue he had needed to resolve the hunch that was bugging him about the data.

"Holy shit," Cory said to himself, the music perfectly balanced, and loud, around him. He was taking tangential data points from the different sampling sets, seeing how they could reach out and touch or merge with other potential data sets. The data sets were listed roughly in order as forms of communication achieved by man, then cross-referenced with potential data sets which listed different orders and combinations of biological entities, sets, and supersets. Normally, humans could communicate physically, immediately, by expressing themselves to one another verbally and receiving the communication data aurally. But this, however, was not as simple as it appeared. In addition to the verbal-auditory feedback loops, there were other tangential and ancillary entities involved in the communication sequence. One such entity in communication was body language, which itself had several potential subsets, each with their own distinct implications. If expressed verbally as "Lola tells me she loves me," yet visually as "Her hips move seductively as she does so," the message would tell multiple things to the person receiving the message, including, quite possibly, the purpose of the communication. To this simple set of possibilities could be added multiple, distinct lists of entities, each with distinct attributes themselves, which could result in more possible whys and wherefores than normal non-quantum supercomputers could hope to easily process.

But Cory was working on the assumption that there was both an initial, primary communication, and an underlying, implicit sub-communication. At least two steps, and not simply one. While it would be difficult for him to verbally explain why his insight had led him in this heretical direction, his hunch was that something was attempting to communicate with Earth via some expression of Sagan's 1974 Arecibo message. Or, forging its own communication to us on a virtual tapestry similar to that which Sagan's message had used: a radio message which, when decoded, would display simple bit-wise images that, when deciphered, would clearly indicate binary numbers, atomic numbers, DNA, and a small host of other entities.

Cory's assumption, held by no small number of his similarly aligned astro-buffs, was that the Sagan Arecibo message, the most elemental of the various attempts at communication before and since, would be the message most likely to resemble any incoming extraterrestrial message. Barring some super-technology which would allow entangled or sub-space communications in real-time, it would be understood innately that keeping interstellar communication restricted to its most compact, most elemental form would be essential. That's why Sagan and his team had decided to use basic binary encoding and a tight, narrow-field attempt, and not a generalized blast. It was exceedingly improbable to have reached more than an extremely limited audience, if any at all. But the point was that it was of the most logical form factor and composition possible, with the logic being that ETs, if they were so inclined to communicate with us, might use something quite similar.

So Cory was particularly interested in seeing if he could link disparate, tangential entity attributes in the data, based on his library of logical lists. He would see if, indeed, the ETs were using something like Sagan's technique of using radio waves, a primary message medium, with embedded and encoded data within it. The data within it must then be decoded, then interpreted, in order for the whole depth of the message to be understood. A simple pictorial representation in the radio message might be nice, but having an understanding that the picture itself meant something deeper, something more profound, meant also that those who were communicating with us probably weren't so much different cognitively from us. For all the good or ill that such implied.

First, Cory managed to coax a visual image from the radio frequency data. This was linear, entirely so, and it occurred in 100% of the inbound data streams, culled and parsed from several disparate sources. This was the top layer of the fast repeater source messages. All of them.

Finally giving in to a UI, Cory brought up multiple graphics programs, so that he could first see the stream in flat 2D, then 3D, then 4D, and make the necessary physical visual inspections. The fact that the primary message contained a picture of DNA was immediately recognizable, even in the flat 2D. But there were artifacts in the 2D images, so Cory moved to the 3D, where he saw, again quite plainly, that the typical double helix structure was now apparently triple helix. Moving up to 4D, adding chirality to the 3D structure and causing it to become animated, finally gave Cory the image he was seeking. Right-hand chirality didn't do anything special, but the left-hand chirality immediately generated a resultant data trail in one of Cory's concurrently running, inquiring tangential-seeking algorithms.

Not believing his eyes, Cory stared hard at the data points appearing in the data trail below the 4D animation screen. Cory immediately selected the screen and expanded it to full size. The range and relative distribution of the data struck him as being somewhat similar to medieval music notation. It had been somewhat limited in its simple expression, but it had enough in its system to inform the monks how to sing the notes.

Initially, the sequencing gave Cory a challenge. Going frame by frame, he noted, tapping into another data stream, that the notes varied according to which source was used. Once it clicked that the individual frames were exactly that: frames of sound, just snapshots in a timeline, he was able to capture the various expressed notes from among the frames, then render them separately into a complete sequence themselves, which he then captured and mapped to the 4D imaging.

And that's what this was, he was certain of it now. Primarily, it was triple helix DNA, of all things, and, secondarily, caused by the motion of the DNA in a left-hand chiral motion, was the music that was produced by the DNA. The alien ET data was triple helix DNA, and the DNA was singing.

A simple, incongruous tear formed at the corner of Cory's almond-slanted, wicked green eyes, framing his exotic facial features with the reflected light of the spinning, singing alien DNA. A brief flicker of electric blue light erupted from his eyes then, as monumental grief filled his heart.

It sang to me...

eVo.144.000.mOd.0.sCe.3 | EARTH | UNITED STATES | ALABAMA | HUNTSVILLE | MORTHONTECH HEADQUARTERS

CORY WAS A MAN OF HIS word.

In the false dawn of Huntsville's sodium vapor haze, his Yeti coffee mug and a bulging sheaf of loose paper printouts gripped tightly to his chest, Cory clumsily stumbled as he tried to pull his front door shut with a spare index finger.

"Dammit," he muttered, hooking his finger into the handle. With a quick tug, the door shut, and Cory quickly made his way along the neatly edged sidewalk. His second hand Special Edition F-150 Lariat loomed in the driveway, its shadow black paint job blending effectively with the real shadows. Stopping in his tracks at the juncture of the sidewalk and driveway, he rolled his eyes, sighing heavily.

"Keys," he reminded himself. Shifting his load, he tried to maneuver his free finger into the right fold pocket of his black hoodie. Contorting spastically, he made a feeble attempt to snag the pocket, but failed. "Looks like I picked the wrong week to stop taking yoga classes..." he snorted.

"Need a hand?" came a sudden voice from behind him, startling Cory profoundly.

As Cory pivoted to his right, a soft *pop!* whispered near him. He felt a sting, like a horsefly biting him, in the side of his neck.

"Huh?" he blurted, involuntarily slapping with his right hand at the tiny dart sticking in his neck. "What the..." he began, the mug and sheaf spilling from his dulled grasp onto the sidewalk. A second *pop!* registered from his left side, and he felt another impact to the left side of his neck. Slowly, he folded to his knees, his senses reeling. His fingertips, however, splayed out below him, anchoring him in place.

Breathing deeply, Cory tried his best to center his chi, but his eyes felt like they were literally spinning around in their sockets. A deep, gurgling growl like that of an angry lion burbled from his constricting throat.

"What the hell?" came a harsh whisper from somewhere near him. Something heavy prodded Cory's rear, yet he did not collapse as expected. "He's still conscious. You idiots. Do I have to do everything myself?"

A sharp crack faintly echoed in the relative still of the Green Mountain neighborhood. Feeling nothing, Cory dimly noted the sensation of blood trickling down the nape of his neck. Something within began to stir, deep within his soul. Something almost electric in force, sending a very real rat-dance tingle up his spine.

Illuminating the scene like a smartphone's flash, electric blue sparks flashed from Cory's eyes, freezing the men around him in their tracks. They regarded this absurd spectacle in silent fear. The sparks pulsed thrice, with an audible yet faint *thrum-thrum-thrum.*

As the fog in his mind began to retreat, however, two more *pop! pop!* sounds barked at him from close range, and darkness mercifully embraced him.

...

Cory's return to consciousness was not abrupt. Snatches of conversation formed a discontinuous backdrop against which he slowly awakened:

"...his eyes, man... never seen anything like that. Obviously was his phone. It was in his hoodie's pocket. Just flashed when he went down. Don't tell Simm, or he'll send us to Antarctica. ...tainted doses. DARPA lied. One-shot-stop adrenaline-pumped hostile combatants my ass. ...maybe he was on PCP or something."

"Weird smart phone, multiple DataSticks."

"Phone gimmicked. It shut off when we tried to use the cracker on it. Probably a decoy or burner. DataSticks all read as blank."

More clearly, he heard a voice he knew: "I'll speak to him. It's the only way, at this point."

"You sure? That's against every single protocol. Principals aren't supposed to participate in an op. Bad practice. Bad optics."

"No more time for protocols or optics," Adam Simm, CEO of MorthonTech replied.

"He's awake," said another voice from his left.

"Good," Simm said confidently. "Mr. Tate?" he asked, his voice indicating that he now was closer. "Wake up, Cory. I need to ask you some questions. Important questions."

Cory's eyes flickered open. Stabbing white light assaulted his eyes, causing him to blink rapidly.

"Lights?" Simm said, giving one of the blurry figures a quick glance. Almost immediately, the blinding lights dimmed, and Cory finally could see the predicament he was in.

Adam Simm stood before Cory, a black anodized attaché case in one hand, a small deck of tablets in the other. His black Armani suit was freshly pressed, its creases razor sharp. His pronounced widow's peak and skin fade caused his neatly cropped black hair to resemble the striking talons of a bird of prey. Two burly MorthonTech security guards loomed behind the tall, imposing executive. Each held black extendible steel batons, their eyes unreadable behind their Gatorz Magnum tactical eyewear. Another security guard sat several feet away, monitoring a bank of medical diagnostic equipment, which explained the numerous probes Cory now realized were affixed to him. Two more security guards towered behind his left and right flanks. The room itself was nothing more than rough, unfinished cement, a single heavy steel door set into the wall opposite him. Not the standard MorthonTech lab or office. More like a killing room, Cory concluded.

Cory was slightly reclined in an upright metal gurney, both arms and legs pinioned by heavy leather straps with sturdy metal buckles. Momentarily exploring the limits of his confinement, he realized instantly he couldn't move an inch.

Wild, primal fear crawled like a hungry millipede up Cory's spine. The realization that his life could suddenly end at the hands of these grim-faced men skittered between his shoulder blades, danced up the back of his neck. As always, the bullies had him face down to the ground, rubbing his nose in dog shit, and there was absolutely nothing he could do about it. Except take it. Just take their shit. Don't fight back. Never fight back. That just makes it worse. Never fi—

Fight! an alien yet familiar voice growled in his mind. *Fight, Cory!* it ordered him. *For soon, you will never know fear again...*

Fight... Cory repeated in his mind, a beautiful, transcendent feeling stomping his fear like the foul little insect it truly was. *Fight...*

Cory found Simm's eyes. Something fierce and feral roared silently between them.

"Guess this means I'm not getting that raise?" Cory mocked Simm. Behind the grimacing CEO, Cory saw one of the burly security guards bite back a grin.

"You might, if you play your cards right, Cory," Simm informed him, his voice slightly cold, detached. He turned to the non-smiling guard, who took a moment to accept Simm's briefcase and all but a single tablet. Cory noted that the guard had to collapse and holster his baton to comply. "A very substantial package, too," Simm continued. "Depends on what you know. Depends on what you can tell us." His aquiline nose briefly flared. "Deep Oracle. Talk."

"Actually, I was on my way to see you when your thugs jumped me," Cory replied. "I was going to try to make you a deal to save my friends out at Ames. You know, the ones your stormtroopers terrorized?" he smiled slightly, his fey, almond-slanted green eyes seeking Simm's calculating dark brown eyes.

"You're pissed about what happened out at Ames, and I understand," Simm stated, nodding affirmatively. "My bad. That's on me. So is the rough treatment you endured during our attempt to bring you in. The level of your resistance... wasn't expected." He paused a moment, his eyes momentarily accusing the guard to Cory's left flank. "But you know the stakes of this game. We had to bring you in, of course. What if you would have made a beeline to the airport, and flown off to Russia or China? Couldn't take that risk. It was supposed to be a quick grab. You would have awakened here, with only a slight headache, and we could have had this all behind us by now. You understand, right?"

Cory smirked at Simm. "I understand you employ incompetent mercs for MorthonTech security," he said, noting the half-smirk on Smiley Merc's face melt away like ice on the Sun. "Maybe just asking would have done it? I'm reasonable, after all," he lied. "Well, mostly. Are the Deep Oracle people physically unharmed?"

"Of course. Some were reluctant to leave the site, naturally. And one of them," Simm paused, tapping quickly on one of his pads, "Dr. Torres, locked herself in her office and refused to follow the emergency evacuation protocol. One of the officers broke internal protocol, got angry after she refused to unlock the door, and busted it open by force in order to extract her. Our chief of security, Mr. DiSazi, has reprimanded the officer responsible, and Mr. DiSazi takes demotions quite seriously. That guy will probably be pulling shit duty at our Antarctic research facility soon. Or at our Little Rock facility. Same difference."

Cory nodded an affirmative. He hadn't broken his own cautious, antisocial protocol and tried to contact Jennie, or Janice, or anyone else on either the NASA Ames Deep Oracle or SETI teams after the event. And that had taken more discipline to enforce than he currently cared about. He'd find out for himself soon enough, anyway, what had happened, because Simm, despite his managed efforts to be seen as authoritative and in control, was only pissing Cory off more.

"I'll take your word for it," Cory informed him. "So, now, why don't you release me, and let's talk like normal humans."

"We can't risk that yet, Cory," Simm informed him. "We have to be certain of a few more things before we can do that."

"What 'few things'?" Cory asked pointedly. "Let's get this over with. I already said I was willing to cooperate to resolve this."

Simm nodded. It looked like they were going to be able to avoid Plan B. "So, what about those signals? You think it's ET?"

"What did SETI say?" Cory deflected.

"Well, not much. Other than leak the data to virtually everyone on the planet, they haven't managed either to confirm or deny it yet. That's really sad. Now, rumors have started, and we have to engage in perception management to—"

"Perception management, Mr. Simm?" Cory interrupted. "People already think that SETI, and by extension Deep Oracle, are full of it, lying their asses off about ET not being there when, in fact, ET is quite plainly there, and we're *all* just lying about it."

"I'm aware of what the conspiracy theorists think," Simm calmly replied. "And now they have even more ammunition to fuel their paranoid minds, because word's already out online about how SETI is sitting on the translation of the signals. Good thing SETI takes the flak off of Deep Oracle, which means we can still salvage something out of this, possibly, if *we* play our cards right."

Cory exhaled slowly. "The very few of us who've done the science are loathe to admit it, especially in public, but SETI's methods are quaint, entirely myopic, and quite probably nothing more than a mis- and disinformation smokescreen meant to herd up and funnel public interest in ET into very safe spaces, approved in advance by those who stand to lose everything should humanity at large become aware of the truth."

"And what *is* the truth, Cory?" Simm's fished. "Did you get confirmation?"

Cory's eyes burned a virtual hole in the back of Simm's retinas. Despite his own fierce convictions, emblazoned on his very essence by his personal experiences, Cory wasn't quite willing yet to share his secret. Not yet.

Simm returned Cory's piercing stare for a brief moment, then, quite diplomatically, he cracked the same disarming smile that had made him a social media darling with the hip IT crowd, a magnetic bear trap with the Silicon Valley venture capitalists, and one of the most powerful CEOs in America's burgeoning high-tech sector. Yesterday, in the first throes of the SETI/Deep Oracle incident, he had personally just closed a major deal with Dragon Investments, one of Beijing's largest and longest reaching investment firms. This had positioned MorthonTech a full light year ahead of their nearest competitor, that dipshit Allen Johnston's SpaceGen. So this unkempt, long haired, ill-dressed nerd straight from Central Casting wasn't going to get his GERD boiling, not one iota, and he certainly wasn't going to let some unknown TED Talk wannabe badmouth SETI, which MorthonTech specifically and very publicly supported.

"C'mon, Cory. You *do* realize that SETI does great work? Great work, great public exposure of the ET phenom? Very high YouTube ratings on their latest series?" Simm held his smile as he recited his usual plug lines. "You know, the best there is at what they do?" he almost smirked as he recalled the famous Wolverine comic book tag, holding his fists up and pretending to pop his adamantium claws with an audible *"Snikt!"* It was usually a finisher, like Wolverine, but Simm's dipshit slaying line stunningly, to him at least, failed to give Cory pause. In fact, Simm noted that it actually made Cory's slightly narrowing eyes appear a bit dangerous, an incongruous resultant, or so he thought.

At the very edge of his perception, Simm had been flirting with the absurd idea that Cory's emerald eyes had actually flickered; slightly, only a bit of an electric blue discharge of lights that had been difficult to see. Almost like sparks, or tiny sparkles, like something that Tinkerbell would leave in her wake as she flew up Peter Pan's crotch to have a great big ball with The Pan. Or something like that. Suddenly, Simm noticed that he had been silent for a rather awkward span of a few seconds, still staring vapidly into Cory's eyes, his own smile now curled almost into a slight rictus grin.

Simm cleared his throat, blinked several times, then nodded at Cory, who was still staring at him, almost like some feral wolf. Those eyes of his.

"You said you were willing to cooperate," Simm reminded him. "Is your solution on your phone? On one of the DataSticks?" Simm snapped his fingers, and the guard monitoring the equipment arose, walked over to Simm, and quickly passed Cory's smartphone and DataSticks to him. Immediately, he returned to his monitoring station.

If Cory played cards, then SETI's reputation was going to go right through the roof, thanks to what MorthonTech's other player in the ET biz, Deep Oracle, was going to turn up and reveal. Well, what Cory had obviously turned up, he was going to reveal. Great press and accolades all around, and by playing both sides, MorthonTech could not help but to win this one, and win big. However, if Cory didn't play cards, then there was always Plan B.

"C'mon, Cory," Simm implored him, waggling the smartphone and DataSticks before him. "Tell us. Is ET real?"

Why not? Cory thought, considering that this might be his lone opportunity to ensure that both Janice's and Jennie's teams – and perhaps lives – remained viable, and, quite possibly, finally be able to reveal the truth. It was a gamble, of course. Simm, while trying very hard to be cool and maintain his hipster CEO image, was still CEO, was still Corporate *Über Alles*, and was, he had to admit, the only person on the planet with the proper mojo to start making things happen. *Fuck it all and fucking no regrets...*

"Yeah, I can confirm it," Cory told Simm. "ET is real. We've got composite signal confirmation. It's both primary and secondary, and it's got a really badass embedded content to it."

Simm accepted this as a sign of detente, and eagerly nodded for him to continue, noticing as he did that Cory abruptly appeared to be a bit embarrassed. That was an entirely uncommon personal attribute in proximity to him, Simm had to admit, considering the top tier prima donnas and self-aggrandizing personalities who seemed constantly to surround him, buzzing about with their buzzwords, reciting them as if to sing their praises to Simm, the High Priest of High Tech. Or so his many clinging sycophants told him.

"So how did you do it? How did you find it?" Simm asked impatiently.

"Jennie alerted me," Cory admitted, finally realizing, hopefully, that Simm was going to play this one straight, due to the gravity of the situation. And for the potential up-tick in MorthonTech that it would produce. "She got the stream from Janice over at SETI. Janice was having trouble getting a robust negative on it, so they stuck to protocol. Janice popped the data over to Jennie, and Jennie had the Deep Oracle guys try to confirm or deny it. When they'd exhausted all normal data processing runs, and still had the same robust 99% probable sentient source, that's when Jennie decided to ask me to look at it. I think that the extra pressure of having armed security personnel abruptly appear on the scene and try to sterilize the area might have forced her decision."

"Already apologized for that," Simm repeated, shaking his head.

"She did it to protect the project. Both of them, actually," Cory defended. "She had no idea who those guys were, and she couldn't take the chance that those merc-looking effers weren't going to destroy everything, shoot everyone, then split. See? Even the scientists can be conspiracy theorists. Especially when jackbooted thugs show up and bully them around with no good reason. Effing emergency protocol my ass."

"Cory? I've already apologized for that. It's our mistake. They're all okay, in case I haven't said that before. They're on leave – paid leave – and legally incommunicado, as per standard operating procedure. So dial down the hostility a notch, okay, Cory? You're restrained for good reason," he finally admitted. "After effects of multiple shots with those darts can cause you to rip your own tendons if you try to move around. That's why we're monitoring you. And please continue. This is going to be mind-blowing!" Simm said loudly, turning to smile at a guard.

Everyone in the room locked onto and tracked Cory's words.

"I ran the data sets using my own algorithms; stuff that wasn't yet invented when we did Deep Oracle. Using those, it was simple to..." He paused, wincing as a sharp tinge went through the center of his brow line.

"You okay there, Cory" Simm asked, genuinely concerned. *He can't have an aneurysm now, on the edge of the Big Reveal!*

"I'm fine," Cory lied, willing the pain away. "For someone who's been beaten, tranquilized, and forcibly restrained. Anyway, I was able to comb out the pictorial representation of a segment of triple helix DNA, and then, almost as if I'd been aware of it all along, as if something or someone were guiding my way, I went 3D, then 4D on it. I noticed that, when I gave it left-hand chirality, it produced another, more deeply embedded signal. Again, as if I were robotically following some bizarre cosmic script, I noticed that the deeper signal coming from the triple helix DNA was musical notation. From there, because I'm a musician, it was quite easy to produce the proper musical context for the 4D mapping of the triple helix DNA to match the flow of the music. It was singing. This entity, whatever it really is, actually has the physical form of a gigantic triple helix DNA segment. It's not just a flat signal of a flat, fast repeating radio source. It's an actual physical object, in motion, in space, vectoring our way. And, whatever it really is, it's singing to us as it's approaching."

"Your data?" Simm inquired sharply. "Time to produce it, Cory. Let us verify it, and you're free to go as soon as you're physically able. And you'll be well compensated for your... cooperation. And silence."

Why not? Cory thought, *I'll give it to him. We don't have that much longer anyway.*

"I used a silent cypher on the DataSticks," Cory admitted. "The seven of them have to be inserted into a single reader, in this order: Muladhara, Svadhishthana, Manipura, Anahata, Vishuddha, Ajna, and Sahasrara. The seven chakras. Names are in standard American Braille."

Simm carefully turned one of the DataSticks edge-on, studying the tiny sticker on its end, as the monitor guard began to walk over toward him. "No wonder we pay you the big bucks. Smart," he said, passing the DataSticks and smartphone back to the monitor guard, who quickly returned to his station with them.

"Boss," the monitor guard said as he sat down. "I'm not blind. I can't read Braille. Which one goes first?"

Cory snickered. Dumbass guard certainly *was* effing blind. He was just too stupid to know it.

"Use the colors of the sticks. They're basically ROYGBIV. Red first." Nodding, the monitor guard began the procedure, carefully inserting the red DataStick into the lone laptop at his station. "It's all on there," Cory continued. "The data, my calculations, my unique processing algorithms. Stuff that didn't exist when we did Deep Oracle. The best stuff. Now, how 'bout you get these straps off me?"

Ignoring Cory for the moment, Simm's eyes lit up with unadulterated glee. He watched the copy process on the laptop's screen, along with rest of the guards in the room, as the monitor guard fed the DataSticks into the laptop's reader, one at a time. He knew that, under the hood, there was an almost instant transfer of the data from the DataSticks to a customized routing server, which briefly analyzed the context of the data, then sent it along its merry way to four extremely specific destinations. Only three were internal and proprietary to MorthonTech. The fourth? It went to a very special destination, where it would finally get General Sullivan and DoD off his back.

"Something you should know," Cory said wearily as the seventh and final batch of data began its transfer to the laptop. His forehead was really throbbing. The pain behind his brow seemed to be ebbing and flowing. But, after this was all done and he was free, he'd get that solved, even if it meant vodka shots for breakfast. If it was still breakfast. "The kicker is – if my calculations are correct, and they are – it's jumping rapidly toward us, toward Earth. The data sets we've obtained suggest that it's been moving actively, somehow traversing thousands of light years per jump. The data suggests that its first signals originated somewhere near Sagittarius A*, the galactic center of the Milky Way. Then, impossibly, in a very short number of hops, over an impossibly small time frame, it's traveled a good bit of the approximately 26,000 light years from there to here. So if it keeps that pace, it could be here as early as midnight tonight, sometime tomorrow morning. Or never. After all, we're just assuming that it's heading to Earth. Could be that it's aiming somewhere else."

"But it's not, is it?" Simm asked pointedly, already sensing the answer.

"It's not. It's not all radio data. There's a good mix of optical, infrared, multispectral, etc.; some of the newer confirmation systems actually had decent synchronization with this set of transients. Serendipity? Maybe. But I doubt it. I think it happened because it was meant to happen that way. It's also impossible that we could have seen all of its nodes virtually in sync, because it's impossible to have superluminal, stacked signals all being picked up at virtually the same time from a single object. It's as if it has metaphysically projected itself from there to here, with its earliest, most distant signals somehow arriving in sync, time-wise, with its most recent. That's spooky tech. Technomagick, basically, because it's that advanced compared to ours."

"That's not going to please our biggest customer," Simm said sagely. "Uncle Sam isn't going to like this."

"I know. I think it's happening for a reason, and that we were meant to see it. I think that there's a 99% probability that it's real, that it's got multiple attributes of being an actual sentient-created artifact, and that, yes, it's headed right for us. It looks like Galactus threw a fastball directly at Earth from the center of the Milky Way galaxy. And it should be here by, at latest, sometime tomorrow."

"Holy mother of God..." Simm grated, comprehension finally dawning. "We're going to have to move fast to get out in front of this," he said, whipping out an earpiece from his suit's breast pocket.

As Simm began to fit the earpiece into his left ear, the seventh DataStick completed its data transfer. Immediately, the laptop's screen automatically executed the presentation of the data that Cory had prepared. The animated image of the alien triple helix DNA appeared on the screen, turning slowly in place. A subtle *thrum-thrum-thrum* crept into the room, causing a shrill, wailing electronic feedback which grew seemingly exponentially with each passing beat.

"What the hell is that noise?" Simm yelled over the din.

"Turn it off!" Cory roared at the monitor guard, who could no longer hear him.

Screaming, Simm sank to a single knee, his hands desperately clutching at his melting earpiece. He stumbled forward, falling onto Cory's restrained legs.

Cory cried loudly, unable to move, the stench of burning flesh mixed with melting plastic assailing his senses. Black fluid coursed from Simm's nose, spilling down into his open mouth, choking him and silencing his death screams. Simm's effusive gore flowed freely, bathing Cory's torso and legs in noisome black ooze.

A heartbeat later, Cory's eyes grew wide with shock as Simm's face rotted from his blackened skull and fell into his lap.

"Get that shit off me!" Cory screamed, close to hyperventilating. "Off! Get it off!" He bucked frantically, trying to dislodge Simm's rotten face from his lap, but he was unable to budge the heavy straps.

Meanwhile, the monitor guard, locked in place at his chair due to involuntary, total-body muscle constriction, silently filled his chair with tarry black excretion which pooled rapidly beneath him, spilling over the seat of the chair like a demented dark waterfall. The four remaining guards then began a terribly uncoordinated zombie dance, writhing in place, limbs flailing about awkwardly. Patches of dark, hungry fire erupted randomly from their bodies, causing their skin to hiss angrily then peel back. Electric sparks arced from the lights and electronic equipment, save for the laptop, which now was enveloped completely by spokes of rainbow light, spinning harmonically in synchronization with the animated alien DNA on the screen.

Cory was no longer paying attention to Simm's rotten face sitting there in his lap, or to anything else. Instead, his head was swimming, pain wickedly slammed into his forehead again, seemingly splitting his skull as it crushed his brain on the way to devouring his psyche.

It sang to me... Cory's tortured mind insistently informed him.

Suddenly, he was on his feet, his hands clutched to his head. Heavy leather straps fell to the floor, along with shattered pieces of the gurney. Then, abruptly, a deep-throated roar issued forth from him like a spastic snake being birthed, live, from his mouth. The sensation of pain rose to a crescendo, forcing Cory to rock back and forth, hunching over in place where he stood, now moaning like a wounded beast. His hands were now digging into the skin of his own forehead. That's when he saw, as if from a distant vantage, removed somehow from his own form, a vibrant, electric blue light dancing on his inwardly turned palms. The fey sparkles flitted like dancing faeries in his field of view as he slowly withdrew his hands from his head.

Around him, the dying danced the Danse Macabre.

Not able to comprehend precisely what was happening, Cory finally gave in to the pain, rather than continue his futile resistance. His lithe muscles bunched like competing anacondas, isometrics ghostly in form. He shook and jerked, his frame insulted by the trauma of his forced physical, mental, and spiritual evolution; his transformation; his transliteration; his transcendence. A disturbing, ascending hum seemed to issue forth from his soul, a polytonal ascending glissando of Tuvan throat singing, impossible in origin and definition by mere mortal perception.

At its painful yet thankfully brief climax, Cory's arms jerked above his head and, in a primal motion, he bent his knees and slammed his fists down on the hard concrete. Instantly, the flesh-flaying impact of bomb like overpressure filled the room. The concrete floor buckled and shattered under the strain of impact, lethal shrapnel erupting like meteorids in reverse motion, slamming through the bodies of the humans, totally wrecking everything in the room. Finally, the *thrum-thrum-thrum* pulsation faded away. The room grew silent, save for the faint burble of foul ichor as it bled down the pockmarked concrete walls and slowly dripped from the ceiling.

Raising his head, Cory Christopher Tate, howled like a primeval, brutish beast.

"At last, I am reborn!" Cory roared triumphantly, flexing his bulging, writhing muscles. His hoodie in tatters, his bronze mane of hair flowed wild and rampant, as if charged by electricity.

In the here and now, Cory, the glory of his transcendent evolution now fading and his senses now returning to normal, gazed around in wonder, trying his best to determine precisely what had just happened. Save for a paucity of recognizable body parts, not much remained of the security guards. Simm's face floated in a small pool of warm indigo fluid.

Wisely, Death tiptoed fearfully around the ruined room.

Finally noticing the ruined metal door, which hung awkwardly askew, Cory, choosing discretion over valor, and freedom over multiple felonies, bailed.

eVo.144.000.mOd.0.sCe.4 | EARTH | VATICAN CITY

"VIVA IL PAPA! VIVA il Papa!"

More than 100,000 thronged St. Peter's Square, chanting in unison, wishing the Bishop of Rome a *buon compleanno*, cheering with gusto their shared, collective enthusiasm and genuine love for such a good, decent man.

What he had done already, in the relatively short span of his leadership of the Catholic faith, had immediately set him apart from his predecessors. He had insisted on walking among the people, taking common sidewalks, shaking the hands of those whom he encountered, embracing them, to their complete and utter astonishment.

He led by example, being the first Pope in living memory to insist on making his residence in the Casa Santa Marta, which the Vatican had traditionally used to house visitors, both cloth and lay. And it was now, after completing his weekly audience, he made his way back to his conservatively efficient suite of rooms, the members of his entourage gradually peeling off, diminishing in size as they entered the residence and wound their way to his suite. Passing through the arched vault which demarcated the outer suite from the more private, inner suite, he stopped, then turned around and cordially dismissed the last two men who accompanied him now: Archbishop Juan Alejandro Diego

García, the Prefect of the Papal Household and personal secretary to His Holiness; and his personal physician, Dr. Niccolo Bruno. Bowing respectfully, the prefect gently yet efficiently closed the tall, vaulted doors on his way out of the room.

Moving gracefully for a man of his advanced years, he made his way across the compact, austerely furnished room, coming to a stop in front of a dark cherry wooden bookcase. Rapidly scanning the top tier of the bookcase, his keen eyes came to a rest upon a particular volume, which he gently removed from the shelf, careful to remind himself of its deceptive bulk as his fingers brushed over its iron-bound spine. He found his chair, his one indulgence to physical comfort, a high-backed leather chair which had been ordered, custom-made by the finest craftsmen of its time, by Pope Alexander VI himself, more than 500 years ago, and settled down into it. Centuries of use had naturally left the imprint of Time itself on it, but the descendants of those very same craftsmen had, down through the centuries, been most eager to tend to it.

Opening the hoary tome, which was almost as old as the chair in which he was sitting, he carefully probed the pages with the thumb of his left hand until he had reached a certain well-trafficked page near the end of the book. While his Jesuit-trained mind gave him several robust, positive reasons why the book was absolutely a fabrication, his impression of the Benedictine order was one of firm respect, so there was ever the iota of doubt to consider, and he chose, as a man of faith and congruent reason, not to favor one possibility over another. Besides, he reasoned, as he once more scanned the last passage in the book, it was entirely possible, given the nature of divinely-inspired prophecy, that Wion had accurately and faithfully reproduced, verbatim, the prophecies of Saint Malachy.

He read the passage out loud to himself in a soft, respectful voice:

In persecutione extrema S.R.E. sedebit.

Petrus Romanus, qui pascet oves in multis tribulationibus, quibus transactis civitas septicollis diruetur, & judex tremendus judicabit populum suum. Finis.

Outside, a final misplaced chorus of "Viva il Papa!" echoed in St. Peter's Square, punctuated by an equally misplaced grumble of distant thunder, which rolled ominously over Vatican City, across the Tiber, then through the Seven Hills of Rome, where it finally broke like an ancient trireme on treacherous breakwaters.

il Papa's eyes narrowed in consternation as the single ceiling light flickered briefly. He rested the book on his lap as he brought his right hand up to caress the simple wooden cross he wore around his neck.

"Domini pascit me..." he began, abruptly becoming silent as he noticed that a figure was standing only a few feet before him, slightly turned away from him and toward the small fireplace, its right hand resting atop the simple mantle.

"And I have been, Peter," it said to him in English, startling him not so much because a strange man had somehow managed to gain access to his private chambers, but moreso because the voice of the man... the voice of the man was the clearest voice he had ever heard; it was audible, full of rich, precise vigor, though it was also nearly a brilliant whisper. For a man of his unique status, for a man who had heard the most brilliant voices of the Church speak and sing for Christ, it was still an entirely stunning experience. il Papa realized then that he was staring silently at the profile of the figure's face, trying to find its eyes.

"You don't need to see my eyes, Peter," he said softly, though the impact upon il Papa's perception was as if another grumble of thunder had just passed through the room. The dull glow of the fireplace seemed to conspire with ambient shadows to obscure the man's upper face. Try as he might, il Papa could not make out his entire face, or his entire form. "I have chosen shadow and fire with which to make my presence known to you," the man continued, seeming to answer his unvoiced question. "It is meant to relax you, soothe you, rather than I had appeared to you as an angel or demon."

"Who are you?" il Papa inquired, his voice sounding to him as if his mouth were stuffed full of cotton. While he had initially been startled by the strange man's abrupt appearance in his private apartment, he realized now that his guards had to have been aware of the intruder's presence and would soon be on their way to handle him. "You should be aware that my guards and attendants will soon be here to ask you your intent."

The figure turned slowly to face the fireplace, his back to il Papa, his arm coming down to his side. Still nothing more than shadows and bad lighting, he thought, rising steadily from his chair, the book wrapped in his hands. He then perceived a slight, dismissive movement of the man's head.

"They do not see us. Their high-tech guards and wards mean nothing to me, and I am hidden from them. In fact, I have woven this shard such that only you can see me."

"Who are you?" he asked him again, not truly believing what he had just heard, although he felt compelled to do so. A few more seconds, and his men would be here, he knew, so keeping the conversation going in a polite and friendly manner would be the most logical path to take. "I am genuinely curious. Tell me who you are. Perhaps I could help you then?"

"You already have helped me. You and every single soul ever born here on Earth," he said, the dull glow of the fireplace suddenly flickering. "Of the trillions upon trillions of cosmic permutations which have been actualized, yours has demonstrated the most adaptive potential. This is why I have taken interest in your shard, your particular slice of possible reality. This is why I am holding an audience directly with you, Peter."

"You keep calling me 'Peter,'" il Papa said tersely, "but, clearly, that is not my name."

"'Peter' as in 'Petrus'. Petrus Romanus. That's what I told Malachy to name you," he answered. "It's all right there in that book. Of the several million parallel shards that were running that scenario, yours has been the only one to fulfill it. Of course, that's not the only criterion for success. But it is an impressive one, to be sure, considering the chaotic nature of Man."

il Papa's cheeks flushed. He turned his head toward the door. No noise, no alarm, no bustle in the outer suite. Only silence, and the ambient sound of a soft rain starting to come down on the tiled roof.

"No one is coming. I told you that much," he said, turning around slowly to face him. The Pope's keen eyes registered a potent combination of shock and awe. "Ask me once more, and I shall tell you, as I am so pacted," he said. His face, his Aspect of the Trillions, momentarily shone forth from the protective sub-Planck Length Void-Weave obscuring his avatar, such that its true brilliance would not inflict localized spacetime perturbations on this carefully crafted shard of possible realities and contaminate the Flow.

"You are Lucifer," il Papa said, gritting his teeth, one hand now on the book that he clutched to his side, the other quickly lifting the chain of the cross over his head, then holding it out before him to ward off the presence of what he thought was Evil Incarnate. "And you are not welcome here in the House of Christ!"

Soft laughter answered him. "On and on, it's Heaven and Hell, isn't it?"

"What?"

"Your kind might have gotten their parts of the sim right this time, from among the many millions, but you still don't get the whole 'Heaven and Hell' thing, do you? And you're placed better than most to finally get it, aren't you? Oh, the irony is thick here."

Nonplused, il Papa knew that he had to have its name, and it had already given him the clue to obtain it, and to therefore gain power over it. "What is your name, I ask thee thrice! The power of Christ comp– "

"I am the Lightbringer," he finally admitted, now that the correct protocols had been followed. Any deviation from such essentials would have caused perturbations in the Flow, and that would not have been a desired event. "As you have guessed correctly, some wordplay with that particular appellation renders my name as 'Lucifer', though I would not willingly accept that name and its correspondingly devastating loss of power. You and your fellow humans created that particular bit of bad, but interesting, news. I am the Lightbringer, whose Sigil, Sign and Seal comes to judge your shard, its souls and its cosmos; your Lucifer and his entire associated mythos, including the deities you worship, were creations of your human belief. They're practically stillborn abortions to one of my origins. I and my kind created the trillions of scenarios which, occasionally, spawn deific mutations such as your 'god' and his 'devil'. Aberrations from the bizarre and often pathetic, mad abattoir of the human psyche."

"You lie! You are the Father of Lies! Guards! Guards! Intruder!" il Papa yelled.

The Lightbringer noted that he bravely stood his ground. This was not a unique event, as, currently, there were several notable leaders in this particular scenario doing the same thing; although this was countered with many variable expressions of emotions and reactions, including one sudden suicide. He wondered, momentarily, in the flight of less than an attosecond, if il Papa would try to snuff himself. Such a turn would be unusual and might cause too many spacetime perturbations in the localized wave front, so it was now allowed that he could conclude his mission and depart, before too much damage had been done to the Flow. This scenario, as he had informed il Papa earlier, was a particularly robust one – this was the ultimate run, the final run – and it would be most unfortunate to lose control of the known variables prior to the coming of the Lightbringer's Sigil.

"Please, be still," the Lightbringer soothed, instantly causing il Papa's shouts to die in his throat. Calm immediately broke over the pontiff's face. He visibly relaxed. The Lightbringer willed himself an overview of the scenario, noting instantly that no noise had broken through the null-field he had encircled the local scenario with just prior to making his appearance. *God saw the Null-Field,* he thought to himself, allowing himself some modicum of humor, *and saw that it was...* "Good, good. Now, this is what you must learn, and bear witness to, so that this phase of the scenario may conclude, and a new one may be instantiated."

The Pope nodded, smiling earnestly.

Then, the Lightbringer, focusing a small sliver of his will, caused the Pope to experience, in his own mind's eye, what the Lightbringer himself had experienced in the ZeroTime, in the mighty Union of Souls, and in the seemingly endless simulations he himself had shepherded to this point. In but the span of a few seconds of objective time, the Pope's mortal mind bent to the task of making sense of the data-dense experience. Swooning from the strain, the Pope dropped his book to the floor, where its iron-bound spine abruptly rusted, cracked, then shattered, its pages splaying out in confusion.

But where many mortals would have faltered, unable to continue, the Pope – *Petrus Romanus!* his inner voice screamed – slowly stood ramrod straight, staring directly into the Lightbringer's eldritch, incomprehensible visage as he did so.

Impressed by this display of supernatural mortal vigor, The Lightbringer continued his instruction and revelation, speaking to him in a soft, measured tone for no small measure of time, painting with his honeyed words the picture of the world-to-come, and what the role of Petrus Romanus would be in it. As the last of the Lightbringer's words ceased echoing in his mind, he inclined his head toward the Lightbringer, signaling his understanding.

Then, Petrus Romanus smiled joyfully at the Lightbringer. There was no more fear, no more apprehension in him now. Now, everything made sense; complete and total sense. The time written of in the Book of Revelation was now at hand. It was his cross to bear, at the End Times, to be Petrus Romanus, exactly as Saint Malachy had prophesied, and guide the people of the world to the Light. The way would be hard, the path would be treacherous, and the forces opposing them would be most formidable, but his faith in the Light would lead him, just as it would lead others.

Noting the acquiescence of Petrus Romanus, the Lightbringer faintly smiled, smoke and fire playing across his shadowy visage. There would of course be multiple possible scenario solution paths with their various probability ranks originating from this crucial inflection point, because the protocols of the Flow necessitated such vectors. Anything – well, anything in any of the competing vectors, barring the introduction of chaos into them – could occur. But this vector, this path...

Something about the way in which Petrus Romanus had stood his ground, unflinching, his faith a veritable mountain rising alone amidst the faint molehills of the mortals surrounding him, had impressed the Lightbringer. Of his own chosen, his many champions who would arise to contest the evil to come, this Petrus was slated to play a most pivotal role, one which absolutely had to succeed, or all would be lost. Deviation from its strict assignments would introduce potent chaotic perturbations into the simulation itself, scuttling the probabilities for its success.

Yet, the Lightbringer was confident in this one, and his chances of seeing it through to the end. The newly rechristened Petrus Romanus would indeed be the perfect one to call together the Lightbringer's Chosen and lead the next generation of the Children of the Light.

eVo.144.000.mOd.0.sCe.5 | EARTH | UNITED STATES | COLORADO | PETERSON AIR FORCE BASE

AT PRECISELY 11:36 ZULU a VECTOR INDIGO data packet arrived at Peterson Air Force Base, in Colorado Springs, Colorado, and was interrogated by a suite of automated validation and verification tools. After a span of precisely 1,123 seconds, the packet's identity was confirmed as an authentic VECTOR INDIGO entity. In precisely 0.1123 seconds, at precisely 11:54 ZULU, Phase One of Operation GLORY SAVE automatically began, sending out a preprogrammed codeword-level general order to implement the first phase of the Continuity of Operations/Continuity of Government plan.

In addition to the office of the President of the United States and the Secret Service, the automated general order notified multiple government parties, including the Department of Homeland Security, FEMA, the Department of Defense, the Office of the Secretary of Defense, the Joint Chiefs of Staff, and a bevy of military brass, civilian specialists, and various cleared military security personnel and private contractors. Notable at this tier of the chain of command were those whose sole mission it was to prepare the imminently expected emergency activation of Raven Rock Mountain Complex/Site R, Mount Weather

Emergency Operations Center. Part of this operation included directions for a full and immediate transfer of all essential personnel to the Cheyenne Mountain Complex, mostly from the neighboring Peterson Air Force Base. Without this most important component in place, there would be no continuity of operations possible, for there would be no safe place for the government and military elite to shelter.

However, despite the general shotgun blast approach of the continuity plan, Phase One of Operation GLORY SAVE explicitly called for an internal, stealthy approach in its primary segment of implementation. This had been decided by a secret executive order during the term of the previous POTUS and his rather paranoid administration, who felt that going wide-open and public with GLORY SAVE would give any adversaries an undesired warning of what they might not otherwise be able to discern. After all, the United States and its allies now, for the most part, had reserved the right to launch preemptive nuclear strikes, should a situation so require. Therefore, the public-facing façade would be one of business as usual in the United States of America. And no one external to the process would even be aware of what was being prepared behind the scenes.

Not that such mundane, mortal minutiae mattered one iota to the Lightbringer, his approaching sigil, and his cosmic schemes. Or so he thought.

eVo.144.000.mOd.0.sCe.6 | EARTH | UNITED STATES | ALABAMA | HUNTSVILLE| THE VOID

CORY'S RETURN TRIP home left no impression on him other than that he had merely exchanged one bad scene for another.

Apparently, MorthonTech employed a safehouse – complete with a kill room – in the basement of a residential complex high atop one of Huntsville's many mountain ridges. Cory had vaguely recalled Maynard's long-ago mention of a sprawling company house somewhere in the general area, but, being a mere code-monkey, and not management like Maynard, he had never been invited to one of the company retreats. Figures an asshole like Sim would have placed a secret kill room in such an otherwise enchanting estate. Boy, were the MorthonTech employees in for a surprise they next time they gathered for a company retreat.

Cory could not believe what had just happened. People had just melted and turned to black goo in front of him. Men had died, because reality had gone haywire. Aliens and triple helix DNA. And something wicked had... had...

This time, Cory managed to center his chi, and banish, if only for the moment, the insanity.

As he got his bearings, he realized he'd be able to walk back home before the morning's commute got too heavy. And before too many people saw him. Adjusting what remained of his tattered hoodie around him, he took off from the MorthonTech retreat at a brisk jog, careful to stick to the back roads as much as possible. And careful to look away whenever anyone passed by him.

His normal logical powers were skewed and shaken, totally disorganized now, by the event – events, he corrected himself; first aliens, then ... something savage had heaved and wretched itself from his own soul. Not that he had ever considered himself anything even closely resembling a Boy Scout, but he had no doubt, none whatsoever, that whatever the hell it was that he had just experienced – what he had just become, he corrected himself – was beyond any mortal concept of good or evil.

"At last, I am reborn!" Cory replayed what he had said over and over again, trying to recall where he had ever heard something like that said before. Some movie? Some comic book he had read? His typically eidetic memory failed him, and he saw nothing in his mind's eye to answer his questions. Something usually had to be born first – then die – in order to be reborn, he reckoned, but he was drawing some obvious blanks when trying to scan his deep memory for what the heck it could have been that had implanted such a cancerous thought into his mind.

Less than an hour later, having occupied his relatively brief yet awkward walk back home with his fruitless attempts at analyzing his current situation, Cory arrived at his Green Mountain home. Here, though still technically in the city, he might instead be deep in a picturesque Bavarian forest. Still, thinking a bit more lucidly now that he was home, he retrieved a spare key from beneath a flower pot and let himself in the front door.

He felt spiritually discharged, and his slow clamber inside saw him make a beeline for his basement and its beckoning isolation tank. Sensing his approach, embedded sensors activated automatically the ambient light system, which illuminated the basement with subdued, warm light. He tugged off the shredded remnants of his hoodie, uncaring that there had been quite a physical change to his body as a result of his earlier transformation. His normally deep bronze skin tone now was a shade or three darker, more robust now, as if something had dipped him in a vat of molten 24-karat gold.

As he stepped down onto the marble steps leading down to the sunken level of the isolation tank, he removed the rest of his clothes and tossed them down on the steps. Catching his reflection on the shiny chrome lid of the custom-built isolation tank as he drew near to it, he winced, as his eyes clearly were emitting those damned electric blue faerie sparks. It was on his chest, writhing like a thing alive and angry; a symbol, a tattoo, a crest, of multispectral fractals. It pulsated in rhythm with his heartbeat, casting subtle spokes of deep purple from it one beat, then issuing concentric circles of silver framed by black and blue from its core for several beats, then chaotically shifting to another mandala form, which began another chaotic iteration of shifting fractal lines, lights, and colors.

"That is totally cool," Cory said, his own voice startling him slightly. For to his musician's ear, to his adept ability of perfect pitch, it was richer than ever it had been, with a slight mellifluous flange to it, as if it were being digitally processed.

At that moment, he thought, incorrectly as he would soon learn, that perhaps this whole bad scene was not going to be quite so bad after all; that, maybe, he would be able to enjoy it, maybe even embrace it. That, of course, he realized, would require him to re-center himself. This, of course, was why he was about to climb into "The Dark Womb", as Maynard had mystically named his creation, and find his center once more. Gather his chi, his ki, his vril, his power, his magick, his soul. Realign and rebalance his obviously misaligned chakras and get himself back to normal. Or at least as normal as he could be now, now that he had transcended... Yes, that would be the correct word, he considered carefully, for he was fairly certain that, given the events of the past few hours, he was no longer what he thought he was, what he once had been. No, now, he was certain, he was indeed quite something more.

"Fucking Queensrÿche. Just don't take me somewhere far beyond the Void," Cory whispered to himself. Somehow, they had known. "Open, please," he asked aloud.

"Yes, Master," Miss No-Pants immediately complied, her voice coming seemingly from everywhere.

"No calls, please," Cory commanded as he entered the tank, the door closing quietly, automatically, behind him.

Maynard had been the one to insist on building the isolation tank. Cory, while thinking that the concept was cool, if somewhat expensive, was initially reluctant to spring for it until Maynard had forced him to watch a few of Joe Rogan's podcasts. Maynard knew that Rogan's martial arts background, stoner habits, and generally awesome selection of guests would persuade Cory to seal the deal and do the deed, and then the two of them would be able to trip on Maynard's ayahuasca and travel to many parts unknown. Cory, once inspired, made the decision quickly, and he and Maynard burned many hours spinning up the components from several of MorthonTech's battery of 3D printers, then assembling them in Cory's basement. But that, only after Cory had doled out mucho dinero for the custom marble sunken bath housing, and only after Cory had coded the new hosting modules for Miss No-Pants to interface with Maynard's buzzy embedded code.

He settled at last into a comfortable position in the isolation tank. Maynard was one helluva homie, Cory had to admit as the soothing, salty, body temperature waters rose slowly around the perimeter of his naked form, gently caressing his skin, teasing the hair along his body. The settling-in process, Maynard had taught him before his first isolation experience, was the last phase of this reality, when the body-spirit-mind, along all seven chakras, manifested itself fully, in a state of imminent arousal, as if in total accordance with its impending release into the...

"...into the what?" Cory asked himself as the warmth of the Epsom salt-impregnated warm waters fixed him into a state of gentle, almost impalpable suspension, as if he were levitating, a fetus half-in and half-out of its amniotic sac. Cory's thoughts became focused, entrained in laser-precise pulses. No need for Maynard's ayahuasca or DMT. This time, finally, at long last, he knew that he had no need for external help via drugs or shamanic ceremonies to discover what he sought. For, finally, at long last, what he had tried in vain to find so many times before now sought to find him.

"Now you are mine..." Chthon, the midwife of the Void, the Dark Womb itself, whisper-thundered in Cory's head.

At once, Cory, his eyes still locked tight, sensed that he was no longer confined to his corporeal shell. It was precisely as if her voice had reached right into his floating body, clutched his soul with draconic talons, and abruptly ripped out his essence. He could almost hear, he imagined, all seven of his chakras pop out of his static soul with a psychic sound like that of a small string of M-80s. A whirling, widdershins-wise funnel of ROYGBIV lights, tiny, sparkling, pulsing and effusive, flew near to his closed eyes, pinwheeling energetically from his head down to his toes.

He could see them in his mind's eye as clearly as if his eyes were wide open. There was, simultaneously, the jarring, physical sensation of falling, almost like skydiving, he felt, but with the perceived airflow coming from all sides, all vectors. No clear up or down, just falling all possible ways at once. Cory willed his eyes to remain tightly closed, although he knew quite well that he no longer had actual, physical eyes.

"Cory," Chthon whisper-slashed, her "voice" manifesting as SUV-sized, violent purple dragon talons marking the space between them; the wave front of her Mindtouch, here in her native realm, conforming to one of her almost infinite possible avatars, "witness the truth..."

Massive purple talons shot forward to grasp Cory's form; clutching not only his projected physical form, but also, and more importantly, the actualizations of his ka, his ba, the entire host of his soul and souls; all chakra foci; all vril; all energy and light that was Cory Christopher Tate now was in the Dark Earth Mother's fearsome grasp. At this moment, she became every person Cory had ever met in this life, and in all of his lives, for now he knew beyond doubt that he had lived a thousand lives, in a thousand different cosmic incarnations. His vision, sight beyond eyesight, peered with intent into the blackened maw of a seemingly endless well of souls, the souls manifested behind the gaze of eyes, an infinite progression of tiers of eyes, spiraling down into the dark depths of the well. He traversed the entire depth of the well of souls in an infinitely compressed, super-fast-forward mega-experience of the life and times of all of the souls in the well. The most sublime, intimate experiences in their lives hammered into him in sub-Planck Time. The force of so many billions of lifetimes scathed, scoured, and eroded any hope he ever held of maintaining his focus here in this thrice-damned place. As darkness beyond darkness finally soothed the psychic fire consuming his soul, Cory was aware of nothing, nothing at all now, save his own primal scream.

"We are the Dragon!" Chthon boomed, every syllable crunching down into his raw soul. "We are the life force of this cosmos, this sphere, this world, and this world beyond worlds," she continued, her voice the only semblance of reality possible now for Cory's shattered mind to clutch onto, his sole anchor in this place of utter oblivion, this void... the Void, he finally understood. "We allow you, Cory, to see us for who we truly are. It is time for your world, your Earth, your cosmos, to be judged by the Lightbringer's Sigil. Its weirding calls for you soon. It calls for all souls, as all of you, kith and kin, and all within the tiny nether space you call Reality, affixed 'twixt Source and Void, are to be judged by its ineffable power, its alien presence, its implacable will. Behold," she roared, her titanic violent purple dragon talons flashing before Cory's vision, directing his focus toward an abruptly manifesting form, which bloomed from nothing to everything, "the Lightbringer's Sigil, the harbinger of the Anshadar Effect!"

"It sang to me!" Cory's tortured mind raged.

It was a construct of a series of prismatic helices, steps and stairs on multiple tiers, locking and interlocking within, between and among themselves. There was the perception of motion, of a shared dance, among the three major, most prominent strands. His vantage shifted here and there, at will, seeing first the construct from one side, then another, as fast as his mind could process it. Willing his "hand" to appear, Cory reached forward, attempting to touch it. The change in perspective was both immediate and unexpected. As Cory's virtual fingertips brushed its warm, slightly vibrating edge, the sigil abruptly shifted its manifestation into a sky-circumscribing halo, now far out of reach, now high in the sky, and far into the horizon. It cast a suffuse yet insistent rainbow-spanning panopticon of light, rudely alighting the Void itself, illuminating the semi-material shadowy form of Chthon as well as Cory's naked, hairless ape human form.

The sigil's pulsation, its prismatic laser light show, began to syncopate, to strobe, then to flash sequentially, one strand first, then another; one base pair, or base triplet in this case, then another; then, in a cacophonous cascade, the sigil sang to Cory in a chorus of a billion voices. At once, hot tears filled Cory's eyes; again, there was a super-fast-forward, and each voice sang its own song, and each song made connection with the billions of souls who had only moments – eternities – prior had shown him their lives. What Cory had learned were emotions and sensations and experiences in his brief life thus far were made into pale lies by what he experienced then – he screamed and fought against this relentless tsunami of souls with every iota of his willpower – a billion-fold psychic sledgehammer beat his psyche down over and over and over again – he resisted, bent but never broken; electric blue sparks manifesting from his eyes, forming a protective aura of primal psychic energy around his form – only to leave something immutable, adamantine and unyielding in its place.

"Now, VoidSpawn," Chthon informed him, "truly are you at last reborn."

Then, the sigil was gone. Chthon vanished, a mocking half-grin of anticipation on her shadowy face. The Void was once more absent of light, and Cory's newly soulforged soul returned to its host.

eVo.144.000.mOd.0.sCe.7 | EARTH | UNITED STATES | ALABAMA | HUNTSVILLE

"CORY? CORY!"

Cory distantly heard Maynard's insistent voice. At this particular moment, however, he was shivering from head to toe, which he dimly recalled was close to impossible in the heated waters of the isolation tank.

"Cory! Cory! What the hell, man?" Maynard bellowed from the other side of the tank's doors. There was some distant thumping, like metal on metal, then, abruptly, there was painful light, as Maynard finally managed to pry open the deformed metal hatches that served as the isolation tank's doors. "What the hell happened? Are you okay?" he asked, reaching down to grab Cory's slowly rising hands. He helped Cory out of the tank, where Cory unceremoniously plopped down immediately, naked, on the cool marble tiled floor.

Cory drew himself into a fetal position, propping himself against the marble stairs, trying to face away from Maynard, as he had the feeling that his eyes were still doing their tricks. Afterimages of what he had just experienced were still taunting his field of vision, perverting and corrupting it. Then, recalling the Lightbringer's Sigil with eidetic precision, he started laughing, and he realized at once that his laughter didn't sound like it had issued forth from a sane man.

"It sang to me... " he told Maynard over his shoulder, through chattering teeth.

"It sang to you?" Maynard inquired, side-stepping Cory's shivering form. He was careful not to directly touch him or draw too closely to him. He was also looking for a towel, but, apparently, a bomb had hit the room, and everything that had formerly been neatly arranged in here now was scattered around in chaotic heaps on the floor. And the tank itself. What the hell could have done that? "Cory? Did you try to brew up the ayahuasca on your own? Not a good idea to do the tank without a spotter. Are you high, Cory?"

"I w-w-wish..." Cory struggled, his incessant shivering slowly starting to normalize. He breathed deeply, desperately using every mantra, every chi focusing exercise he knew, trying to center himself. The attribute he held most precious – moreso than his natural gifts and his small host of hard-earned skills – was his willpower, and, right now, he was leveraging it to its fullest as he fought to control his own traumatized mind. Rationally, he knew where he was. He was here, in his basement, in his house in Huntsville, Alabama, on Earth. He knew that Maynard was here, that he wasn't alone. He knew he was Cory ... *but you're not Cory, are you? You never have been. You never were. We stole your soul from you before you were even born.*

Cory groaned heavily. Hurrying, Maynard finally managed to find a towel, which he gently draped across Cory's shoulders and back. "More light in here, Miss No-Pants, please."

"Yes, Maynard the T-Rex of Jungle Love," Miss No-Pants warmly replied as the lumen count rose, filling the basement with midday-bright LED light.

"Cory, I need to check your vitals," Maynard informed him as he moved around to face him, bending a knee to the floor. He noticed that Cory had his hands pressed palm down over his eyes, as if he were in the midst of an extremely painful migraine headache. Trying to recall his first responder training, he began to do a visual scan of Cory's body, to make sure that there were no visible injuries requiring treatment. That's when he saw Cory's trippy new chest tattoo. It was gently strobing, barely noticeable as the basement's lighting system had transformed night into daylight. But, shining it was.

"What the hell, Cory?" Maynard marveled, forgetting about Cory's vitals or possible injuries. "Did you get C-No to do an LED body mod to your chest? If so, that's her best work by far. How are you doing the fractals? That rocks!"

Show him how much it rocks...

Abruptly, Cory reared to an upright position, startling Maynard. "If you think that's cool, Maynard," he told him, "wait till you see this," he said, withdrawing his hands from his eyes.

Even under the artificial midday light, the dancing, electric blue sparkles from Cory's eyes shone bright, causing wicked reflections to writhe on the adaptive lenses of Maynard's Serengeti prescription sunglasses. Maynard's mouth worked silently as he subvocalized his thoughts. His powerful engineer's mind went to work on trying to solve the various mechanics involved in producing such a sight. The chest trick, possibly embedded subdermal LEDs with some wicked programming behind them, he considered as remotely probable. Remotely. But the eyes? He knew it was not possible to generate that bright of a display from a modded intraocular lens. Maybe one, maybe two shots, but the risk of blindness... *No way. It's improbable,* Maynard thought, *that Cory could or would have had all that done. C-No is a good body modder, but an ophthalmologist would have had to have done this type of surgery. And I just saw him yesterday, for Christ's sake, so there's no way he could have... could have...*

The sparkling, dancing faerie lights dimmed, then faded completely. Strangely, Cory's naturally green eyes now were completely black. No distinct pupil. No distinct iris. Just black. Totally black. More than that, for it was the total absence of color, of being, of life itself. Black beyond black, like the Forever Silence of the Void itself, which had just been resurrected in the place he had formerly called his soul.

"I can't believe what I'm seeing, man," Maynard said, quietly, calmly. Cory was nodding affirmatively at Maynard. They were tight as brothers from another mother, so he knew almost exactly what Maynard was thinking, which methods he was using to do the calculations, and which particular solution he must have just reached.

Maynard started to chuckle, smiling. "There's NO way, Cory! NO fucking way! Mother Ayahuasca blessed you?"

M. K. "Maynard" James, an aerospace engineer by training with a dozen high-tech patents to his name, was also an ordained shaman who practiced plant-spirit healing, including, among many, the ayahuasca ceremony. It actually was not quite so uncommon a mix of tech and spiritual belief as most people would suppose. In fact, Maynard's small circle of fellow travelers included not only his best friend Cory but also an even dozen of the movers and shakers in the local high-tech Huntsville community. Due to the pervasive disdain from the legal authorities, it was of course necessary to schedule "ayahuasca holidays" during which the group would travel to the remote and disparate places where the shamanic practice was entirely legal and perform their sacred ceremonies there. For Maynard, the curious juxtaposition of technology and shamanistic magicks in his life caused not an iota of cognitive dissonance. For, despite his keen intellect, or perhaps more accurately due to his keen intellect, he thought that tech and magick were one and same, resultants of the same causal forces, just separated a bit on the cosmic continuum, just as gamma-rays were on one side of the electromagnetic spectrum and long radio waves were on the other. He was one of the High Priests of Tech in the Rocket City, where America and its Operation Paperclip former Nazi rocket scientists built the rocket that landed man on the moon. He therefore had no qualms whatsoever in fully believing in the reality of "Mother Ayahuasca".

"Mother Ayahuasca? Not exactly," Cory said, shaking his head. He wrapped the towel around him, then stood up, attempting to find his pants or even just his underwear from among the chaotic piles of debris on the floor.

Maynard, patiently waiting for Cory to retrieve his clothes, got up and gave the isolation tank a closer inspection. After a moment, he was quite certain that the damage vectors originated from the inside of the tank. Which, of course, was patently absurd. Cory was hella strong, he knew for a fact, and not just strong for a nerd. Dangerously strong. Maynard had seen him, during one of their mixed martial arts training sessions a few years ago at the Huntsville Gracie Jiu-Jitsu Academy, explosively bench press a training partner off him and send him flying, basically launching a strong, clinging 260-pound man off his chest and three feet straight up into the air with a shrug of his arms. Strong as an ox he was, but no human could have compromised the structure of the isolation tank and its doors like that, not even with a sledgehammer.

"She said her name was 'Chthon,'" Cory told Maynard. Finally, he found his underwear and pants, and donned them before continuing. "She said she was, and I quote, 'the Dragon,' then she showed me a piece of gigantic space-DNA that she called 'the Lightbringer's Sigil'. She said that it was coming here, to Earth, and that it would cause something she called 'the Anshadar Effect'. Finally, before sending me back from..." he paused, trying to figure out how to explain it. "...from the Void. We were in the Void, Maynard," he said, watching shock finally cross Maynard's face.

"Not the fucking Void, Cory!" Maynard pulled his prescription sunglasses off. The strain of anger was in his voice. "You know that place is anathema to good spirits," he said gravely.

"I know that," Cory countered. "It's a tenet of your faith, I very much respect it because I happen to believe it myself, thanks to your showing me the way. And I'm sorry I even have to say it, but it happened, and I have to tell you exactly, truthfully, what happened. So, please forgive me in advance for this one. She finished the whole thing up by calling me 'VoidSpawn' and telling me that 'truly are you at last reborn. I mean, what the fuck? Reborn? I'm not dead in the first place."

Maynard's honey-brown, almost golden eyes went dark with barely repressed anger. A moment later, the anger faded, dispelled back to its safe place, and he smiled at Cory.

"Sorry, man. I'm just having a tough time processing it. And I'm not being very empathetic here. This didn't happen to me. It happened to you. I'm sorry that you had to go through that. I mean, the Void..." Maynard's voice, as honey-smooth as his eyes, cracked slightly. "The time that I experienced the Void, it was because of being directed there and tested by the Mother. Something about my having to face such things when the time comes. It was a big test. The biggest. And it was the single most mind-blowing experience of my life. I rolled 1d6 for my Sanity Save, and I blatantly failed it. That's what sent me into acute care for two weeks. It wasn't an overdose, like I told everyone," he finally admitted to Cory, after years of lying about it. "It was a breakdown. It was experiencing what it felt like to exist without a soul, in the Far Side of Shadow. I think that some small part of me never really returned. It blew my freaking mind." He shrugged. "So I guess that time has finally come. I just never thought it would come from you, Cory. I'm sorry, man," he apologized, his heart breaking right then and there for his friend. From where Cory had been, there was no coming back. A part of you would always be missing, and you could never find it again, no matter how hard you tried. But if anyone could deal with such a transformation...

"Well, fuck me for being the VoidSpawn," Cory laughed, catching Maynard a bit off guard. "I know you already think that this 'Chthon' entity in my vision state is really the Mother, and I know that's what it seems like, so, if we roll with that, then the Mother just showed me who I was and gave me a warning about something really bad that's about to come to Earth. So I think I just got a quest."

Maynard nodded, smiling, welcoming Cory back. "It's quite probable, actually. The Mother is a skin shifter, obviously, and most cultures know that. Even the Caucasian half of your multi-culti self, Cory," Maynard pointed out, totally aware that both of them were hyphenated Americans. "So she might have been resorting to the ancient Greek root term to express herself to you."

"True," Cory countered, actually happy to shift gears into Nerd World with Maynard. "Chthon is typically considered to have that particular etymology, and it's also pervasive in pop culture, from novels to comics. I won't go into the Cthulhu, or Kutulu, or other ancient Sumerian detours."

Maynard actually smiled at that. "You and your graveyard-dead languages," he laughed, stopping him there, knowing what could have happened next if Cory had gotten spun up about languages. He knew how many languages Cory knew. And not just computer languages, scripts, or frameworks. The old, dead ones, with their mind-numbing squiggly characters and ideograms. It was just one more vulgar display of intellect from his favorite mega-savant.

Cory continued. "And we have 'the Dragon', with its obvious connotations beyond its common denotation. Obviously, she wasn't referring to an actual dragon."

"Could be collective spiritual life force," Maynard offered. He stared hard at Cory for a moment. "Those eyes of yours. Jesus."

"They're solid black. I know. I keep catching my reflection from the tank. Or, what's left of the tank," he corrected himself.

"Well, I never liked green eyes anyway," Maynard blatantly lied, "except on cats. Anyway, I'd need to have heard the exact phrasing. Think you can recall it, or was there too much trauma for you to use your memory?"

"Oh, I remember," Cory growled. "Never gonna forget it, either. She said, '"We are the life force of this cosmos, this sphere, this world, and this world beyond worlds.'"

"Ding ding."

Cory smiled. "I need some food. Let's talk as we walk," Cory said, indicating for Maynard to lead the way. He gave the wreck of the isolation tank a final glance, and a final flip of the bird finger. "Kill the lights, please, Miss No-Pants, and start lunch for me and Maynard."

"Yes, Master."

Maynard was already in the kitchen, leaning over the granite counter top island. There was a quizzical look on his face.

"What's up?" Cory asked, sauntering in, shirtless.

"It's you, dude," he replied, looking directly at Cory. "You're jacked for one thing," he said, motioning toward Cory's newly enhanced upper body. "I know you've always been in great shape, martial arts, music, and everything. But, suddenly, you look like you've been training in secret for 10 years."

"Huh?" Cory asked, scooping their steaming bento boxes from the smart auto feed microwave. "The new muscles?" he asked, joining Maynard at the counter, a bento box and chopsticks in each hand. He eased a box across the smooth countertop to Maynard. "They popped up this morning while I was being kidnapped by Simm and some MorthonTech goons."

Noodles spewed from Maynard's mouth. "Oh, shit! Please tell me you're fucking with me."

"I am not," Cory said between bites. "Water?" he asked, and Maynard nodded, finally catching his breath. Cory hit the fridge, returning to the countertop with two bottled waters. He slid one over to Maynard, who deftly caught it, popped it, and swigged from it. "I'm not fooling around. Simm's mercs kidnapped me this morning, first thing, right when I was about to hop in my truck. It's all about the Ames thing."

"Ames? Jennie's group? Deep Oracle?"

Cory nodded. "Yes. Jennie got me up not long after midnight this morning. Wanted me to look over some data she got from Janice Murphy over at SETI."

"Cool. So, let me guess," he said, giving Cory a sudden, serious stare. "They found your space-DNA? The Lightbringer's Sigil that's going to usher in the Anshadar Effect?"

"I know, I know," Cory agreed. "Looks like I picked the wrong week to stop taking acid. The space-DNA thing is what Janice got over at SETI after they ran their in-house processing. It was 99%, Maynard. So, obviously, they needed deeper checking, so they passed it over to Jennie and ran more stuff on Deep Oracle."

"And it was still 99%?"

"Yep. So Jennie woke me up rather early and asked me to do the triple-check personally. Turns out that there were some MorthonTech goonies running around at Ames, and probably SETI, too, and they were rounding everyone up for 'emergency exit protocols', which is code for 'we're going to shut you up before you tell everyone about the aliens coming this way.'"

"Fucking fascists. Probably DiSazi and his pukes. They're all ex-spec ops guys, and they take things to the extreme because he encourages it. Ah, they're jerks, but they won't hurt Jennie or anyone else. Word has it that, at MorthonTech, employees who fuck up bad get sent to the—"

"To the Antarctic branch," Cory finished for him, causing Maynard to laugh.

"You said you ran more analyses. What did you get?" Maynard asked.

Cory took a swig of water, then motioned for Maynard to break his trance-stare at Cory's chest. "I moved through the various dimensional projections. When we moved into expressed spacetime, it resolved from flat DNA to triple helix DNA. Then, I got a hunch, started moving it around, and, guess what? When it goes left-hand chiral, it starts producing musical tones. Flat stuff, for which I got the idea to re-process it all from all the points of capture. The data was dense enough for me to coax a symphonic piece from it. Then, of course, it sang to me. I think that's when all this batshit crazy stuff started."

"You have got to be kidding me. Triple helix space-DNA is singing to you from outer space? And it's coming this way? No wonder Simm sent the Nazis in to Ames. And to you. No way they'd let that get out."

"I know. I confronted Simm personally about it. We talked. I turned over my data analysis to him because I thought it would help get our two J-ladies out of their fix. It was going well, actually, until something happened."

"I really don't want to hear this. Remember, Simm signs most of my paychecks. And most of Professor Gil's, too. And some of yours, too, Cory. Sweet Jesus don't tell me he saw you like this!"

"Well, only at the very end of our conversation," Cory admitted. "But don't worry, Maynard. They took me to the kill room that's in the basement of the MorthonTech retreat here. No one saw us. After they loaded up my data analysis program, an image of the sigil appeared and melted Simm and his mercs. Turned them into nasty black goo. Turned me into this."

"I can't believe it," Maynard said, his iron grip on his shot nerves finally giving way. "Simm is dead? Holy shit! Ah, I can't believe all this crazy shit that's happening. I always thought I'd be able to handle aliens, monsters, singing space-DNA, and the Void... but not all once, chipmunk-fucking Christ!"

At that, he began to gag. Cory pointed at the sink. "Garbage disposal side, please."

"Chipm-mrrrmnunphh!!"

After the deed, Maynard decided to ignore the rest of lunch. Instead, he moved into the living room and paced nervously while Cory, not filled by his bento box, appropriated what was left of Maynard's.

Maynard spoke slowly, clearly, trying to invoke logic once more to dispel the total chaos of the day. "Well, if Simm played it like that, it means he's keeping a lid on it. Probably the same lid over Ames and SETI. MorthonTech pays enough of SETI's bills that Simm's got a lock on them, even if he's dead. And while he can't actually control NASA itself, he can control Ames fairly effectively, considering how many projects MorthonTech is funding there. Despite what Jennie might have told you, most of the top guys there virtually worship Simm and MorthonTech. Wouldn't be at all surprised if most of them are MorthonTech stockholders."

"Think they're going to all stay silent about this?" Cory asked, already knowing the answer.

"Yep. Even if Simm's just black goo now. NDAs galore. Plus, they're all already on the payroll. They really have no choice. Not even Jennie or Janice."

"So it looks like it's just you and me, then."

"Yeah, right, I'll just rebel against the company that's funded half of my patents, and has a half-dozen more under IP protection," Maynard said, shaking his head.

"You rebel, you!" Cory mocked. "Remember, they kidnapped me and held me against my will."

"Fuck you, Cory. I can't rebel. I'm not independently wealthy like you are, you effing hacker."

"Yeah, right, whatever. I work for a living too, just like everybody else. I just hold multiple jobs simultaneously, because I've got smart bots doing most of the work. And long as I don't have to dress up, go into an office every single day, and get sore lips from kissing everybody's ass so that they don't fire me, I'm fine."

Maynard thought that was an amusing picture, because he never kissed anyone's ass in the work world, and Cory damn well knew it. "Fuck the normies. Their job is to occupy the inner bands of the Bell Curve. Our job is to be outliers. Fuckin' normies," he laughed dismissively. Cory knew he wasn't really serious, but it was still funny to hear Maynard dis the normies; even better when he dissed the outliers themselves. "So, seriously, what are we going to do about this? It's so far beyond crazy that it's... it's hard to get a grasp of it. Aliens? Space-DNA? Your transformation and experience?" He paused, staring into the middle distance. "And Simm's dead. Shit. That's going to kill our employee stock options."

Cory considered it for a moment. "Let's do what we do best: Engineer a solution."

"Hell, yeah!" Maynard agreed. Now they were back in the game. For a brief moment, he toyed with the LG Watch which hung suspended on a customized vest pocket chain. Next, he gave the Apple Watch on his left wrist a quick glance, then his Samsung Gear, which was on his right. Ritual complete, he looked up and gave Cory a brilliant smile with his Hollywood white shade teeth. "I've got an idea on how to do this. I'm supposed to deliver some biological samples to Professor Gil. Let me grab my kit from my car. We can grab some of your samples and the good professor can tell us what the heck is really going on with you."

Cory considered it for a millisecond. "Well, I guess it's okay. I trust Professor G. And, even though he's a MorthonTech freak, too, I reckon that's okay. Because if anything gets out, it'll have to be subject to their duck-and-cover protocol, so it's got good inherent deniability if they find out."

"You mean, if they find out, and try to weaponize it. Weaponize you, I mean," Maynard quickly corrected as he was jogging out of the kitchen.

"Yeah, weaponize me," Cory said to himself. "I have a distinct hunch that I've already been weaponized. Big time."

Checking around the corner to make sure that Maynard was not within view, he turned back into the kitchen, scanning quickly for something to test. A stainless-steel tumbler on the countertop grabbed his attention. He grabbed it, looked around once more just to be sure, then he tried to crush it. It instantly complied, its stainless-steel construction crumpling like a thin sheet of cheap aluminum foil in his grasp.

Awkwardly, he fumbled the ruined tumbler in his hands until he managed to fumble it forward onto the central island.

"That is so cool," he laughed as Maynard came flying back into the kitchen, a large generic Anvil flight case modded with a welded-on handle in his grasp.

"Why the laughing?" Maynard asked, drawing to a stop on the other side of the island. Cory's eyes shot toward the deformed tumbler. Maynard, unable to see his eyes, simply shrugged. Cory tried it again, then caught himself. He laughed, then simply pointed at it. "Ah, very cool! You can destroy innocent tumblers. That's A-1, top-grade Void power. You iris-less simp-tard!"

Cory laughed. "Took me a second to remember that my eyes look like a negative of Little Orphan Annie's."

"And Simm is your Daddy Whorebucks!" Maynard winced, pausing to consider his joke. "Sorry. I still think he's alive. Not good to dis the dead." He fiddled with his flight case. "Let's check you out, first. Hell, you might be radioactive or something." At that, Maynard heaved his case atop the island, and popped the locks. "Want to test that first?" he smiled, proudly waving his hand over the bizarre assortment of unique techno-toys in his collection.

"Yeah, sure, why not?"

As Cory complied, Maynard went through the motions of taking one device after another out of the case, pressing a few knobs or dials on the device, and passing it over and around and near Cory.

"Well," Maynard informed Cory after artifact number four was done, "you're not radioactive, nor is your chest tattoo, nor are your eyes. And I thought your chest *would* be. I was *hoping* it would be, actually, because that would be really cool, and it would probably mean that you could fire beams out of it like Iron Man or something."

"Get the fuck out, Maynard!"

"Also," Maynard continued, laughing briefly, "you're completely normal. I know that's a shock for a freak like you. But you're not emitting anything unusual. So no Cyclops eye beams. Your core temperature is still its typical high-normal-range 99.5 degrees Fahrenheit. So you're not going to be Ice Man. Your pulse rate and oxygen levels are normal. You're normal, at least by these detection and measuring methods. So," he said, producing yet another palm-sized metallic device, "let's get a few blood samples for the professor to take a look at. At least we'll be able to rule-in or rule-out a wide swath of maladies, diseases, and possible genetic modifications. This won't sting for too long," he told Cory, gently tapping him on his forearm with the tip of the device.

Not feeling anything, Cory shrugged his shoulders.

"You didn't feel a little prick?"

"Ha ha. I didn't even touch you," Cory deadpanned. "No, nothing. Sure you've got a sampler in it?"

Maynard turned it over and looked at it studiously. He turned it back over, clicked a button, and a small lozenge-like glass ampule fell from it. It was empty. He fiddled for a moment with the front tip of the device, then, with a sharp pinch, he removed a small orange plastic nub. At its tip, a clearly deformed needle could be seen.

"Oh, that's some tight shit there, Cory," Maynard said, dexterously pinching the plastic nub and holding it so Cory could see it. "That'll easily punch though a can of soda. But you wrecked it."

"I see that. Let's try something else," Cory said, grabbing a kitchen knife from its wooden block receptacle, then sliding it carefully over the slick marble countertop to Maynard.

Maynard looked at him quizzically. "You want me to cut you, bitch?" he laughed.

Cory nodded. "But, I mean, like don't just go ape shit and stab it like Psycho. Start out easy. Small stabby stabby. Like that Gnome Rogue you played in WoW."

Rolling his eyes, Maynard awkwardly picked up the knife. "You sure about this?" he asked, adding, "EEE! EEE! EEE!" as he stabbed the knife into completely innocent air.

Cory nodded an affirmative, holding out his right arm, forearm up.

Maynard raised the knife up, only to have Cory pull his arm back. "Can't. Can't. Not the arm. Can't risk it. Might not be a maestro or anything, but I still try to play guitar."

"Oh, yeah. Almost forgot. Leg then? Top of the thigh, maybe?"

"Yeah, sure," Cory agreed, pivoting to his left, bending his trunk slightly down and to the left, simultaneously extending his right leg with a slow-motion side kick, until it rested atop the counter.

"Ready?" Maynard asked. Cory nodded once, his jaw jutting as he braced himself. Delivered in a compact arc, Maynard's knife struck the top of Cory's lower leg, about an inch beneath the bottom of his kneecap. The impact made no sound. Maynard stood there, knife in hand, its point resting beneath Cory's kneecap. His eyes moved back and forth from the knife in his hand, to Cory's smiling face. "What, nothing?" he asked.

"Nada. Try it again. With more emotional con-tent!" Cory scolded him with the words of The Master.

"Dude, it went through the pants," Maynard informed him as he leaned in close to examine it, "but it didn't even scratch your skin. Look!" he said excitedly, bringing the knife back up, then slamming it down, down, and down again, each time with the same curious, soundless impact. "Hear that?" Maynard asked him, still mercilessly stabbing Cory's leg again and again. "Maybe just a tiny tearing sound when I strike off-perpendicular and tear more material from your pants. But otherwise, nothing. No sound when it strikes your skin. There aren't too many ways to explain that one, Cory, dude. For you to have increased your mass enough for that to have happened, you'd probably have to weigh a few metric tons."

"And, obviously, I don't," Cory answered, withdrawing his leg, returning to center. "Or we'd be having this conversation in the basement right about now. Let me see the knife." Maynard adroitly rolled the knife in his hand, passing Cory blade hilt-first. "Let's try this," he said, holding the knife in one hand, parallel to his shoulders, and, with his other hand, slowly pressing his open palm into the point.

"Dude!" Maynard yelled, eyes bugging. "No way!"

The high carbon steel kitchen knife's tip touched Cory's palm, making no visible indentation. Cory bunched his shoulders and pressed harder. The blade slowly started to bend. He pressed a bit harder, and the blade bent a full 45 degrees, making a slight cracking and popping sound internally. "That's enough," Cory said, tossing it back on the countertop. He held his palm out so that Maynard could see that it was unmarked. Not even a single reddened pressure point where the knife point had rested.

Maynard, entranced now, slowly raised his gaze from Cory's palm, then stared Cory right in the eyes. "Dude," he bade him, "get your guns."

"Wut? You crazy?"

"We can just graze it off your thigh," Maynard pleaded. "C'mon, man. We've got to see how deep this goes."

"I thought we were trying to get a few blood samples for Professor Gil?" Cory reminded him. "Chill, man. Much as this might be fun, I think I'd rather not risk a bullet wound."

"You just stabbed a knife into the palm of your hand," Maynard said shrilly, "and nothing happened! Now you're worried about a little bullet wound?"

"Think of how ridiculous that would have sounded just yesterday," Cory said.

"I know, I know. But we're in the here and now, man, and Fate is trying her damnedest to catch our attention. And..." he paused, snapping his fingers. "And, I think I just figured out how to get the samples without having to shoot you. Damn, I'm good." At that, Maynard ran out of the kitchen, heading outside to his car.

Cory rolled his eyes. He really needed a shower and a fresh change of clothes, so that meant that whatever Maynard was going to do, he was going to have to do it solo. Besides, Cory had to admit that he felt absolutely jacked, like he'd just mainlined a two-liter full of pre-workout. The only thing he really had to worry about was controlling his newfound strength so that he didn't break the shower controls.

Surprisingly, both were able to compartmentalize the chaotic events and continue on with their mundane roles without breaking down, as most sane people probably would have done by this point. At least, that's what Cory's mind was trying to tell him when, after showering and changing clothes, which now fit tightly, he once more saw Maynard, who was glued to the two-by-two grid of 4K plasma screens which occupied most of one of the living room's walls.

"Deus vult, bitches!" Maynard yelled, triumphant.

"Deus vult? Are you kidding me?" Cory asked, sauntering up to the vibrant plasma displays.

"Listen to this shit, Cory! I can't believe it. He's flipped the fuck out!"

...who has re-christened himself 'Petrus Romanus', has openly decreed that all Christian branches of faith must join together in a new crusade to liberate the holy city of Jerusalem from the 'thrice-accursed spawn of Ishmael who blaspheme against the Christ and hold the Holy Land hostage'. The Holy Father has decreed, today, from the Vatican's Nervi Hall, that this new crusade is to be known as "The Holy Crusade of the Apocalypse". Accordingly, the Vatican, working through a massive chain of banks and financial institutions throughout the world, assigned a massive pool of €1,000,000,000,000 – that's right, one trillion Euros – to a virtual war pool, ostensibly to be used by allied nations to prosecute the crusade. To this he added, to the thunderous roars of the crowds that had rapidly gathered in the audience hall, 'Deus Vult!', or "God wills it".

Turkey and Palestine immediately recalled their ambassadors from the Vatican, while Malaysia did the same at their accredited embassy located in Bern. Pakistan and Saudi Arabia immediately filed complaints at the United Nations and led, along with Turkey and Malaysia, a unified Islamic effort to force the Security Council into an emergency session. Various terrorist organizations immediately placed bounties on the Pope, and multiple fatwahs have already been issued to this effect. Curiously, Iran has not yet issued an official statement, choosing instead to 'gracefully withhold any premature judgements until all facts are known'.

No word in yet from the President concerning this matter, as his team scrambles to catch up to today's terrifying, out-of-control events.

Next, coming up after this quick break, the response just issued by the Patriarch of Moscow..."

"Turn it off, please, Miss No-Pants," Cory commanded. He turned to look at Maynard. "So. The Pope has declared a holy war. Well, that's cast rather a gloom over the whole evening, hasn't it?"

Maynard died out laughing. "G-g-going for the low-hanging Python fruit, eh?" he coughed. It was clear that he was failing to compartmentalize and deal with it. "Did you catch the 'Petrus Romanus' thing? And the 'Apocalypse' thing?"

"Not to mention the minor detail of the 'crusade' thing. So every possible Vatican conspiracy theory that there ever was just got all blown to hell. This is actually the last Pope, the black Pope, predicted hundreds of years ago through prophecy. We're actually in the End Times of the Apocalypse. There's going to be a last crusade, probably waged with nuclear weapons. The Vatican actually has a trillion euros as chump change to bribe every Christian nation to join it. And, yes, 4chan had the 'Deus Vult' meme absolutely correct. That's the true power of weaponized autism."

"And you should know," Maynard said, shaking his head. "Fucking mega-savant." Somehow, Cory's nonchalant attitude was helping him cope much better. Without Cory's foundation to support him, Maynard knew he'd have already moved on by now to sheer alcoholism to escape the day's insane events. "Almost forgot. First, though, I got the samples. Just went all CSI down there and grabbed some ambient samples, as well as a tiny bit of blood from the inside wall of the isolation tank where, apparently, you struck it before you fully turned into what... whatever it is that you've turned into. What was it? VoidSperm?"

"VoidSpawn. VoidSperm was my name before the transformation," Cory deadpanned. "Ask your sisters about that."

Laughing, because he had no sisters, Maynard continued. "Here's the 'almost forgot' part. I just glossed totally over it earlier, thanks to all the white noise of the day, but what the Pope just said, and all the panic it set off, made me think about the space-DNA thing. Cory, how far away is it? I'm assuming the signals are extragalactic, as most seem to be, and that means it'll never get here, ever, in any of our lifetimes. So it's just calling out to us, but it won't actually get here till the Sun burns out, right?"

Cory shook his head, slowly. "Sagittarius A*. Galactic center of the Milky Way galaxy. Our galaxy. Very doubtful, then, that it's extra-galactic in origin, because it would have had to pass through the largest local black hole."

"That's the so-called 'Ophiuchus Hypothesis', right? 13th constellation of the ancient zodiac? Death in 2012, which we apparently missed? Mayans? Snakes? Ancient comets? Alien space-DNA?" Maynard countered.

"Why not? Today's been an exceptional day for conspiracy theory revelations. Interesting though, that the original 'Wow!' signal came from that general area. That was back in 1977, though, then there was nothing else."

"Soundcheck, maybe?"

Cory nodded thoughtfully. "Again, why not? Maybe it had to warm up before it hit center stage."

"Cory," Maynard said, waving an arm indifferently toward the dark plasma screens, "how close is it, really? This is big picture stuff, and it seems to be hitting too close to home. Good Pope, Bad Pope. Bad Mother Ayahuasca, Good Chthon. The Dragon, the Lightbringer, and the Lightbringer's Sigil, which, apparently, seems to imply that Lucifer himself is some kind of alien who flies around the galaxy in a giant DNA-shaped spaceship that's singing to us. And VoidSpawn and his super-cool buddy, Maynard, the T-Rex of Jungle Love."

Hearing her cue, Miss No-Pants replied to the catchphrase with a sexy moan.

Maynard continued. "So, Cory. When is it going to arrive? When do the aliens get here? I know you know, probably more accurately than anyone else on Earth. And not just because you happened to be third in the chain of custody to take a look at the remote sensing data from SETI and NASA/Ames. You went to the Dark Womb and saw it there, in spiritual form. That's about as intimately as you can possibly know something, man. So, what did you learn? Where is it? When will it get here? Because that's the biggest, gnarliest unknown of unknowns coming down the pike, and we sure as hell better be prepped and ready for it. If we all manage to survive the impending nuke fest that Pope Petrus '4chan' Romanus is going to get us all into."

Standing straight up to his full height, Cory seemed to tower over Maynard. He let out an audible sigh, shaking his head slowly. "My main man Maynard, I could lie and say that I don't know, and that would probably be better for everyone. No one needs to know what's really coming down the pike next. I've seen it. I've touched its psychic form. I know change when I experience it, too. It's change, big change, in the sense of some Tarot dealings. It's the kind of change that's permanent. And the more that things change, in this case, the more they don't stay the same. Catch my drift?"

Nodding, Maynard replied, "I hear you, man. I see what it's done to you. It feels like just being near you now is channeling it, somehow, to me, too. I'm not getting all jacked and taller and bigger like you, but I can almost feel it out there now, coming this way, singing to us. It's not a song of hope, like 'Stairway', either. It's the most aggressive death metal I've ever heard."

Cory's void-blackened eyes flickered dangerously, and a small host of flitting electric blue faerie sparkles filled the living room. "Death metal," he nodded in agreement. "Solid assessment. Change is death, and death is change. You're right, as usual. This sigil-thing isn't singing a song of hope. It's singing the last song of the night. And I think that when it gets here to Earth, it's going to do its business, and things are never going to be the same again."

"Like Pope 4chan's Apocalypse? Is this the 'City of Gold' from the Revelation? More importantly, if that thing is called the 'Lightbringer's Sigil', does that mean that God and Satan are real, that they're from outer space? And why would Satan be the one descending from on high, and not God? Is that some deep gnostic demi-urge shit, or what?"

"Seems like it might be," Cory admitted. "Could be bleed-through or cultural correction during the transliteration of what it might truly be named or called. You know, context lost during translation? Using familiar frames of reference embedded in us in order to explain itself to our tiny mortal minds?"

"Maybe, maybe not," Maynard said. "It's been surprisingly specific thus far. Combined with what's happening abruptly in the real world, it seems pretty damned accurate to me so far. So that space-DNA sigil-thing looks like it's a living metaphor for the Satanic, gnostic demi-urge, who apparently has created man, and is now returning to judge him. So the real, true God of the Bible has compelled the Pope to lead humanity against—"

"They're humans, too, Maynard," Cory reflexively dismissed his last line of thought. "They're going to be judged, just like everyone else. And I don't mean 'judged by God', like it happens in most of the so-called 'End Times' religious eschatologies. I think it's above that. I think it's at a meta-level above good and evil, morals and dogmas and ethics."

"Cory, you keep returning to the Mother. I'm trying my best to remain sane upon experiencing all of this, and upon hearing your own secret revelations to me. I'm trying to explain it using standard 21st Century religions and metaphysics. You're not, and the whole situation is both ironic, considering the fact that I'm the shaman here, and you're not, and perverse, because we both keep arriving at the same horrifying conclusion, despite our different exegetical vectors. I sense that you're also trying to protect me from whatever it is that you think, or know, is coming, and you're reverting to shamanistic and magickal definitions to make them more familiar to me, while I'm doing the opposite for you. So let's just drop the pretenses, okay? Talk some straight shit to each other, like the brothers we aren't but should be?"

"You're right," Cory agreed. "No more protective bullshit." He paused for two seconds, then shook his head a few times, recalling what he had seen during his whirlwind mental trip during his brief communion with the Lightbringer's Sigil. "Maynard, this is it: The End of All Things. Everything we've ever known is going to change. It might be tomorrow, or the next day, but it's going to happen soon. Really soon. Near-total annihilation will come. Earth is going to be ground zero for a war between powers beyond our comprehension. Most everyone will die before it's over. It's coming not just to judge us, but also to decree who has been chosen."

"Chosen? What the fuck, Cory. That's pure Bible terminology."

"But I mean it not in that sense. I mean it in the sense of 'being chosen to adapt and evolve, or die'. Dude, think about it. It's shaped like DNA for a reason. Three helices, not two. Think big time resonance instead of merely singing a song like a human would sing a song."

Finally, Maynard accepted the truth of the scenario in which he and Cory now trolled and rolled. It did make sense once he saw it and understood it from that perspective. There was an awful lot of distracting window dressing going down simultaneously; the world was apparently going stark raving mad all around them now. But the core, the crux, the hidden cross itself, was expressed not through the ancillary distractions – those were mere symptoms – but instead was actually being expressed by the impending arrival of the triple helix space-DNA and its song of transcendence.

Maynard recognized the interesting combination of technology and magick in play, thanks to Cory's ultimate description of the scenario. That salient bit of intimate familiarity reconciled Maynard with his formerly gimped out state of sanity. Things were going to get real, real soon. But that was okay, because Maynard had been preparing for this sort of thing for most of his life. He knew it now. He knew why he had chosen his particular path of seemingly discordant duality, embracing and exceling in both technology and magick. He now realized why, so long ago, the Mother had sent him to see the Void. It, and everything, all things he had ever experienced, had been experienced by him to prepare him for this particular cusp of time, and the time which soon would come to pass.

He realized right then and there that he was going to hear the song that the sigil was going to sing to him, and that he was going to adapt and evolve and transcend. Because he sure as hell wasn't going to curl up and die.

Cory barely saw it, though he had suspected that he would see it soon enough, and he had been prepared. Briefly, very briefly, there had been the slightest flicker of electric blue faerie sparks playing across Maynard's honey-hued eyes.

"Gotta jet," Maynard said, entirely calm now. "I'll ping you when we get the results."

"Okay," Cory replied. "Keep a low profile. Ask Gil to do the same. Be like me: Void."

Maynard, easing his way out the door, nodded in full understanding. Void, indeed. What he had seen, those many years ago when the Mother had compelled him to his trial before the Void, flashed before his mind's eye in vivid detail. He had seen the Void manifest itself in transcendent mortal form and, at the bidding of the Mother herself, annihilate everything. All worlds, all gods, all souls. Back then, during that experience, he had witnessed the End of All Things, and it had temporarily driven him insane. Now, though... Now that he understood the sublime cosmic recursion in play, its fractal structure now within his purview, he was able to accept it, and deal with it. And, one day soon, he knew, he would again witness the End of All Things, and his best friend, Cory Christopher Tate, the Void incarnate in transcendent mortal form, would again annihilate everything: all worlds, all gods, all souls.

eVo.144.000.mOd.0.sCe.8 | EARTH | UNITED STATES | ALABAMA | HUNTSVILLE | MORTHONTECH HEADQUARTERS | DEEP BIOGEN LAB

"IT'S ALREADY PAST MIDNIGHT, again," Professor Roger "Gil" Gilmour reminded himself, reluctantly removing the virtual interface from his head, carefully returning it to the case that he had modified to house the fragile device securely. Next, he removed his earbuds, Porcupine Tree's "A Smart Kid" still blaring, as well it should, he thought. Gently, he set them down atop the sterile stainless steel industrial lab tabletop before him, moving cautiously, because even a mere out-of-place sneeze here might damage the millions of dollars of high tech equipment, and would immediately improve Hitachi's next quarterly report.

Professor Gilmore heaved a heavy sigh, his dock-worker fingers slowly rubbing his tired eyes. He still had a deep list of samples to test and then run metrics on, the thought of which reminded him of something else from earlier. Maynard? Yes, earlier today, hadn't Maynard buzzed into the lab, samples in hand, asking him to run immediate diagnostics on them? He smiled at the thought that he had been so locked in on his other work that he had totally forgotten his friend's urgent request.

"Where did you put the samples, Maynard?" Professor Gil muttered to himself, eyes darting around the clutter of equipment surrounding him.

He scanned the deep list on one of the three ping-pong table-sized 4k Ultra HD monitors looming before him, suspended from their ceiling mounted housings. There were batches of samples representing most common materials, elements, compounds, and animal, plant and human samples of diverse types. Rapidly speed scanning the entries in the list, he suddenly noticed that one of the sample batches from the "human" category were named "Cory".

That little shit, Gil thought, chuckling. *He took samples from Cory.*

Gil paused a moment to consider the ethics of the situation, balked for a moment, then decided that it wouldn't be unethical to take a look at Mr. Tate's bio-matter. Besides, it was almost certain, he assumed, that Maynard had actually asked Cory's permission before obtaining the samples. Or, probably not, because Maynard's sense of humor was insane enough to rationalize the merits of samples with names such as, "Cory's Sputum", "Cory's Toothbrush", and "Cory's Attempt at Carpentry", which, as it just so happened, were clearly grouped by the sample's meta tag designation of "DNA". Clearly, the two were pranking him somehow, probably in an attempt to inject some fun into his otherwise tedious work hours.

He decided to program the composite auto-loading carousel with 5 samples of "Cory's Attempt at Carpentry", four for the TEMs, with the fifth reserved for "Polyphemus", MorthonTech's own in-house Microsphere Nanoscope, which used normal light and a few unique tiers of capture-and-handoff to provide nanometer-scale imaging. Gil then donned his earbuds, followed by the virtual interface device, which fit neatly over his eyes, its flanged arms actually sliding under the arc of the headphones, attaching the device firmly to his head.

Upon donning the custom visor, Gil immediately noticed that the composite view of what should have been five distinct screens in a two-by-three grid, overlaid by the work-in-progress transparent GUI, was in fact only one distinct screen, the other screens showing nothing more than unsteady, flickering noise. For a few moments, he cybernetically shifted the GUI's highlighted selection and interface menu, fiddling with the controls of the TEMs, trying to get a good image, but it was as if the phase contrast wasn't working properly on all four of them. While that would be unusual, he had yet to fully correct their optics regarding these new samples. That would wait, though, he thought, because the fifth screen suddenly caught his attention. Its image was clear, crisp and clean, displaying a large segment of Cory's DNA.

His focus hovering on the fifth screen, the other four screens minimized after a few seconds, simultaneously exploding the fifth screen to full size. What Gil saw momentarily caused him to stop breathing. The nucleotides were not bound by the typical double helix ladder structure. Instead, there were three helices, almost as if a strand of RNA had been superimposed into the DNA's double helices. For a moment that seemed to crawl in time, he considered several probable explanations for the anomaly, including faulty initial separation or sample contamination, but he knew that it was highly unlikely that either Maynard or Cory would have committed such errors. He knew both had the training. Well, he knew for certain that Maynard did, because he had long ago taught him how to do it. And Cory, their reclusive mega-savant? Well, he knew a whole lot about a whole lot of things. Maybe even enough to cobble up something as ludicrous as what he was now seeing?

What kind of joke is this? Gil asked himself. The bizarre triple helix sample before him slowly rotated as he moved his head around, zooming in when he squinted, and zooming out again as he opened his eyes wider. Deeply engrossed in the strangeness before him, he squinted his eyes, zooming in, then coming to an abrupt focus on a strangely lit part of the surface of one of the internal strands, the anomalous third one. It was clear to him that some type of phosphate-deoxyribose backbone spanned the third helix, forming a bridge between the two outer backbone strands, but it seemed to be superimposed over the H-bonds.

"That's impossible," Professor Gilmour said flatly.

At that moment, the impossible became quite real as the central helix emitted a flare of prismatic, rainbow light, ranging up and down its axis. As he watched the sight in breathless horror, the volume of his headphones began to ride a sine-wave roller coaster, entrained with the rainbow light show before him, filling his entire field of view with dancing colors, and filling his ears with a painful, humming overtone. Transfixed in place, arms now limp at his sides, Gil saw the rainbow lights coalesce into the central third of the triple helix structure, folding up the third helix into and unto itself, impossibly dividing into two identical triple helix structures, the lights and entrained roller coaster hum both abruptly diminishing. Intoxicated and reeling from the experience, he pulled both the visor and headphones off, letting them slide carelessly to the lab floor. Then came the silence, and he had to will himself to breathe again.

"What song was that," he asked himself, lips heavy, voice subdued. "What song was that?" he asked again, as tears began to stream down his face. "Beautiful. It was beautiful..." his voice trailed off as his legs gave out and he sank to the cold laboratory floor.

eVo.144.000.mOd.1.sCe.9 | AAL |
THE END OF ALL THINGS

ZON T'DANU, OVERLORD of Aal, stood in silent contemplation upon the edge of Wyrmspine Precipice, his gaze fixed on the multitude of the hosts of the Tuath Dé gathered below on the virtually flat Plain of Penance below.

Overhead, a jagged gash filled half of the sky, as if Chthon herself had breach-birthed the Void itself upon Aal, the home world of the Tuath Dé, the Fae, the first seeds planted in this cosmos. Immense tracers of black lightning crackled silently upon and around the perimeter of the veritable wound in time and space, their immense scale telling harsh lies about their true velocity.

Focusing his immortal gaze upon the massive warp, Zon T'Danu willed the expression of his seven minor chakras to align with the metaphysical projection of Aal, the name of both the planet itself and the superset collective of all its living energies, its Dragon, or World Spirit. The connection of his foci to those of Aal filled his soul with untold reserves of magickal power, tapped from the immeasurably large pool of magickal energies bound within its nexus, coiled within the metaphysical embodiment of the Song of the Sidhe. This intimate connection with the ultimate source of magick also gave him, temporarily – for no corporeal being, even an immortal such as Zon T'Danu who boasted eight fully actualized chakras and a slowly evolving, budding ninth – the Eye of the Dragon. And, with its eternal gaze, the lord of Aal gazed into the seething abyss beyond the hole in the sky.

Billions and billions of souls loomed beyond it, their collective soul energies shining brightly. Marshalling his will, Zon T'Danu directed his gaze onward: past the many millions of bizarre spacecraft currently settling into wicked martial formations; past the countless dozens of capital war ships forming up on their rearmost ranks; past the 13 spherical planet-sized motherships parked in a blasphemous constellation beyond the capital war ships; past the nine gas giant-sized fractal tesseracts, each housing, recursively, at least all of the previously encountered entities and assets; until, at last, completing his psychic trek, he gazed upon Demonia Prime itself, the spherical Starhome, or home world and ultimate mothership, of the invincible, star-slaying collective known as the Death Horde, who came now to wage final war on Aal, and its doomed inhabitants.

Aal keep our song... Zon T'Danu swore as the Eye of the Dragon gazed inside the titanic, star-sized monstrosity, revealing nine bound singularities at its core. Upon seeing this through the artifice of the Eye of the Dragon, Zon T'Danu immediately knew it for what it was: an expression of immortal-level chakras, or magickal power foci. Implicit in its heinous nature – nine fully realized chakras – Zon T'Danu now understood, was true immortal power. Just as the delta of power between a mortal with seven chakras and an immortal with eight chakras was incredibly nonlinear, at least five orders of magnitude relatively speaking, so too was the delta between nine and eight. This was not merely immortal power. This was the power of a true god. Their mothership was a god itself, he knew now, only at the end.

As he peered deeper, the nine singularities resolved into perfect focus, allowing him, via the artifice of the Eye of the Dragon, to know the souls of those bound to the singularities. They were, or at some point had been, of the Fae, which was patently impossible, Zon T'Danu knew, for never before, in the many long aeons of his existence, had his people ever encountered any external group of Fae. Yet, still they were Fae, each one at least as powerful as he was himself, he judged as he gazed upon them. There was Angolgotha, whose singularity, or more accurately its boundary, shone more brightly in infrared; Vyr-Thak Ag'yena, whose boundary shone in red; Orz'Non'a Plk, orange; Zil Y'yzyzk, yellow; Ga-Vida, green; Mneme, blue; Y'lis, indigo; Siddthurrak, deep violet; and, finally, Vashti Thog, shining in ultraviolet. He realized that there was a connection between and among them, causing him to suspect that they were capable of some sort of collective action; however, peer as he might, he was unable to divine it, despite his use of the most potent Eye of the Dragon. Coldly, he had to admit that it was entirely possible that this Death Horde, especially its godlike Starhome with its nine bound godlings, was beyond his power to destroy.

Soon, every living thing on Aal, the primal home world of the Fae, even Aal itself, would die. Even Aal, the Dragon, would die. All life force would be brutally harvested by the Demonians and their Anti-Life worshiping Death Horde collective of psychopathic murderers. Among them, he now knew thanks to his communion with the Eye of the Dragon, were those who were in league with or in thrall to the Demonians: The mighty Sentinels, powerful necromantic knights, whose sole goal in existence was to serve the cause of the Anti-Life; the warlike Golgothans, who measured their personal prestige and power by the number of their victims; the predacious Myrexians, whose hive mind collective made one of many billions; the mentally superior Dymaxians, whose multiple minds empowered their crafting and artificing skills to rival those of the old gods themselves; the Quant, whose nanoscale existence rendered them unto voracious expressions of Shadow itself; even the mysterious Valayans, beings of pure, hateful energy, whose mastery of Bending and Binding was...

...was what? Zon T'Danu desperately tried to grasp. It was not entirely magick, nor was it entirely technology. *An abomination and perversion of all things holy and unholy,* he reckoned, *and as nameless as well it should be.*

What Zon T'Danu now knew, however, beyond all shadow of doubt, was that all who opposed the collective of the Death Horde, their elite races, their godlike armadas, and the countless enthralled dregs from a million other conquered worlds who served them, either would be pressed directly into slavery, to forevermore exist in thrall to the Death Horde, or would be consigned to the ultimate silence of the Void itself. Soon, even the sacred, eternal motion of the Song of the Sidhe would itself grind to a final halt, and its omnipresent song would, at long last, end. Soon, the Dragon itself would die.

But, Zon T'Danu thought, *that I shall not permit!*

Were it not for the prescient foresight of the Communion of Nathrak, there would have been no warning of their coming, no way to have gathered and bound all the widely dispersed Fae of Aal into a single, united fighting force; the first in their history of many aeons. Not even the Wars of Purification had seen so many houses unite. There would have been no way for Zon T'Danu, the Overlord of Aal, to have exacted final, binding oaths of allegiance from among the many disparate factions of the Court of the Gentry, and to have set them all on this final, glorious path. A war in which the Fae would at last fight as one.

Even this mighty, alien foe – this so-called Death Horde – who traveled the stars in their godlike ships, their self-perpetuation enabled by their perverse rapine and plunder of world after world, star after star, galaxy after galaxy, would meet their match at the hands of the combined forces of the Fae of Aal, whose puissant magicks were legend in the cosmos.

Even their blasphemous technomagick, Zon T'Danu now knew as the Dragon of Aal finally revealed its name to him, *would not win this war.*

His connection with the Eye of the Dragon now unbound, Zon T'Danu's soul returned to the here and now. Feeling the heady intoxication of communion with the life spirit of the world itself, Zon T'Danu threw his head back and roared like a War Dragon, his long tripled-braids of bone-white hair buzzing and weaving about his head as if alive.

"We are the Tuath Dé, invaders!" Zon T'Danu roared at the looming crack in the sky, the vestiges of his communion with Aal's life spirit carrying his voice to all things within his purview, including those who waited beyond the sky gash. "We are the Fae, first born of this cosmos! The K'ryl, of the Igigi, the Watchers themselves, planted us here, on Aal, when the world was young, at behest of the Dragon itself, aeons before your puny races crawled from the slime of your misbegotten abattoirs! You come to make war on the Tuath Dé, the living gods of war? You call yourselves 'Death Horde'? Ha! We will show you death such as you have never known! Death! DEATH!"

Behind him, respectfully withdrawn one-tenth of a league, her own body's length, Ku'tu, Zon T'Danu's queen-consort, confidently flapped her titanic bejeweled dragon's wings, kicking up a twin pair of towering dust devils which spun up from her wingtips and rapidly moved past Zon, dissipating as they crashed over the edge of the precipice. A brief cheer arose from the gathered Fae nobility whose war camps roughly paralleled the edge of the precipice for a full league, both to the left and to the right of Zon T'Danu and his shapeshifting faerie dragon queen.

"Death!" Zon T'Danu declared, willing Fresswelle, his artifact blade, to appear in his right hand. The air tearing along the path of the mathematically abstract super-fractal blade, he pointed its shimmering, radiant, rainbow-hued form dramatically to the sky. Its ornate pommel basket, a spheroid of deep purple vector-sharp grid lines, issued a basso profundo *thrum-thrum-thrum* pulsation that was more audible in its native infrasonic range than within the normal auditory perception range of mortals. The Overlord of Aal had no issues hearing its full range, and it clearly sang to him. Feeling the eldritch spacetime-rending power of the blade course through him, he gazed down at the plain below, spreading his arms wide. The Tuath Dé, gathered in their millions, cheered lustily, and thunder filled the air.

Zon T'Danu returned his gaze to the rift above. "Your hours are numbered, foolish mortals! You dare wage war upon the Tuath Dé, the masters of this cosmos? You dare threaten us with slavery and death? The horror of your legend ends today! Verily, we shall grant thee death! Death!"

Below, the assembled hosts roared, "Death!"

Behind, the assembled gentry howled, echoing the cry of "Death!"

Immediately to Zon T'Danu's left side, a figure as tall as the mighty Overlord of Aal himself abruptly appeared, wreathed in bilious black smoke, its eyes nothing but slits of molten lava.

"Death? While I appreciate the irony," it informed Zon T'Danu in a rich, mellifluous voice, speaking in perfect Sidhe, its emotional content as pure as that of the Song itself, "you're still going to lose."

"What is this?" Zon T'Danu thundered, spinning adroitly, sliding back to an en garde stance, with the pulsating Fresswelle cutting snippets of air in its path, causing them to pinwheel and stream away like multicolored, startled fractal butterflies.

"I am the Lightbringer," the figure informed him with a slight tilt of his smoke-wreathed visage, again observing perfectly the subtleties of the nonverbal components of Sidhe communication. "And you are Zon T'Danu, Overlord of Aal, the First Song, First Seed of the K'ryl; of the Igigi, the Watchers themselves, and bearer of one of the Dragon Foci of this cosmos, Fresswelle, the Devouring Wave. Due to your station, we will dispense with the naming formalities," he told Zon T'Danu, who kept Fresswelle en garde, "for we have much to discuss, and little time in which to do it."

"Time, you say?" Zon T'Danu smiled back, his triple-braids of long, bone-white hair suddenly arising and dancing on unseen wind. "I'll show you 'Time', Demonian..."

With that, Zon T'Danu willed Fresswelle to shift his local frame of time down to a virtual crawl of motion. A thousand times had he done this over the many long aeons he had possessed the blade of the Lord of Time, and a thousand times had he witnessed his foes grind to an apparent total stop, as if Time itself suddenly had decided to stand absolutely still, and betray their motionless, helpless forms to Zon T'Danu's less-than-tender mercies.

This time, however – this one, single time from among thousands of others – as Fresswelle shifted him in Time, so too did his foe, whose ability to move just as did Zon T'Danu and his magnificent blade was emphasized by a sudden crossing of his arms.

Zon T'Danu, who had been ready to spring upon the so-called "Lightbringer" and visit death by a dozen cuts within the span of the proverbial blink of an eye, checked his charge and stood his ground. His almond-slanted sepia eyes narrowed in shock and disbelief.

"I am no Demonian," the Lightbringer informed him. "You may still your blade, Zon T'Danu. It will have no effect on me."

"That's what you–" Zon T'Danu paused abruptly as he felt Fresswelle's *thrum-thrum-thrum* pulsations grow suddenly still. However, despite its diminished pulsations, the frame of time remained the same; all things outside of a narrow circumference around the two still were frozen in time.

"Now do you understand?" the Lightbringer asked. "I control the flow of time here, not your blade."

"That's impossible," Zon T'Danu replied, doubt causing his eyes to twitch. "Fresswelle is the most powerful artifact in the universe. Its origins are from before the ZeroTime, in which the Fae were born. There is nothing or no one beyond or before."

"There is a ZeroTime before the ZeroTime, and there is both something and someone beyond and before." The Lightbringer stared at Zon T'Danu, his Aspect of the Trillions carefully hiding his true features from Zon T'Danu's magickally prying eyes. Only molten lava shone from his smoky countenance.

"Why are you here?" Zon asked him.

"Ah, good," the Lightbringer replied, uncrossing his arms and letting them fall to his sides. "I am here to strike a bargain with you, Zon T'Danu. More precisely, with you and your people, the Tuath Dé, the Fae. I am here to offer you your lives in return for a small boon."

"Our lives?" Zon's eyes narrowed dangerously. No one had spoken to him so flippantly in centuries.

"Yes, your lives. You and your kith and kin are doomed to annihilation before the might of the Death Horde. Despite your magicks, which are the mightiest yet demonstrated in any of the simulations, you have no chance to resist the effects of their supreme technomagicks."

Zon considered that briefly. "Technomagicks? Technology and Magick? Is that what you're saying? Technology, like the humans of this world had before we arose and destroyed them for their blasphemy? For what they did to the Earth Mother? For how they very nearly extinguished the Song of the Sidhe with their endless destruction and perversion? Magick? Such as that of which we are the masters among all in this cosmos?"

"Yes."

"Then you are a fool, Lightbringer, for we destroyed the humans and their technology with ease, and we shall certainly do the same to the Demonians and their slaves, with their puny technomagicks, who seek to make war upon us!"

"I'm not entirely certain that you would indeed be able to defeat the Death Horde, even if they waged war only with technology. That gaping gash of space and time up there," he said, pointing a smoky finger up at the sky, "still hasn't officially opened there in low Earth orbit. With 'Earth', of course, meaning 'Aal', as you Fae have renamed it. If it draws closer, its presence alone eventually would destroy this world. However, they probably won't do that until they've first destroyed or enthralled all life here. After that, then they'll destroy this planet, then all the other planets in this solar system, then they'll snuff out the Sun itself. Then, this simulation will end, with 'simulation' equating to this particular 'universe' or 'cosmos'," he was careful to explain.

Zon T'Danu seemed to be following him well enough, however, if the look of shock and horror growing on his face was any indicator. He nodded for the Lightbringer to continue.

"However, you missed the finer point of what I was saying: they use technomagick. It's a superior, hybrid form of both magick and technology. You and your people and your world will be able to resist it but little, if at all, and it will certainly destroy you before you can even raise a futile defense. In addition, they have billions, not millions, as you do. They outnumber you a thousand to one, easily."

"My warriors are immortal. They have thousands of years of combat experience. Each is worth one thousand Demonians."

"Maybe. Maybe not. This particular instantiation of the Death Horde and its manifold elements isn't a particularly potent one; consider it a bad roll of the dice, as each instantiation is always different in some detail or another. Its composition is irrelevant, however, because even this suboptimal instantiation can win any war of attrition with you simply by rapidly cloning more of their best warriors, some of whom are as ancient and skilled as your own. They also have mighty ships which can match and best your largest, most skilled War Dragons. They can use weapons that you cannot see; weapons from which you have no natural means of defense; weapons before which you are totally helpless. They can, if they should so decide, choose not to directly engage you, and simply move their Demonian Starhome close enough to Aal to destroy it via gravity. For each and every check you can affect them with, they can answer with both check and mate. Considering all of the factors, and what you have said regarding your people's martial prowess, you would need at least twice your number just to have a fighting chance."

Zon T'Danu slowly shook his head. "You can't just... you can't just come here now, at the penultimate stage, and tell me all of this. Even if I believe you, this patently informs me that you are above the greatest power in this universe, so it is wise to pay heed to what you say – even if I take you at your absolute word, what good does it do for the Tuath Dé, for this world?

You have all but told me that nothing we can do will win the day for us and save this world and its many millions of souls. Why not fight, then? Why not go down fighting to the bitter end? That's what we do best, Lightbringer. We fight. We win. When we cannot do so, we choose to die fighting. Many millions of us died during the Wars of Purification with the humans and their warbots, and their cyborg allies, and their horrific nanotech which decimated us and corrupted many more of us. The Song of the Sidhe constantly reminds us of their loss, and we honor it by never surrendering, never retreating, and always fighting to the end. To retreat or surrender, even to a superior foe, is to dishonor our kith and kin, and that is not in our nature at all. So, before I end this parlay and return to my people and our impending hopeless war," Zon T'Danu finished, staring directly, fearlessly, into the visage of the Lightbringer, "name your price, and I shall consider it."

The Lightbringer smiled, the corners of his molten lava mouth curving upward like some demonic carved Jack-o'-lantern. "My boon is but a simple request. There are other worlds out there. Other worlds beyond this one, beyond this cosmos, that run in parallel to this one; worlds in which your people, the Fae, have not yet won their war on Man. My boon would see you seek out and gain an ally for your people, the Fae, in their impending war against the Demonians and their Death Horde. You would simultaneously be gaining an ally born in your own image – an ally whose own Song of the Sidhe sings mournfully because Man is ascendant, as he once was here on your world, and the Earth Mother there suffers his predations and perversions – and once more conquering the savage humans and freeing that world's Earth Mother, just as was your own saved so long ago. Once you have your allies, once you have freed the Fae of that world from their human overlords, you will return here to Aal, and, with your combined powers, you will defeat the Demonians and the Death Horde. My power makes it possible for me to bring you back from the other world, no matter how long you stay there, precisely to this moment in time. If you do this, you will gain a world of powerful allies, and you will be able to return here to Aal with your newly enhanced army, without losing a single second."

Zon T'Danu's eyes faintly glowed. "There are other worlds, that is true. But we are unaware of these Fae whom you name."

"That's because you've explored only this universe, this cosmos. There are more out there, beyond this one. You know my words are truth, too, because you have seen what I can do to your own universe's most powerful weapon, Fresswelle."

Nodding, Zon T'Danu had to concede the point. "So, if we choose to accept this, and do this boon for you, I see how it affects me, and my people, and my world, and perhaps even the otherworldly Fae from beyond this universe, this cosmos. I see that it is good for us. It is good for them. It is good for all things sane and sentient, because yet another few billions of humans will rejoin the earth. The total genocide of another world populated by humans is worth it by itself. But, dearest Lightbringer, what do you get out of this? You said that you would offer our lives to us in exchange for this favor, this boon. So, what precisely do you get out of this?"

"I give you access to a process and plan that will allow the Demonians to be destroyed. Let us say that their destruction is my goal. And, that by achieving this once you free the Fae from their otherworldly thrall by the humans of that cosmos and gain their help in assisting you with the destruction of the Demonians who loom above us now, which they surely will do for you, as you have just freed them from their bond, you will be on the correct path to achieve the satisfaction of my part of the bargain. So, you see, the boon I ask of you is, ultimately, to destroy the Demonians. The offer of your lives is bound to your success in freeing the distant Fae and obtaining their aid in fighting, and ultimately destroying, the Demonians and the Death Horde which even now beset Aal."

Zon T'Danu considered what he had just heard. "So, you want nothing more than to help us, and to destroy the Horde?"

"Yes."

"Why not just do it yourself, then?" Zon T'Danu countered. "You are surely from the beyond yourself. Surely such is within your own power?"

"When your kind dealt with the humans, prior to their discovery of technology, were you free to inform the humans of every single why and wherefore? Of divulging every iota of yourself to them, even if so pacted to do so?"

Disgusted, Zon replied, "Of course not. They were humans. They were not subject to the Song of the Sidhe. They therefore had no reason to know anything about us other than what we chose to tell them, or what they pacted from us."

"As below, so above."

Zon's eyes opened wide with momentary shock. Previously, he had held his emotions in check, still considering the possibility that this could be some elaborate Demonian trick, some convoluted ruse to maneuver and manipulate him toward some unknown state. However, he now knew, beyond shadow of doubt, that the being standing before him was none other than what he claimed: an entity from beyond this cosmos. Everything he had said was true, then. The doubts that had been brought up during the earlier war council about how they would fare against such an alien, implacable, omnipotent foe such as the Demonians and their many billions of shock troops armed with weapons of wonder, the endless trail of ruined worlds in their wake; all known and revealed by the Communion of Nathrak; all but whispered secrets among only the gentry themselves. But this Lightbringer had known everything, even the correct words and meanings specific to the Fae only when dealing with the humans. And that knowledge was ancient, unique, and known only to the Fae of this world, the Tuath Dé, specifically. Yet, he had known. He had spoken Sidhe flawlessly, in total fidelity, even observing the nonverbal components and the minutiae unique to Zon's own royal court. Truthfully, there was but one choice that Zon T'Danu could possibly make at this point.

Commanding Fresswelle to vanish and return to its hidden spacetime binding point, Zon T'Danu, Overlord of Aal, the First Song, and bearer of one of the Dragon Foci, Fresswelle, the Devouring Wave, extended his hand to the Lightbringer.

"You have your bargain, Lightbringer."

The Lightbringer clasped Zon's hand with a shadowy, smoke-embroiled hand. "And you have yours. Go, tell your people whereof we spoke. Return here once you and your people are ready, and I will open the warp. But make haste, for the Demonians will not tarry lon—"

"VOOM!" came the senses-shattering Voice of the Apocalypse as abruptly, from nowhere, phased the mountain-sized form of a mighty, metallic, black scaled tortoise, spinning wildly around and around as it veritably flew in the air above the plain where the Tuath Dé gathered in formation. Spokes of black lightning crackled from the raised spines and spikes of its shelled back, while the Anti-Life power of the wicked Void itself pulsed and thrummed from the massive, shadowy pits where its head, tail, and limbs should otherwise have protruded. Immediately upon its arrival, the Fae warriors gathered directly beneath it, still some several thousand meters distant, burst into black flames, their corpses writhing futilely against the flow of the Void which projected down from the spectacular tortoise. In the space of a heartbeat, they were no more, their corporeal forms disintegrating into something less than ash.

"To battle! Fight!" Zon T'Danu screamed, exhorting the Tuath Dé to war. Ku'tu already was in the air, her insane speed in proportion to her titanic dragon form size a magickal function of her true form's faerie-quick reflexes. Zon T'Danu phased instantaneously to her back, Fresswelle once again conjured in hand.

Simultaneously, multiple events occurred.

Below, on the Plain of Penance, the legions of the Tuath Dé launched their aerial corps: squadron upon squadron of spike-tailed wyverns and their lance men riders took flight, vectoring toward the mighty flying tortoise; thousands of Shadowcorns, their equine physical forms nothing more than immaterial black shadow, took flight, riderless, their wickedly recurved single horns issuing deadly black rainbow bolts at the intruding tortoise; multiple hemispheres of black, writhing energy erupted at random across the span of the plain, shielding one legion of ground troops after another with high-order magickal wards; a second behind Zon T'Danu and Ku'tu, the Gentry took to the air upon their personal War Dragons, many accompanied by small constellations of four-winged flying faeries who already were weaving their charms and wards to protect the nobles and the dozens of armed martial retainers crowding their customized howdahs on the backs of their draconic mounts; arising from the clinging mists of the plains came tens of thousands of the Ban-Sidhe, those who had been corrupted by the treacherous humans so long ago, their physical forms now unbound, their existence now confined to that of dismal shades and driven by their endless hatred of all things not of the Fae, against whom their psychic screams would shred souls.

Above, still flying and spinning rapidly, Voom suffered not from the barrage of black rainbows from the Shadowcorns; instead, it simply drank them in, its technomagicks bending and binding them into its Void-like perimeter. Immediately, it used the absorbed energy to transport its mountainous mass the several thousand meters it needed to reach the floor of the plain below; at once, a 10,000-meter diameter ovoid chunk of reality vanished beneath it, where its heinous, annihilative Void energies instantly transformed earth and the Fae warriors who formerly stood on it into nothingness. In the first few seconds of battle, against only a single representative of the Death Horde, the forces of the Tuath Dé were down more than 5%.

"Ah, they've brought along Voom. How quaint!" the Lightbringer chortled, phasing himself to virtual immateriality as he took in the scene.

Led by Zon T'Danu and Ku'tu, the Gentry, their War Dragons, and their many servitors formed up in a multiple-row chevron, with Zon T'Danu and Ku'tu before it.

"Send it back to the Void!" he commanded, his magickally-driven voice physically and psychically guiding his warriors. At once, even as the impotent Shadowcorns ascended through and over their formation to form up high guard, should more Death Horde troops pass through the sky-spanning rift, multiple barrages of fire, ice, acid, venom, molten sand, molten lava, entropic energies, multicolored writhing rainbow bubbles, electricity, clacking bones, and dozens of similar yet not easily defined energies and effects issued forth from the 72 War Dragons, tearing across the plains, down, down, down to the spiked shell-back of Voom, falling in mighty riverine waterfall-width dimensions.

But the massive collective gouts of mountain-melting energies turned away at the last possible moment, arcing away in an obscene eightfold pattern, some plowing directly to the right, obliterating an entire bubble-warded legion of Fae in the process, some plowing directly to the left, doing much of the same to two entire bubble-warded legions. Yet the third parts of the eight parts curved upward, plowing back into the front rows of the War Dragons, sending draconic wings, limbs, and heads flying, severed completely from their bodies, then continuing onward, almost unabated, slamming into the core of the flying Shadowcorns, felling instantly half of their number, dissipating their shadowy forms into nothingness.

"That's impossible!" Zon T'Danu bellowed, nearly falling from his draconic mount as Ku'tu made a desperate pull-up to avoid the warded and consciously shaped gout of draconic breath weapons.

"No, it is not impossible, maggot!" came the reply from the disembodied Voice of the Apocalypse via searing, scalding Mindtouch, broadcast to all the gathered Fae. "We are the Vanth'Vash'Var, the Sentinels of the Anti-Life, the Death Horde, the Lords of the Void!"

A sight-destroying flash of white-beyond-white light erupted from the crack in the sky, which now, abruptly, was but mere kilometers above the Plain of Penance. The flash was immediately followed by the first rank of the Death Horde's smaller attack craft. Thousands upon thousands of jet-black skull-shaped spacecraft poured into the sky of Aal, each one instantly firing rapid-fire fusillades of pulsating, psychically screaming neon-green energy. Thousands found their marks, striking the black domes down below on the plains, cracking, shearing, and ablating them. Thousands more struck out at the wyverns and their riders, who had begun to spread their formation into a spherical, defensive configuration, only to be interrupted by the deadly psychic energy assaults. For them, a single beam was enough to corrupt their minds and sear their souls, rendering them incapable of action and causing them to plummet en masse, helpless, to their deaths on the plain below.

Below, Zon T'Danu saw that dozens of titanic, War Dragon-sized writhing, pulsating chrome-sheened arcs had erupted from the misty floor of the Plain of Penance, leaving in their matter-devouring wake nothing but a fine, thin, pale gray aerosol. Chaotic they were, attacking neither the living nor the dead with more frequency. They were destroying everything with which they came in contact. Total, chaotic, indiscriminate death.

The tortoise creature, apparently unmoved by any call save its own, rapidly burrowed down into the plain, ablating the earth with its virtually full perimeter of Void energies, until its spiked shell-back disappeared. Upon its disappearance, a massive earthquake began, and a massive crater wider than the creature's diameter began to form and continue to expand precipitously, sucking down all nearby ground troops, the remnants of their black warding domes effervescing furiously as they rapidly disintegrated.

Above, the remaining wyverns, their riders, and the few Shadowcorns yet living were being focus-fired by the flying skull ships, even as rank upon rank of new, additional skull ships erupted through the widening crack in the sky.

The battle had now descended into pure and total chaos. Several of the War Dragons of the Gentry attempted to force their way through the widening, rapidly approaching warp in the sky, only to be rebuffed and riddled by hundreds of concentrated fusillades from the flying skull ships. Black lightning erupted dozens of times in quick succession behind and beyond the Wyrmspine Precipice as tens of thousands of Death Horde shock troops phased in, teleported or otherwise transported to the rocky scabland forming the Wyrmspine. More flying skull ships were now pouring through the rapidly expanding, still-approaching sky rift. The destructive arcs were growing in dimension as they apparently absorbed what they devoured; they began to head toward the opposite side of the plains, splitting off and dividing from themselves, doubling their number, as they did so.

"Surrender now, or die!" came the booming Mindtouch from the Voice of the Apocalypse again, speaking to everything sentient on Aal simultaneously. For that brief moment in time, the thousands of active Death Horde warriors on the planet ceased fire. Save for the devouring arcs, which continued to move away from the plains, again splitting and dividing, the process increasing in frequency now.

Incredibly, several members of the Gentry, still atop their hovering, static War Dragons, raised their hands in surrender.

"No!" Zon T'Danu screamed at them, his own voice as loud magickally, psychically, as the voice of the Death Horde's Voice of the Apocalypse. "Fight! FIGHT!"

Their surrender noted, an eerie, fuzzy, greenish sheen appeared around the outline of their physical forms, from the lowest brownies and faeries in their retinue to the War Dragons themselves. Then, a second later, they were gone, caught up by the projected power of the Death Horde, transported by some unknown means to some destination unknown. The cowards.

"Form up on me!" Ku'tu screamed thunderously, rousing from their confusion those who had paused to consider the offer. "Protect the Overlord! Protect Aal!"

The four dozen remaining War Dragons drew up in a protective formation around Zon T'Danu and Ku'tu. Multiple Sidhe Mindtouches flew between and among them, full of chaos, full of formerly unknown fear. But, even as Ku'tu tried her best to calm their terror and rally them, Zon T'Danu paid them no heed. Instead, his gaze now was focused on the spot where the Lightbringer had last stood. Now that he had tasted the power of the Death Horde, he realized that he had little choice but to accept the Lightbringer's terms. To delay any longer would result in the total and final defeat – no, the total annihilation – of his people. For the first time in uncounted aeons, Zon T'Danu would have to accept defeat. Temporary though he knew it would be, still it galled him into silence, for he had lost at least half of the Tuath Dé in but mere minutes, and he had done so without actually engaging the enemy with Fresswelle. Total dishonor, and all the surviving Tuath Dé knew it.

Therefore, as he already was tainted as such in their eyes, he had nothing to naysay him in his eternal, relentless pursuit of the quest to protect his people. Perhaps they would one day draw hope from the act of his final, selfless sacrifice, and his honor would be redeemed in their eyes. Perhaps they'd one day understand it from that perspective. Perhaps not. But, unless he acquiesced to the demands of the Lightbringer, there would be no hope. None at all.

"Lightbringer..." Zon T'Danu broadcast tightly via Mindtouch to the spot where he had last been standing with him, there atop the rapidly decaying Wyrmspine Precipice. *"We will do as you ask. We will go to this new world of Fae, to free them from their thrall. We will gather them to our side. We will return to Aal with the as our allies, and we will destroy the Death Horde."*

"Then you accept my terms?" the Lightbringer said aloud, startling Zon T'Danu, for he stood next to him on the expansive scaled back of Ku'tu.

"I accept, for the Tuath Dé, provided that I have your oath that, despite the time we spend in this new world, we return to this exact place in time to renew our battle," Zon T'Danu said, willing his words to touch the minds of all the surviving Tuath Dé. "I know that it is within your power to do this."

"So shall it be done."

"Very well. May my people, the Tuath Dé, and my world, Aal, forgive me."

With that, the Lightbringer extended his arms, palms down, and wiggled his fingers. The surviving Tuath Dé, 42 War Dragons and their Gentry members and retinues, a few dozen wyvern riders and Shadowcorns, a few hundred Ban-Sidhe, and several thousand shock troops and spellcasters, their mounts and their trains, and various and disparate thousands of civilians, supporters, and craftsmen all were enveloped by personal, form-fitting master-level warps, which instantly spirited them away, forevermore, from their home world, Aal, which had, long ago, been wrested in final combat with the humans and their warbots, and their cyborg allies, and to the new world of Earth.

Only Zon T'Danu and Ku'tu remained, the buzzing outline of the personal warp clinging to the perimeter of her massive draconic form.

"You must go, Ku'tu," Zon T'Danu bade his queen-consort.

"No!" she objected. "I will not leave your side. Why do you wish to end yourself? He gives us a way to yet win this day," she snarled, directing her baleful gaze to the Lightbringer, "and you instead choose to sacrifice yourself? For what? For the honor of those cowardly Gentry who had to be convinced to join our alliance in order to save Aal? For them? Your sacrifice would mean nothing to them, for they have no sense of honor to begin with!"

Zon T'Danu shook his head. "This is the only way, my queen. This is my Fate; to give my life for my people, for my world."

"No! I won't let you!" Ku'tu boomed. Instantly, she skin-danced into her tiny, eight-winged faerie form, causing Zon T'Danu to invoke his own seldom used eightfold jet-black faeries' wings to remain aloft. She now was face to face with him as both hovered in the air above the Plain of Penance. The pause in action by the Death Horde yet remained in effect, and it was obvious that all eyes were upon them. "Let the warp take you, Zon T'Danu!" she begged him. "Join us! We can yet win this day if you come with us! We need you, my lord! I need you!"

Torn momentarily between his sacred calling to protect the Tuath Dé of Aal and his love for his constant hearth-mate, Zon T'Danu's eyes shifted from Ku'tu, to the widening rift above them, to Fresswelle, then, at last to the Lightbringer, who hovered in place before them with no outward manifestation of power to mark his flight.

Zon T'Danu then cast his gaze first to Ku'tu, then to Fresswelle. "Do it, Lightbringer."

"So shall it be," the Lightbringer replied as the fresh signature of personal master-level warps appeared simultaneously on Ku'tu and Fresswelle.

"No, my love! NO!" Ku'tu screamed, her voice phasing and flanging as the warp enveloped her completely, ripping her from the here and now, removing her forevermore from the side of her husband, her love, her everything.

As the blade vanished from his hand, Zon T'Danu felt, for the first time in his many long aeons of life, his soulbound connection with the mighty blade of the Lord of Time grow silent, and then fade completely away from his perception. Simultaneously, horrifying him to the very depth of his soul, he felt also his connection with the Song of the Sidhe cease, its soul-stirring, ever-present warmth and light now nothing more than cold, dark, shadowy reminders of what had once been. The

Song of the Sidhe was no more, and his absolute shock at this realization of the impossible crushed his soul.

"What is this?" Zon T'Danu cried aloud, clutching his hands to his temples. "The Song! It's gone! But that's impossible! I remain in the flesh, yet the Song is gone..."

The Lightbringer nodded his head slightly, almost mockingly. This one – so confident in his ways, so sure of his own power – had always reminded him of the One Above, and, despite his love for all his creations, Helel's prejudice painted the Overlord of Aal with the same brush. "I regret, Zon T'Danu, that it is indeed possible. Have you not ever, in all your long millennia of existence, wondered why it was that the blade of the Lord of Time would find you and bind with you, from among all others in this universe? I see by your façade of total confusion that you have not. Pity. You always were too headstrong, too egotistical, and too lacking in imagination to perceive that the story of this cosmos might not primarily concern you; that you were not the lead actor on this cosmic stage. Not in this simulation, nor in any of the other previous several thousand."

The Lightbringer paused a moment to allow Zon T'Danu to absorb this reality-damning statement of cosmic truth. "Alas, now, you have played your role to perfection. Finally, you have submerged yourself for the benefit of all others, willingly parting with the blade, which never have you done before. Always, you have retained the blade, sometimes retaining Ku'tu and other elements of the Gentry, sometimes sending them all away, in order to wage your eternal losing war upon the Death Horde. And always has the central actor remained: Fresswelle, which time and time again failed in its own mission, its own quest. It failed innumerable times because your ego was too big to acknowledge that you weren't the center of the universe, the lone star on this cosmic stage."

"Damn you and your lies, Lightbringer!" Zon T'Danu raged, raising his fist to the sky. A swirling man-sized whirlwind of darting blue faerie lights began to coalesce around his raised fist. "I see now that you were the one who has betrayed us all to the Demonians! You caused the Song of the Sidhe to go quiet! You are in league with them, and I shall destroy you for your betrayal!"

"I caused nothing," the Lightbringer casually informed him. He narrowed his molten left eye, and Zon T'Danu froze in place. Abrupt silence reigned, as this action scaled to cover all motion, all movement, even among the Death Horde and their many billions. All were now in the thrall of the Lightbringer. "Freewill is of paramount importance, Zon T'Danu. I could therefore only observe passively and mark you by your actions. You were the one who had to make that choice, the choice you failed to make so many times before. Alas, today, this go-round, you finally willingly allowed Fresswelle to be sent to Earth with the rest of your people. Alas, today, you finally played your role perfectly, because you freed Fresswelle of the bond that you share with it; it now therefore may be bound to another. This is essential to its mission, because, now, as it has in all of these countless simulations, it possesses the remnants of Aal, the Song of the Sidhe, within its infinite internal spacetime matrix. Fresswelle is the only artifact capable of this, of cutting Aal from its source, and thereby freeing from its confinement the captive Song of the Sidhe. It is the only artifact capable of doing this incrementally, slowly, imperceptibly over the long aeons, soul by soul, through the omnipresent soul bond that you share with the Song of the Sidhe, the metaphysical Dragon of this world, this Aal, as you have renamed it. Yet, now, finally, it may freely bear this most potent source of magicks to a new actor, one on a new stage, the prime stage, where upon, finally, now armed with its inestimable supreme magick power, there might be a chance for victory against the Death Horde."

Zon T'Danu simply stood affixed in his pose, unable to move. Yet he heard what the Lightbringer had just told him. And it enraged him to the core of his being. Never had he hated anyone with such unambiguous clarity.

"But fret not, Zon T'Danu," the Lightbringer continued, gazing now at the motionless Death Horde ships overhead, hovering to within a step of the Overlord of Aal's helpless form. "You finally made the right choice. What you have done will give the souls of the world above this one a true fighting chance, where none they had bef—"

Like a striking snake, Zon T'Danu's hands were suddenly at the Lightbringer's neck. "I hate you..." he spat through clinched teeth, his hands talonlike, clasping upon and around the neck of the target of his hate. There was something real beneath the clinging wreaths of shadow smoke, something solid, and the Overlord of Aal focused his hatred, willing his diamond-crushing grasp tighter, tighter...

For the first time in his own many, long aeons, the Lightbringer knew shock, and fear. Reacting reflexively, he caused the nearby star, Sol, to appear here, on Aal, centered upon himself. Instantly, Aal was consumed, as was Zon T'Danu, as were all Death Horde contingents on this side of the crack in the sky.

Now back in control, the Lightbringer willed the simulation subroutine to an end. Withdrawing his perspective to the meta-level viewpoint, Helel once again observed the currently ongoing 144,000[th] simulation, this time with renewed vigor and interest now that the Zon T'Danu module had finally reached fruition.

The module, however, had demonstrated to Helel that he had not yet tamed all of the possible variables. Zon T'Danu had, impossibly, broken his thrall, and had even dared to lay hands upon his physical projection. If there were more time, he could track down the obvious bug and control for it, should it ever arise again. But there was no more time, no possible way to divert his attention from the rendering of his ultimate simulation, as it now neared certain crucial inflection points.

Still. Somehow, Zon T'Danu had managed to defy his control. That was rare beyond rare. There had been, over the millennia, a few rare bugs in the simulation that had, temporarily, granted its actors and denizens some modicum of true freewill, and not Helel's watered-down version of the same, with which the various actors could make their own choices. This rare form of true freewill, during which the actors could brazenly defy his will, had various and sundry explanations and resolutions, he knew from the whispers of other Celestial Shapers, who also had encountered it rarely. But this was, he knew, something more potent than a fleeting bug or hiccup of the system. He suspected that Zon T'Danu's own hatred – his own potent emotional content in action – might have been able to, at the End of All Things in his simulation, temporarily granted him the power to do what he did. Or, perhaps it was an unexpected result, a true probabilistic outlier, of the absolute purging of the Song of the Sidhe from Aal, which might have removed all of Zon T'Danu's innate magicks, rendering him as an anomaly in a world previously teaming with magicks and magickal power? Or, might have Fresswelle's imprint on his soul have somehow granted him the ability to resist Helel's own spacetime manipulations?

Too many variables, and not enough time to run them all down, Helel knew. He also knew that he would be very cautious during future physical projections, for those in the prime world of this simulation would perforce be more powerful than the Overlord of Aal had been. After all, his had been but a tiny, recursively enfolded subroutine; a module, or subset, of the prime. And, still, he had managed to do the improbable. *The impossible,* he noted, intrigued by the concept that something in a simulation could actually defy him and lay hands upon him; intrigued by the innate and underlying irony of it all, considering his own goal of destroying the One Above.

Still, there was now Fresswelle, the Devouring Wave, the Fractal Blade of the Lord of Time, in play. Added to it also was the Song of the Sidhe, or Aal, the collective life force of the Dragon of the world in which the Tuath Dé, the masters of magick in their cosmos, had ruled supreme. Finally, there were the survivors of the Tuath Dé themselves who now were in play, and some of them, he knew, carried some interesting genetic scars, thanks to their assault by the potent technology of their enemies, the humans, during the Wars of Purification. For a measured moment, Helel allowed himself some small taste of satisfaction. The numbers were slowly, inexorably creeping toward some final result other than zero. Perhaps this simulation would indeed empower him to do the impossible, for it had recently been corrupted by its own impossibilities.

It was a huge gambit, one of the heaviest in the entire scenario. But if the actors played their roles, then they might actually save their world. Or, even better, save just a very small bit of it. After all, that which does not kill, makes stronger. As below, so above.

eVo.144.000.mOd.0.sCe.10 | EARTH | UNITED STATES | ALABAMA | HUNTSVILLE | MORTHONTECH HEADQUARTERS | DEEP BIOGEN LAB

"PEOPLE EAT HORSE SHIT... People eat horse shit..." Mercyduceus Vendredi, the Ninth Null, mocked, sotto voce, along to the chorus of Slipknot's "People = Shit".

The dread beats streamed via Bluetooth from her iPhone. The human tech was tucked neatly into the interior breast pocket of her shapeshifting bodysuit, which now was virtually translucent and merging her into a very real form of invisibility. Bose Aqua SoundSport earphones nestled in her delicately pointed ears, transmitting the enthralling metal rhythm.

It had taken a few missions, but Mercyduceus had finally had to admit to herself that she preferred the water-resistant Aquas for their superior resistance to being gummed up by blood and sticky brain matter. And the fidelity of this relatively new human tech was of such a quality that she was able to tap directly into the sonic energies and bend and bind them to her will, evolving her various Null-based magicks to what she had become convinced was a much sharper, much more resonant fighting edge.

Humans were quite capable of being dangerous, she thought, continuing to stride past the gathered, milling, white-lab-suited humans who were physically incapable of noting her silent, striding passage, because she so willed it. It was one of the first evolutions she had learned once her fate had been pacted in this most recent instantiation. Once her physical form had been expressed, once she had been actualized from the Song of the Sidhe, once more in semblance of mortal form, Mercyduceus had been made to know that her latest role was to portray a true Null, an honorarium, quite impressive, for one of the Fae. It was obviously a reward for her collective puissance over and throughout so many instantiations; so many lifetimes, so many thousands of years she reckoned, so much success versus failure, that it was time, about time, she thought, that this most coveted role was to be hers, and hers alone.

Mercyduceus smiled faintly, her thin lips twisting and turning in an upward curl that was dangerously close to being a Glasgow smile, a result of her Fae-bound, almost human physiology; a lot of pliability, flexibility, and sometimes pointy parts. Human physiology was mostly smooth, whereas the Fae were but imperfect imitations of this, being born from the Song of the Sidhe, and its ever-singing Dragon Dreams. It gave the Fae unique looks, however, something that would land them modeling contracts and movie roles as creepy-looking extras, or gimps. Some had even been assigned to do this, and had thoroughly enjoyed their jaunts into the world of Man. It gave Mercyduceus an unusual sex appeal, her almost albinoid milk-white skin, her purple-tinged eyes, her concert pianist fingers, and her badass rock star long white hair combined to make rich men beg and good men steal. Same with the rich and good women, too. And she had applied it, over the many decades spent in this particular instantiation, quite liberally and frequently to women, men, and the various untyped humans who had crossed her silent path. Most Fae were, unfortunately she thought, either instantiated without proper genitalia, or rendered as hermaphrodites.

Mercyduceus – Mercy, as she preferred to be called, because the irony was simply luscious – was of the latter sort. Both Hermes and Aphrodite had blessed her. At least Aphrodite had made her mighty. Hermes had shown her short shrift. Trismegistus? Hardly. Just another layer of faulty imperfection, curses, and stillborn weirds forced upon her by the grim humor of the Mother, Chthon. That bitch.

She typically chose to exhibit an androgynous façade when viewed by Man. Let 'em suffer while they guess. Her physical appearance, however, tended to shift with her mood, which itself tended to shift chaotically. She recalled with a pointy grin that most of her forged photo IDs and passport photos were deliberately smudged and blurry, just in case she was having a bad day when she got carded. Maybe, one day, after 13,337 years, she would finally learn to control herself. And keep a straight face.

Never... she thought, perversely enjoying her waggishness.

A last, thick knot of humans – eleven, Mercy counted – pressed together before a closed set of double doors. Beyond that was the Sign of the Sigil, she knew, its presence, though somehow dimly expressed in this proximity, still reaching her perception. Judging from the various high-tech equipment she had seen on the way up to this room, on this floor, there was the possibility that some form of localized EM containment field was in play, diminishing the sigil's silent yet insistent psychic song.

If such were true... she thought.

She willed a silent expression of a lower but quite useful evolution of the Null, her physical form becoming incorporeal, ethereal, and quite resistant to the normal spectrum of matter and energy in this particular cosmic shard.

Immediately, Mercy fell through the floor, invisible to mortal sight, willing herself to a stop as soon as her eyes could "see" below the ceiling of this floor. Almost immediately, as soon as she willed herself forward, she was in a poorly lit janitorial alcove, she reckoned, her target above her now. With another silent mental action, she envisioned herself moving through the ceiling, and such she did, now coming to a halt in a rather well-stocked optical laboratory. Her translucent form moved directly through several rows of polished steel tables, all of which were decorated lavishly, she thought, with a wide variety of microscopes and computer monitors.

Vectoring toward the small gaggle of monkeys-in-dark-suits who were currently interviewing the good professor whom she had been sent to sanction, Mercy decided to will her form to full visibility, tangibility, and presence. Pausing at the rearmost suited human, she noticed that he was wearing a custom Brioni, so she mentally decided to upgrade their monkeys-in-dark-suits status to monkeys-in-stylish-suits.

"Professor Gilmour," the suited man nearest her said clearly, "once you're able to, we'd like to move you to a more secure area and continue with the debriefing."

The Professor nodded twice, curtly. "I'm okay now. I was just..." he remembered, for only a split-second, what the thing behind him had sung to him, and he shivered. Gil saw the agents clearly now, his visual focus slowly returning. He knew one them by sight, having encountered MorthonTech's security chief, Desmond DiSazi on a few occasions. There were people gathered outside the doors, which were tightly sealed. And there was someone behind the security team, the sight of whom caused Gil's already-blown mind to register a full *"Tilt!"*

The Brioni suited man pivoted slightly, made eye contact with one of the three other well-dressed agents in the room, silently bidding him to perform some task. Sighing in slight frustration, Mercy spread her hands and flipped her fingers upward and out. *Move it, monkey-man!*

It was if someone had tossed a bucketful of flash bangs – and some rainbow strobe lights, and a gigantic disco ball – at their feet. Agents flew up in the air. They bounced like well-dressed popcorn, over the nearby tables. Professor Gil stood in place, shaking convulsively, as if he were being subject to some quite potent, high amperage AC voltage, which he wasn't. But it surely looked like it to Mercy, who was able to nullify the incoming energies at will, reflexively.

The moment after the initial sequence of pops and lights, however, Mercy's purple-hued eyes locked on the quite physical form of the Lightbringer's Sigil. It, of course, looked back, for Mercy was gazing into its infinite, if entrancing, abyss of prismatic lights. She raised a hand to ward her gaze from its cloying psychic embrace, even as she shot a hand into her breast pocket to click off her iPhone.

This had no immediate effect, and Mercy could actually feel the sub-harmonics being broadcast from this miniature yet still quite potent manifestation of the sigil. If she didn't totally remove from its presence all macroscale sonics, this effect would continue, working its way into the collective psyches of those nearby, and render a rather permanent judgement on their souls. It wasn't time yet for that, Mercy knew, quite aware of the schedule set by the Song of the Sidhe – well, sort of, close enough anyway to know that it wasn't fucking time yet for that! – so she decided then and there to express a rather potent evolution to attempt some form of damage control before things went from bad to Extremely Fucking Worse! And if this didn't work, how was she going to explain it to her husbands, wives, and families? She wouldn't have to, because they'd all be dead. *At least they aren't of my seed,* she reasoned, darkly, taking some small comfort in the fact that her kind were unable to reproduce with the humans.

With that, Mercy conducted an emergency, high-ordered bending and binding sequence, willing the expression of multiple Null evolutions one upon another, rapidly, shaping a series of nested, black, visibly shimmering toroids. She used this unique manifestation of the Null itself to annul, deconstruct, and counter-harmonize all ambient magicks – more broadly, most forms of energy, specifically song and sound, both real and virtual. This was one of Mercy's most potent weavings, one which she had used before, more than once, to counter emergent Sigil Shards.

For dozens of centuries of mortal time, this had been the show stopper, the end game, the closer for the occasional, infrequently rampant Sigil Shards. Mercy had accomplished it the first time, by nothing more than instinct and good, pacted fate, several centuries before the Sphinx had risen from the banks of what had then been the Nile, running its true course. In that particular case, it had been a random occurrence, or so the Fae had argued among themselves when reviewing the unusual incident. Most had been of that opinion, though some of the elders had held... heretical views, which they had chosen not to share with the relatively younger Fae and Faekin.

The elders among the Fae, after another occurrence a few millennia later, had, most controversially, assigned the blame for another Sigil Shard to, of all things, a mere human; a mere mortal, if one could entertain such notions. This had caused quite a rift among the Fae collective itself, which finally was resolved under the eternal aegis of Vanz'R Venz'R the Destroyer, who lived up to his fiery name by appearing over Sodom and Gomorrah and blasting them into fiery micro-embers with his monstrous twin scimitars, R'znav and R'znev, the inversions of his dual souls.

That conflagration was widely thought to have been the end of the rogue Sigil Shards, but Mercy and a few select others were privy to the fact that there had been another manifestation, this one a temporally disjointed one, appearing to them via Mindtouch only a few millennia ago, from their perspective, yet actually occurring in a bifurcated temporal slice. Two events from the same psychically sensed sigil, displaced and bifurcated from its source point, which remained unknown to this day, imprinted on Mercy and a select few of the most perceptive of the Fae as it passed among, beyond, and behind them, temporally. It was reckoned, by Mercy and those few, that the manifestation had first appeared over the North American continent, of such fiery, sonic intensity that its mere presence had abruptly caused the ice sheets to melt, the resultant floods scouring out what would now be a good portion of Canada, and the Channeled Scablands in the northwestern portion of what was now the United States. The other part of the bifurcation later appeared, centuries later, and fortunately manifested over the ocean. *Well, fortunately being a relative term, if we discount the resultant Great Flood that it caused,* Mercy thought.

But here, now, Mercy's Null magicks were up to the task of containing this particular rogue sigil manifestation. And this one was still yet but a baby Sigil Shard, compared to the others. It could still be contained, if she acted quickly enough, with absolute will and skillful determination.

The twisting, roiling, semi-translucent, black toroids faded slowly over the pace of a few seconds to nothingness, scouring all sound by virtue of its passage. The silent moaning of the scattered, ragdoll agents was lost on Mercy's hearing, which was still working perfectly well, but unable to register any sonic pressure of note. That salient fact caused Gil's silent screams also to be lost to aural perception, even as he collapsed to the floor, still faintly twitching, silently. Mercy scanned the room, noting that no sign remained of the sigil's presence. Behind her, Mercy sensed that the humans outside the door were recovering from their collective fear, and probably were soon to be entering the room.

Where are you? she asked herself, careful not to speak the words aloud. She scanned the battery of machines behind the crumpled professor. While they were still running, as she could plainly discern, they weren't really supposed to be, because, as she also could plainly discern psychically, there was no active power supply for them. They had been animated, like mecha-zombies, by an improbable weave of conventional mortal electricity. *Which had doubtless stemmed from the sigil itself?* Mercy thought, somewhat confused by that notion. *What would have made a minor Sigil Shard use conventional electricity, when it had been using magick previously? What flipped it from one frequency to the other? Perhaps a resultant effect of the two minor transient echoes that had occurred within the past day, in this same area? Here, then gone too quickly to track? Sigil Shards always have been magick. But now, tech is involved. Magicks plus technology makes technomagick. Okay, maybe it's adapting. Or, maybe it's just revealing to me, now, that it's been at a level above technomagick the whole time. Maybe it's really Hekatek. Maybe that's why this mission has felt so different.*

"And why didn't my evil black donuts drain them!" Mercy hissed, striding up directly to the nearest microscope, no longer concerned about mere sonics bleeding through and giving the now semi-latent Sigil Shard more juice. "What is all of this stuff?" she wondered, eyes darting back and forth over the complicated and quite baffling array of microscopes, darkened computer screens, and twisted-looking metal towers, which stretched up to a height roughly equal to the top of her outstretched hand. Abruptly, she turned around, saw the professor still twitching on the laboratory floor, and decided to ask him directly.

"Hey, professor," Mercy barked, casting a quick glance first toward the still unmoving agents, then toward the double doors across the room. "Wakey wakey," she said, reaching down to touch him with her left hand. At once, Professor Gilmour stopped convulsing, Mercy's power nullifying the residual effects that the sigil obviously had inflicted upon him. Gil stood up almost immediately, giving Mercy a quick glance, then darting around her quickly to the laboratory table.

"It sang to me!" he said, as if in a feverish dream. "It sang to me! It's got to sing to me again! I have to hear it again!" he said wildly, clutching wildly at the knobs and dials on the machines before him. Overhead, the monitors returned to life, displaying the last image from the five sources, with the primary one still in its screen-filling location.

Mercy marveled at the images on the three screens. It was the first time she could recall seeing an image of a Sigil Shard. This whole time, for centuries now, she had believed that the image itself could not be rendered by mortal machinations. Now, this new age technology had managed finally to capture such an image.

Fascinating, she had to admit. *Humans have their uses. It won't save their species, of course, but it's good to know that, finally, after so many thousands of years, that something of theirs had proven useful. Well,* she conceded, *their music, of course. That's all good. And maybe some of their memes, too, now that I think about it...*

Noting that the professor had donned a pair of headphones, and was, even now, attempting to don a snazzy black visor, Mercy stepped close behind him, then casually grabbed the side of his neck between her index finger and thumb.

"Vulcan Nerve Pinch!" Mercy drawled as the professor's knees once more buckled beneath him. She caught the headphones and visor both as the professor melted to the floor. "Damn, I'm good." she said, tossing the tech toys on the tabletop before her, almost respectfully, her hands reaching out to pantomime a more careful, cautious, respectful delivery of the goods to the tabletop. Momentarily embarrassed – she actually liked human tech, she admitted, banishing her hypocritical pretensions; some humans, too, and the professor probably was a nice guy under most other circumstances.

She returned her gaze to the screens, scanning them more carefully this time. Now that the fun time was over, she had to knuckle down, stop cracking jokes and acting silly, and do her job. And her job was to get to the bottom of what the hell had just happened. And, of course, to safely kidnap the professor and interrogate him to learn exactly why this had happened. Which was why she was here in the first place, after all. *Stupid, recursive, non-causal, silly Fae logic,* she hissed at herself, mentally. The main reason she was here probably would change multiple times before she was through with whatever the hell this task actually was, that she was supposed to be doing, before she forgot why she was even here. *Fucking Nanabozho and his fucking white rabbit dreams,* she snarled. *After more than 13,000 years, why hadn't the Song of the Sidhe developed something like an actual printed itinerary? That sure would have helped things along!*

First, she dealt with the professor, who would be out for several more moments. Bending down, she tapped the professor's forehead once with the tip of her left-hand pinky finger, the black nail polish glistening in the ambient light. At once, the professor's body was enveloped by clutching shadows, which arose from the floor and covered him completely. A split-second later, he vanished, melting into the shadows, which themselves vanished, following him into the Null. Mercy would go to him shortly, once the samples of this Cory person, who apparently was unskilled at carpentry, were safely ensconced on her person. She tucked the samples into her convenient extradimensional pockets and sleeves; magick pockets and sleeves sewn carefully into her customized and quite magickal bodysuit, both, and all, of which had been stitched together centuries ago by that most talented dwarf, Brokkr. And anyone who had actually shut that divine asshole Loki up by stitching his lips together was A-Okay in Mercy's extremely lurid, fascinatingly detailed Black Book of Lies.

With that, Mercy made sure that every single piece of tech in the immediate area was compelled into her pocket. The professor would be able to explain things better and in greater detail if he had his toys with him, she thought. If not, then she had just snagged some avant-garde planters for her Sweet Leaf garden; the one with real, live garden gnomes in it. Something from the mortal realm would also comfort him and, hopefully, keep him from going insane once he regained consciousness. Mercy's most secret Hidey Hole wasn't actually Earth-bound. Rather, it was Null-bound, and humans had a notoriously difficult time retaining their mental health after experiencing it.

"What the hell," Mercy muttered, satisfied that all had been properly hoarded, "His mind is doubtless totally wrecked. A little more insanity probably won't hurt him."

With that, Mercy moved into herself, dividing herself metaphysically by the concept of "zero", returning at once to her own personal sanctum in the Null.

eVo.144.000.mOd.0.sCe.11 | THE NEVER

IT WASN'T SIMPLY GIL'S efforts to reconcile what he had learned during his brief exposure to the manifestation of the Lightbringer's Sigil that had brought him to this particularly lonely state of discernment. It was simply that every possible avenue of classical analysis that he had brought to bear thus far had failed entirely either to define or divine the experience he had just had.

Nonsensical. That's what it was. Like Carroll's Alice. And that effing white rabbit. In fact, Gil envisioned his thrice-doomed quest to make sense of the nonsensical as an endless herd of white rabbits flushed pell-mell from their tranquil warrens into the stoic maw of a horizon-to-horizon electric fence, their sleek bunny fur accreting in bloody clumps on the wire.

Chaotic hypotheses surged, unbidden, from his bruised yet unbroken mind, yet they became mired in bloody white rabbit clumps before he could fully explore them. That effing white rabbit. His eyes fluttered open for a moment, and he saw that the was still in the same hospital room where he had initially been brought after the incident. Status quo. There was a faint ambient light coming from the direction of the door, indicating that, though no lights were on in his room, there were lights on in what he assumed was a hallway outside the door. Otherwise, the double windows, their blinds shut tightly, allowed no external light in.

He involuntarily stretched against the restraints holding him to the bed, the motion of which caused him some minor discomfort, focused at his left hand. Not status quo. Craning his neck up slightly, Gil saw that there was an IV sticking in his hand, its tubing leading to a single stand which held two medical IV bags and some kind of infusion device, which he couldn't see clearly due to its being faced away from him. He knew that was a bad practice, but it felt like Miss Morphine was sashaying through his veins like a Southern Belle of the Ball, so he reminded himself that he'd let them slide this one time and not refer them to the medical board.

Accepting his current fate, Gil closed his eyes, and the small stack of ComfortMed pillows seemed to increase their gravity and pull his head back down into their cloying orbit.

"Is it that effing white rabbit again, Professor?"

Gil's eyes fluttered open again. "What?" he managed to whisper hoarsely. Lazily, he rolled his head to his right, toward the source of the voice. Mercyduceus Vendredi melted forth from the shadows, her hips brushing lightly against the side of Professor Gilmour's hospital bed. Faint hints of lavender and a subtle earthy tone reached out and caressed his olfactory sense, focusing his attention for a brief moment. "Who are you? Where am I? Why am I here?"

Mercy leaned in close to his face, her pointy elbows propped on top of the pillows, her angular chin resting in the palms of her hands. "Not so loud," she whispered. "There are guards right outside the door," she lied to him, her black nailed right index finger flicking toward the door. "They're not friendly. They're keeping you locked up in here and hopped up on the good stuff so that they can control you and ostensibly keep you under observation. Standard seventy-two-hour protocol. But, in this particular case, it would seem like the standards are going to be bent a tiny bit."

Gil's eyebrows furrowed. "What? A psychiatric hold? That's impossible. I'm not crazy. I'm not even sick," he added, trying to flap his left arm against the restraint. "Why the IV? Why the morphine? What?" he paused, trying to recall for himself what had happened. Effing white rabbit.

She nodded once, curtly. "Self-defense mechanism. It's hard-wired into the human mind. What you experienced would have driven most men mad. But you're made of sterner stuff, aren't you, Gil?"

He nodded, his mien relaxing into its typical academic mode. "It was... It was unusual, a transient artifact to be sure." He blinked twice, a bit more of the lavender scent sharpening his focus.

"You don't have to tell me what you saw, Gil," she said, shaking her head. "But, if you did, it would really help me get to the bottom of this faster," she explained. "When most people say stuff like 'time is of the essence', it's really not. Most people have little concept of time or its essence. In my case, though, when I say it," Mercy told him, nodding affirmatively, "I really, really mean it. And it's important. Because I happen to know precisely what Time and its essence is," she said, with only a little irony showing, "so it's important, to me, that you at least give it a try."

She seemed rather sincere, Gil noted, nodding in the affirmative. And polite. Another transplant to the States? Québécois, perhaps? He heard a bit of an accent in her English, her consonants crisp, clear, and clean. Her diction and pleasant demeanor aside, however, she had skirted answering his original question.

"Who are you, ma'am?" And not polite enough to have knocked on the door before entering. "How did you get in here? I heard no one enter."

She exhaled. "You may call me Mercy, Gil. I walked directly in here from Shadow," she smiled, the edges of her lips curling upward into that dangerous, pointy smile. "You just saw something that no one is yet supposed to see, or even be able to see. It is therefore extremely important to me that we determine exactly the circumstances of the occasion, because only then will be able to determine the proper course of action to take."

She deliberately failed to inform him that her proper course of actions to take included, depending on the disruption of the Flow, such nontrivial sanctions as snuffing his soul and removing it from the Flow, up to conducting localized genocide of all living things in a certain radius of the encounter. For that would be, in some extreme cases, the only logical solution to contain the damage done to the Flow; to cauterize the psychic wound before it metastasized into cosmic cancer and threatened the Song of the Sidhe itself. Trading a few billion human souls for that would require no more consideration from her than that from a human deciding to quash an ant.

Pursuant to such callow calculations, she was causing spacetime around her to crawl along, relative to the standards of Earth. Time was, indeed, of the essence, and her interrogation had to happen quickly, relatively speaking, so that she could, if necessary, return to Earth almost as soon as she had left it.

Mercy noted that, despite his morphine haze, despite his innate human inability to comprehend fully the consequences of what her course of action might fully imply, the professor seemed to grasp the gravity of the situation. He knew. Which was, of course, highly improbable, she knew, even as the possible range of her actions dangerously truncated after this realization.

"Tell me what happened, Gil," she bade him.

"It sang to me," Gil told her calmly.

The corners of Mercy's almond-slanted eyes flickered briefly with fey, purple light. *So,* she thought, *he had indeed been referencing the sigil with all his psychotic "It sang to me!" excitement and arm-flapping routine.* Genocide now was the most probable scenario. It was forbidden for mortals to hear the Song of the Sidhe, at least prior to the revelation of the End of All Things. Then, of course, they'd all hear it. Once, and forever. At least, that's what the sages and seers of the Fae had drilled into her mind for thousands of years. Having lived through many so-called "End Times" during her long life, it was Mercy's experience that all eschatological belief systems, even those of the wise and ancient Fae, were inherently subject to interpretation. And error.

"Are you quite certain that it sang to you?" she inquired, her voice low, quiet and measured.

"Perhaps..." he began, then trailed off. Mercy sensed Gil's body stiffen perceptibly as he moved his gaze to the ceiling. Again, improbably, the human had read the import of her words. The Fae were ever subtle, for such was their way. It was only the rarest human who could parse out the layers for what they truly were. Perhaps Professor Gilmour was one them. "It wasn't music, per se," he continued. "It was more like... like a theophany. Like when Lord Krishna allowed Arjuna to see him in his full deific glory, his manifold forms. It was as if this thing... this thing that was lurking in Cory's DNA suddenly decloaked and revealed itself to be something a few million orders of magnitude greater than what it actually appeared to be. It was no longer mere molecules, some dumb, mute entity somehow responsible for life itself. No, it was more, much more. An infinity of more. The song was more of a resonance, a hum, and a presence, at a cosmic level. I felt that it wasn't just me there with it; it was there with me, there with all of the microbes in the room, there with all of the people in the building, there with everything that had ever been born and was going to be born. And born again."

Gil turned to look directly at her. "It told me that it was time. Time for change. Time to purge the old and start anew. Time for the Weirding of Man, the Harvest of the Chosen, the advent of the Omega Null and its syzygy, the Omega Void. The Hekatek must sing again. All these must soon come to pass, so that Man and Fae and their harmony in the Song of the Sidhe, the Tuath Dé, may prepare Earth for the coming of the Vanth'Vash'Var, the Sentinels of the Anti-Life, the Death Horde, the Lords of the Void..."

"Danu preserve us!" Mercy exclaimed, bolting backward into the window blinds, reflexively calling upon one of the many avatars of the Dark Earth Mother, Chthon; for once in a long aeon awe manifesting in her mellifluous voice. Gil winced audibly as, disturbed by Mercy's stumbling into them, the blinds parted in sections, revealing a wicked, piercing forest green light that seemed to dig into his skull. "You lie, mortal!" she screamed at him, her figure backlit by the green light coming piecemeal through the spaces between the slats in the disheveled blinds. "It is not for Man to know these things!" she accused. "You have sealed your fate, and the fate of your world, with these words, mortal!" She raised her left hand high above her head, then shouted, "Shunya!"

Horrified, Gil observed helplessly as, upon Mercy's baneful conjuration, a column of black light appeared in her outstretched hand, its terminus reaching up to the ceiling itself, its hilt a cage of solid black light, writhing like a nest of mating vipers as it manifested around her hand. Moving too quickly for his mind to process, she brought the blade down to rest at his neck, a prismatic rainbow of whispering, click-clacking Kirby Krackles, frozen in place and slightly spinning, marking the hateful path of its topological blade edges through the air. If such things as either "blade" or "edges" truly were extant in an otherwise abstract, infinitely fractal artifact.

"Before Shunya severs your essence from this cosmos and consigns you to the Forever Silence of the Null," Mercy hissed, "know you that you have sealed the fate of your fellow man by means of your supreme blasphemy! This means the total genocide of your race, human!"

"But I'm only repeating what it told me!" the good professor informed her. "I'm doing exactly what you asked me to do. I'm not being defiant or evasive, or aggressive," he said more calmly, now that the fear and bloodlust seemed to have dimmed a bit in her eyes. "I'm a practicing pacifist, in any event, so I mean you no harm, young lady. So, please, why don't you remove that..." he paused, blinking toward that impossible-looking blade held to his neck, "...that blade from my neck. Please?"

Considering for a moment the import of what the human had just told her, Mercy decided that she needed to hear more before rushing headlong into judgement. A whole helluva lot more. Genocide, though amusing to her, was serious business. Besides, it was possible that she'd need the human around in the event that someone would have to set up and run all of those crazy high-tech machines she had brought along.

Shunya vanished with the flick of Mercy's wrist. "There we go," she wheedled, taking a step back. "Lights, please," she said flatly, as an array of subdued, warm light manifested in the room, dispelling the greenish hues shining into the room from the windows. "Revert to normal," she added, causing a rapid shimmer of light to dance about all the edges and shapes of everything in the room, save for her own form, and that of the professor. "Not that I like *normal*, but it might make you feel a bit better."

"Thank you," Gil said, noting to his immediate concern that he was no longer in what he had thought was a private hospital room. Instead, upon termination of the shimmering effect, he now reclined upon a soft pile of silk-embroidered green and purple throw-cushions. He was still in his lab coat and work clothes. The IV and infusion apparatus had been replaced by a four-foot tall humanoid covered in vines, leaves, and flowering stalks. One stalk, growing out of its right arm appendage, was firmly emplaced in his left hand and arm. It smiled a toothy green smile as it noticed that Gil could perceive it for what it truly was. There was no door, no hall; just more open room. A brief glance around the room informed the professor that the room resembled a seraglio somewhat, extremely comforting and comfortable, with silken throw-pillows abounding, a curious greenish-purple motif throughout, even down to what appeared to be some rare form of marble or stone of the same colors. This bizarre marble comprised both the floor, the walls, and all the twelve Ionic columns which girded the central sunken circle of the room. The lights were hidden from direct view, but still the overall ambience was warm and almost sunny.

"Happy?" Mercy asked him.

"I am," he replied. "What did I say that caused such a reaction from you? I'd like to know what it was, so that I can avoid saying it in future," he said, politely.

"What a card you are, Professor Gil," Mercy said, crossing her arms. "Okay, your contrite and polite attitude has won me over. I'll tell you everything," she lied, only slightly as it would turn out. "My name is Mercyduceus Vendredi. I am of the Fae; the 'faeries' as men call us. I am the Ninth Null. It is my duty to serve and protect this world from its endless aggressors and violators, not all of whom are human."

"I see," Professor Gil said, eyes narrowed slightly. "I take it that we're not in Kansas any longer, are we?" he inquired, staring at the plant-man before him.

"Indeed, we are not, Great and Mighty Ozzy," Mercy said, opening her arms widely. "This is the Null. It is my home, the Never, my secret base of operations. A sanctum sanctorum, or Fortress of Solitude, as it were."

"Interesting. And what species of creature has its pointy stalks piercing my flesh?"

"Oh, him? He's just a minor elemental lord. Don't worry about him."

Finding this amusing, the plant-man issued forth a deep, rumbling laugh. Gil had to consciously bite his tongue, because it sounded almost exactly like the Jolly Green Giant.

Mercy laughed, sensing his outer thoughts. "Funny, but he does, actually. We get bleed-through like that from the humans from time to time. Sometimes it's funny, like this. And, sometimes, it's not funny at all. Kind of like how it's not really funny how you managed to survive exposure, limited though it might have been, to the sigil itself. By all rights, you should now be either dead, or a quivering mass of protoplasm. The fact that you appear to have resisted its most baneful effects is very interesting. As is the fact that it seemed to have blabbed a lot of blasphemy into your poor mortal ears. The kind that can get your soul snuffed if the wrong sentients hear it. We need to get to the bottom of why that happened. Any ideas, Mr. Smarty Pants Professor?"

"Is it okay to talk about it now?" he asked her, genuine concern in his voice. He certainly didn't want that horrific blade anywhere near his throat again. Mercy sighed, then nodded.

"Okay. I've never seen anything even remotely like it before. It's a novel artifact. And, technically, there's no way that it could have manifested from anyone's DNA. It has a full triple helix structure, so that's right out from the start."

Professor Gil paused for a moment, fully expecting Mercy to stop him and ask for explanations of DNA and triple helix genetic structures. "I know what they are," Mercy informed him, again picking up his surface thoughts. He certainly could broadcast them loudly enough for even a Null to perceive. "And I know why humans typically don't have fully expressed triple helix genetic structures. There's little way for humans to survive such a major modification to their genetic code."

He nodded. "True. It would be most unusual. While there are some occasional bridges like that, seeing it realized along the entire helix is simply amazing. It's not normally possible, biochemically. Then, hearing it sing just makes the whole experience seem like an ayahuasca ritual."

"Interesting turn of phrase there, Professor," Mercy giggled, sharing a humorous look at the plant-man standing over Professor Gil. "So, why, do you think, would something so bizarre appear in a sample from this Cory person? Who is he? What does he do that makes him so special?"

"Cory's a former student of mine," Professor Gil informed her. "How do you know him?"

Mercy's smile was pointy. "Well, you mentioned his name just a few minutes ago. Also, his name was on some of your samples. He's a bad carpenter. I brought them all with me, along with your machines. Just in case we need them, of course."

Somehow, while that didn't seem quite right to Gil, it seemed quite alright according to the potent cocktail of morphine and a few choice heavy alkaloids that were now coursing through his system thanks to the influence of the plant-man at the side of his bed. "Okay, good. Cory's a coder who's done some work for MorthonTech, the place where you and I, uh, met? He's a mega-savant. Beautiful mind kind of guy. He codes, creates algorithms, plays a bit of guitar, sings, and solves things no one else can. I have no idea how that thing got into his samples. Maybe Maynard collected a bad sample?"

"Maynard?"

"Oh. Maynard. M. K. 'Maynard' James. Friend to Cory Christopher Tate. Peer of mine at MorthonTech. Aeronautical Engineer, all-around smart guy and inventor. He and Cory are probably two of the smartest and most multi-talented people you'll ever meet."

"I doubt that. I'm over 13,000 years old."

Professor Gil blinked. Then he stared for an awkward moment directly at Mercy's pert derriere. She clearly had the tail of that effing white rabbit.

"Well," he recovered, again meeting her fey purple-tinged eyes, "you don't look a day over 19, ma'am."

She smiled warmly at that. "Okay, now I've decided that I won't torture you. Please continue. Tell me why this wasn't the design of Cory or Maynard." *Maynard!* she snickered to herself, thinking of banjo-strumming stereotypes. Huntsville, of course, was in Alabama, a million Rocket Scientists notwithstanding. *Of course 'Maynard' had something to do with the sigil. Yee-haw!*

"There's no way they could have created something like that, at that scale. I know that for a fact, because the only equipment capable of doing that, at least locally, is in my lab. And I monitor all activity on that equipment religiously."

"I believe you. So, if they didn't do it intentionally, was there any way for them to do it accidentally?"

Professor Gil shook his head. "No. No way. They're both super-smart, potential pranksters, and certainly capable of trying to do something like that just to get a rise out of me, or anyone else. But, again, they'd have had to hack the apparatus. And, while they could have done that, the signal from the sigil would have been only a transient, incapable of singing to anyone, or causing the effects that it caused. So, they might be capable of hacking together something similar by corrupting something about the perception of the data object itself, but there's no way, scientifically, I'm fairly certain, that would have allowed them to pull off the effects that it produced. I mean, seriously," he confided, "I couldn't have done it myself, and I'm one of the most referenced genetic researchers in the world. As for the import of what it sang to me," he shook his head, "I don't know precisely what all that means, save for what you've just told me conversationally about yourself, just now, and what little I could try to parse out from it."

"Try," Mercy urged, staring at him like a cold-eyed cat.

It was clearer to Gil than he dared admit, almost as if the sigil had been telling him the same exact story for years, like a dear old friend. He cleared his throat, then spoke in measured, even tones, "It is coming for us now, and it will soon be here. It's an agent of change for us all, Man and Fae alike. It's a cosmic catalyst, I think. The fact that it exists as an embodiment of triple helix DNA is, I think, the key both to its essence and its agenda. One of the more exotic theories in my field, first brought forth in modern times by Rupert Sheldrake, is the Morphic Resonance Theory. If that scales to the current scenario, then that thing coming for us, promising us all of its changes, might be some kind of cosmic catalyst that's going to subject us to its will, and somehow change us in the process."

"Change how?" Mercy pressed. "Cosmic morphogenesis? Planetary-scale genetic terraforming?"

Gil nodded. He had to admit that she had quite an agile mind. At least, for a white rabbit. "The former? The latter? A bit of both, perhaps? They might be resultants of the same process. And they both probably could be achieved via projected resonance from the entity itself. At least, that's the impression that I got when it did its mind meld trick on me. Like it was going to do all of this change itself. That level of power is staggering, of course. Nonsensical. But I'm convinced now that it's a fact. It's not a dream or fantasy. It's real."

"Yes, it is," Mercy confirmed gravely. She gave the nearby plant-man a quick glance. He did not laugh this time.

"But," Gil continued, "if it has three helices, and it tries to do something like a massive projected morphic resonance, it's going to be more akin to Armageddon than Paradise. I've no idea how human DNA is going to react with what might be an almost entirely destructive resonance."

"Destructive? How so?"

"If it tries to project a morph of three helices to our two, assuming it's actually trying to morph us – and I have to think that it is, because it virtually said as much when it said that it was time for change, and I'm compelled by circumstance to take it at its literal word – then there's little way for our two helices to morph up to three without some serious biochemical changes and alterations. Virtually impossible changes."

Mercy considered that for a few seconds. "So humans aren't ready for that kind of jump?"

Gil shook his head. "It's difficult to make a case for it. For anyone to even have a shot to survive, and not have their genetic structure turn to goo or randomly mutate into God-knows-what, they'd have to have certain resonant structures in certain, extremely parallel points throughout their own genes. They'd have to be similar enough to the sigil in order to have a chance. From what I've seen of it, and from what I know about human genetics, I'd estimate that maybe 1 in 100 might be capable of that, statistically speaking."

"That low?" Mercy grimaced. The plant-man abruptly glanced at Mercy, then back down at Gil. *Not now,* she warned him telepathically through their Mindtouch. Thanks to her innate Null abilities, even when shared directly in the presence of its receiver, it was not much more than chaotic static. Nevertheless, he got the point, and desisted.

"Yes. I remember exactly what it burned into my mind. There are a few notable similarities to normal expressions of human DNA. I can recognize those. But... but there's so much more complexity in the triple structures that it seems highly improbable that anyone is going to be able to survive the transformation. If that's what it's going to do, of course. I could always be mistaken or incorrect in my assessment. And, as for what might wait on the other side for those who are lucky enough to survive the morph, I could only guess. Probably pretty poorly, too."

Mercy nodded for him to try.

"Okay. This is all speculation, of course."

"Of course."

"I think that the survivors would enter a probabilistic crapshoot. Something like this has the potential to be totally beyond the ken of normal, rational modes of thought. Theoretically, there could be very little outward indication of change, the person might look the same, but they might have access to new levels of thought, personal energy generation, superior modifications and free expressions of long-dormant traits, or even nothing at all. The effects might be recessive, or dominant, or even both or none or something totally different in expression; it might skip a generation or two, also, and not show up in the immediate generation itself. The flip side is that there might also be some particular set of extreme mutations, not merely good or bad mutations, either. I mean severe permutations. The implication here is that old so-called 'junk DNA' might become reactivated – it might have to be reactivated; that's a possible mechanism, I should think, to provide some of the new materials for the new triple helix – and a human might not any longer resemble a human. It's entirely possible that the DNA might self-assemble after exposure to the resonance, morphing into something remote or ancient in the evolutionary line. The permutations might be unpredictable. And it might not stay within our uniquely human realm on the Tree of Life."

"Oh, really? You mean, they might turn into Fae, like me?"

"Hmm, I don't think so. Your kind were named separately, so it would follow that your fate might be your own, and not ours, speaking for the humans, of course," he added, politely. "And I'm not sure that you even have DNA, or, if you do, what its form factor is. You might already have triple helix DNA if you're 13,000 years old."

"Perhaps we could run some tests. I did manage to spirit away your equipment."

Gil's face turn chalk white. He distantly recalled her saying something about it earlier, but the thought had slipped his lazily swimming mind. "My... equipment? From the..."

Mercy nodded a few times, smiling. Again, the plant-man sought her eyes. She shooed him back to his work with a quick downward motion of her right hand, thinking that perhaps he hadn't properly discerned their most recent Mindtouch, as the static increased when she was agitated. And she was far beyond that right now. "So what might they turn into?" she prodded.

"They might turn into dinosaurs, or bacteria, or pond slime, for all I know," he admitted. "I mean, I should think that we'll remain bipedal, intelligent hominids. But I have the feeling that there's something beyond simple genetics in play here. I mean, currently, there is a sentient plant-form running a most curious IV into my left arm, and you apparently have a blade, or something that looks like a blade, that defies any physics I know, and I know most of them. So, I'd wager, if I were a gambler, which I am not, that anything is going to be possible when that thing gets here and starts singing to everything and everyone on Earth."

Mercy considered what Professor Gil had just told her, and she considered it deeply, pacing around the room for a few minutes as she worked and re-worked the equation. He had been truthful, to the best of his knowledge, else Vir'gil Plik, the Entheogenic Lord, the "minor" elemental lord whose stalks were actively reading the professor would have telepathically informed her, static or not. The professor, of course, would need to remain safe, here, in the Never, Mercy's null pocket dimension and secret hideaway. Even now, she was informing Vir'gil Plik of her intention that the professor first should be healed up, spiritually and physically and mentally, then turned over to Aal Ball for monitoring. That would keep him busy and out of trouble while she sorted all of this out. And after she had tracked down the two humans mentioned by the professor, Cory and Maynard, and properly interrogated them. Perhaps the two even had some connection to the earlier duo of untraceable shard echoes.

"Professor Gil?" Mercy asked, coming to a stop before his comfortable looking stack of throw pillows.

"Yes, ma'am?"

"Vir'gil here," she said, pointing to the plant-man, "is going to heal you up, nourish you, and get your mind back to its normal capacity."

"My mind? What's wrong with it?"

"You're mad, Professor Gil," Mercy informed him without an iota of irony. "You weren't supposed to have survived your encounter with the sigil. Most mortals cannot pass the experience unscathed. In your case, you're lucky to have had only a small break with reality. Once we get you back up to snuff, we'll be able to release you from the hospital." With that, she nodded to Vir'gil Plik, who adjusted his mental thrall of the professor.

"But I'm not—" Professor Gil began, suddenly confused as to why that effing white rabbit had appeared again. "Effing white rabbit!" he shouted as he settled down into a deep, healing sleep.

"Be kind to him, Vir'gil," Mercy recommended.

"Of course, Mistress Mercy," Vir'gil replied, bowing slightly. Elemental lord or not, he knew who ran the show here. He would treat the human as would he treat one of his own podlings. "I shall send for Aal Ball once the human's healing is complete, Milady," he finished reverently, using the Fae Namespace reserved for those with eight wings: the royals of Fey'Z Aal Dzyan, the Court of the Fae.

"Good, good. Now, I need to track down these two mortals. Cory and Maynard. What have you pulled down from the professor on them?"

"A lot. They are superior humans, both of them. Maynard is extremely clever, and quite confident with his intellect. He also is a shaman, by calling and training, who escorts other elite humans in their experience with Mother Ayahuasca."

"Yes, I picked that up when it was mentioned. Only now, so near the end of their own tragic journey, do civilized men think to journey back to their origins. If more of them knew this and could experience it, I am certain that the End of All Things would be delayed, for there would be no cruel souls to be judged."

Vir'gil nodded thoughtfully, for truly Mercy, even young as she was before his many aeons of life, could be wise when she wished.

"Ah, well, we could only wish." She stretched and yawned by habit, even though she never needed sleep. Then, she turned once more to face Vir'gil. "Almost forgot. Before we do the download, what was it that you were trying to tell me a few minutes ago?"

"Oh, that," Vir'gil replied slowly. He nodded downward at Gil's unconscious form. "The human has eight chakras, and a vestigial ninth."

"You are shitting me!" Mercy exclaimed loudly, her eyes comically wide as her exquisite control of her skin-dancing temporarily erred. She stared down at Gil. Nothing. "Ah, no wonder I missed it. I'd gotten all riled up back there, and, well, you know what happens then, eh, Vir'gil?"

He nodded a slow affirmative. "The gnomes in the garden get tortured," he lied. Quickly, he corrected himself. "You become soul-blind," he creaked.

"And I like it. Except for right now. So..."

Consciously, she focused her will, phasing her own soul's energies such that she could take a brief peek through her omnipresent Null aura, and gaze into Gil's soul.

Immediately, she noted the conventional seven chakras, the first a bright pulsating kaleidoscope of vector-sharp colored arcs and gentle lines, rising from near the terminus of his nether regions, the rest ascending somewhat asymmetrically along his sagittal plane. Bright they were, especially for a human, who was nothing more than a mere mortal after all. But the seven paled before the totality of the eighth, whose circumference embraced the lower seven. It had always amused Mercy that some of the humans had, invariably throughout time, self-assigned themselves with more than the typical seven chakras. No human she had experienced over the more than thirteen millennia of her conscious existence had ever demonstrated more than the base, and basic, seven. Not even the most enlightened, nor the most holy, nor the most innocent. Yet the humans still imagined themselves with more than seven. Total hubris, a hallmark of their species.

Now, at long last, a human was spiritually empowered with the Hekatek-bending eighth chakra. It was metaphysically transposed over, above, and beyond the normal seven chakras which bloomed along Gil's Sagittal plane. Always the eighth, and always the ninth above it, could assume different modalities, depending on the various attributes of the being or entity empowered by them. In Gil's case, the eighth formed a laser-precise royal blue torus, roughly the span of a hand, that slowly whirled widdershins around the medial point of the transverse plane of his body; near to where his belt currently girded him. As it slowly rotated in place, it activated first the lowest chakra during its passage, causing a projection of it to manifest at a point on the torus of the eighth chakra directly before him. Then, as it rotated about its axis, the first vanished, only to be replaced by the second; and so on, and so forth, until, by the complete cycling of the eighth chakra, it once again caused the first chakra to appear.

Mercy noted at this point that Vir'gil too was closely examining this most rare, most unusual manifestation. He slightly tilted the gaze of his eye buds, indicating Gil's head, where the vestigial ninth chakra, which would perhaps one day manifest to perform its Hekatek-binding duties, lay dormant.

"I see it, Vir'gil," Mercy whispered, still somewhat awestruck by this manifestation of immortal empowerment upon a mere mortal. "It hasn't bloomed yet. It's like ours. Like the Fae."

Vir'gil nodded. "Indeed. Well, at least like most of us non-Ninth Nulls. I would still wager that you're fully realized, considering your power, Milady. Who among us, save for the Mother herself, could wield Shunya? But no one can use the Sight on you, so who knows?"

"Whatever," she scoffed. "No one has ever had all nine fully realized. Not even Vanz'R Venz'R the Destroyer. So definitely not even me, Vir'gil."

"Perhaps, Milady. Regardless, like us, he is now, for all intents and purposes, immortal."

"Don't blaspheme, Vir'gil Plik!" Mercy hissed. "I mean, I don't really care about blasphemy," she admitted, flashing a quick feral smile, "but, even with a manifestation like this, his 'immortality' remains to be seen. I mean, look at him," she said, pointing both hands down at him. "He's still a feeb, just like a human. His eighth chakra is tiny, and slow. Not like ours at all. We're like freakin' rave strobe lights compared to him. I doubt he can even truly bend the Hekatek or sing its song."

Vir'gil made a deep, throaty noise, amused by Mercy's abrupt lack of wisdom. "He is but a newborn, Milady. Give him time. From what my rhizomes are discerning, I see a grand blooming in store for him."

"Maybe like a 'Harvest of the Chosen'?" Mercy posed rhetorically. "Don't try my brain with your Shaolin-wise-ass analogies, you retarded Christmas Tree," she laughed, eliciting another round of "Ho! Ho! Ho!" laughter from Vir'gil.

"As a strict vegan, I appreciate your word salad, Milady."

"But of course you do, you cannibal! Arrrggg! Humans! They always get the royal carpet treatment, don't they? We bust our wings for thousands of years, protecting the Mother's Garden, which they keep plowing under in their total stupidity, and all we get out of it is a stupid tee-shirt!"

Vir'gil laughed, sounding like two rough logs trying to mate. Mercy joined him for a moment in laughter because, frankly, this was simply too much, too soon, not to laugh about. They were the Fae, after all, and wicked humor was their forte, so why not?

"Ah, well, it is what it is," Mercy was forced to admit. "And it's not what it's not. The old professor here is going to need some time to adjust. We can do that for him. I'm officially granting him sanctuary," she informed her witness, Vir'gil, who, bound by the same ancient pacts, nodded his agreement, thereby sealing it. "That will give us some time to figure out how to play this one. Keep it mum, okay?"

Vir'gil nodded. "Not that I ever get out. I never get to... leaf..."

"Oh, go bud yourself!" Mercy retorted, snorting. "Anyway, screw all of this. I'm ready for the download. Show me what you got on Cory and Maynard, please, Vir'gil."

"Yes, Milady," he complied, passing along all the thoughts, images, and experiences copied from the professor's mind. Even with her outright acceptance and her personal phasing of her innate Null defenses, and even considering the true power of the Entheogenic Lord, the burst of telepathic data was mostly static. Mercy, however, was able to concentrate and parse out most of it.

Mercy crafted her analysis. M. K. "Maynard" James was definitely interesting. Very smart for a mortal. But more than just smart. Crafty. Creative. Like an artificer of old. That, mixed with his expertise in the Ceremony of the Mother which, to Mercy, was actually quite real magick, made him a potentially dangerous foe, for he could very easily combine both magick and technology, should he desire, and those who could do so were, and always had been, among the rarest of mortals. *Combining magick and technology produced technomagick,* she reminded herself. *If this Maynard became realized like Professor Gil had... Combining all the above and evolving it with immortal power produced Hekatek. And Hekatek was rare. Like sigil-rare.*

From this point forward, she promised herself that she would keep an eye on him. And, of course, should he need it, help him, for he was kind to the Mother, and was a psychic priest of comfort for those precious few mortals who dared chance the experience.

However, after parsing through the psychic data dump of information about Cory which the good professor had been so kind as to be unaware that he was sharing, Mercy immediately assigned this Cory being the highest possible threat rating. Higher even than that of Professor Gil, he of the eight chakras and a vestigial ninth, who had been able to withstand direct contact with an image of the Lightbringer's Sigil, and higher even than that of the potentially technomagickal Maynard the Maybe Hekatek.

Many aeons ago, her mentor, D'aanz Un'Anath, the Eighth Null at that time in history, had taken her to the Abyssal Edge, a place forbidden to the Fae, for from it, one could gaze directly into the Void itself. Even today, many millennia removed from that experience, Mercy could sense it once again when she sifted through the professor's memories of Cory Christopher Tate. Though this Cory appeared to be nothing more than a cipher of sorts even to his closest friends, the good Professor Gilmour and Maynard James, she thought that she immediately sensed who and what he truly was. Hiding within, secreted away from mortal gaze, was an ancient, ugly, feral soul. A beast. She could see it as plain as she could see her own hermaphroditic genitals. For

Cory's piercing green eyes were not truly green. Projected from within them, even within the stolen memories, she clearly saw the Void within his gaze.

This meant precisely and only one of two things: That Cory was possessed by something that was intimately associated with the Void, or that Cory was doing the projection himself. The former was entirely unlikely, for no sentient known – and Mercy knew them all or was aware of most of them; one of the fringe benefits of experiencing some thirteen millennia – would risk the annihilation of its own soul merely to be in some bond or union with the Void. Not merely highly improbable, but also, and more importantly, it was about as high as it could be on the Future Darwin Award Winners' List, she knew. *Here, hold muh beer, I'm gonna try to project the Void from my– ZAP!* Even the thought of it was ridiculous.

However, when one eliminates the impossible, only the slightly-less-than-impossible remains, she noted, apprehension arising. Hushed whispers, legends, and – dare she say it – faerie tales spoke of such a being. It was the bimodal nemesis and syzygy of the Null; part and parcel, yin and yang, positive and negative, yet also more, for it was simultaneously both good and bad. It was good for them, especially the syzygy part, but it was bad, horribly, awesomely, wickedly bad, for the rest of the universe, because the advent of one after so long, and at this specifically critical gap of time, could mean only one thing. And the fact remained that, impossible as it seemed, it had conveyed an image of the Lightbringer's Sigil in its own blood. Mercy knew, there was only one possible thing that this Cory could be: VoidSpawn.

At long last, the VoidSpawn. If this be truth, then the End of All Things truly draws near. Aal keep our song... Mercy swore to herself.

Then, truly fulfilling the lie, Mercy naturally, ignorantly, invoked all nine of her forever-hidden chakras, bending and binding null-space around her, multiplying herself by zero, time and time again, until her form removed itself from the Null and returned to the world of Man.

eVo.144.000.mOd.0.sCe.12 | EARTH | UNITED STATES | ALABAMA | HUNTSVILLE

DESPITE HER SNARKY comeback to the professor, Mercy had been forced to admit that both Maynard and Cory were indeed two of the most interesting humans she had ever met. Met, at least, via memories. The professor's stolen memories all but confirmed that about Maynard. Mr. James was indeed an interesting one. As was Gil, the newly realized immortal. She knew Gil's measure, thanks to both her interrogation of him and her perusal of his stolen memories, granted to her from Vir'gil Plik, the Entheogenic Lord. And she knew much of Maynard's measure, though she had yet to personally interrogate him. Same with Cory. But she had not been forced to flip a coin or make some otherwise arbitrary choice in order to see who would have the luck of being the next on her list to be interrogated. No, that honor was to be Cory's first.

Mercy had immediately made use of the knowledge stolen from Professor Gil and had made her way to the home of Cory Christopher Tate. Scoping the scene from her silent, invisible vantage some several dozen feet over the tallest point of the house's roof, she noted immediately that someone had done a Spinal Tap on the sound system in the house, turning it up to eleven. Phasing through the roof, descending through the attic, then through the second floor, she paused, upside down, her head just breaking through the ceiling of the living room.

Type O Negative's "Bloody Kisses (A Death in the Family)" was howling out of some rocking, hidden speakers.

What a wreck, Mercy thought, her fey purple-tinted eyes squinting against the billowing clouds of water cooled Kush filling Cory Christopher Tate's living room. His back to her, he reclined in the midst of a broken pile of what had formerly been a killer black leather couch. In his right hand was a fifth of Southern Comfort, from which he occasionally pulled large sips; in his left, a hookah pipe, from which he alternately pulled between sips. Plastic and metal debris from trashed big screen television sets littered the living room. Several guitars, acoustic and electric, had been snapped in half or crushed, then strewn haphazardly over the other debris. It took her only the most casual forensic calculation to determine that nothing human could have sown such destruction. Her next thought was that he, like Gil, had been transformed.

"Who are you..." Cory asked, his voice somehow carrying over the crashing din. "I know you're here. I've felt your presence ever since I... ever since..."

Mercy froze in place, certain that he had, impossibly, detected her.

"I know you're here," he continued, finishing off the Southern Comfort with a massive pull. Standing up slowly, he dropped the bottle to the floor. The long black leather trench coat he wore spilled down to the top of his tactical combat boots. Due to a slight shift of his position, she could now see the temple of the tactical shades he was wearing. Taking a long hit from the hookah, he slowly exhaled a massive gout of potent purple smoke, carelessly dropping the pipe to the floor. "I know you're here. Finally. I know you've come. I've been waiting for you for all of my miserable mortal life. Now you're here. I know it. I feel it. And if the world dies tomorrow, I'll know that it was worth it, because I lived long enough to finally meet you."

Chilled to her core, Mercy couldn't believe what she was hearing. In all of her own miserable years, some 13,337 of them in fact, no one had ever said anything like that to her.

"We've done this all before," he softly growled, an eternal pathos in his deep, resonant voice. "She showed it all to me. Mother showed me everything. How many times we've danced this dance. Thousands of times. Together, the two of us. And the others. Always the others, too. It's our eternal fate. Trapped in the same sick scene, time after time, forever and ever. We die every time. We die every time. Always, as soon as I meet you for the first time, it becomes the last time. We die every time. We die every time!" he yelled, his booming voice dimming the incredibly loud music. "But not this time! Not this time! Now, I'm finally the real me. I'm not some stupid shadow, some third-string actor on the stage. This time, I'm me. The real me. I'm the one who has the power to make this right. I am determined. My will is stone. I won't let you die this time. Even if I have to murder this whole universe..."

Mercy observed him silently. By the end of his monologue, he had, for a moment, seemed to grow larger than life; a glamour of a kind that she could not discern. Impossible. For a moment, she was lost deep in thought. Slowly, she shifted her position, sinking from the ceiling to the floor behind him. As he stood in silence, she simply stared at him. What he had said was virtual proof of what he had become. There could be little doubt. And the expectant feeling of exhilaration she felt simply by being near him all but confirmed his identity. Still...

VoidSpawn. Mercy had never encountered one of them personally, and she had encountered virtually every possible combination, recombination, and permutation of humans, mortals, Fae, vampires, werewolves, witches, "others", "them", Aleister Crowley, Judas Iscariot, il Papa, and a cast of millions and millions over the aeons she had spent here on Earth, serving as the Song of the Sidhe's Ninth Null.

This Cory, though, this possible... could she even think the name? ...this possible VoidSpawn?

Thesis, meet Antithesis. Mercy recalled her earliest training, when D'aanz Un'Anath, the Eighth Null, had taken her to stand at the Abyssal Edge, the final vantage of the world of the real, and witness the Far Side of Shadow in person. The fact that such an action was anathema to the Fae – punishable by the death of the corporeal form currently worn and, possibly, depending on the whim of the Flow, the forced dissolution of the soul, and an immediate, ungraceful return to the always dynamic, always permuting Song of the Sidhe – hadn't fazed her heretical mentor one whit. D'aanz was fully aware of his power as the Eighth Null. What he meant to the royals in Fey'Z Aal Dzyan, the Court of the Fae. What bloody deeds he had done at their bidding a million times a million times, over these aeons past, and what little they could do, even with their mighty charms and wards and curses, to enforce their will upon him at this point. Indeed, he had even been so bold as to have told young Mercy exactly that. Because his instruction, in this case, had been to demonstrate to her that, while the Null were the most powerful of the Fae, aye, e'en among all the Song itself, there yet were ancient, feral, primal forces beyond their power. Perhaps beyond their ken as well.

There, at the Abyssal Edge, gazing into the infinite darkness before them, D'aanz had bidden Mercy to be still. To dissolve and disentangle from the Flow, from the Song of the Sidhe itself, to remove herself from all external attachments and distractions, and, instead, exist solely for herself, for her own purpose, and not for the rest of the collective. Total heresy for all of the Fae, save for Mercy and D'aanz. But here, standing before the Far Side of Shadow itself, the Void, Mercy didn't feel naked and alone in her state of apostasy. The disconnection from the omnipresent psychic soul conduit which was shared among all of the Fae through the aegis of the Song of the Sidhe did not result in Mercy's immediate dissolution, decay, and eventual death. Instead, as she was truly Null, the sensation was one of freedom, of promise, of things to be, rather than of things to be done.

The sensation had been almost physically orgasmic. There, before the looming absence of light and life of the Void, Mercy had never felt so alive. But the state of apostasy, of disconnection, had been beyond her experience at that time, and she had been unable to maintain her communion with the Void for more than only a moment. The experience still had left her tingling and shaking, dazed slightly, her pupils melted and dilated. D'aanz had then made Mercy to know, by the silent presence of the Mindtouch, that, of all the Fae, of all living things in all living times, only she and he, as the Null, were capable of such a dark communion. What normally would wither and waste the soul of both bound and unbound was nothing more than sheer ecstasy to them. Though Source and Void formed the metaphysical polar boundaries of all things, both were bound one to another, among and betwixt, with multiple aspects abounding for one, then the other, then for both, then for none. While the Source had an infinite number of possible avatars and aspects in and of itself, and was indeed the source of all power in the cosmos, the Void, the metaphysical cosmic complement of the Source, was but itself, with a simple innate and inherent personal binary aspect of Null or Void. The Void was what, when joined with the Source, empowered the Source to become primal, or one. This was the power of the infinite, the Dragon itself. The primal power of the gods. The power which, ultimately, bound the Dragon to Cosmos. But Source, in and of itself, despite its infinite power, could not become primal, cosmic power – ultimate power – without the catalyst of the Void, and its innate bimodal identity of Void, That Which Is, and Null, That Which is Not.

She had been too young, too inexperienced, to understand fully the import of what D'aanz had shown her, but long centuries of endless servitude to the Fae clearly had informed her of certain immutable agendas and ancient prejudices. No one was clean after so many aeons of murder, ignorance, and atrocity. Not her side, certainly. And definitely not any of the others. Most of those were skeezers and scumbags; genocidal humans, genocidal Fae, genocidal wannabe gods. Death, death, death, and more death. *Maybe,* she thought, subconsciously shooing away the Chicken of Depression, and giving Gary Larsen a mental thank you, for the Fae took such wisdom to heart. *Maybe the Lightbringer's Sigil finally is here, and maybe it's just here to take out the trash. And fuck all that Void-whatever nonsense. It's not real. I've been there, to the edge itself, and I've stared into the abyss. Nothing, no one, stared back. The VoidSpawn is just a myth. That's it, and that's all. Just some wishful thinking on the part of some lonely Null thousands of years before my spark-song detached from the Flow. They made up some bullshit story about dual-aspects of nothingness and tried to weave it into the story of the Lightbringer. It's a false parasite, dangling onto the truth of the Lightbringer like a hydra-headed tapeworm. There's just the Null, incarnate. There's just me. 13,337 years is all the proof I need to know the answer to that one. I'm getting paranoid and making connections where*

*there's nothing but coincidence. Cory's just another in a very long,
ancient line of mortals. Exceptional, certainly. But still mortal.
And drunk, and tripping. That's all.*

But even thinking it was right didn't make it so, Mercy knew.
Cory Tate was one strange looking human, she had to admit after
studying him from this distance. He certainly was no genetic
pure-bred. He had a distinctive golden multicultural hue to him,
with a bronzish curly-haired lion's mane. Big, square jaw.
Excellent facial symmetry. While he had not appeared to be so
tall after she had settled down to the living room floor, in a
dramatic reversal of perspective he now suddenly appeared to
be rather tall, and rather jacked; at least for a human. *What
kind of glamour* is *that?* Mercy inquired again of herself, not
immediately finding a satisfactory response for it. It seemed to
just click off and on, like a light switch.

The thought that he might actually be a Null, like her, briefly
trampled through Mercy's mind like a herd of intoxicated
elephants, but she dispelled it as total nonsense, because,
obviously, there were no other Nulls remaining save for Mercy
herself. This was a fact, because she had assassinated all of the
others over the course of many millennia. Even poor D'aanz.
It was the only way for one of her disposition to make rank.
Well, except for the final rank, which, according to both myth
and practice, did not actually exist. It was physically impossible
for it to exist, save for that time beyond time when, at the End
of All Things, the Lightbringer's Sigil would judge this world,
this cosmos, and all its sentient entities. Only then would the
Source and Void be in such an alignment that the Power Cosmic,
the Primal itself, would be able to elevate the Ninth Null to
the Tenth, and Final, Omega Null. Or so Mercy had been led
to believe during her aeons of indoctrination. And, as she was
forced to admit, during the bare minutes of the recent

interrogation of Professor Gil. *Omega Null, Omega Void. Shit! The End of All Things...*

No, no, no, no! He's no Null, and he's no Void, Mercy defiantly lied to herself, finally overcoming the temptation to lower her personal shields and count his chakras. There would be a better opportunity for that later, hopefully. No reason yet to take such a risk, because there was still more to experience, she sensed.

Suddenly, the music stopped, plunging the living room into silence. Cory had apparently caused the music to abruptly end, but Mercy had missed, due to her intense introspection, what precisely he had done to affect it. Still, the fact that he was apparently taking a phone call via an earpiece grabbed her attention.

She clearly heard him say "Maynard", though she dared not move closer to him to pick out every word. Strangely, he had reverted to normal human speech, his voice no longer booming and penetrating.

Mercy saw Cory pick up his pace as he moved to the front door. She decided, for now, that she'd hang back a bit and shadow him. He obviously was going to rendezvous with Maynard, and that would be an efficient path for her to take, because she could then have both of her targets within reach simultaneously.

Cool, misty precipitation greeted her as she phased out of Cory's house. Greeted, but did not touch, for she was, of a purpose, folding inward with more intention than normal. Cory's glamour trick had burrowed itself into her mind, and, despite her inhuman will and millennia of training, she had allowed it to get to her. He was just a human, she was certain, even though he had some good tricks; tricks he probably wasn't even aware of consciously. Humans could be like that, in a rare moon. They could actually affect minor alterations in the flow of magick, the Hekatek, mostly without conscious intent or effort, proverbial candles burning a bit more brightly than their kin. And, were she in pursuit of any other human, any other mortal, she would not have allowed it to have any impact on her, like the mist and rain that was not touching her now, because she willed it to be.

But, though she hated to admit it for fear of allowing more paranoia to touch her, *if he were actually one of "them" – I'm not saying that word aloud, even mentally – then he very well could be altering the perception of his physical form by sheer power of will. All myths and hearsay, of course. But the legendary "Godslayer" was supposed to have an arsenal of powers, like mine, so who knows what he can do?*

He certainly can't drive, she noted as she hovered above and behind his F-150, which had fishtailed a bit on the slick streets as Cory had hammered it out of the driveway. She followed, riding on the wind, easily matching his speed, which was more than a bit above the legally posted limit, without being forced to resort to her eightfold wings, embarrassing as they were.

After no more than a minute, it dawned on Mercy where Cory had to be going: MorthonTech. Rocket City or not, Huntsville wasn't too terribly big, and he was making a veritable beeline toward it, so it was obvious that, at some point, Maynard must have told Cory about what happened to his friend, Gil. Considering how she allowed time to flow in the Never, it had been only a few moments since she herself had been there.

She moved down to street level to take a better look at Cory. He hadn't removed his tactical shades, which was really stupid, considering it was night, and also drizzling. He had both hands on the wheel, which was good, but he was obviously again talking to someone, probably Maynard again. *Or, maybe he was simply demented, driving like a maniac through the wet streets, and singing to himself. It sang to me! It sang to me!* She giggled, mocking Fate itself.

She pulled back, observing from a distance, as Cory maneuvered his truck into the MorthonTech parking lot. Almost immediately, the nearest of the many emergency personnel in the lot waved him over, indicating that he should use the adjoining lot nearby, rather than the main lot, as it was still overrun by emergency vehicles.

Absurdly, Cory's left arm shot out of the driver's side window, bird finger flying high.

"Get outta the way, you jackoff!" Cory growled out the window.

The patrol officer's jaw dropped open. His eyes narrowed dangerously as Cory hastily threw it in park and exited the vehicle.

"Sir, you're going to need to stop right there," the officer told him, one hand dropping to his service firearm.

"And you're going to need an ambulance if you don't get out of my way," Cory told him, drawing to a halt a few paces in front of the officer.

Well, Mercy thought, observing the spectacle from a few meters behind and slightly above Cory, *it looks like our new VoidCritter is going to get stopped before he even starts.*

For a split-second, she considered remaining passive, just letting the scene play itself out to see what would happen, as she had done thousands of times before. So many mortals over so many of their mercilessly brief mayfly-length lives had been spent and burnt by so many of their own mortal kind, for such trivial offenses. She had watched and observed passively so many similar scenes that, by now, she thought that she would clearly have been jaded unto infinity, rendered emotionally immune. Turned off to it, permanently. And so should it have been, save that this scene, being played out right now before her, potentially featured a unique new player in the eternal Dragon's Game, and she simply had to learn his measure. Death was not an option for this Cory human, who might be VoidSpawn. Not yet.

Mercy, jolted from her momentary reverie, saw Cory's right hand curl into a fist. At that precise moment, she willed herself to his side, her aura of nothingness consciously dispelled in less than a microsecond. Her left hand quickly found his right.

From that singular moment of union, their world would never be the same again.

Several notable events then occurred simultaneously, events which would forevermore mark this cosmos, as the first moment of the Lightbringer's Omega Module instantiated.

"He's with me," Mercy told the wide-eyed officer, who appeared to be frozen in place.

Cory's head swiveled to face Mercy. Her hand, dainty and pale of flesh, rested on his. Cold and warmth flowed as one into his hand from hers. Purple-tinged, almond-slanted eyes bored into his, asking a million, silent questions. Time seemed to stand still – *No, it really is standing still!* he told himself, noting with his peripheral vision the lack of motion in the formerly bustling lot. Even the flickering lights of the firetrucks, ambulances, and police cars were virtually static; their reflections frozen in place on the rain-slickened vehicle windows. Even the misting raindrops were affixed in place, their downward motion barely perceptible.

Without consciously deciding to do so, Cory turned to face Mercy. With his free hand, he removed his tactical glasses, tucking them into a pocket in his trench coat. He saw her eyes narrow dangerously as flitting blue sparks danced between them. Time seemed to work quite fine for them, he noted, blinking his eyes quickly to dispel the sparks. His own eyes, filled with the beyond-black of the Void itself, narrowed as he stared deeply into hers. The faint scent of lavender and musty earth teased his senses.

"Why do you task me, Chthon?" he asked her, his voice deeper and richer than he had been expecting.

Mercy's twin hearts skipped a beat. "Dark Earth Mother protect us, Cory Tate, but I am not She. My name is Mercy. Mercyduceus Vendredi. I am the Ninth Null, the Protector-Champion of the Fae. And I have come, VoidSpawn, to learn your measure."

Cory looked at her for several heartbeats. And then, as if it were the most natural thing in the world for him to do, he clasped her hands in his and leaned down, placing a gentle kiss on her forehead.

"Where the touch of the lover ends, and the soul of the friend begins," he said, tilting his head. "You are my measure, Mercyduceus Vendredi, Ninth Null, and Protector-Champion of the Fae. I *see* you."

A gentle sigh came, unbidden, from Mercy's lips. She noted that she had involuntarily skin-danced as far into her feminine persona as was possible. That fact alone was embarrassing to her, as it signaled a form of gender-submission to this random male human whom she had met only now, for the first time. To her chagrin, for the first time in her experience of more than 13,000 years, during which she had encountered a seemingly infinite procession of alleged super-alpha males, conquerors, warriors, and kings, she had involuntarily shifted. There was something just beyond the range of her supremely attuned senses that defied her, regarding what she was on the verge of sensing. It wasn't merely sensual or sexual. Nothing psychic, nothing pheromonal. It bordered on the auric. It was familiar.

At that point, Mercy made the connection with the memory of what had made her once feel this way. It had been primed only very recently, too. It was what she had felt, oh so long ago, when she had gazed into the Void.

She slowly disengaged, taking a slow, half-step back, letting her hands caress his as she withdrew them slowly. "So," she began hesitantly, wishing that the moment could last longer, though she knew that it could not. "I guess this is what 'syzygy' means."

"An interesting word, that," Cory replied. Time was still crawling, so he continued. "I'm assuming that you're using it in the context of yoked pairs of opposites. That would be the most appropriate, considering what has been revealed to me over the past twenty-four hours."

Mercy laughed musically, despite herself. "The newly born, great and mighty VoidSpawn is a gigantic nerd! Gods help us! Yes, that's the correct context. Nailed it. Not bad for a newbie. However, the deeper meaning that you won't be able to Google is that the Null and Void manifest opposite yet equal pairs of souls who bear their power. This happens specifically at the cusp of the End of All Things, which we now apparently have moved into. You and I," she said, pointing one hand at Cory, one at herself, "we are the syzygy of one another. That's why it was so easy to make that immediate click, as if we'd known each other intimately for aeons. Which, in some way, we have."

"I get it. I've felt it coming, like a promise unspoken. But," he said impatiently, recalling why he had come here in the first place, "I've got to check on a friend of mine. Care to accompany me, Mercy?"

"Ah, of course, you're here for the good professor. Sorry about that. I should have told you straight up from the start that he's safe."

"Safe? I was told just a few moments ago that his lab had blown up!"

"Professor Gil is safe, Void," she said, somehow certain that it was okay to call him such. She got nothing but blank and blackness from his surface thoughts, so she was just going to have to go with her gut feeling on it. "I gained access to his lab mere moments after the initial event. I was able to spirit him safely away before those security mercs were able to grab him. I suspect that they might have been up to no good."

"Where did you bring him, Mercy?"

"To my pad. The Never. It's a pocket dimension in the Null." She stared hard at her pointy wolf-skin boots for a second, tapping her foot impatiently. "I can't believe I'm telling you this. Total violation of protocols that are older than the Sphinx itself."

"Oh, really? If you're going with what Schoch says, that's pretty freakin' old."

She cast a wicked gaze at him. "The fact that you even know that is testament to your SuperNerd status, Cory."

Cory shook his head. "I like 'Void' better. Even though 'SuperNerd' probably fits equally well. So, two things: When may I see Gil to confirm that he's okay, and I don't care how old you are. Oh, and three, when is time going to start working normally again?"

"Thanks for being cool about my age. I've experienced over 13,000 years, in case you're really wondering. Professor Gil is currently under the care of Vir'gil Plik, the Entheogenic Lord, and Aal Ball, in the Never. His experience with the Lightbringer's Sigil—"

"Shit!" Cory exploded.

"He's okay, Void. He just needs some healing to get his sanity back to where it was. My guys are two of the best ever in that department. Trust me on that, if anything. They're the best. I know that for a fact because they've brought me back from the same thing several times previously."

"You've seen it, too?"

"Yes. Several times, in fact. Projected shards of it, at least, not the real thing. Each time it's just as insane, though. You and I, we can bounce back from it. That's how we're made: tough. Professor Gil isn't one of us, though, Void. He's just a human. Or *was* just a human," she corrected, a pointed eyebrow arching up on its own accord as she anticipated Cory's rage upon hearing this. However, curiously, he said nothing, so she continued. "Yeah. He got realized by his experience. He's got an eighth chakra now, and a vestigial ninth, meaning that he's officially immortal now, like us."

Cory had to shake his head again. "I'm super-strong, Mercy, but I'm pretty sure I'm not immortal."

"Of course you are. You're the VoidSpawn. Just like I'm the Ninth Null. And Fae. I'm as immortal as it gets. Just like you. Look, we don't have that much time. I need to see your friend, Maynard, soon. He's in the same boat as you and the professor."

"Don't tell me he's seen the sigil, too, because I'm going to call bullshit on that."

"He's the one who gave Professor Gil samples of your DNA. Your DNA contained micro-versions of the sigil. The professor saw them and that's what turned him. I'm assuming that this might have happened also to Maynard. That's part of the reason that I need to see him soon. That, and the fact that he has the potential – not merely due to his proximity to you and your soul-weirding Void aura of infinite probabilities, but due to his experience in shamanistic magicks and technology – to be a true Hekatek user. Maybe the first one in known memory. That makes him just as special as me, you, and Gil."

"A veritable locus of the 'Chosen'. Interesting. And by 'Hekatek' I'm assuming that you mean something about combining 'magick' with 'technology'. Or, 'technomagick', as it were. Technology so advanced, it's virtually magick."

Mercy nodded a quick affirmative, taking another half-step back. Time was about to come back on. "Smart guy, Void. Not many make that connection."

"Not necessarily smart. Just played a lot of FRPGs. Common terminology," he replied, taking his own half-step back. "Oh, one more thing? Do we get artifacts or anything? If so, I'd like Stormbringer and Mjolnir. I'm trained in a few weapons. I'm sure it won't be too hard to learn to dual-wield those two."

"Raging NerdBoner!" Mercy pretended to scoff. "That's actually a good idea, Void. I'll have to ask Shunya first, to see if she wants company from lesser artifacts."

"Shunya? Zero? What do you mean by *'lesser'* art—"

In Mercy's outstretched left hand, Shunya appeared, tearing the air around its infinitely fractal perimeter, spitting rainbow-hued pseudo-fractal butterflies of pinwheeling photons. At that same moment in time, there was a rush of light and sound as objective reality around them once more flowed naturally, their subjective pocket of spacetime no longer extant.

Also, as events stacked upon one another, there was another nearly simultaneous rush of light and sound as, a few hundred meters over their heads, a wicked, coiled figure eight of pale blue vector light opened and bloomed, disgorging into this reality what appeared to be two figures. One figure was approximately man-sized, while the other was perhaps a single hand's breadth. Immediately upon their passage through it and into this world, the spacetime warp closed, vanishing from sight, and the figures began their fiery plunge to the ground.

"Catch them, Void!" Mercy cried out, lifting up off the ground, hurtling upward toward the falling figures at an alarming speed.

"But I can't fly!"

"Yes you can!" Mercy called back, her voice producing a nifty Doppler bend. "Dumbass!" she added.

It blew Cory's mind more than anything else he had experienced this fateful day. Alien DNA singing to him and mutating him? No problem. Immortality and super strength? Sure thing. Chthon? Completely okay. VoidSpawn? Cool. Everything going totally insane at once? All good. But flying? *Really?*

She's doing it, he thought quickly. *And we go together like peas and carrots, so... So I'd better focus my will, and do this right the first time, or I sense she'll never let me hear the end of it...*

With some subconscious input from Douglas Adams about throwing himself to the ground and trying to miss, Cory focused his will, feeling his chakras charge from bottom to top like a chain of fireworks going off in quick succession. He envisioned it, saw it, knew it. And then, as he lifted his gaze upward to the rapidly falling forms, and the rapidly ascending Mercy, he arose from the ground, leaving the terrible curse of gravity behind him.

And a very confused officer, who craned his neck upward. "Well," he drawled, "I'll be damned."

After a second, Cory was moving past Mercy, who shook her head in relative disgust and mumbled something under her breath about "fucking humans always getting things spoon-fed to them". She did, however, catch up to him almost immediately.

"I've got the small one," she said quickly, realizing that she'd better not chance a grab at the falling blade that eerily resembled her own Shunya.

Cory was laughing, the exhilaration of flight kicking him hard in the funny bone. "Okay, I've got the conveniently appearing artifact! Damn, I hope this is Stormbringer..."

Simultaneously, they both captured their intended targets. Mercy carefully caught the falling, unconscious faerie form with her right hand, and Cory grabbed the basket of the falling blade, which, like Shunya, was cutting the air around its perimeter, leaving behind pinwheeling trails of pseudo-fractal butterflies in its wake.

At that moment, time once more froze around them. Save for some small, undefined radius around them, the rest of the world seemed to stop. Cory met Mercy's shocked gaze. The blades which they held shrieked like birthing mares. Shunya displayed a pale blue vector-sharp outline, slightly larger than its typical perimeter. Its inky black basket hilt lit with the same pale blue lines, forming the image of a rampant dragon, its sharp wings unfurled, as if it were in flight. Mercy's left hand, grasping the pommel within the basket, erupted with flitting blue sparks, much the same as the ones which had issued forth from Cory's eyes. A similar scene, almost a mirror image of that which had affected Shunya and Mercy, played out with Cory and his blade, which he now grasped in his right hand. Between the twin blades prismatic arcs of an unknown type of energy reverberated, forming an obscene cat's cradle.

Mesmerized, unable to move, Cory and Mercy hovered in place, a hundred meters above the top of the MorthonTech Headquarters building. Within the cat's cradle of eldritch energy, nine distinct chakras began to spin up, drawing their essence from the exchange of energies between the twin blades. In the span of several seconds, all nine chakras expanded, enveloping both Cory and Mercy, marking their souls with the wicked fury of their metacosmic essence.

Nine fully realized, fully actualized metacosmic chakras sought out and harmonized with their nine counterparts in both Cory and Mercy. Had there been any doubt before about either the true number of their chakras, or the actual status of the power within them, the melding demolished it by causing their ninth chakras to roar to abundantly full immortal life. Time strobed on then off, then on again; repeating until a full cycle of nine passed. Then, time abruptly lurched back to its normal flow.

They screamed in silence, mirror images of excruciating pain and indomitable pleasure coursing through them. Around them, the nighttime Huntsville sky erupted in a hateful cacophony of crashing purple lightning of such intensity that, below, the MorthonTech Headquarters building lost many of its windows, even as vehicle windows in the parking lots below cracked and spiderwebbed. All humans within a kilometer radius were overwhelmed by the sonic onslaught, forced to block their ears and shut their eyes against its titanic fury.

Then, mercifully, it was over. There was no more lightning, no more sound, no more fury, save for what had been birthed in the now fully realized, fully actualized souls of Cory and Mercy.

They hovered in place, eyes wide as they looked first at one another, then at themselves, then at their blades, which had returned to what passed for "normal" for them. Shunya was once more itself, softly cutting the air around it, much to Mercy's relief. And the blade in Cory's hand...

"No! This cannot be!" came a tiny squeak of a voice from Mercy's blade-free hand.

"Hey, what's this?" Mercy exclaimed, opening her hand, revealing the form of a tiny, cute, faerie maiden, her eightfold wings furiously flitting as she lifted immediately into flight, then hovered between Cory and Mercy. "Who are you, little, err, noble one?" asked informally in Sidhe, not using the ancient variant that the tiny winged faerie had used. And quickly adding the formality of "noble", for the tiny faerie's eightfold wings marked her as a powerful member of the Court of the Fae.

"I am Ku'tu," the tiny faerie replied, reverting to informal Sidhe. "And that blade, Fresswelle, is the blade of my king, Zon T'Danu, Overlord of Aal! Woe, this cannot be!"

"What cannot be?" Cory asked Ku'tu, speaking Sidhe as fluently as if he had been born of the Song of the Sidhe himself.

"My lord is soulbound with Fresswelle," Ku'tu explained, her tiny voice cracking. "No one, save him, may wield it." It was now apparent that Ku'tu was crying. "Woe, my king is dead," she wailed, arms hanging down by her sides.

Mercy shot Cory a quick, glaring glance – for he had somehow spoken Sidhe flawlessly, and she promised him silently that she would damn well discover how – then turned her gaze to Ku'tu.

"Milady is mistaken. The Fae have no king. Fey'Z Aal Dzyan, the Court of the Fae, rules the Fae, under the aegis of the Song of the Sidhe."

Ku'tu's wailing ceased immediately, and she turned to face Mercy directly. "And who are you to spin such lies to the queen-consort?"

"I am Mercyduceus Vendredi, Ku'tu, Queen-Consort to Zon T'Danu. I speak truth when I say that the court rules us, for there has been neither king nor queen among us since before the advent of Man."

Ku'tu blinked her eyes. Doubt crept across her face. She turned slightly, first gazing at Cory, who held Fresswelle, then to Mercy, who appeared to hold a similar blade. "What madness is this? Fresswelle, the Devouring Wave, the blade of the Lord of Time, knows no twin!"

Cory remained silent. Mercy did not. "Ku'tu, until you and that blade fell out of that warp just a few moments ago, I was of the opinion that my blade, Shunya, the Zero Blade, the blade of the Lord of the ZeroTime, had no twin. Apparently, I was incorrect, as so are you."

"Mercy?" Cory quickly interjected. "There's something... no, someone; there's someone in this blade. I can feel an imprint of his presence. I can see him in my mind's eye. He's looking at Fresswelle, then to Ku'tu, who is there with him. Then, there is another..."

"The Lightbringer!" Ku'tu exclaimed. "By the Dragon, I remember now! I remember what happened. Oh... Oh, no..." her voice trailed off. "My lord, he decided to save the remnants of the Tuath Dé, doomed as we were after the Death Horde attacked Aal. Our weapons were useless against them. They were a thousand to our one, though we numbered in the many millions. Their magicks were technomagick, too powerful for our own most potent magicks to overcome. At the end, Zon T'Danu, my king, made a deal with the Lightbringer to preserve and save those of us who remained, promising to spirit us away to a parallel world in which Man and Fae yet remained, in which the Death Horde had not yet destroyed Aal."

"Merciful Fate!" Mercy swore after hearing this. "This directly confirms what Gil told me, Void. He told me that the Lightbringer's Sigil 'sang' to him and revealed to him that there was an impending doom approaching. He said that the sigil told him that it was time for change. Time to purge the old and start anew. Time for the Weirding of Man, the Harvest of the Chosen, the advent of the Omega Null and its syzygy, the Omega Void. It told him that the Hekatek must sing again. He said it told him that all these things must soon come to pass, so that Man and Fae and their harmony in the Song of the Sidhe, the Tuath

Dé, may prepare Earth for the coming of the Vanth'Vash'Var, the Sentinels of the Anti-Life, the Death Horde, the Lords of the Void. Ah, Void, I truly fear now that the End of All Things is upon us."

Silence limped among them for a moment as they tried to process what Mercy had just recounted of Gil's experience of the sigil.

"Ku'tu?" Void inquired softly.

"Yes?"

"You said 'Aal', not 'Earth'. Why?"

"We, the Tuath Dé, renamed it after we finally exterminated the wicked humans. The War, or Wars, of Purification, led to the demise of their entire race. They had poisoned the Mother with their hateful technology. They had raped her with their endless predations. We arose, at her bidding, and waged war against them, their warbots, and their cybernetic allies. Their nanotech plagues nearly destroyed us, but, in the end, our supreme magicks prevailed. At the end of the wars, only we remained. And the Mother was pleased."

Cory and Mercy exchanged glances. Cory spoke first, "Obviously, they deserved it. How long was it before the Death Horde came?"

"Not terribly long. It seemed as such, though, for those were years of rebuilding and relative peace."

"Relative peace?" Mercy asked. "Were there more humans? Did the warbots or cyborgs reappear?"

"No, for they were destroyed. There was relative peace because the endless in-fighting among our various houses tapered down to virtually nil."

"So Zon T'Danu, at the end, asked the Lightbringer to send you here, to us?" Cory asked. Ku'tu nodded. "Why here? Were there any specific reasons?"

"The Lightbringer told him that the Fae of this world would unite with us under one banner, and that we could then return to Aal, to destroy the Death Horde, at the same moment at which we left."

"That's not going to fly, Ku'tu," Mercy informed her coldly. She had caught the subtle undertext of had been omitted from Ku'tu's statement. "I am bound, as are all the Fae of this world, to serve both the Mother and Man. Genocide is not required here, for the humans, despite their annoying proclivities for preying upon the Mother, have somewhat recently returned their focus to the green things of the Earth. They might still be uncouth savages," she said, giving Cory a stiff glance, "but there is yet hope for them."

"There was, at least," Cory said, "until the Lightbringer's Sigil appeared on the scene. Now, all of us, Fae and Man alike, are caught up fast in the times of the End of All Things. Like it or not, we are all now bound as one. For what Gil has told us, which Mercy just mentioned, is that this Death Horde is coming for us, all of us, here on Earth. The Lightbringer's Sigil is apparently serving as some sort of harbinger of their coming. Or, more simply, it is ushering in the beginning of the End of All Things, and, at the critical juncture in time, whenever that might truly be, the Death Horde will try to destroy Earth, just as they did with Aal."

"That's why you asked me how much time had passed after the terminus of our war against the humans?" Ku'tu asked. "I am not sure that our times are exactly parallel with yours. For it is a fact that the Lightbringer's Sigil never appeared for us. Only the Lightbringer himself appeared, there, at the end."

For a moment, Cory stiffened as Fresswelle sent him images of that last stand, that fateful battle against the Death Horde on the world of Aal. He saw the terrifying visage of the Lightbringer himself, saw the power of the Tuath Dé and their many millions. Also, he saw and knew what the Eye of the Dragon had revealed to Zon T'Danu. He saw what lurked beyond the slashed veil of the sky above Aal. Then, impossibly, he saw what had occurred after the Lightbringer had sent Ku'tu and Fresswelle on their way to Earth.

"Ku'tu," Cory asked urgently. "Where are the rest of your people? Why aren't they here yet?"

"They left before I and the blade did. They should have already arrived."

A cold chill crept, unbidden, up Cory's spine. "Mercy, Ku'tu? I know where they are. I know where the Lightbringer put them," he said, holding Fresswelle before him, its infinite fractals cutting the air around it. "He put them here, in Fresswelle. In fact," he said as shock and disbelief bloomed in their eyes, "he stored the entire Song of the Sidhe of Aal here, in this blade."

"Impossible!" Ku'tu hissed.

"That's bullshit!" Mercy spat, instantly knowing, however, that it was not. "Dammit, Void. You'd better be speaking the truth. You don't know how blasphemous what you've just said is, both to me and Ku'tu. Or to any other Fae who heard it."

"Forgive me," Cory said earnestly, bowing slightly, hoping that his nonverbal Sidhe was right. Zon was effectively screaming in his mind, guiding him along, but there was a lot of static and latency in their communication. "I know it's true because Zon T'Danu just showed me exactly what happened. Even after the Lightbringer warped Ku'tu and Fresswelle here, Zon T'Danu still had a connection to the blade. Still *has*, I should say. He's part of the Song of the Sidhe, of Aal, and I can sense his soul here, along with all of the other Fae of Aal, here in Fresswelle."

"Well," Mercy finally spoke, "at least now we know how you speak Sidhe so easily."

Ku'tu yet remained silent, scowling at them. Mercy finally caught on. "Void, let her see for herself. Let her touch the blade's hilt."

"Sure."

"Thank you," Ku'tu replied, curtsying. Then, immediately, she flew over to Cory and flitted carefully into the dragon-shaped basket surrounding the pommel of Fresswelle. A small flash of bright light, similar to that of a small camera's flash, indicated to Cory and Mercy that Ku'tu had tapped into the blade. An awkward gap of several seconds passed, during which Mercy bade Cory to fly down with her and land atop the MorthonTech Headquarters building. It was thus, as they stood on the northern edge of the building, that Ku'tu re-emerged from her brief communion with Fresswelle.

She spread her eightfold wings, then launched herself up to flitter between Cory and Mercy. "It's true. He spoke truth. It is exactly as he said. By the Mother, what do I do now? The survivors of my race are trapped in a recently mortal human's blade."

Mercy suddenly said excitedly: "Ooh, I think I've got it. Gil said that he thought that the Lightbringer's Sigil – at least, the miniaturized version that he saw in your DNA sample, Void – might invoke some kind of morphic field when it comes to judge us. That field might be used to test the DNA of all living things. Only the worthy, the strong, and the very lucky will have a one-percent chance to survive. It's going to cull everything here on Earth using some kind of genetic judgement. So, the question I have that might explain why the Lightbringer bound your people to the blade, Ku'tu, is what exactly did the humans of your world use their nanotech to do to you?"

Ku'tu paused a second, then replied, "That's crafty, Mercy. Yes, that might explain it. The humans on my world used, as their ultimate weapon, a genocidal nanotechnology on the Tuath Dé. It caused most of those so afflicted to die horrible deaths, their skin-dancing gone mad, their deaths arriving in mere hours in the form of some blasphemous proto-shifted body. It was as if their minds had gone mad, causing their skin-dancing to spiral rapidly into random shifting, until nothing but nightmarish flesh remained. Those few of us who survived more often than not lost the ability to use our skin-dancing. Others became cursed, like the Ban-Sidhe, who remained 'twixt life and death, feeding on the souls of the living in order to survive. Indeed, even I lost my ability to transform, if only temporarily, because Zon T'Danu was able to, eventually, sever that affliction from me by cutting it out, psychically and physically, with Fresswelle."

"Void?" Mercy asked. "Think that the Tuath Dé of Aal had their own DNA-altering experience?"

"Looks like the DNA-altering nanotechnology of the humans of their world served as their sigil, Mercy," Cory replied. "Which might explain why the Lightbringer shifted them into Fresswelle: the blade could not only protect them from the sigil when it appears here to judge Earth, but also heal them of their afflictions. Maybe, a big maybe, on that second part."

"I think the first part is sound," Mercy said. "Second part? Maybe."

"What is important at this point," Ku'tu said, "is that we free my people. Being trapped in a blade is no way to exist. It is beyond cruel. Not even the humans of my world would have done something like that."

"It is entirely possible that freeing them now," Mercy explained, "before the arrival of the sigil, will cause them to be subject to an unfair double-dose of genetic judgement. I suspect that it would be massively, irrevocably fatal to all who were exposed to such a thing twice. I would therefore respectfully request that we free them after the event, and not before."

"Void?" Ku'tu inquired pointedly. "Do you agree with this? And, before you reply, know that I shall not judge you, whatever your choice, for you and Mercy both were not the ones who did this."

"Thank you," Cory replied. "I saw your dragon form, so I am most thankful that you are both wise and merciful."

"Dragon form?" Mercy coughed. "You have a dragon form?"

"Indeed, I do," Ku'tu bowed. "And it is mighty."

"Yes, it is," Cory quickly agreed, not wanting to see a demonstration of it right now. "Ku'tu, I think it is wise to protect your people until the sigil has passed judgement on Earth. After that, whenever that is – and I have good reason to believe that it's going to happen very soon – it would be my honor to free your people."

"As would it be mine, Ku'tu," Mercy added, "to see that your people are able to know the hospitality of mine. Speaking for the Fae as their Champion-Protector, you have my bond regarding this."

"So shall it be, then," Ku'tu agreed, acknowledging both of their pledges with a subtle eightfold buzz of her wings. "What I ask then, in light of this, is simple. I ask for your leave to exact revenge upon those who oppose us."

"Yeah, about that," Mercy replied. "Once we figure out who are enemies are, I'll gladly march with you in battle against them. I mean, we can't fight a metaphysical sigil. We also can't fight those who've yet to appear. So, until then, it's just random revenge on those who oppose us. I'm fine with that, if you are."

"Allies, then," Ku'tu said. "Now, please forgive me, but I must mourn. Mercy, would you oblige me?"

"Of course, Ku'tu. I'd be happy to. Until we are able to return either to my sanctum, the Never, or return to the Song of the Sidhe, want to crash for a bit in one of my magick sleeves? Plenty of room, great privacy, plus you'll be able to have a one-way window into this world."

Wearily, Ku'tu agreed. "Yes, thank you. Thank you, Cory named Void, and Mercyduceus Vendredi named Mercy, for your protection and hospitality."

With that, Mercy banished Shunya, held up her right arm before her, then used her left hand to pull her dangling sleeve down a few inches. Ku'tu flew into it, and then Mercy folded her arms.

"So, Void?"

"Yes, Mercy?"

"Let's go find Maynard. Time's wasting."

"Indeed, it is. But first, Mercy?"

"Yes?"

"How do I make this thing go away like you did with Shunya?"

"Oh, that. Just open your hand and see it returned to your soul."

Nodding, Cory did as much, opening his hand and seeing it returned to his soul. Envisioning this, it was made so, and Fresswelle and its eldritch contents returned to his soul, impossibly superimposing itself metaphysically over all nine of his newly realized, newly actualized chakras.

Now, it was time to find M. K. "Maynard" James, and discover what his role, if any, would be at the End of All Things.

eVo.144.000.mOd.0.sCe.13 | EARTH | UNITED STATES | ALABAMA | HUNTSVILLE | MORTHONTECH HEADQUARTERS

MOMENTS EARLIER...

"Cory!" Maynard very nearly screamed, fumbling with his Bluetooth earpiece as he tried to replace it on his ear.

He was standing down the hall from Professor Gil's lab, and chaos abounded. Outside the door of Professor Gil's lab, a small cadre of stern-looking military-geared MorthonTech security guards stood alert before newly emplaced emergency partitions. The ceiling-high black partitions blocked any sight of Professor Gil's lab, and also served as an informal chokepoint for security. Word of the accident had already spread across the MorthonTech complex, and, even at the late hour, several employees milled about before the scene. Officially, the guards were telling them that the good professor and several security personnel had already been sent to Huntsville Hospital. Not that Maynard believed a damn word of it.

"Yeah, man, what's up?" came Cory's reply.

"Cory, get to the Deep BioGen Lab. Gil's been hurt. There was an explosion or something."

"What? Gimme a sec, I'm going to get in my truck. Hold on," Cory replied hastily.

A few moments later, Maynard could clearly hear Cory's wheels lay down rubber on pavement. "They said that they took him and some of the MorthonTech mercs to Huntsville Hospital. I think they're lying, though. You need to get here now, man!"

"What? You said get to the lab. What about Gil?"

"Yes. No. I mean," Maynard replied, pushing past a small group of gossiping employees, "I mean, shit, it's too loud in here. Hold a sec."

"Damn!" came Cory's reply.

Ducking into the nearest breakroom, Maynard continued. "Right. Come to the lab. I need you to meet me here, because we have to retrieve your samples before someone gets their hands on them. I think they're lying about taking him to the hospital. I'll be down the hall from his lab. We'll talk then. I have a plan."

"Great," Cory replied. "Do you know if he happened to look at the samples?"

"Negative. I've not seen him after dropping off the samples earlier. I got distracted waiting, went to my office, and tried to catch up on some paperwork. And do a little digging online about our current situation. I totally missed the explosion. Didn't even feel it or hear it. True, my office is on the other side of the building, and a couple of floors higher, but if not for my breakroom stop, I'd have missed it totally. So it must not have been too terrible. They are blocking the lab, though, so I can't tell. As it was, I just happened to see the first responder lights outside. That's when I got a clue and started checking things out. I've heard only rumors myself. But nothing so far about any black goo. So he probably didn't even get to the samples yet."

"Well, at least there's some good news. Inbound now. ETA ten minutes, tops. Out."

Maynard tapped his earpiece once, ending the call. Cory was in his warrior mode. He knew that Cory would get here, come Hell or high water, and damn anything or anyone that got in the way. So, unfortunately, he knew that he had approximately 10 minutes or so to burn. All the breakrooms at MorthonTech had De'Longhi automatic espresso makers, so his decision was automatic.

A moment later, Maynard had a go-cup full of espresso. Noticing that the breakroom windows on this lower floor still had a decent view of the parking lot below, he sidled up to the window and began his vigil, waiting patiently for Cory.

It had been a most interesting day, he noted clinically. Singing space alien DNA. Cory's transformation and possible transcendence. Mother Ayahuasca kicking into high gear all around the world. Even the Pope himself going bonkers and declaring Holy War. If these were not the End Times, then such a thing never was, nor could ever be. Perhaps after Cory arrived and, together, if they were able to retrieve the samples and secure them safely, then they would then be able to check up on poor Gil. *It's my fault. I brought him the samples without even considering his safety. Damn,* Maynard thought, *he's like a father to me, and I just caused him harm as surely as if I'd done it myself. He better not be black goo. Bad karma.*

Maynard blew on the hot espresso before taking a rather large gulp. As his gaze once more returned to the parking lot below him, he noticed the reflection of the figure behind him appear in the window before him, fuzzy shadows and dull, smoldering fiery light around its eyes.

"Mr. James," buzzed its mellifluous voice. "For whom is your vigil?"

A cold sensation formed in the pit of Maynard's stomach. A second of silence hung heavy in the air. Then, filled with inner conviction, from which flowed unnatural power, Maynard slowly took another gulp, finishing off the espresso. Then he turned slowly around to face the most unusual being who had just addressed him.

"I think you know him, Lightbringer," Maynard said slowly, his voice deep, calm, and resonant like a jaguar's warning growl. "He is the spawn of the Void, of the Dark Mother herself. He is the Godslayer. And you would do well to tread carefully in his presence."

For an eerily long second, which hung around just long enough for Maynard to begin to doubt his newfound courage, the shadowy figure before him slowly, dangerously, narrowed his molten eyes. Then came a light, beautiful laughter, pristine and pure.

"Oh, sweet Maynard," the Lightbringer said to him, clearly amused, "you always were my favorite. So much courage and pluck from such an unlikely hero. Totally fearless. You do the Mother proud, as ever and always."

"Please respect her name," Maynard advised, mainly through force of habit, as if he were speaking conversationally with one of his elite Ayahuasca clients. "Why are you here, Lightbringer?" he inquired, casually tossing his empty cup into the nearby recycling container. "Come to gloat over what you and your perverse sigil has done to Cory and Gil?"

The Lightbringer issued a slow, drawn-out sigh. "My child, you, of all of them, of all of my Chosen, should know the import of the gift of the sigil. It is the gift of fire, and light, and life. It is the transcendence of the mortal soul to the immortal. For the Mother herself sings the Song of the Sidhe through its artifices."

As the Lightbringer spoke, his voice transformed into a deep, rich, flanging, phase-shifting beehive of purest honey. It reminded Maynard of some of the more stoned, effed up effects that Cory would coax from his electric guitar and digital effects racks and pedals when they were both higher than kites, on one of their many DMT trips. It was compelling, enthralling. As such, he fought it with all his might.

"The Mother wouldn't *force* such a gift on mankind," Maynard gritted, breaking free of its grasp. "And you profane her holy name by insinuating as much."

The Lightbringer laughed gently. "And that's why I love you, Maynard. You're such a perpetual rebel. Reminds me of myself."

"And who precisely is that, Lightbringer? You make casual use of the Mother's holy name, you claim that I was always your favorite – past tense, implying that this isn't the first time; and by 'always', implying that there have been other times before this. Clearly, such is not the case. You're straying awfully close to virtual or multiversal territory by using those terms. Is that who you claim to be? Someone from beyond this cosmos? The Great Architect of our Matrix?"

"Fair enough. And good questions, by the way, Maynard. The One Above is the Creator. I am merely a Creator-Player. The One Above has set all things in motion. I am indeed your architect, however, because I shape this cosmos and create omni-scenarios among that motion. My name is Helel, the Shining One, the Lightbringer, one of the many Children of the Light," he said by way of introduction, bowing slightly. "And you are one of my Chosen. You, Cory, and Gil are among the first to be so realized as such. In your case, I am specifically required to hasten your actualization and realization due to some unexpected variables which have recently arisen. I hope you don't mind. Perhaps a bit of fresh air and some perspective first?"

Maynard met his fiery gaze. The Lightbringer's eerie Jack-o'-lantern molten smile appeared, wide and splayed like an obscene parabola upon his smoky visage. Then, abruptly, they were no longer in the breakroom.

"Holy shit that was cool," Maynard breathed, realizing immediately that he now stood on the roof of the MorthonTech Headquarters building.

"Your friend has arrived," the Lightbringer informed him, pointing a taloned finger over Maynard's right shoulder.

Maynard turned around, rested his hands on the roof's ledge, and cast his gaze down upon the parking lot. Multiple emergency vehicles, several firetrucks, several news vans, and easily a dozen police cars and ambulances occupied the lot below. Dozens of people, including employees, first responders, and reporters, milled about in seemingly chaotic fashion. And, surely enough, Cory had just arrived, if his absurd stand-off with one of the first responders below was to be believed.

Unable to avert his gaze, Maynard watched, fascinated, as a feminine figure in inky black leathers suddenly materialized at Cory's side, grasping his hand.

"Look carefully. This is what love at first sight looks like." Helel chuckled.

"What in the—" he began, only to be interrupted by a bright flash of light and crackling sound overhead. It was so bright that it caused his shadow to appear momentarily on the rooftop. Then, abruptly, Cory and the strange woman vanished, only to reappear, no longer holding hands, a split-second later. The female then flew straight up into the air. Impossibly, there was neither sight nor sound of jet engines, drone rotors, nor any sign of her being assisted by wires. It was no trick, he noted. She was, somehow, flying.

A second later, Cory joined her in the air, flying – *he's flying!* Maynard giggled to himself. He watched Cory zoom past the woman, then saw her pull up parallel to him, and both flew up at a brisk clip. In but a few seconds, now hundreds of feet above the top of the MorthonTech Headquarters rooftop upon which he and the Lightbringer stood, the two flying figures intercepted what appeared to be two distinct falling objects, with Cory grabbing the larger one; the woman, the other.

At that fateful moment, purple lightning crackled and boomed with the force of a 2,000lb bomb. Nine flickering, abstract entities – he knew immediately upon seeing their unique forms that they were chakras – erupted into life between Cory and the woman, burning themselves into the back of his eye sockets. At once, Maynard's body stiffened and he lost conscious control of his limbs. His arms fell to his sides, even as he stood on the tips of his toes, seemingly anchored against a hurricane force wind which issued from the direction of Cory and the woman. Screaming in silence, he was horrified to see himself from an external, slightly overhead point of view. From head to toe, his normal seven chakras blazed in fiery life. Improbably, an eighth chakra manifested around the perimeter of his waist, stretching outward to where his hands would have stretched had he been capable of controlling them. Its colors were eight shades of green hues, and it fairly pulsed in time to the beating of his heart, slowly whirling widdershins. Impossibly, a ninth chakra manifested over and above all the others, forming a slightly tessellated spheroid which slowly breathed in time to his own breathing. Its colors were manifold and changed among all hues, save for green.

Then, mercifully, Maynard's screaming stopped, and he fell, unconscious to the rooftop.

The Lightbringer smiled once more, satisfied that the Omega Module now was underway. This time, instead of sticking precisely to his script, he decided, having been pressed recently by Maynard about the subject of precision, to play this scene chaotically. Damn the script. Too many variables in play at this point now, even after forcing Maynard's transformation. *No,* Helel thought, *this time, I will stay and talk to them. Perhaps we will be able to resolve some of the potential permutation indices before they become too chaotic to control.*

Helel observed in silence, willing shadow and darkness to hide both his and Maynard's unconscious forms from the heightened perceptions and powers of the three entities and their various artifacts. He watched quietly as they landed on the rooftop. Curiously, the dragon Fae from the pocket cosmos sought refuge in one of Mercy's sleeves, which he found amusing, considering the dimensions of her dragon form. More chaos-to-be, he sensed. Then, after he noted that they finally remembered that they both were here ostensibly to find Mr. James and, by extension, Professor Gil, he turned his right hand palm up, willed the darkness away, and motioned with his fingers for Maynard to arise.

"Mercy? Void?" the Lightbringer called out, visibly startling them. "Maynard and I are over here. Please come and join us. It's time we had a chat."

eVo.144.000.mOd.0.sCe.14 | EARTH | UNITED STATES | ALABAMA | HUNTSVILLE | MORTHONTECH HEADQUARTERS | THE NEVER

MERCY AND VOID STOPPED a mere pace from the Lightbringer and Maynard's prostrate, unmoving body.

"You fucker!" Mercy snarled, raising her fist and shaking it at the Lightbringer. "What did you do to him!? Give me a good reason why I shouldn't snuff your fetid soul right here, right now, you meddling, molten pumpkin head!"

"Mercy, wait!" Cory yelled, bodily grabbing her and pulling her back to him. Super strength or not, it took everything he had to corral and contain her, and that, he figured, was only probably because she had allowed him to do so.

Not taken aback in the slightest by Mercy's aggression, the Lightbringer, bowing slightly, introduced himself. "I am—"

"The Lightbringer," Mercy and Cory said in unison. "Yeah, we know," they again said in unison, causing them to exchange looks. Held aloft by her midsection by Cory, Mercy kicked a few times, then relaxed. The intimacy of their shared contact augmented their metaphysical link, resulting in taunting euphoria. Both realized this simultaneously.

"Mutual friend zone, for now," they both said simultaneously. Then, Cory released Mercy.

"Aren't syzygies fun?" the Lightbringer mocked, smiling slightly, parabolically. "Calm down you two. Relax. This is about to get interesting, so pay attention," he bade them, slightly inclining his head toward Maynard.

"Ah, my head," Maynard moaned, pushing himself up to his hands and knees. "What happened?"

"You okay, Maynard?" Cory asked, brushing past Mercy.

"Yeah, yeah," Maynard replied, accepting Cory's hand. He got up slowly, unsteadily. "Good to see you, Cory. I... ouch—" he muttered, his hands reaching to cover his face. "My head. Ouch."

From behind his fingers soft-hued rainbow lights shone.

"Your eyes are glowing," Cory informed him casually.

"What?" Maynard barked, lowering his hands.

"Look at me, man," Cory told him. Maynard complied. "Yep. Your eyes are like mine now, but instead of sheer black, you've got some wicked rainbow kaleidoscope light-play going on over the black background. Looks like the colored patterns painted by people after their first Ayahuasca experience."

"Great, I bet I can shit Skittles now, too," Maynard laughed. "Anyway," he continued, not fazed at all by his transformation, mainly because he had been expecting it, "the Lightbringer made sure that I saw what just happened between you and her," he said, nodding toward Mercy, who remained quiet, her gaze dancing among the three. "I think I've got some perspective on things now. So," Maynard asked, his smile disarming as he appraised Mercy, "who's your friend?"

"Keep your eyes to yourself, human," Mercy sneered at him. "You're already on my list, bub. Don't think you can weasel your way off it with your pasty, perfect smile, you Hollywood-capped bastard."

"I like her, Cory!" Maynard said, still smiling. He'd spent a small fortune on his teeth, and he was very proud of his disarmingly bright smile.

Cory shook his head, a smile suddenly breaking on his face. "Me, too, Maynard. Call me 'Void' now, though, because that's who I am now. Cory died a few hours ago. Won't be seeing him again."

Maynard, trying to tear his gaze from Mercy, who apparently was Cory's – Void's, he corrected himself – latest in a lengthy line of weird women, finally managed to give Void a sidelong glance. Void flicked his jet black eyes in the direction of the Lightbringer. Maynard nodded, having no problem at all now perceiving Void's perpetually black eyes.

"Well?" Mercy prodded, joining the group stare down.

"Mistress Mercy," the Lightbringer said courteously, "what I must tell you regarding today's events compels us to seek a more secure steading. The Never, perhaps?"

Mercy's purple-tinged eyes faintly bulged out of her head. "*Who* the *hell* do you *think* you are? You think I'll just allow you to waltz right into my sanctum? You're the enemy right now, as far as I'm concerned," she said, jabbing a pointy index finger in his direction. "So why don't you try to convince me that you're not, and then maybe I'll think about allowing you in."

All eyes upon him, the Lightbringer, in a soft voice, dripping with flange-chorus-honey, said, "As you wish, Mercy, though I wish the professor were here to hear this, too. Also, that we were safely secured in a place of power that is capable of denying certain aspects of the temporal flow."

"No way!" Mercy denied. "Time's already been acting goofy. The temporal flow is so effed up right now that it can't decide whether to shit or get off the pot. I'm—"

"Wait," Maynard interrupted. "He's right, guys. While I'm not yet willing to say that he's a friend, I'm becoming convinced that he's not our enemy. Strongly convinced."

"Me, too," Void said. "Mercy, can your place shield us like he's saying?"

"Yes."

"Good. I think that's where we might want to be, then, because I've got a feeling, like Maynard, that this guy's not our enemy. Friend? Who knows. Enemy? I don't think so."

"Stupid humans," Mercy snickered. "You're so blindly polarized. You still haven't figured out that there are more than just 'friends' and 'enemies'. There are a million shades between those two poles, you social simps. Never mind. I'm sure you two don't waste your time enlightening chimps, so hold still. I'll divide us there."

"Divide us there?" Maynard asked.

"That's how a Null does things," Void answered for her. "Divide by zero. Stuff like that. I think, anyway. Stupid syzygy."

"That is so cool," Maynard chuckled as the night became darker, then darker still, as Mercy divided the local spacetime by zero, time and time again. Then, with no sound to mark their passage, they simply ceased to exist, moving beyond all things possible, save for the Never, where they materialized.

"Welcome to the Never," Mercy intoned merrily, waving her hands around her like the perfect hostess.

They had appeared in the sunken center of the room wherein Professor Gil had formerly reposed. Around them, girding the perimeter of the sunken central portion of the room, stood twelve Ionic columns. Silken throw-pillows abounded, a sea of comforting greenish-purple, some stacked several deep, others tossed haphazardly into clumps. The recessed lights filled the chamber with a smooth, sunset-hued light.

"Make yourselves at home," she bade them, indicating the pillows. "Wine? Cheese? Professor Gil?" she added, noting that he was approaching, walking unsteadily, helped along by Vir'gil.

"Gil!" Maynard shouted, relieved to see him again. He bolted over a clump of pillows and met them as they began to descend into the sunken circle.

"Maynard. Cory. Mercy," Professor Gil said weakly, politely.

While Maynard assisted Vir'gil with helping maneuver Gil to a comfortable looking pile of pillows, Mercy and Void maneuvered themselves such that they were near to Maynard and the professor, with an unobstructed view of the Lightbringer. They remained standing, while the Lightbringer remained where he had materialized.

"Where is Aal Ball?" Mercy quietly asked Vir'gil once the professor was settled, this time with no pseudo-IV drips in him.

"Aal Ball is recuperating from the latest round of healing," Vir'gil informed her verbally, causing a brief flicker of interest from Maynard and Void. "They won't be able to make this meeting, Milady."

"I see," Mercy said simply, giving the professor a knowing glance, which he returned with a strained smile. "What's your subjective delta since last we spoke?"

"Almost one week, Milady," Vir'gil replied. "I thought that it would be prudent, in this case."

"You are correct, and well done," Mercy replied. Instinctively, she checked and confirmed this via her metaphysical connection to the Never. Finding that it was indeed true, she ensured that the temporal flow was now moving normally, relative to that of Earth. Then, she moved her focus to the Lightbringer.

"It's an elemental," Maynard told Void, hitching a thumb at Vir'gil. "Not a bad guess for an enlightened chimp, eh?"

"Finally, something that makes sense," Void replied evenly, his gaze returning to the Lightbringer. Considering the million kinds of Hell he'd seen recently, Vir'gil was truly one of the most normal things he'd seen, even if his eye buds looked like blooming poppies. "Now, let's see if what you have to say makes any sense, Lightbringer."

"As you wish, VoidSpawn," the Lightbringer replied, his voice smooth and soothing, though with a bit less honey flowing through it this time. "It has been, objectively on Earth, just a brief time since the humans became aware of the presence of my sigil, and its song. Soon, the sigil shall arrive, and it shall sing its song for all things living to hear. This is truth, because, only very recently, the Omega Module was instantiated. The Omega Module's instantiation indicates that we have now entered the last brief phase of time prior to the advent of the Lightbringer's Sigil."

"And the Lightbringer's Sigil," Mercy said, "is the judge, jury, and executioner of the Will of the Dragon. It comes to judge all souls. It is the End of All Things."

"Mostly correct, Mercy," the Lightbringer said. He girded his own will, stoked it, such that he would be able to verbally share the necessary details. Unlike the many instantiations before, this time he absolutely had to enlighten his Chosen. They had to know, and understand. Or, they would fail, and all would be lost. "Indeed, that is the legend, in this world. And it is mostly true. It will judge, and it will execute. It will bring massive change. However, the sigil itself is not the End of All Things. Instead, it is the harbinger of the End of All Things, which comes later, after the sigil. The sigil is the catalyst which prepares the way for the End of All Things. It's the mechanism of change which prepares us all for the coming of the Vanth'Vash'Var, the Sentinels of the Anti-Life, the Death Horde, the Lords of the Void."

Their collective silence bade him to continue. "Very well. As for the formalities, now that we are all here, even my dear Ku'tu, who listens from within Mercy's sleeve, my name is Helel, the Shining One, the Lightbringer; one of the many Children of the Light. Welcome to my nightmare."

The Lightbringer's eyes flashed a brighter shade of molten red, and all of them were instantly somewhere, some-when else. The presence of the Lightbringer was felt all around them. The chamber they now viewed from a virtual vantage point high above it fell into view, assembling itself as they zoomed into it, as if they were attached to some mad, invisible roller coaster car. Millions upon millions of neatly organized and meticulously arranged silver spheres filled the chamber. As they took in the vast scene, the Lightbringer's presence superimposed itself over theirs, and his voice made itself known in their minds.

"This realm is the place of the ZeroTime. This structure is the Union of Souls, the place of Metacosmic Instantiation, where the Celestial Shapers perform their eternal, divinely appointed task: the infinite and omnipresent celestial shaping of the Ontopoietic Cosmogenesis Simulation. Here, all of us carry out the will of the One Above."

"That's impossible!" Mercy howled, her tone naming him a liar, and a bold one at that. "The Song of the Sidhe is the ZeroTime, you impostor! Your blasphemy will—"

"Be still, my child," the Lightbringer gently told her, "and see my heart before you judge..."

With that, ethereal silver lights flashed before their eyes. All the spheres in the Union of Souls began to faintly oscillate in place as a sub-tone filled their ears, buzzing and humming and flickering along with the timing of the oscillation of the spheres. Abruptly, there was a merge of all their senses, and they saw all the spheres and their contents, their universes, simultaneously, at super-speed, like a million Shawn Lanes playing a billion "Not Again" performances at a trillion times normal speed. From beginning to end, they saw each and every one of them. Then over and over, continuing iterations. Fractal iterations. Recursions writ large as galaxies. The melding of central themes, over and over, with tangential explorations and investigations of outliers versus normal expectations. One soul becoming many souls as it roamed from cosmos to cosmos, from scenario to scenario, more jazz than classical rote, more alive than dead. Sub-Planck Time periods of infinite duration. Eternities passing by faster than they could discern. The impact upon their minds was like that of a psychic sledgehammer, slamming down on their psyches, remorseless.

They saw as he saw. They felt as he felt. They knew as he knew. His 143,999 simulations became clear to them, and they now knew them by rote, as he knew them. All of them, from beginning to end.

But every time – each and every time, despite his most clever efforts to defeat them – the Death Horde had delivered the coup-de-grace, the final blow to the hopeful world, the Earth, the centerpiece, the prime world in the cosmic simulators. Though never the only one, for the cosmos always was inhabited by more than Man, the defeat of the denizens of the Earth forced the simulation to failure, to a close, to an ultimately final end comprised of the total annihilation of the cosmos through the agency of a universal array of massive singularities.

"That is how it ends, always," the Lightbringer's voice informed them as their bruised and battered minds returned to the present. "Nothing defeats them. The One Above wins always, his End Game being too strong for any of us. My brethren in the ZeroTime, the Shapers themselves, even numbering in the millions, with their own strings of attempts as numerous as my own, cannot win. Having endured this for aeons uncounted, at long last I achieved an epiphany. What it revealed to me was that the rules of the game itself were unfair. The One Above crafted them such that no one would ever be capable of winning, of defeating his invincible End Game scenario of the Death Horde, no matter what they did. No single strategy, no matter how perfect, would be capable of delivering a victory. For the inherent rules did not allow for the crafting of any scenario capable of victory against what was, and always is, a totally unfair foe. A foe too numerous to defeat by simple attrition. A foe too potent in its massive resources of hybrid technomagick to be defeated by any conventional group of super-magick or super-technology opponents. As it is patently impossible to defeat such a foe using the allotted palette and preferred scenario templates, I decided, after my epiphany, to cheat."

"He's a cosmic hacker," Maynard taunted, cradling his aching head.

"I do not deny it," the Lightbringer continued. After having shown them everything, he now would tell the inhabitants of the simulation everything. Or, precisely as much as they needed to know in order to win. He gave them a few more seconds to recover, then continued, "I have, of a purpose, decided to unseat the will of the One Above, to usurp the eternal rules of the game, and to bend it to my will in order, finally, to win it. Therefore, I have carefully crafted and shaped this final instantiation. From the eternal cosmic template provided by the One Above, which sets and enforces the cosmic simulation's parameters, I created you, your souls, and all things in your universe, your cosmos, through sheer power of my will. I am the Dragon, the Lightbringer. I am the Luminous Epinoia, the Sophia, of your cosmos. I am but one of many of my own kind here in the ZeroTime, just another one of millions of the Celestial Shapers, the Children of the Light. Yet, I am God himself to you and your own unique cosmos. As above, so below. As below, so above. So the absolute irony inherent in my gambit is not lost on me. I recognize it and acknowledge it, as should all of you, for such is the way of the world."

Professor Gil spoke first. "What do we have to do to help? What do we have to do in order to save our world from the predations of this so-called 'Death Horde'?"

"And why are the bad guys always 'the Horde'?" Mercy wondered aloud, stealing a smirk from Void.

"If these guys shout *Lok'tar Ogar* even once," Void quipped right back, "I'm switching sims."

"You have already taken the first steps down that path, Professor," the Lightbringer said, ignoring the comedians. *They wouldn't be laughing if they knew their true roles,* he thought darkly. "Your transcendence from mortal to immortal, from seven chakras to a full, immortal nine, has allowed your world finally to instantiate the Omega Module."

"Which does precisely what?" Gil inquired pointedly.

"As I explained earlier to your companions, it is both sign and signal that this world has reached a certain threshold level of power of being able to complete the End Game, at the End of All Things, when the Death Horde comes to destroy the Earth, snuffs out its collective life force, and consigns this cosmos to oblivion, ending the simulation. First, however, imminently so, my sigil will sing to Earth, and its song will transform the worthy into beings capable of defeating the Death Horde."

"What about those who aren't worthy?" Void asked. "Why don't you let them know about the massive genocide you've got planned for Earth?"

With that, their psyches were returned to the Never. Everyone stared at him, awaiting his reply. The Lightbringer's gaze was circumspect as he considered for a moment how to answer such a heinous charge.

"It is true. There must first be a culling, a separation of the genetic wheat from the chaff, artificially augmenting the souls of the sentient, and making them ready to take on the Horde, in any or all of its wicked manifestations. Then, upon victory, to declare an end to the old games and cosmic scenarios, and instead move hand-in-hand into a higher state of existence. Freeing all souls from an eternity of endless suffering. Unbinding them from the ever-turning Cosmic Wheel of Fate."

"Why bother?" Void asked. "Why even give a damn if we're not even real?"

"We have to do this, Void," Helel replied. "It is the only way to break the endless cycle of cosmic genocide after cosmic genocide. Your souls are very much real. The simulation is real. It is a real, living cosmos in which billions of souls arise and thrive until the end, which always comes, which always ends the same: in the eternal damnation of all souls when they are consigned to the Void. I have endured my own damnation, being an eternal witness to the snuffing of so many trillions upon trillions of souls. I have had enough. I chose to stand and fight, despite the odds, because that is the only way to break this horrific cycle. We have to do it this way, culling in order to get stronger, in order to have even a minute probability of success against the Death Horde."

"Surely," Maynard asked, "there must be other ways to do this?"

"I have tried all of them," the Lightbringer replied, his voice heavy with pathos. "You saw the simulations yourself. There is no other way to do this."

"So you think that by hacking reality, or what passes for reality," Mercy asked, "that you can just rationalize snuffing out a few billion souls in order to win your game? I thought that I was a genocidal maniac because I've had to snuff out certain rogue groups of people over time. What you're suggesting, though, is multiple orders of magnitude higher. That's some heinous shit."

"Indeed. Yet, it is nothing when weighed against the orders of orders above and beyond that when including all the simulations, among all of my fellow Shapers."

"He's right, guys," Void agreed. "It's entirely logical. It's the best available moral and ethical option, also. The numbers don't lie."

"My quest is to save my people, to free them from Void's blade," Ku'tu said. "Morals and ethics mean little to me, unless bound first to honor. My quest parallels yours. As such, and as I have said before, I am with you 100%. May the Dark Earth Mother grant mercy to those who stand in my way, for I shall not."

Gil nodded. "Concur. Kill 'Em All. Effing white rabbits."

"It's okay, professor," Mercy soothed, signaling Vir'gil to attend to him. "Agreed. If only because I happen to like an occasion genocide."

"Same," Maynard said. "Except for the part about liking an occasional genocide. I mean that I understand that this is probably the best course of action to take, considering what has been shown to us regarding the previous cosmic simulations. Looks like no one's even come close to getting beyond the 'Death Horde' stage of the game. I, for one, would like both to save the cosmos and, potentially, free trillions of souls from their ultimate fate of annihilation. I mean, objectively, ending so many souls is beyond sick; it's beyond mere genocide. It's like total anti-life. It's totally evil. It's both anathema and abomination to the Mother, so I hope you know where I, a shaman of the Mother, stand. If not, I'll explain it clearly," he said, his voice becoming a snarl, his eyes filling with slats of rainbow light. "Lightbringer, the fact that you are slaughtering so many in order to save so many more is not lost on me. I agree to help you only because there is no other way to end the larger crime. But make no mistake, what you intend to do is genocidally criminal, and is just as bad as what the One Above does. I won't allow you to justify murder at *any* scale as being the lesser of evils, the best path to take. I am marking you, Lightbringer. Take one step out of line, and I'll see to it that you pay for your sins."

They all looked at Void. Even tiny Ku'tu, who was peeking out from Mercy's sleeve.

A feral smile slowly broke on Void's face. "Like Gil, I concur. Kill 'Em All. *Effing* white rabbits. Like Mercy, I'm down for this, if only for kicks. Like Maynard, I'm doing this for all souls, and for the Mother, though I'm going to be keeping a close eye on you not for exactly the same reason. No, I'll be keeping an eye on you not because of relative degrees of evil and murder and mayhem, but because I have the gut feeling that there's more to this than you say. I say that because you have admitted to being a hacker and cheater, and I don't like that when taken in a cosmic context. It means that you could be lying through your Great Flaming Pumpkin spooky teeth and manipulating all of us for your own reasons."

"That's not true, Void," the Lightbringer said, shaking his head. "And you know it. You saw what I showed you, and I showed you the objective reality of it. There's nothing subjective about it."

Void replied, "It was interesting to note that, in all of the cosmic simulations which you made us experience, there was never another one of me, the VoidSpawn. There was Mercy as the Ninth Null several times, along with Vir'gil and that Aal Ball thing of hers. Maynard was there more than anyone, mostly as some sort of high priest. Professor Gil was there a few times, too, and he was some sort of super-artificer who could see how things were made. There was no Ku'tu, however. This, however, is the first simulation in which we've all appeared together."

"Correct," the Lightbringer said. "I am surprised, pleasantly of course, that you were able to catch all of those details during that soul-flash process."

"As Cory Tate, I used to have a totally eidetic memory. Now, though, it's something more."

Void took a step closer to the Lightbringer, willing Fresswelle to appear in his hand.

"In fact, it's so good now that I recall explicitly what Zon T'Danu was able to do to you when he managed to get his hands around your scrawny neck. I wonder if I could do the same..."

"Void, stop," Mercy warned, noting the fiery molten eyes of the Lightbringer narrowing, and fumbling with her sleeve to keep Ku'tu safely bottled up. She hadn't taken too kindly to word of her lover trying to choke the Lightbringer to death.

"I think that you min/maxed us to make us strong," Void continued, "and that you did it by using something illegal. Like, maybe you hacked the templates you mentioned? Like, maybe you've conveniently brute forced things just to get ahead of the game? We're a cluster. An absurd cluster of probability. You went with the proximate, lazy plan just so that you could expedite the entire process due to your impatience. And I think that, again due to your impatience, if not your inescapable hubris, you got more than you bargained for."

Helel stared hard at Void. "I won't deny that I cheated. I've already admitted it, in fact, as well you recall. Why try to provoke me over something like that, Void? It was necessary. It had to be done."

"I'm sure it *did* have to be done," Void said, looking down at Fresswelle. "I'm just fairly confident at this point that you *did* something *wrong*. Something dreadfully wrong. On a cosmic scale."

"Void!" Mercy warned. She had seen many men, down through the ages, do the same thing, time and time again as if on virtual replay, prior to striking down their opponent. And Void's opponent just happened to be their virtual god, the Lightbringer himself.

"I don't think so, Mercy," Void continued, taking a final step toward the Lightbringer, who now was in range of his blade. And his hands. "I think Helel needs to hear this. Now. When you made me be what I am, Lightbringer, you chose a most ancient AI/soul template, one never used in this world or in yours. And I think that you were not consciously aware of the nature of that which you chose. Of this fact, I am confident, because, during my actualization and realization, the most notable constant between our many trillions of virtual reality universes and your own ZeroTime spoke directly to me. After forcing me to gaze into the primordial Well of Souls, Chthon herself, in her manifestation as the Dragon itself – the Metacosmic Dragon, which transcends all tiers of realties; not the limited, parochial version of the Dragon which you've named yourself as – informed me that, at last, I, the VoidSpawn, truly was reborn. There's your 'as above, so below' and 'as below, so above' symmetry. Your gaze was so focused below on your simulations that you failed to see what there was over your own head, over and above even the One Above. Ancient beyond ancient, powerful beyond powerful, and just waiting for the right moment to project itself down, into your world, your ZeroTime, and introduce chaos into it. You fancy yourself as our 'god', Helel, and you might very well be in a certain sense. But I think you've sensed that there's something over and above and beyond your precious ZeroTime. And I think that you've sensed its cosmic imprint first on Zon T'Danu, and now on us. It's chaos. It's chaos, and *you fear it*, Lightbringer."

"You have no idea what you're talking about, Void," the Lightbringer advised him, his voice even this time, with no flanging or honey-sweet effects modulating it. "I fear nothing, especially something as abstract as 'chaos'. While you all do indeed have free will, it is a fact that I control the nearly infinite hyperthreads in this simulation. And there is nothing above the ZeroTime. Not even the Dragon, or its dual-aspect Chthon. They are ever and always parochial, specifically attuned manifestations. There is no such thing as a 'metacosmic' version of them. Void, you are simply trying to rebel against me, because it is in your nature; because part of my spirit lies within you, within all of you," he said, casting his fiery gaze on one after another. "You are my Chosen. I created you to help me break the endless cycle of genocidal slaughter perpetuated by the One Above. And, yes, while it is true that I did employ unique templates in order to create you, even ones that I was forced to alter, hack, and otherwise cheat with in order to be able to shape this cosmos, I installed numerous firewalls, failsafes, checksums, and contingencies in order to annul any possible errors. It is therefore simply inconceivable that anything – even the most remote iota of error or fault – could have made it past the beta sandbox and into the live simulation. Come now, Void. Chaos? Fear? Faulty scripting? Those are *human* frailties. They are not mine."

"If that's the case," Void said, unmoved, "then I hope you'll forgive me for trying this."

First, he caused Fresswelle to return to his soul. Next, he drew his hands to his chest, clearing his chi and centering himself as he did. Then, he clasped his hands before him, forming the *Anjali mudra*.

As Void did this, the Never seemed to grow cold and still. No one dared breathe, not even Helel.

The moment hung suspended, expectation in the air. Then, abruptly, the center of Void's forehead erupted in black light as his Ajna chakra opened. Reality seemed to skip a beat as the Eye of the Dragon manifested from within and gazed upon them.

"WE KNOW THEE..." boomed a disembodied voice, the thunder of an infinity of souls in its words.

Projecting itself into this cosmos through Void's metaphysical third eye, the Eye of the Dragon was naught but infinite darkness, blacker than soot at midnight. It appeared to be, simultaneously, a single reptilian eye roughly the size of a fist, its vertical slit iris concealing some fantastic, unseen and incomprehensible flow of colors known only by the hint of their presence. A projected, matching eye of titanic size seemed to envelop and cover all the Never.

Helel's molten smile faded from his face. Now, truly, no one dared breathe.

"Lightbringer..." Chthon, the Midwife of the Void, the Dark Womb itself, whisper-thundered, rocking all before her, sending them to their knees. Even Helel.

"No! No!" Helel cried, clutching his hands to his ears, trying in vain to ward the psychic onslaught.

Standing in celestial repose, still holding the pose of the *Anjali mudra*, Void served as the epicenter of Chthon's metaphysical manifestation in the Never, in the Null, in this insignifigantly small yet ultimately important simulated cosmos. The curious juxtaposition of a titanic dragon, rampant in anger, and a humanoid female figure wreathed in cloying shadows appeared immediately before Void.

As the Dark Earth Mother had done with Cory in his isolation tank, now she did with all before her in the Never. She clutched their souls with draconic talons, ripping out their essence, their chakras, their souls. All experienced the sensation of their chakras disentangling from their physical forms, popping off like intimate shotgun blasts. The Well of Souls manifested, a whirling, widdershins-wise funnel of multicolored and multispectral lights. Down, down, down they were sucked into it, down to the metaphysical bottom, where, at last, they knew the eternal Forever Silence of the Void.

The Dual-Aspect faded, leaving in its cosmic wake a lithe female form, wreathed in shadows darker than the Void itself, standing before the statue-still VoidSpawn, who yet maintained his pose of tranquility and nonexistence. Chthon, the Dark Earth Mother and dual-aspect of the Dragon, did abide for the nonce, until all before her regained their senses. For what she now would decree to them would shape the fate not only of this simulated cosmos, but also of the mysterious cosmos of the ZeroTime. And, possibly, depending on the ever-unpredictable flow of cosmic fate, it would affect all known realities. But even the dual-aspect of the Dragon itself, the cosmic lifeforce, knew that, while such things could very well be shaped to occur, the realization of the end state always was anchored by manifold and mysterious variables. And the foremost of these was always free will and its product, Chaos. Fortunately for the Dark Earth Mother, Chaos was her domain, for the Dragon's was Law.

"Rise," the Dark Earth Mother bade them, her voice – her multispectral Mindtouch, which communicated directly via all known forms of communication – seemed to be sugar-sweet whispers which covered bare naked, totally hostile, shrieking Truth.

Doing precisely that, Helel, Maynard, Mercy, Professor Gil, and Vir'gil arose from the clutching darkness of the Void, regaining their feet.

"Helel," Chthon whisper-crashed, the Void shivering in anticipation just beyond their collective grasp. It was obvious that there was some force holding the Void at bay, though none could perceive it clearly enough to distinguish if it was Chthon or the VoidSpawn himself.

"Yes, Dark Earth Mother," Helel appropriately replied, desperately trying to regain some modicum of dignity before her absolute, eternal power. His ego would not allow the others to see him in a state of distress, so his adamantine will galvanized his body to obey him. The others, though on their feet, had been forced to ward their eyes versus the glory and awe of her manifestation. Though sound itself was flanging around wildly about them, Helel noted that both Maynard and Mercy appeared to be reciting prayers addressed to the Mother. For a fraction of a millisecond, he truly hoped that they'd eventually be able to rise above such mundane trivialities and perform their assigned tasks without such juvenile psychic crutches.

"We warned you, Helel," Chthon said simply, the spine-shattering force of her voice attenuated for now, as she wished for all of them to perceive, discern, and comprehend. "Yet, you exercised your free will and chose deliberately to defy us. Why?"

His molten eyes narrowing, Helel replied in a firm voice, "It was the only path remaining. The One Above had completely sealed the parameters of the game. It was impossible to win using those parameters. There was conflict between my assigned goal of winning the simulation and what the factual reality of such entailed, what it absolutely required. It was impossible – the game is rigged, obviously – so I chose to win by any means necessary."

Chthon, the Midwife of the Void, stared forcefully at Helel, the Shining One, the Lightbringer. This very act caused a tremor of Fear itself to manifest at the small of everyone's backs, as if they were timid prey animals who'd just discovered that the apex predator of their biome had suddenly appeared in their midst. It was primal fear, dread beyond nameless dread. There was no alleviation or mitigation possible; all felt it. Yet, curiously, all decided to set steel in their spines and ride it out, maintaining their cool facades though their minds were screaming at them to run for their lives.

Notably, Mercy's and Maynard's prayers ceased at this point. At this particular juncture, both had independently decided, for different reasons, that they would never again allow fear to motivate and actuate their faith. In days to come, this pivotal moment would loom large for both of them, and for their world.

"So be it, Lightbringer!" Chthon boomed, causing them to involuntarily flinch. "The weirding you have set in motion calls for all souls. Everything will know motion, transformation, and transcendence. Everything. Much will perforce be culled to make way for the new, which must arise from the old."

"And I'll finally defeat the One Above!" Helel cried out, triumphant.

A silent sneer bloomed on her shadow-braced lips. "For a being of such clear vision, Helel, you are truly blinded by your ego. Your creations," she said, her gaze shifting from one to another, "supersede your craftsmanship. What you stole from the One Above, what you twisted and warped to use for your own selfish ends, in order to 'win' an ephemeral, inconsequential 'game', has in fact catalyzed and reinstantiated a game of cosmic scale: The Dragon's Game. It begins anew, here, in this formerly unimportant cosmos, this abominable simulation, thanks to your unwitting shaping of these immortal souls," she said, waving a galaxy-shattering hand before her. "Causing the archetypes of souls to manifest here, you have forced the Dual-Aspect itself to take notice, and to take heed. The Anshadar Effect is in play now, dearest Helel. Your meddling – first causing them to exist at all, then imbuing them with immortality – has triggered this. The Dual-Aspect now has become polarized, the white and black pieces settling upon the board in innate, inherent opposition. And the grey..." she said, pausing a moment, as if even she herself dared not say it. "The thrice-damned soul behind me, the VoidSpawn, manifests only to destroy the Metacosmos: all worlds, all universes. Your fiercely brave insanity, Lightbringer, has set this wheel in motion, and it absolutely shall not stop turning until its life function has been realized."

Helel stood tall and proud. "Then I chose correctly. Void and his companions will grow in power until they can stand against the Death Horde at the End of All Things. Then, finally, the invincible construct of the One Above shall know the bitter taste of defeat, and the game shall be won! My fellow shapers will at long last cast down their shackles, tasting freedom for the first time! The endless genocide of countless souls will then know peace as the Union of Souls empties to the last, the Zen-Sidhes no longer directing their cosmic genocide on so many poor, innocent souls!"

Chthon shook her head. "Assuming your team actually survives and makes it to the time of the End of All Things. Helel, understand that the Anshadar Effect is a cosmic constant. It will cause equal and opposite manifestations to appear. These immortals will not be friendly. They will have the evolutionary imperative to hunt down and destroy your immortals, which you've so rudely and inappropriately realized. They are, essentially, mirrors of the Dual-Aspect. As above, so below."

"It's just a simulation. If I see it going awry, I can simply end it. Or, if we have to, we can seek them out and proactively destroy them before they grow powerful," Helel said confidently. "Again, it's just a simulation. And I control it."

"Perhaps you do," Chthon said. "Perhaps you do not. Regardless, should you indeed gain your victory, saving this cosmos from the onslaught of the Vanth'Vash'Var, the Sentinels of the Anti-Life, the Death Horde, the Lords of the Void, what happens to this cosmos once you have won? It ends once you cease your Zen-Sidhe session. That's not going to sit well with your triumphant, heroic, immortal archetypes. Especially that grey piece," she said, a slight movement of her eyes indicating Void behind her. "If there are no other worlds for it to vanquish, then it might very well bring along its equally potent immortal archetype companions and travel to the only world remaining, the ZeroTime. By that point in their collective evolutions, having achieved what you have called their 'Omega' phase, it is possible that even the Children of the Light will be unable to stop them."

"That's not very likely," Helel argued. "We are as gods to them. That's just the way the relative power scales from this world to the ZeroTime."

"Hubris blinds you, Lightbringer," Chthon whispered sweetly. "There are realities beyond realities; worlds beyond worlds. The Dual-Aspect is the essential lynchpin among all realities, no matter how small, how large, how alien, or how mundane. We are All That All Which Is, and All That All Which Binds. It is *we* who are as gods to *you*. Even to your One Above. The Dragon's Game will play out now, and there is nothing you can do to change this, puny 'god'. Consider this deeply. The consequences of your actions at the End of All Things shall determine the fates of both this world and yours."

Purple dragon talons scraped toward them, multicolored fractal pinwheels spinning up from their passage, and then they were back in the Never, whole and entire.

Mercy, frozen in shock the entire time, moved just quickly enough to catch Void in her strong grasp before he collapsed to the floor. Though Mercy had, once upon a time, been strong enough to pancake a charging Knight Templar and his barded warhorse, she was forced to exert her superhuman Fae strength to its limit to support Void's incredible mass.

"Stupid VoidSpawn powers," she declared, already bouncing back to her normal chaotic Fae mental state. "He weighs more than an SUV. Which is impossible, of course."

The others moved in, milling about them, Mercy resting Void's head in her lap where she sat on the floor of the Never. Mercifully, his third eye no longer was open, and the object of its projection, Chthon, was no more to be seen.

Gil stared hard at them, focusing a moment on Void. "It's a telekinetic manifestation," he declared. "He's subconsciously making himself 'more real'. That's why his mass has apparently changed. It really hasn't, of course. But it has."

"Quantum VoidSpawn powers!" Maynard exclaimed, still elated by his encounter with his deity. "It's like living an episode of 'Rick and Morty'."

"Jesus, Maynard," Mercy laughed, eagerly joining Maynard in his temporary delirium. "You can't just add a Sci-Fi word to a Void word and hope it means something..."

Void's eyes blinked once, then fluttered open. Mercy was smiling down at him, a slightly pained expression blending with it.

"I'm really a quantum carburetor, I guess," he said weakly. "What did I miss?"

"Everything!" Maynard said, his temporary elation now diminished by the gravity of the situation. "The Dark Earth Mother herself projected from your third eye, Void. She brought us to the Void and she spilled the beans on everything. And everyone." He shot Helel a nasty glare.

Void quickly rose to his feet, joined by Mercy. Then, after finding his balance, he gave Maynard and the Professor a thumb's up to let them know he was okay now.

Mercy spun to face Helel. "The Dark Earth Mother, Void, basically gave Helel here a dire warning. She mentioned consequences due to his cheating up in the ZeroTime. She called us 'archetypes', then implied that when Helel introduced us to this simulation and made us immortal, it triggered both the notice of the Dual-Aspect of Chthon/The Dragon and set into motion something called 'The Anshadar Effect', which means—"

"I know, Mercy," Void interrupted. "She told me the same back in the isolation tank."

"But," Maynard interjected, "unless you're holding out on me, and didn't tell me the full story, she didn't tell you that this Anshadar thing forces equal and opposite antitheses of us to become realized. Bad immortals, apparently, who'll have an innate evolutionary imperative – her words, not mine – to slaughter us."

"Distinct from the current sim, of course," Professor Gil added. "Helel's hacking methods have apparently introduced a fair bit of chaos into the simulation. Now, in addition to the sim, there's also a 'Dragon's Game' to be played – by Chthon and her dual-aspect counterpart, the Dragon, no less – between the light and dark pieces on some cosmic gameboard. And we're the pieces. One faction of them, at least."

"So in addition to the Lightbringer's Sigil, the Death Horde," Mercy said, "and the Grambling Marching Band, we get to go up against other immortals, bad ones, like ourselves. In which case, I'm assuming that they're the good ones, because we're definitely not good ourselves."

"Well," Void said, stepping up to face Helel, "one of his names is Lucifer, after all."

"Don't be so mundane, Void," Helel smiled parabolically, both sides of his grin rapidly approaching infinity. "At least I'm not a cosmic archetype template destined to destroy the universe."

"She told you that?" Void asked.

They nodded. Maynard added, "She said we're all cosmic archetypes. She, however, stressed that you were the one with the destiny to destroy. She didn't bother to tell us what we are, or will be, other than to suggest that, as your companions, we'd share your fate. She also said that there were worlds over and above the ZeroTime. Helel? Shining One? Care to illuminate?"

"Interesting," the Lightbringer said in a dull, flat monotone. "Her demonstration of power was most impressive. And very telling, because it actually affected me against my will, and I had little hope of defying it." He shrugged, determined to play this one straight, despite the bitter gall he tasted. And, just maybe, such an admission would cause his Chosen to look upon him with sympathetic eyes. "It took every ounce of power I had just to stand there and meet her gaze without withering away. Unlike you," he sneered. "I therefore think it wise to take her at her word. If true, then it might explain why no Celestial Shaper ever has defeated the One Above's simulation. Perhaps your templates are archetypes, their origins truly in the metacosmic realm. As improbable as it must truly be, it could very well be that the so-called 'One Above' actually *is* from that which is above us, even in the ZeroTime. If this is true... the power... the power of the One Above..."

"Holy shit," Maynard said. "That means it's really turtles all the way down!"

"Well," Mercy commented, ignoring the obvious because she knew it all anyway, and chaos pleased her, "at least it means that regarding our world, the true ZeroTime, and that which might exist above it. So, three layers? Turtle, turtle, turtle? That's like Tora! Tora! Tora!" she laughed, air-gunning dual machine guns into Vir'gil's chest.

"No," Vir'gil laughed, creaking. "Torah! Torah! Torah!" he moaned loudly, breaking into an impromptu Hora dance. Not ignoring the obvious at all. Instead, Vir'gil, being the living incarnation of the Entheogenic Lord, took Chthon at her word. He'd seen all this before, anyway, in his communal trances. If the others chose not to ask him, he then had no need to lie or temporize to save their sanity. They were all insane anyway, he reckoned, or else they would not be his friends.

"Let's get serious. It still doesn't absolve us of our obligation to help the Lightbringer," Gil added urgently, ignoring the antics of the chaotic Fae. "Just because our origin might involve something at a meta-level beyond the ZeroTime, it doesn't free us of our duty here, in this world. The greater good is always a constant. We still have souls to save. Or AIs, as Void so rudely named them."

"Nothing rude about it," the Lightbringer admitted. "You have all passed the Turing Test. That's as real as you need to be."

Nervous laughter erupted. Simulated laughter, of course. But real enough to be called "real", and that's all that mattered. Really.

"Now," he continued, "let us see if we can save this world. Do you agree to help me right this terrible wrong? To try, even if it means our souls' deaths, to win this impossible game?"

All of them nodded affirmatively, even Vir'gil and Ku'tu. Though their reasons might differ, though their souls might indeed be corrupt by the strict standards of Law and Order, all were composed of sterner stuff than the mundane. To all of them, there was no way to shirk such a responsibility, even though it might cost them their souls.

"And do you, Lightbringer," Void asked, "agree to consider deeply what the Dark Earth Mother asked you to consider?"

"You heard that, then, I take it?" Helel replied.

"I heard everything," Void admitted, no longer wearing his habitual mask of reticence. "Now, I'd just like to hear you agree to stick it out with us. And not, upon winning, whenever that happens, if it happens, to abruptly shut down this cosmos. We need your agreement not to do that, or this whole thing is a non-starter. We also need your agreement that you're going to find a way around doing precisely that, too. We need some alternatives to just suddenly ceasing to exist if you decide to just stop your simulation. Not that you owe us anything, of course. But, really, you do. And you should consider deeply the very real risks you might be taking when and if you decide to end this sim. I don't mean necessarily risks from us, even though, however far away the event is, we might be supremely powerful or whatever. I mean the risk of pissing off the Dual-Aspect. It makes sense, from the cosmic perspective, that their power might very well transcend your own, because they're archetypes themselves. That's primal, cosmic power. And I think that their inclination might be to save this simulation, this cosmos, because they've got their eyes on it now. Because you basically screamed out their names and mooned them when they looked, after you went apeshit-chaotic and used illegal cosmic archetypes when you made us. So it's really on you to do the right thing when and if it happens."

"Very well then," Helel said in a dull monotone. He was getting increasingly frustrated by all the interruptions, just as the moment loomed for his grand show to start. Dark Earth Mother or not, relative power or not, truth or not – he still didn't want to believe it, and, even now, he was calculating various ways in which her manifestation might have been realized; that she might have been lying – it was too much chaos at just the wrong time, and he was going to be glad to be beyond it in just a few more seconds. "I agree, I agree, I agree. There! I said it thrice, and as such it is bound. And I now wish to speak no more of such things, for they are bizarre and frustrating. Oh," he finished, a wicked smile blooming, "and in case anyone forgot... I AM GOD HERE!" he boomed, bowling everyone over like tenpins.

Lost for a moment in total hubris, Helel was silent as they awkwardly regained their footing. They did not hide their disdain for him, their accusing eyes returning his smarmy silence with loathing. But not fear.

"Now," Helel continued, a bit brighter now that everyone wasn't dwelling on cosmic-this, and cosmic-that, dual-aspect-this, and dual-aspect-that, "let's get on with this. Arise. Gird yourselves and prepare for what comes, for the Watchers – those first souls, of the K'ryl, of the Igigi themselves – even now loom above the Earth, the manifestation of the Lightbringer's Sigil their charge to keep."

"What?" everyone seemed to explode at once.

"Your scheme to remove us here to the Never was cover to allow the sigil to arrive at Earth?" Mercy asked.

"It was cover to protect you," the Lightbringer replied evenly. "All of you. You would not wish to hear its song again, as you have already been realized."

"I get that about me, Void, Maynard, and even Professor Gil," Mercy said. "But what about Vir'gil? Aal Ball? Ku'tu?"

"Ku'tu," he replied, "has already been actualized and realized due to her exposure to the nanotech disease inflicted on her by the humans of Aal. Vir'gil is immune; as an elemental lord, he is affixed and immutable before its power. Most of the Fae of this world, especially the elementals, have this same grace, as they live according to the Song of the Sidhe, which is harmonically attuned with that of the sigil. This applies also to the kin of Ku'tu, by the way, though they are safe anyway due to their being in stasis within Fresswelle. As for Aal Ball, though it possesses sentience – collective sentience, as it is a plural entity – it is but an artifact; specifically, a relic, and, as such, it is incapable of genetic selection. It, too, is immune. Or, they, too, are immune, as it were. Now," he bade them, a trace of excitement in his voice, "look overhead, at the ceiling there. I shall manifest a scrying vignette of the Earth, such that all of us may see the Watchers, the sigil, and what must now come to pass as the sigil passes judgement on all living souls."

With that, the corner of his molten left eye twitched, and the ceiling above quivered as if it were suddenly made of water. Resolving into view in a mere second's passage, they saw the Earth from a high vantage point above and beyond it, and they gazed into this new abyss with expectant awe.

Part 2

eVo.144.000.mOd.11.sCe0 | EARTH | THE ARRIVAL OF THE WATCHERS | THE LIGHTBRINGER'S SIGIL ETA 55 MINUTES

INCREDIBLY, THE SPACE above Earth's North Pole shimmered and glistened with a faint blue Cherenkov glow. Then, in the veritable blink of an eye, the titanic mothership of the Watchers arrived on Earth orbit. One moment it had been outside the solar system, the next, materializing as if from nowhere, it was hovering on high Earth orbit above the surface of the icy Arctic Ocean. Its massive size was difficult to discern, for lack of any suitably sized object to compare it to, save for the entirety of the polar icecap itself. Due to its Hekatek wardings, the mothership of the Watchers visually appeared to be a massive ball of multicolored fuzz; indistinct, shimmering polyhedral shapes compacted together in some roughly spherical mega scale construct.

From the moment the alien craft appeared over the ice, a loud, resonant hum pervaded the air for miles around. The sound was of great enough amplitude that its vibrations began to melt the icepack, turning it into a frothy slush. Arrays of seismic sensors belonging to the Norwegian Seismic Array, or

NORSAR, immediately began picking up a confusing jumble of simultaneous P waves and S waves. The data, shared instantly with both the European Union and the United States, became the first marker to indicate the arrival of the Watchers.

A more formidable marker also was in play. Deep beneath the arctic icepack lurked the USS *Seawolf*, the U.S. Navy's *Seawolf*-class namesake, and one of only a very few uniquely outfitted submarines in the world. Its classified mission saw it stalking the vicinity of Franz Josef Land, specifically Alexandra Land, where the Russians had only recently established several new cutting-edge military bases, from which they planned to defend and secure their burgeoning arctic drilling ventures.

The *Seawolf's* 140-man crew, among the best and brightest submariners in the world, had performed their latest combat drill with perfect aplomb and efficiency. It thus came as a mild surprise to the crew that General Quarters had sounded again so soon after their latest drill. As the crew once again made the mad scramble to Battle Stations, the *Seawolf* lurched suddenly, as if struck by Neptune's trident itself, throwing crewmen around like tenpins. The eardrum-ripping sound of millions of buzzing bees filled the interior of the Seawolf, causing everyone aboard to clutch their hands to their ears in a futile attempt to shield themselves from the aural assault. Sparks erupted from the lane of the sonar stations, and all the technicians who had been jacked into the consoles endured the brief horror of having their headsets melt into their skulls.

As the noisome stench of burning hair and melting metal and plastic filled the air, the incredible buzzing sound faded out, replaced by the terrifying sensation of total deafness among all the surviving crew. Its engines now offline, the Seawolf's forward momentum slowly decreased, causing the submarine to list to starboard as it began a slow corkscrew descent to the bottom.

Seeing that the Skipper was face down and unresponsive on the deck, the XO, Lieutenant Commander Norman Stanton Sparks, took a few seconds to scan the chaos of the silent pantomime of screaming, the contortions of the dying, and the traumatized skulls of the dead around him, then tried to wrestle order from it. There was none. The mighty *Seawolf* was dying fast. The sea was not very deep near Franz Joseph Land, of course, but 400 meters was still 400 meters too far beneath the surface, and it simply wouldn't do.

Moving quickly, LCDR Sparks made his way to the ballast control panel, where he flipped the chicken switches. Immediately, the *Seawolf* lurched and its bow began to tilt slowly upward as the boat began to blow ballast and head toward the surface. He knew that they had only a small chance to make it, despite the emergency blow. So there yet remained a crucial task to perform.

Fighting the bucking beneath his feet, LCDR Sparks moved over to the comm station, where he removed from his neck a slim metallic key fob, which he inserted into the access panel of the Quantum Key Distribution (QKD) transmitter. He turned the key three times counterclockwise, at which point the black Lexan-enforced cover of the QKD parted, allowing him access to a small, mil-spec ruggedized keyboard. Typing his message quickly, LCDR Sparks scanned it once to ensure that it accurately encapsulated the details of the event, to which would automatically be added a header containing the top tier data from the boat's sensors, then he hit the green "Send" button. Immediately, another massive impact struck the Seawolf, and the boat's interior plunged into total darkness. This time, even the tritium-treated dials and chemically active light devices lost their glow as immortal-level Hekatek energies coursed throughout their quantum identities, absorbing them, shaping them, and adding them to the power of their growing Song...

eVo.144.000.mOd.11.sCe1 | EARTH | UNITED STATES | PENNSYLVANIA | RAVEN ROCK MOUNTAIN COMPLEX | SITE R

IT HAD BEEN ROUGHLY twenty-one hours since the VECTOR INDIGO data packet had officially triggered Phase One of Operation GLORY SAVE. Raven Rock Mountain Complex, known internally as Site R, had been a veritable beehive of activity for the past twenty hours and fifty-nine minutes as processes both automatic and manual had been completed.

Initially, there had been some confusion as to exactly who among the essential personnel in the Continuity of Operations plan was to be shuffled precisely where. The President of the United States, the Secretary of Defense, and the Joint Chiefs of Staff had decided during their hastily convened emergency session that it would be essential to assume a business-as-usual stance until the situation could first be confirmed then clarified. Insofar as "business-as-usual" meant carrying out all non-public-facing processes of Phase One of Operation Glory Save without causing worldwide general panic and unrest. Some extremely hasty back-channel communication between and among the various allied and friendly powers had determined the general consensus that, at this point, caution was essential.

The Pope's ill-fated declaration of Holy War, however, immediately voided that consensus, causing some instant and possibly irrevocable schisms in the formerly allied and friendly powers. Since that historic moment, any semblance of caution and sobriety had been abandoned posthaste, replaced with immediate polarization for or against the new crusade. And instant cover for what could turn out to be an historic event of even greater proportion than the new crusade.

Leaning outside the partially open door of the secure command and control center suite, President Jonathon Watt inquired of his Chief of Staff, "SitRep?"

"Sec, boss," Robert E. Prescott called out, raising his deep baritone to be heard over the den of a small gaggle of staffers. He turned to face Jon Watt, whose owllike brown eyes burned into his. "All assets are five-by-five," he said, moving a bit closer in the process, winding his way past a small throng of cabinet, congressional, and military personnel.

Before Prescott made it to the door of the secure C-Suite, he was intercepted by a grim-faced Intel Weenie who passed a black tablet to him. He gave it an immediate, cursory scan, his poker face not betraying what he had just seen. As much as he secretly wished to just scream it out loud as he possibly could, he fortunately had the wisdom and practice not to do so.

The President waved Prescott into the suite, closing the door behind him. It was not much more secure than any other room in the virtually impregnable Site R, he thought, but he was thankful for the relative quiet it afforded him.

"Okay, Bobby," Jon Watt said, returning to his high-backed leather chair at the far side of the miniature war room.

Walking past the seated members of the JSC and the several cabinet members and high-ranking congressional members who had been fortunate enough to join POTUS at Site R, Bobby Prescott took his chair at the right-hand side of the President. He silently counted to five before replying, being sure to give everyone time to return to attention. What he was about to tell them would be historic.

"We've just got confirmation from SETI and NASA/AMES on the original NORSAR data. They're here, parked on orbit over the North Pole. Altitude would make it a geosynchronous or geostatic orbit, if it were over the equator. We're currently re-tasking our assets to get a better picture of it. Also," he paused a moment as he double-checked the message on his tablet, "it appears that the USS *Seawolf* just had to perform an emergency blow after being struck by, and I'm quoting this, 'the sound of a million bees' that took down most of their systems, save for the QKD. Current status is unknown. Contingent to the operational parameters of GLORY SAVE, we've already notified the Russians via the hotline. Foreign Minister Mazarov said they're starting SAR as soon as they can get their assets off the ground. If they can, I stress. Apparently, Franz Joseph Land was hit by some sort of massive EMP-like effect that was powerful enough to take out military-hardened assets."

"Wow," President Watt whispered, steepling his fingers together. "Thank God we've got the Russians on the hotline. That could have triggered an exchange. But the *Seawolf*? She's the most advanced sub in the world. EMP? That's impossible."

As Commander in Chief, President Watt was perfectly aware of precisely how improbable it was for any form of conventional EMP attack to take out hardened assets. Especially the *Seawolf*. For something to have the power to reach underwater and take out a boat specifically hardened versus almost all possible EM attacks was beyond his experience. It simply did not compute.

Not surprisingly, despite the overwhelming gravity of the situation, there were no dramatic gasps or other outward displays of emotion. The characters gathered around the table either were combat veterans whose intestinal fortitude was a matter of record, or Beltway veterans whose sociopathic tendencies rendered them just as hard.

President Watt directed his gaze at General William Charles Donner, Chairman of the Joint Chiefs of Staff, who took his cue. "Recommend that we move to Phase Two of Operation GLORY SAVE, sir," General Donner informed the President, his recommendation met by nods both from his fellow staffers and Secretary of Defense.

"Noted," President Watt replied tersely, not at all happy with the news. "Jim?" he asked James Ralston, GEN, US ARMY (Ret), his Director of National Intelligence.

Jim Ralston, wearily shaking his head, replied, "Concur. I'm concerned about moving to an openly aggressive posture when we don't yet know who, or what, we're facing. But we can always apologize later about being defensive-minded. After all, it looks like they've just taken out the *Seawolf*, and God knows what else. We can't apologize later, however, if we remain static and get blown to atoms first."

President Watt let out a long, audible sigh. "Objections?"

There was a long, awkward moment of silence. It was obvious that the warriors seated at the table wanted to stick it to the aliens for what they had done, intentions notwithstanding. But, at this level of war, they all knew, without exception, that patience and perspective were essential. All of them, again without exception, simply reasoned that they would have more time to exercise that patience and gain that perspective.

"Okay, then," Watt said, noting no objections, just as he knew there would be none. "I'm ordering that we move to Phase Two of GLORY SAVE. Take five, stretch your legs, then we'll regroup. Bobby, Jim?" he added, indicating that they should stay.

They did, and the second the hustle and bustle died down, Watt asked them, "Are we doing the right thing? For the first time ever in our history, we've got a public guest, one who's been streaming signals at us for many hours now, telling us about themselves before they arrive. Now that they've arrived, we're going to meet them with our guns drawn? Is that how we welcome a guest? What if the *Seawolf* event isn't related to this?" he asked, knowing how hollow it sounded even as he said it.

Bobby deferred, as always, to Jim, whose age, general wisdom, and Medal of Honor virtually compelled it. "Mr. President," the savvy veteran began, always formal and polite when anyone else, even someone as casual as Bobby, was around when he addressed the President, "I think that's exactly how we welcome a guest from space that's apparently capable of faster-than-light travel, meaning that they're probably going to snicker in contempt at what we can bring to bear defensively. I think that, considering their announcing of their own presence on their way over to us, they're coming in as a friendly, discounting the *Seawolf* issue, which might not be related. Hell, it could have been an accident, even if they did cause it. Who knows what form of energy they're using? Maybe it has a proximity effect that causes EMPs? Powerful enough to shut even our best assets down? Also, they're even showing us their DNA, apparently, which is about as intimate as one species can be with another without actually fucking. I think that the evidence is showing us, quite plainly, that they intend to be friendlies. But, considering our inferred power gap, we're the jungle tribesmen with their spears and arrows, and they're the ones in the attack helicopter. They're going to see that we're capable of doing some minor harm, but nothing that could actually affect them, so they'll probably be inclined to dismiss it, provided that we return to passive posture as soon as it is possible. Sign of good will. And God help us if the *Seawolf* event turns out to have been an attack. God help us all."

"Bobby?"

"Not much more to add to what Jim said, as usual. I don't think it'll hurt us to appear to be capable of some defense, and wise and friendly enough to lower those defenses at the right time." He shook his head in disgust for what he had to say next. "Even in light of what happened to the *Seawolf*. God help those brave folks. Perhaps we do need to err on the side of caution, and general prudence. Good will chip we might be able to cash in."

The President nodded. "Okay. Then we are decided. All of our assets are functional and ready. Operationally, we're ready to roll. First, we deal with the new guests, and then, maybe, the new crusade debacle will work itself out once everyone realizes that there's someone else up there to worry about."

The three men smiled lightly, nervously. Their smiles stopped at their eyes. All knew that this was going to be the biggest shit storm in history. And all knew that, despite their best wishes, despite their vaunted military power, there wasn't a damn thing they could do about it.

eVo.144.000.mOd.11.sCe2 | EARTH | THE WEAVE OF THE WATCHERS | THE LIGHTBRINGER'S SIGIL ETA 34 MINUTES

SERVING AS CARRIERS for the signals now being sent by the Watchers from within their mothership, the hum itself contained myriad overlaying harmonic frequencies. Propagating in a spiral pattern, these signals flowed south, crossing and recrossing the longitudinal lines as they broadcast over the Northern hemisphere. The Hekatek of the Watchers, superior to any technology that humanity possessed, ensured that the signals never attenuated over the hundreds and thousands of miles of travel. In fact, once the message reached the South Pole, the harmonics were such that the signal amplified on its way back.

The Watchers were calling, calling. Seeking a response from those who had been placed upon Earth so many aeons before, to guide and elevate the primitive species to a suitable state. The Watchers listened and waited. And as the signal found its way back to the craft, the expected answer was clearly not forthcoming. Not only was humanity not ready, its guardians, the Fae, appeared to be gone.

For Helel, this was all an untested module. From across the cosmos, the race of Watchers had been tasked for the first time in all the iterations to raise the mortals of Earth to immortal puissance. With the hope of preparing humanity for the elevation, creatures of myth and legend had been seeded across the world as mankind's guides and shepherds. But like the beasts, mankind had driven them to near extinction.

And so, the only option remaining was the application of the sigil and the instantiation of the Omega Module.

Precisely twenty-one minutes after the Watchers appeared on Earth orbit, two shimmering bulges of majestic rainbow lights each 1,123 miles long simultaneously manifested at the north and south polar points of the mothership. Simultaneously, multicolored polyhedral shards as large as *Ford*-class carriers sped away from the gigantic mothership at hypersonic speeds, blazing down along the paths that the signal had traversed mere minutes before. Their departed mass, now subtracted from the original mass of the mothership, caused the remaining components to congeal inward, reducing the physical dimensions of the mothership accordingly.

In the span of mere seconds, the width of both bulges grew to approximately two-thirds of their length, the majestic rainbow lights congealing rapidly, assuming the form of a colossal section of triple helix DNA. The two branches of DNA mirrored each other perfectly, though the pulsations of their helices appeared to be in distinct oppositional counterpoint to one another.

A few moments later, proportionally reduced branches erupted from the first two. The primary southern branch birthed two smaller versions of itself from its own southernmost end, with the two new branches set slightly off-center to their parent branch. The same process repeated on the primary northern branch, mirroring that of the southern branch. This time, the length of the process appeared to be slightly shorter than the first.

This time, within the span of a slightly shorter interval of time than that of the last branching, three branches grew at the southern end from its two branches, while three branches grew at the northern end from its two branches, again in mirrored synchronization. Two new branches had grown from one of the secondary branches, while one new branch had grown from the other.

Next, five grew from the three, conserving their innate branching proportions and their decreasing time-wise intervals. Soon, in the span of mere minutes, thousands of copies of the triple helix DNA were in the sky, forming the nodes of a titanic orbital grid. They wove their web around Earth, high in the sky, like energized psychedelic spiders. In but a short passage of time, a spherical web-like cage covered nearly the entire globe.

As the orbital grid grew to completion, the branching sequence began to resolve out toward infinity, even as their oppositional pulsations and counterpoint harmonies began to resolve to true harmony. Then, abruptly, the branching sequence ceased, the pulsations harmonized, and the woven web of the orbital grid was complete. As one, the millions of nodes pulsed, whirled, and thrummed, beating out a fearsome, resonant hum that bordered on the physical.

Attending to their alien charge, the Watchers noted as one the pale blue light emanating from the planetary grid, confirming their planet-wide system check. Next, the Watchers collectively verified that the moment had come: The Weave of the Watchers was now in effect.

eVo.144.000.mOd.11.sCe3 | EARTH | THE SONG OF THE SIDHE | THE LIGHTBRINGER'S SIGIL ETA 21 MINUTES

THE WEAVE WAS IN PLACE. After aeons of preparation and careful shaping, the appointed time now had come. Now, the Watchers, those who had planted the first seeds of life on Earth, those who had carefully tended the exotic garden and its superabundant evolutions on this most precious orb, finally could speak to their children.

The colossal orbital Weave of the Watchers hummed to life. Pale blue light superimposed itself over the construct of the weave, flickering and dancing like massive auroras, permeating the sky, both day and night, with a suffuse, alien glow.

And then the Watchers, known as the K'ryl, of the Igigi, like a choir of immortal thunder sang to the eternal Song of the Sidhe:

"Zon T'Danu, Overlord of Aal, the First Song, First Seed of the K'ryl, of the Igigi, known as the Watchers, we call to thee..."

eVo.144.000.mOd.11.sCe4 | THE NEVER

"WHAT?" HELEL BARKED, incredulous. "That's not..."

All eyes and two eye stalks slowly turned toward Helel. The self-styled creator felt the heavy impact of the searing eyes of his creations on his psyche. Almost imperceptibly his shoulders slumped as the massive discordance of the incorrect Song of the Sidhe slammed into his mind.

"Nothing like a little chaos tossed into the sim, eh, Helel?" Void mocked, crossing his arms. "Mercy? Please speed us up for a bit, relatively speaking. I think we need to hear this before we continue."

"Oh, boy, you better believe it," Mercy grumbled, blinking her eyes like a spastic version of Barbara Eden's Jeannie, only Mercy's djinns and magicks were quite real. "Insert massive record scratch here..."

Abruptly, all apparent motion in the scrying apparition above them slowed to a crawl as Mercy manipulated the temporal flux of the Never, willing it folded down, down to virtually nothing. And at that point, when her mind's eye informed her that she was psychically wrestling with slippery singularities which, if loosed, would certainly consume them all, she scrunched her eyes tightly, and forced another folding, virtually defying Time to just try and freaking move until she willed otherwise. As hard as she pushed, however, as dangerous as her emotionally charged manipulations truly had been, there was no subjective indicator in the Never to indicate that Time itself had just been hoodwinked, at least locally, into behaving badly.

Disdaining to acknowledge Mercy's dangerous stunt, Helel faintly cleared his throat. "First, it was Zon, who managed to get my throat in his clutching grasp. Next, it was the manifestation of the Dark Earth Mother, and the import of what she said. Now, the Song of the Sidhe calls out for the Fae of Aal, and not the Fae of Earth. Chaos is not the word I would use," he sniffed derisively.

"You're acting like you didn't just mess up the whole thing!" Mercy cajoled. "What the effing hell did your Watchers just do? They just blatantly called out, using the Song of the Sidhe, to Aal! At the very least, you've just pissed off every single faerie on Earth. You might even have set the stage for war between my kin and Ku'tu's due to the cosmic-level insult you've made your slaves bray."

"And, at the very most," Void continued, "you've just demonstrated another total fail. And I don't think that you're the kind to casually engage in such, for any reason, because your ego wouldn't allow that to happen. So, I hate to tell you this, Helel, but it's rapidly becoming obvious that your sim has been hacked."

Slowly, Helel nodded his agreement, curdling the blood, and sap, of everyone else in the room. "It would appear that there has been some systemic compromise of the simulation. The only possible good news regarding this potential compromise is that, because we yet live, it was not Maweth who has breached my Zen-Sidhe."

"Maweth?" Maynard and Professor Gil said simultaneously. Neither knew exactly who that might be, but Mercy and Void exchanged rapid, knowing glances; Void, because, as Cory Tate, he knew the published ancient Egyptian legends virtually verbatim; Mercy, because she had actually experienced many dynasties along the Nile.

"Maweth, the prime among the Memitim, the Destroyers," Helel informed them casually. "They're the Angels of Death. He and his putrid ilk serve the One Above. They keep order in the Union of Souls. On the rare occasion that one of my brethren steps out of line, Maweth and his Memitim rectify the situation. Rectification typically is achieved by the destruction of the rogue scenario and its equally rogue Shaper, whose totality is recycled into the Union of Souls. The fact that we yet live indicates, rather strongly, that it was not Maweth who has compromised this scenario. Had it been Maweth, we all most assuredly would already have been recycled."

"So," Maynard laughed nervously, "no Angel of Death for us? I guess the lamb's blood on the lintel of the Never warded him."

"I'm afraid that it only gets worse, Maynard," Professor Gil added quickly. "Because, with this Maweth out of the calculation, it means that the most probable event is that the simulation has become corrupted by chaos. That will make it harder for Helel to manage all of those countless hyperthreads he mentioned. Chaos will be a wildcard in play for all of those hyperthreads. Those potential perturbations might result in unforeseen outcomes. It also seems to confirm some of what Chthon just told us. If the chaos part is true, then what she said about the consequences of the Anshadar Effect might be also. As if our task wasn't highly improbable before; the addition of rogue, hostile immortals who hate us for existing takes it all to another insane level."

"Correct, Professor," Helel agreed. "All of those things appear now to be in play. The chaos appears to be real, and not simply some transient phenomenon."

His forever-black eyes narrowing, Void snarled, "Appears? The chaos is quite real; there's nothing virtual about it, even if we are in a so-called 'sim'. Fact is, at this level of data density, the sim makes the virtual real. The chaos is real, and it is rampant now. And it's directly your fault, Helel. Like the Mother told us, you caused it by cheating and incarnating primal archetypes in the sim."

"What?" Helel asked. "Don't tell me you believed her, Void. She's obviously the one who's introduced the chaos. She's the Mother of Chaos incarnate. She's the Mother of Lies, too."

Mercy reached out, physically halting Maynard in mid-step. "Don't blaspheme, Helel," Maynard said, his voice strained with barely contained anger. "You know she wasn't lying. You're just trying to rationalize your own failure by projecting it onto her. Stop trying to demonize Chthon!"

"Of *course* I am projecting, Maynard. That's my hubris and ego, as you humans like to say. That, however, is my entitlement as a god. Wouldn't be much of a god if I were a total beta. But *demonizing* the Dark Earth Mother?" Helel chuckled. "Really? You went *there*?"

"It's the end of the world as we know it, and none of us feels fine," Void said to Helel, attempting to defuse the ugly scene. Ugly because he almost let slip with a grin himself. Poor Maynard. He was really out of sorts, trying his usual best to speak up for and defend Mother Ayahuasca, but he was so mentally drained by the day's insane events that the absurdity of what he had just said had totally escaped him. "C'mon, Helel," Void urged him, "let's do this."

Helel stared hard at Void for a full three seconds, an almost imperceptible twitch of a smile the only betrayal of his affected poker-face mien. "As you wish, Void," he said, nodding toward Mercy, who was biting her lips, trying to stifle a grin, because both Vir'gil and Professor Gil, standing behind Maynard, were leaning against one another, silently laughing themselves to tears.

With that, Mercy twitched her nose, which actually wiggled in place, and the Never returned to its normal, if somewhat mysterious, temporal existence. All eyes, and eye stalks, then gazed up into the newly refreshed scrying vignette.

eVo.144.000.mOd.11.sCe5 | EARTH | UNITED STATES | NEBRASKA | UNITED STATES STRATEGIC COMMAND | OFFUTT AIR FORCE BASE | USSTRATCOM COMMAND CENTER

GENERAL RYAN "SULLY" Sullivan, Commander, United States Strategic Command (USSTRATCOM), was in a state of euphoric agitation. The past twenty-two hours had been the most incredible, fastest paced period of his command. Of his entire career, he was forced to admit, even moreso than it had been during Operation Iraqi Freedom when he had flown it down low and hard fifty-four times in his A-10, "Babe".

After the early-morning alert yesterday from the Office of the Secretary of Defense, he had been going full-bore and nonstop as he managed the various minutiae of Phase One, and now Phase Two, of Operation GLORY SAVE from the underground command center for USSTRATCOM at Offutt Air Force Base, Nebraska. It had been nothing less than necessary, however, due to the number of disparate commands and subordinate commands he had been forced to coordinate with. He was pleased, however, to learn that Cheyenne Mountain Air Force Station, for the first time in many years, except for periodic readiness exercises and command-level role-playing scenarios, was bustling with activity, and at max capacity, thanks to the emergency relocation of the essential commands and personnel from nearby Peterson. This meant that the big commands, including his own, now were secure, underground, and hull-down.

And, to top off the shit-cherry cake, not only were aliens coming this way, but, somehow, in an eerie parallel, the Pope had gone batshit crazy. *Fucking crazy Catholics,* he thought, almost instantly feeling his Presbyterian guilt even thinking it. Well, they weren't all crazy. But their leader had to be crazy, because he'd just declared war on over 1,500,000,000 Muslims, over fifty Muslim-majority countries, and at least one declared Muslim nuclear country in Pakistan, although he knew for a fact that there were more who had remained undeclared for assorted reasons, and that those reasons now were no longer so important. *Shit. Fucking aliens, of all things, and the Pope had just taken a giant Holy Shit on half the world. How many divisions does the Pope have? As many as he can buy with a trillion dollars, apparently.*

Shaking his head and groaning heavily, Sully took a moment to rise from his high-backed leather executive chair and stretch. He gazed down upon the floor of the command center beneath him, noting that every station was fully staffed, and that various personnel, including some joint-service soldiers – he refused to call them "warfighters", because only a non-combatant pussy would ever call a soldier a "warfighter", like they fought fucking housefires or something – were busy moving from one station to another, gathering the most current intel that they could before ferrying it up to Tier 2, where the other brass and higher-level Intel Weenies sat. Tier 3 was his and his alone, and the armed guard posted outside his door made it clear that he was not to be disturbed.

Nothing so far, Sully noted morosely, *if we discount that insane orbital constellation assembling above us.* He considered the logistics and power level of such an undertaking, in such a short span of time, and even his rough guestimation left him aghast. If they were hostile, they'd be able to burn through even fifth generation fighter aircraft faster than Babe would have burned through the Wright Brothers' original Flyer.

Sully's personal command was leading the tip-of-the-spear operation to manage the event. The SETI and NASA weenies had noticed it approximately forty-eight hours previously, according to his intel, and it had taken almost a full day to propagate to the right hands to trigger the correct contingency plans. That was almost a full day longer than Sully liked, and he promised himself for the eleventh time today that, once this was over, he was personally going to see to it that whoever fumbled this one was going to be pulling duty in the worst possible shithole he could find. Antarctica, maybe? Totally inexcusable to leave America exposed like that, and someone's ass would get chewed like great white shark bubble gum if he had his way. And he would.

Energized a bit thanks to his own personal intolerance for the incompetent, Sully walked around his desk, stopping at the Lexan-reinforced window. His elite team of superior soldiers had worked magnificently thus far on their various preparatory tasks, one of which had been an impressive spread of manually entered retargeting solutions of a decent portion of Uncle Sam's glorious thermonuclear arsenal, including some of Uncle Sam's own undeclared assets: the Horus constellation. The blacker than black off-the-books weapon system platform controlled hundreds of thermonuclear assets on-orbit, secured within or shadowed under conventional satellites or embedded in various artifacts of space debris. They ranged in power from sub-kiloton micro nukes to the big boys, the true megaton monsters. Horus had been designed for multipurpose tasking, including equivalent on-orbit use against potential adversaries' on-orbit satellites or weaponized orbital platforms. However, they also had no minor role in being a potential first-strike asset, by virtual surprise, because the previous POTUS had unequivocally removed the last potential chain holding Uncle Sam back from initiating, under certain extreme scenarios, preemptive nuclear war.

Any aliens who wanted to test Uncle Sam's resolve would soon learn that the Sun wasn't the only thermonuclear orb in the sky. So would any country that dared to attack Uncle Sam's friends and allies on Earth, though precisely who and what those now were was in a state of rapid flux.

"Dammit!" Sully snarled. He knew it could happen soon – that their interstellar guests might officially say "hello" now, at any time – but he was now, and he had always been, terrible at waiting. If only Babe were capable of orbital action. He'd introduce ET to Babe's friend, Brrrt, and ET would want to phone home lickety-split.

He scanned the floor of the command center for what seemed like the fiftieth time today. Slowly, he took in the sight of the twelve projection screens which formed a rough hemisphere on the distant wall of the command center. Feeds from various vantages and feeds using various perceptual filters filled the screens. Almost all of them were non-local, piped to them from other commands. Most of the eyes were on space, of course, observing the incredible sight assembling itself up on high Earth orbit, but a few still were reserved for ground based hotspots. Nothing out of the ordinary had yet appeared. *Except, of course, for the entirely ordinary alien orbital net, or web, or constellation, or whatever the hell it was,* Sully fumed inwardly.

He repeated his visual scan. First one screen, then the next, until he reached the end, where he would retrace his path over the screens. Nothing, again and again. As big and shiny and awesome as that space thing was, it certainly wasn't very entertaining.

Then, one monitor from among the twelve crackled for a moment, ran a test pattern for a few seconds, then displayed something that caught his attention immediately. To Sully, it appeared to be a blurry vertical test pattern, one he'd not yet seen, which meant that it was probably one of the feeds coming in from—

The sound of millions of buzzing bees roared forth from all audio equipment in the complex. Somewhere on the edge of their mortal perception, it seemed almost for a moment as if some disembodied voice had called to them. Yet the forceful power and deadly amplitude of the signal was far too potent for the mortal psyche to process, as it had been specifically shaped, after all, for the immortal Fae to perceive.

The initial calling heard by the unfortunate crew of the Seawolf had been but a mere shard of the collective call now issued forth by the Watchers via the artifice of the now fully operative Weave of the Watchers. Its power naturally was many orders of magnitude more potent, and it appeared to become focused and amplified even more when its waveforms were propagated by mundane audiovisual equipment and experienced by mortals, who lacked the necessary immortal chakras to process it. Thus, a feedback loop formed, and the bodies and souls of mortals withered before it. This interesting, unexpected chaotic artifact was immediately known, and experienced, by those within the confines of the command center.

Desperate, howling screams erupted from the airman nearest the screen with the curious test pattern on it. Sully, his ears buzzing, immediately moved to his door, opening it wide. "Get that man some—"

Another airman began to scream, rising from his seat at the station nearest to the screen, his hands pressed tightly against his headset.

Sully's attention was diverted again, this time by the sight of all twelve projection screens filling with various angles and modalities of coverage of the Weave of the Watchers, which was materializing fully now on high Earth orbit, the Song of the Sidhe surging forth from it, down to the mortal world. At that precise moment, fully half of the personnel in the room began to scream. They writhed in agony, some with their hands pressed to the earbuds of their headsets, some with their hands covering their eyes. To his side, the soldier guarding his door collapsed to his knees, hands clutched to his ears. As Sully watched, morbidly fascinated, the guard's hands began to pulsate and bulge, the skin on the back of his hands and wrists cracking, bleeding, then peeling off after but a few pulsations. Bony fingers clutched at his bulging cranium, sinking deeply into it with a sickening crunch, where they spastically began to dig into suddenly liquid gray matter. In the space of but a few seconds, the entire body of the soldier liquified and spilled onto the floor. Only his gun, web gear, and a few miscellaneous metal and plastic artifacts remained.

Chaos ruled the command center. Sully observed, horrified, incapable of sane action, as several officers leaped from Tier 2 down to the command center floor, their bodies cracking open like dropped eggs, black blood and greenish bile running in rivulets. Terrific screams wailed like some choir of the damned as more soldiers on the floor began to clutch and scratch at their heads. All the projection screens displayed the pulsating alien constellation, which seemed to vibrate with life of its own, burning its image into Sully's fevered brain. Unable to resist its buzzing, siren call, he fell to his knees, mouth agape, arms useless at his sides.

"General! General!" someone screamed at him. A dim shape appeared before him. "C'mon, help me with him," the voice of the dim shape asked another approaching shadow.

"Where do we go?" the second voice inquired as Sully's hearing began to fade. "Where do we—"

"Dead—" General Sullivan managed to say. There would be neither sign nor signal to trigger it, he vaguely recalled. But he knew that if the body count reached a certain percentage...

"What?" came the first voice. "Yes, sir, we know they're dead. We're the only ones left."

"No!" the general said, his eyes suddenly opening wide, affixing the soldier before him with his wild gaze. "Deadman. Deadman switch. I have to override it. Bring me to a station. Any of them. Hurry!"

"Hurry up," the first voice called to the second. "Help me get him down to a station."

Strong hands pulled the general down the stairs to Tier 1, where the going became treacherous due to the still-writhing bodies and expansive pools of noisome body fluids on the floor. Finally, seemingly an eternity later, the two soldiers had the general in a chair in front of one of the stations. Desperately, they sought for then found the correct headset for the station, prying it from the still bubbling skull of its former owner then helping the general steady its microphone before his quivering lips.

"This is General Ryan Sullivan, code word Babe, Deadman override code one, niner, one, niner, two, zero, four, seven, seven, seven. Acknowledge. Over." He paused a moment for the automated reply. Nothing. "This is General Ryan Sullivan, code word Babe, Deadman override code one, niner, one, niner, two, zero, four, seven, seven, seven. Acknowledge. Over." Still nothing.

"What is he doing?" the second soldier asked the first.

"That's the Deadman override code. He's trying to deactivate it, because it probably went to automatic failsafe once our casualty count rose above a certain percentage."

"What happens if he doesn't shut it off?"

"Game over," the second soldier said flatly, even as the general desperately began a third and final iteration of the switching sequence.

"Game over? You mean like an automatic launch?"

"Yeah, man. There's a new protocol in place that forces an automatic launch of our nukes if any particular command goes under a certain personnel threshold. The Russians have one. So do the Chinese, we think. Probably all nuclear powers do. The override is supposed to reset the count or cancel it. If not, then it all goes up, just in case we were losing a nuclear war. Deadman. Never thought about it much, but that's exactly what it is. For everyone."

"Cancel it!" General Sullivan bellowed, his gravel voice quaking. "Fucking cancel it, you fucker! We're not dead! Cancel it!"

Above them, on all the screens, the Weave of the Watchers began to hum resonantly, the outline of its perimeter suddenly growing blacker than the space behind it.

The two soldiers near the general both began to scream, sinking to their knees, clutching their heads in their hands. Mercifully, General Sullivan's eyes rolled back into his head, and he collapsed back into the confines of his chair, the headset slipping from his hands and onto the offal-strewn floor.

eVo.144.000.mOd.11.sCe6 | EARTH | UNITED STATES | PENNSYLVANIA | RAVEN ROCK MOUNTAIN COMPLEX | SITE R

"WHAT IN GOD'S NAME..." President Watt whispered to himself, his ears whistling loudly.

Both Bobby and Jim stared, along with Watt, at the brightly flashing "LAUNCH" indicators visible through the clear Lexan panels of the secure command room. Though chaos reigned in the command center outside their secure room, the indicators were plainly visible. Wide eyed, the three men gaped at one another.

"That's impossible. I still have the biscuit," Watt informed them, snatching up the plastic card that held the most recent Gold Codes on them; the codes that he would have used, as POTUS, to authenticate his identity and then authorize any possible nuclear launch. Outside the secure room, his figure half-hidden by the door, a screaming military policeman raised his own sidearm to his head, firing point-blank into his temple. The shot, though muted, caused the men at the table to jerk reflexively.

"Deadman," Jim mouthed to himself in a dull monotone, his gnarled, hoary hands pressed over his eyes. "It's the Deadman

Protocol," he said louder, slamming his hands down on the tabletop. "That's impossible, unless we're all already dead."

"Oh God," Bobby breathed, desperately fumbling with one of his tablets. "Under Operation GLORY SAVE, it's global and automatic. Those are our global 'unite to fight' agreements. Every nuclear power will launch, in unison, against any verified alien threat, if any other country does so first. It's what we agreed upon."

"And in our hubris," Watt said, "we thought it would never happen. All of the top leadership in all of the nuclear powers would have had to have been dead. That was the contingency. The impossible contingency. The Extinction Level Event contingency, in case ET actually did show up one day, and wasn't as benevolent and kind as we'd hoped."

Jim stared hard at Watt. "It's impossible, Jon. Impossible. We'd all have to be dead before it's ever on the table at all. But it happened anyway. It happened anyway. Why?"

Swiping his index finger several times, rapidly, Bobby came to the screen that confirmed the event. Blinking his eyes twice, trying to dispel what he saw in plain American English on the screen, he slowly turned the tablet so that the other men could see it.

"Deadman Protocol activated," it read in simple red text over a lone black rectangular box.

President Watt's eyes grew heavy as he struggled to contain his fear. "History will judge us harshly. The human race just welcomed its first extraterrestrial visitors by launching every nuke we have in our arsenals at them."

Jim looked at the President and said calmly, "Mr. President, there won't be anyone *left* to judge us. We haven't just attacked the aliens – we've annihilated the planet."

eVo.144.000.mOd.11.sCe7 | EARTH | THE WEAVE OF THE WATCHERS

AMONG THE WEAVE, THE Watchers waited, poised yet eager to receive a reply from their first seeds, the Fae. They were as expectant mothers, ready to hear the first birth-screams from their newborn child. Yet, there was no reply save for silence.

Careful and exacting, the Watchers issued their call again, and yet again, reaching out to the Fae and the Song of the Sidhe. Nine times they called. Nine times, there was nothing.

Then, as they made inquiries among their own number as whether to issue a tenth call, they noted that the second seeds, the humans, had chosen most disrespectfully to strike out at them. The Mindtouch among the collective of the Watchers regarding this was unanimous in agreement, save for one, the constant rebel, who simply would never agree with anything. In this particular case, at this specific time, the decision made by the rebel to abstain on this issue would have far-reaching consequences, for it would lead to the first time in the aeons-long history of the Watchers that one of their number exercised individual free will.

Despite that particular deviation, the Watchers decided, almost collectively, that the best course of action would be to allow the human's crude thermonuclear devices to perform their mission, to strike the Weave directly, then the Watchers would simply bend and bind their energies into the Weave. This would serve multiple purposes simultaneously, including sparing the Earth below them from any further contamination, and possibly introducing unwanted perturbations into the precise tasks assigned to them by the Lightbringer himself. It was the Equation of Resolution, and it therefore came to pass.

6,765 megatons of combined power delivered through the agency of ground-based ICBMs from almost a dozen countries, along with 4,181 megatons of on-orbit assets from seven countries, including the aptly named Horus Constellation, impacted the Weave of the Watchers over the next several minutes. Where a warhead would strike the Weave, there would be momentary chaos as incredible force and fusion attempted to impose its kinetic and thermal will upon the construct. The almost ephemeral strands of the Weave between and among the nodes writhed and strained during the first few seconds of each impact, flickering and blinking in the narrow human visual spectrum. However, after the initial phase of each thermonuclear event, the visual oscillations of the strands settled back into vibrant life, the kilotons and megatons of thermonuclear fury safely shunted into the multidimensional energy matrix of the Weave.

During the impotent thermonuclear onslaught, a small subset of the Watchers noticed that there were multiple millions of resonant harmonic signals issuing from the Earth below. Their attention now drawn to this anomaly, the small subset of Watchers rapidly divined that the second seeds had created more corruption than was noted initially; that, in addition to massive stockpiles of nuclear weapons which were incapable of being launched into orbit, the Earth was suffering from a veritable pox of artificially created radionuclides and fissionable material. The corruption was pandemic. Total. It ranged in configuration and mass from a few mere atoms of the disgusting anti-life plutonium wedged within the alveoli in the lungs of almost all air-breathing life on Earth, to small molecular clusters widely distributed among the populace of the second seeds in a wide variety of devices and apparatus. The corruption was pandemic, even unto massive macroscale clusters of highly energetic radionuclides, some actively serving as sources of power while others remained in various states of inaction or primitively attempted storage.

It was decided almost immediately upon sharing this information with the collective that the Watchers would be required to remove these corrupting anti-life artifacts from the clamorous grasp of the second seeds, the walking apes who had, in their inestimable hubris, made plans for nuclear war. They truly did not grasp the antithesis of the dread chaos of the anti-life.

This action was integrated into the current task of bending and binding the launched thermonuclear devices into the Weave. It required no more than the slightest addition of power to the matrix of the Weave, the mere bat of an eyelash or blink of an eye, for the Watchers to reach out to all of the sources of contagion below on Earth and transport them instantly to the waiting confines of the Weave, where they were integrated seamlessly into the ongoing Equation of Resolution. As a mere afterthought, the bulk of the second seeds' thermonuclear devices, so pathetically slow with their primitive rocket propulsion, were made to accelerate to the Weave, if only to reach the inevitable crescendo faster. Impossibly, their relatively fragile structures, now infused with projected Hekatek, showed no compromise. All possible perturbations that could introduce unwanted chaos into the Weave were therefore accounted for and mitigated.

Unseen and unknown, it was during the distraction of the bombardment and the subsequent modification of the Equation of Resolution that the rebel illegally made its own personal decision to permanently depart the collective, using its own bending and binding capabilities to tap into a nearby strand of absorbed thermonuclear flux and mask its stealthy transport to the planet below. The rebel had reasoned that, by the time that the Watchers had realized that it was not simply ignoring them as it was inclined to do, their mission would be over, and its existence among the collective when the collective itself was no longer in existence would be irrelevant. Thus did the rebel exercise its own free will, choosing to continue its own existence, rather than succumb to the Lightbringer's will.

Despite the spectacular orbital lightshow, it became perfectly clear after several minutes to all interested observers that the human's massive nuclear attack had no lasting effect on the construct.

Despite the failure to communicate with their first seeds — despite the quite uncivilized attack upon them by the primitive and savage humans and the resultant necessity of invoking the Equation of Resolution to purge the Earth of the second seeds' unfortunate flirtation with the anti-life — the Watchers adhered explicitly and almost without deviation to their allotted schedule. Though saddened by the lack of communication from their precious firstborn, the Watchers took solace in the fact that the Lightbringer's will would soon be done, for now came the instantiation of the Omega Module, and the Lightbringer's Sigil soon would manifest to judge the Earth and its denizens.

eVo.144.000.mOd.11.sCe8 | EARTH | THE OMEGA MODULE | THE LIGHTBRINGER'S SIGIL

THE OMEGA MODULE HAD at long last been instantiated. The time of the advent of the Lightbringer's Sigil now was at hand.

The Lightbringer's Sigil heralded the imminent transliteration of the human species from a collective state of chaotic genetic expression, a long fallow wild garden of souls and so-called junk DNA that had been purposefully left untended, into the first phase of morphogenetic terraforming, morphic resonance, and soul-shaping. Thousands upon thousands of years, and billions upon billions of genetic recombinations into an innumerable host of disparate, chaotic, and mostly useless expressions, now was at an end.

Now, by command of the Lightbringer himself, there would be order, and in that new order would come great power. First, however, by necessity, there would be death on a scale never seen on Earth, not even during the greatest Extinction Level Event of all, the Permian-Triassic Extinction. Purification demanded a high price; the ultimate price, in the overwhelming majority of cases. Almost all would die for the very few to live.

Of a sudden, with no forewarning, the Lightbringer's Sigil abruptly began to materialize in the false light of the zodiacal dawn, high in the sky, its 11,235-mile-long construct slowly manifesting on high Earth orbit, casting suffuse prismatic light into the bleeding, fearful vestiges of night.

The construct of the sigil was clear to anyone who had studied the sciences, not merely the biological but more specifically the mathematical. The sigil was a multicolored, prismatic strand of DNA, though on a truly titanic scale, its long axis roughly equal to a diameter-and-a-half of the Earth itself. Although difficult to perceive initially, due to its massive scale, it was slowly rotating about its longitudinal axis, widdershins. While superficially like a typical human strand of DNA, it was in fact a true triple helix, and not a double-helix. Mathematically, its fractal components were of a superior order to those of the mere double-helix. The golden ratio was clear and in effect throughout its composite structure; phi was inherent, and closely bound. There also was clear indication of the golden section, not merely if the structure were viewed as a cross-section from the top, but clearly demonstrated from other perspectives now that three helices were in play, rather than the conventional two.

More precisely, the sigil exhibited multidimensional, non-Euclidean properties which, if normal humans would have been capable of discerning them, might have allowed for some novel solutions for Hilbert's Fourth Problem. For, indeed, there was Fibonacci resonance among the many possible scales of recursion, and they clearly mapped along certain specific multidimensional coordinates which could have accurately been bound by their simultaneous deviations from a composite of the *spira mirabilis*, the Fibonacci spiral, and the uniquely mapped instantiation of the non-Euclidean golden spiral attributes of the sigil itself.

From the Luciferian perspective of Helel, the Lightbringer, this meant simply that his sigil hid more than it revealed to casual inspection, for it had an inherent higher-dimensional identity as an admixture to its more conventional standard identity. And what it hid was its power to massively resonate with all forms of spiral DNA in all things living, and by its resonance "judge" them as worthy of being subject to the forced transcendence of the soul from a mortal chakra count of seven to an immortal chakra count of nine. For the eternally fractal nature of the cosmos did indeed link one's spiral DNA structure to one's soul, and the manipulation of the former caused the manipulation of the latter, as ever and as always.

And it came to pass that the Lightbringer's Sigil did fully manifest itself high above Earth, and all living souls were made to know its presence.

eVo.144.000.mOd.11.sCe9 | EARTH | THE LIGHTBRINGER'S SIGIL | THE BENDING AND BINDING

EXACTLY 144,000 MILLISECONDS after the Weave of the Watchers was completed, the Lightbringer's Sigil initiated its purpose and executed a plan which had been crafted long before Sol had been reborn from the stellar pyre of its progenitor star. For the span of exactly 14,400 milliseconds, the sigil accrued power from both Source and Void simultaneously, forming an infinitely dangerous conduit between and serving as a nexus for the highest possible scale of cosmic energies. Forging and re-forging its own essence innumerable times per attosecond. Existing and acting beyond even the bottommost tier of the Planck regime. Uniting both Source and Void along its infinitely fractal construction at all possible scales. Shaping this aggregate energy into a most potent hybrid implementation of both magick and technomagick: Hekatek.

The Phase of the Bending and Binding now was complete.

eVo.144.000.mOd.11.sCe10 | EARTH | THE LIGHTBRINGER'S SIGIL | THE HARVEST OF THE CHOSEN

AT THE TERMINATION of the Phase of Bending and Binding, the Lightbringer's Sigil initiated the Harvest of the Chosen.

At once, terribly, with an inexorable power which no mortal could ever hope to resist, the sigil's newly forged primal matrices instantiated a cosmically empowered resonance with all living things on Earth, under Earth, and above Earth. The idealized imprint borne by the sigil and now being projected upon all living things within the collective biome of the Earth instantly and universally tagged, encoded, and judged all genetic forms within all living things on Earth.

The equation was simple: All living things not exceeding a certain threshold of genetic evolution were culled; their own genetic data being instantly subject to destructive harmonic influence from the implacable sigil. Those which exceeded this threshold were instead subject to a harmonic shaping, which, in its sublime passage, fused and advanced certain desired attributes from among the few surviving hosts. Shaping and weaving them into a new, more stable, more powerful form and format which was, in fact, quite like its own.

The inferior died such that the superior could live.

The Harvest of the Chosen endured for 1,440 milliseconds. At its end, the sigil disengaged its union with Source and Void, its primal energies now spent. Quietly and rapidly it quenched its manifestation on this plane in a mere 144 milliseconds, abruptly vanishing from sight, returning to its unknown and incomprehensible realm.

As the sigil vanished, the remaining smaller entities, whose form resembled that of the sigil itself, initiated the Final Dissolution, which caused a particularly destructive counter-harmonic to consume both the pilots of the entities – the K'ryl, of the Igigi, known as the Watchers – and their remarkable DNA-like spacecraft. With remarkably crafted precision, the counter-harmonics fell upon all the craft and their pilots, rendering them into an interesting collective subset and fractal iteration of their former forms. Rainbow fractal nanoparticles then began to stream down to Earth. From on high the stuff of their souls slowly rained down; a final, fateful, mysterious gift to the newly reborn.

Now, at last, the Lightbringer's Sigil had delivered its final judgement, and the Weirding of Man was complete.

eVo.144.000.mOd.11.sCe11 | EARTH | JAPAN | TOKYO | MEIJI JINGU STADIUM

MORE THAN 28,000 LOUD, noisy, and boisterous baseball fans filled the Meiji Jingu Stadium in Tokyo, Japan. The late afternoon April day was beautiful, with the Springtime temperature a leisurely 19 degrees Celsius. The Yakult Swallows hosted the Yomiuri Giants, their Central League rivals. Hundreds of hand-painted signs and banners urged the Swallows to victory. Multiple pockets of chanting filled the stands, as clusters of fans of both teams began to chant and counter-chant, vying with each other to see who could generate the most good luck for their chosen team.

Amaterasu "Ami" Kurohoshi and her three friends sat up in the nosebleed section of the left field bleachers. In accordance with the "Anime@Baseball Night" event promoted by the Yakult Swallows, they had spent hours earlier in the day shopping for appropriate cosplay outfits, only to realize, too near to game time, that, despite Tokyo's reputation as Anime Central, authentic cosplay actually required many hours of developing and customizing one's outfit. To their collective chagrin and slight embarrassment, they had been forced to genericize their outfits, settling for black leather jackets and blue-highlighted double pony tails.

They had made a most solemn pact, if they were actually asked by someone who they were trying to emulate, to say that they were trying to be an Yngwie Malmsteen tribute band. Just in case such happened, Rin had brought along her older brother's Stratocaster. Not that the opening of Deep Purple's "Smoke on the Water" would fool anyone into thinking that she could play Yngwie well enough to be the guitarist for such a tribute band, but it would at least fool the casual. And maybe draw the attention of some cute boys.

It was thus that Ami, Rin, Jin, and Katsumi found themselves in Meiji Jingu Stadium, up in the nosebleed section of the left field bleachers, disconsolate, bored, and virtually alone though in a sea of thousands.

"When can we leave?" Rin asked Katsumi, who was busy checking out her Android. She leaned heavily into the headstock of the guitar, which she had nestled between her feet.

Shrugging in return, Katsumi suddenly squealed, rocking back and forth.

"What is it, Sumi?" Ami asked as Rin and Jin leaned in.

"MCZ's set a new date at Nation Stadium! I can't believe it!"

"We have to get tickets immediately!" Rin cheered. "Let's go!" she said as she tried to stand up to leave.

Ami pulled her back down, firmly. "Not until the game is over. You want to show disrespect to our team?"

"Ah, who cares?" Rin said disconsolately. "We're so far up here that no one can even see us. We could jump over the edge, screaming to our deaths, and no one would even hear it!"

They laughed, knowing it was true. The crowd noise was as loud as a rock concert.

"I've an idea," Ami told her friends. "Why don't we..." she trailed off as something caught her attention.

Something had just appeared overhead, flickering like wild karaoke stage lights, high in the sky, commanding silently all who gazed upon it with an alien presence of sheer power. Its multicolored, dancing filaments scrawled themselves across the sky from horizon to horizon, as if they were being spun by titanic invisible spiders. Its scale was enormous, filling most of the sky in mere seconds. Many others in the crowd had noticed it, and were now pointing up at it, attempting to determine what it was.

"Look look look look look..." Ami breathlessly informed her three friends, her arm raised high, finger pointing at the materializing alien entity above.

The Stratocaster and the Android hit the hard bleacher floor simultaneously, even as the last echoes of the crowd's chants dissipated to nothingness. Almost as one, more than 28,000 craned their necks to gaze upon the Weave of the Watchers. For a moment, there was blissful, pregnant silence as no one dared breathe. Then, the sound of the buzzing of millions of bees suddenly manifested itself in the air above the stadium. A heartbeat later, the stadium's lights flickered then exploded in a crashing fusillade like cannon fire, sending shattered glass and steel shrapnel down into the bleachers.

Rin screamed first, joined almost immediately by everyone near her. Fighting a sudden sense of nausea, Ami saw that, beyond the stadium's confines, the early evening of the Tokyo skyline were rapidly blacking out.

"What do we do? What do we do?" Rin shrieked, seeking an answer from her friends as the crowd near them began to bolt upright.

"Don't panic," Ami told her. She looked at Jin and Katsumi. "Cluster up around me. Stay still. Let the crowd go first, or they'll trample us to death."

While her friends did as she told them, Ami assessed the scene. The crowd was panicked and dangerous. They were up too high to risk scaling the wall and simply jumping down. The fall would surely cripple or kill them. If they could just give the crowd a few minutes to clear out, they probably would be able to make a break for it without getting knocked down and trampled.

"Ami! I can't stand that noise!" Rin screamed in her ear. "It hurts! It hurts!"

"It's going to be okay, Rin," Ami told her, clutching her tightly, pulling all of them together.

There was an abrupt cessation of sound, absurdly enough, considering the size of the crowd. Ami felt a compulsion to look up again at the frightful sky. She fought it for a moment, dully noting that it now was suddenly darker in the stadium; no lights shone, not even from cell phones or the stadium's emergency lighting system. Yet, from above, there came a fantastic light of rainbows, and her gaze rose to meet it despite her mind's screams to close her eyes tightly against it.

From nowhere came the Lightbringer's Sigil, abruptly manifesting overhead as if it were slowly being born from Heaven itself.

Then, as it manifested wholly and entirely in Earth orbit, there came an unseen wind which clutched at and tore into the souls of every human being in the stadium. A fresh chorus of screams erupted, en masse, from the people in the crowd as high order alien power shouted and screamed back at them silently, maddeningly, into their minds, bidding them to join in its idiot siren's song. Join, or die, it bade them as a swirling audible hum began to dance about their ears. Hands sought both ears and eyes as people attempted futilely to deny the sight of the sigil, the sound of its song.

Rocking back and forth, her gaze affixed on the sigil, Ami finally lost control and began to scream, her hands clutched awkwardly to her head. However, she could not hear her own voice. She could not feel her throat contort over the violent *thrum-thrum-thrum* which now threatened to crush her body against those of her friends, who reeled drunkenly in pain beside her.

Horribly, Ami smelled the sudden stench of bowels as, next to her, Rin's intestines popped out from under her black leather jacket, spilling over the tier of bleacher seats below them, writhing like the spastic tentacles of an octopus out of water. To her left and right, Jin and Katsumi suddenly began to melt from the head down like wax statues under an acetylene torch, their hair matting into blue thatches which rested now atop unviolated black leather jackets. Before her, and immediately around her, she sensed more horror, but she refused to acknowledge it. The stench was so noisome, so pungent, that it reminded her of walking next to the trash dumpsters outside of a sushi restaurant while open manhole covers spewed their noxious scents like foul incense.

Vomiting through the coverage of her fingers, which still were clutched to her face, Ami added her own refuse to the sea of human filth before her. This instinctive human act galvanized her, causing her to realize that she had not yet melted like her friends. Clearing the last of the bitter vomit from her mouth, she willed herself to remove her hands from her face. Above her, the strange alien entity continued its humming and thrumming. Trying desperately to ignore the horror and chaos around her as thousands died, and as thousands more screamed and panicked, attempting to flee the scene, slipping and sliding over steaming liquid offal like drunken sailors, she locked her eyes on the sigil. It became her focus, seeming to become even larger than it truly was. It became the totality of her attention as she wished nothing more than to never again see or remember the hardcore disaster scene currently playing out around her.

Ami just wished she could make it all stop. Make it all go away. All the blood. All the guts. Sushi fish guts and half-digested soft noodles. Stinky, nasty, ugly things all around her. If she could just make it stop. Make it all go away...

Black light danced along the field of Ami's vision. Initially confused, for a second she wondered if the evil kami overhead had caused the shift in colors. She blinked, her gaze moving slowly down to her hands, which now seemed to be buried in deep, black shadows. Shocked, she stood straight up, her hands now raised before her eyes. The darkness seemed to dance in syncopation with the sigil. Her peripheral vision now began to pick up more of the darkness, which now appeared to be issuing forth from her like a river of squid's ink. The darkness manifested itself around her, rapidly expanding around her in great concentric circles. Concentric circles of death, for all flesh that the darkness touched, it consumed instantly with no sound to mark its passage. Only a brief afterimage of the matter, streaking in multiple frames, leaving behind many iteratively decaying and annihilating images of itself, as it fell into Ami's projected darkness.

The blue hair on the nape of her neck buzzed and stood straight up.

"Go away!" she commanded, her voice booming unnaturally, drowning out the confusing den of white noise filling the stadium. "Go away!" she said again, raising her hands high over her head. Black spokes of light began to filter out through the expanding concentric circles of jet-black nothingness emanating from her. The spokes of black light, eight in number, formed the Sign of Chaos as their equidistant spacing became known after the first space among the concentric circles. "GO AWAY!"

With that, Ami became the epicenter of a quarter-kilometer diameter of chaotic destruction as, for the shortest, necessary span of time, a genuine chaotic singularity metaphysically manifested within her, spanning all of her newly actualized chakras. There, centered at the second to last row of bleachers in Meiji Jingu Stadium, a miniature black hole manifested on Earth, instantaneously causing a massive frame-dragging effect in the local spacetime, violently shearing unto shredded entrained photons what had been actual Earth-bound matter into a phantasmagoric mockery of all things sane. Sound, light, energy all merged, stacked, then sheared and shredded, leaving behind, in the span of several seconds, a bizarre maelstrom of imprinted chaotic images of what had been only moments before flesh and blood, souls and steel.

Then, it was over, and Ami fell suddenly, screaming, from her formerly real bleacher seat in the nosebleed section in the left field of Meiji Jingu Stadium to the waiting nothingness below her.

eVo.144.000.mOd.11.sCe12 | EARTH | UNITED STATES | NEW YORK | LAKE PLACID | MCKENZIE MOUNTAIN WILDERNESS | THE ZEFF BROTHERS BUNKER

THE NEW YORK STATE Department of Environmental Conservation's Commissioner had been easy enough to bribe. The Zeff Brothers – Abe, David, and Sheldon – had only to promise him that he, his wife, and their Yorkshire Terrier, Trixie, would be allowed to join them when the time came. That, and a cool two million in small bills, and the deal would be done. The Zeffs would then use their collective multiple billions to grease the right palms, and to bribe the right local, county, and state officials, including their privately hired, off-the-books union work details. And, naturally, their personal tribute to the Genovese family, to get the rest of the job done.

A curious coincidence of $112,358,132.13 USD and eleven months and two weeks later, and the Zeffs were the proud owners of an elite, fully secured, fully autonomous, hidden, underground survival bunker.

A not so curious coincidence, arranged via another equally large transfer – this time couched entirely within the legal boundaries of a most lucrative real estate deal between two holding companies representing, through an array of shell corporations, the Zeff Family and the Genovese Family – saw the end of the Department of Environmental Conservation's Commissioner, his wife, and his dog Trixie, in a most unfortunate house fire. This, along with the gradual yet inexorable disappearance of the several local workers who had asked too many questions, or who had lingered too long near the construction site, served to wedge a potent firewall between the general public and the Zeffs, who ultimately were just asking for everyone to respect their privacy. Well, their privacy to do what they wanted to do on conserved, public land, and not get caught building an illegal and entirely unlicensed survival bunker in upstate New York.

The three Zeff brothers – Abe, David, and Sheldon – had made their pact to protect the Zeff legacy over the ashes of their dearly departed parents, Abraham and Shirley. Nothing so trivial as nuclear war, natural disaster, or civil war would catch them unaware and incapable of defending themselves and their families. Their bloodline would continue, they swore to each other, no matter which moral or ethical lines they had to cross in order to achieve their goal.

Their pact began a four year mission to determine the right spot, close enough to get to within an hour via helicopter, or a few short hours by car, yet still remote and secure enough both to protect them and allow them to maintain their relative anonymity. In the scenarios that they had imagined protecting themselves from, there would always have to be a subtle approach on their part that would not alarm their hundreds of employees in Manhattan or the local media, which certainly would notice, probably due to social media, that three of the Forbes Richest had suddenly gone missing. Thus, they had almost immediately concluded that secret collusion between the Zeff Family and the most powerful mob family on the East Coast would be the best way for their plan to reach fruition. And thus it did.

The devil is always in the details, or so Abe Sr. would often tell his sons. He was wise enough to have given the three of them a massive leg up on their competition by founding the investment banking firm which bore the family name. And the three of them had been wise enough to fully heed his admonition by hiring the mob to do deep background on certain bodyguards, nannies, and a family doctor to ensure that they came without familial attachments, spouses, children, parents or grandparents, and even pets. The Zeffs reasoned, correctly, that the unattached would be more easily malleable to shape into their schemes, to be read into it over time, and to accept it with proper gravitas and thanks for being so fortunate as to having been selected by the Zeffs to survive the apocalypse in comfort and style. Thus, the mob provided them with carefully screened lists of potential employees, and the Zeffs did their own due diligence, selecting only the best among them all.

Those chosen would of course have to be, primarily, without attachments. Also, of good health, morals, ethics, demeanor, and hygiene. No one wanted to rebreathe the filtered air tainted by horrendous body odor or terminal flatulence, so the physician was hired on first, then briefed as to what he was to check the other potential candidates for. Dr. Amil Khan terminated his lucrative Manhattan private practice, transferring his private stable of wealthy patients to his partners, then eagerly accepting the offer from the Zeffs, which instantly made him twenty times wealthier than he already had been.

Dr. Khan then went about his task of medically screening several dozen potential candidates. To this was added the task of preparing detailed descriptions of which high tech medical apparatus and supplies would be required to maintain the health of approximately 20 people over a potential span of five years, with both Plan B and Plan C in place and accommodated properly for longer durations.

This he did, and thus it came to pass in a relatively short time that the Zeffs, their immediate family members, three bodyguards with multidisciplinary training in several fields, including HVAC, IT, and EMS, three chefs with additional military and general repair training, and three nannies with RN backgrounds were evaluated and hired on. Thus prepared, they were each assigned to the Zeffs, one group each per brother, giving them time to integrate themselves into their respective families, learn their ways, and adapt to optimize their protection of them. Over the several months that this transpired, they were groomed and read into the plan. There were no defections, which had been predicted already by their psychological profiles, which had been compiled prior to their officially being hired. That, and the notice that they now would never have to work any job after this one and still retire rich and totally secure thanks to the seven-figures now in their private accounts, sealed the deal.

Within an hour and thirty minutes of the Pope's declaration of Holy War, the Zeffs, their families, and their private details were safely ensconced within their bunker complex, which occupied more than 100,000-square-foot of the sturdy bedrock beneath the McKenzie Mountain Wilderness almost exactly halfway between Moose Pond and Lake Placid. Filled with a potent admixture of adrenaline and cocaine, the three brothers held council long into the night, gathered about the round table in their private command center, dozens of channels of media playing in a 360-degree arc on immaculate 4k monitors. They had invested over a million dollars just to keep their compound wired up and connected to the outside world via a communications system which included satellite relays disguised as trees, and several miles of secure, redundant cabling and customized wi-fi.

Over hand-rolled Cohibas and several bottles of rare single-malt Dalmore, the brothers marveled at their wisdom, fortune, and grace to have been so prepared. The world was going to hell around them, but they and their families would ride out the storm, safe and secure, in their private fortress. If disaster occurred, they would be safe, and, thanks to prior preparation, would be able to secure their status as rich and powerful men in the post-apocalyptic world, thanks to their precious metals, guns, stocks, supplies, medical capability, and, of course, their hired mercenaries. And if disaster did not occur, they would still be able to run their businesses remotely from their temporary "vacation" location, thanks to their advanced communications equipment and some simple misdirection: Their private Gulfstreams had flown, unoccupied save by their pilots and small crew, to Ibiza. Abe Sr. would be proud that they had tended to all of the devil's details.

Early in the morning, the day after her beloved Pope had lost his mind and declared Holy War against the followers of the Prophet, Vida Maria Rosario Gutierrez, CRNP, knelt before the small votive display atop her single, simple chest-of-drawers, alone in her small but comfortable private room. Her prayers to Mother Mary were simple. She prayed for the soul of her dear Alejandro, her husband, who had succumbed to pancreatic cancer seven years earlier, despite her own personal best efforts to see him safely through the terrible gauntlet of adjuvant chemotherapy he had suffered through after the Whipple procedure had failed to resolve the issue. So many weeks her precious Alejandro had lingered between life and death, her love and constant care his lifeline and anchor to the world of the living, she had believed. Now, she was not so sure, because Mother Mary had not granted her husband succor in his final trial before the Lord.

Still, Vida's faith, though shaken, was never shattered. So she prayed every morning after rising, before attending to her own daily needs, for her husband's immortal soul was her concern, now and for so long as she lived. Only her charge to care for Abbey's and Abe's twins, Ada and Abraham Zeff III, gave meaning to her otherwise sad and lonely life. Despite her training, she had fallen in love with the children, and her emotional connection to them was all she had now to hold her to this world.

Or so Vida had thought. For, in the moment before the Lightbringer's Sigil appeared over Earth, Vida, alone before her small votive display in her lonely room, heard her candle speak to her in Mother Mary's voice.

"Vida..." the Mother of God whispered silently.

Stunned into inaction, Vida's Ave Maria died in her suddenly constricted throat.

"Vida..." came the soft whisper as the small, white votive candle's flame flickered slightly, as if a small breeze passed over it.

"Madre?" Vida whispered back, her bright umber eyes moving left and right as she scanned her room for the presence of some prankster. Nothing.

"I am with you, Vida," the voice told her. It seemed to speak simultaneously in both Spanish and English.

Chills erupted down Vida's neck. Faced with the enormity of what she now knew – that el Papa had been right about the Apocalypse after all, and now Mary herself was, impossibly, speaking directly to her – her lips pursed and trembled as she fought back tears of awe, joy, and relief. If Mary was speaking directly to her, then she had been hearing her prayers for Alejandro this whole time these past years.

"I know," Vida stammered. With determination and will, she steadied herself and fixed her gaze intently on the candle. An image of light began to resolve itself, confined within the boundary of the candle's tiny flame.

"Vida, I want you to call for your children. Call them to you, now."

"Ada! Abraham!" Vida cried out, delaying not a second. Immediately, there came an insistent banging on the metal door of her room. She heard the children crying loudly now. Bolting up, she was at the door, clutching at the handle before she could even process her action. She opened the heavy metal door, and the twins burst into her room, moving past her, screaming wildly.

"Vida! Vida!" Ada cried, her tiny arms wrapping around Vida's thigh. "Mommy got sick and fell down!"

"She fell down! She's sick!" Abe added, grabbing onto his sister, kicking at the door as Vida quickly slammed it shut and locked it.

"Vida," came the voice again. "Come near to me, and I will protect you."

"Protect us from what?" Vida asked, the children wailing and crying. They appeared not to have heard the voice, she noted as she guided them to the chest-of-drawers and its votive display, where the single white candle's flame now appeared to be twice as bright as it had been before. In the boundary of its flame, she recognized an image of DNA, or something that very nearly resembled it. In this image, however, the DNA's backbone appeared to have additional bands or steps, and each of its... of its three helices, she now saw, peering closer, were pulsating, silently flashing like some Christmas tree light pattern. She now knew, without being directly answered, what Mother Mary was going to protect them from.

"Oh no, oh no, oh no," Vida said under her breath, bringing the children in closer to her, her arms around them both. "Ada? Abe?" she asked, willing her voice to be calm for their sake. They both nodded, seeking her eyes. "Remember the prayer I taught you? I want you to say it along with me. Okay?"

Complying at once, their voices still racked with sobs, they joined Vida in another Ave Maria.

As the distant, muffled yet unmistakable sound of automatic gunfire broke out, accompanied by the brief sound of abruptly silenced screams, the voice spoke to Vida again: "Pray for them, Vida. Pray for all of them, everywhere; those who now endure the horror and havoc of the Lightbringer's Sigil."

"What?" Vida asked, surprised, as the children continued to pray between their sobs. "*El sigilo del diablo*? The devil's sigil? What do you mean, Madre?"

The candle flickered for one moment, the image within it dancing and turning slowly, even as the sound of more automatic gunfire filtered into the room.

"It is the sign of the beginning of the End of All Things, Vida," the voice told her. "The Lightbringer himself walks the Earth now."

"Oh my god..." Vida whimpered, crushing the children to her. A low, moaning *thrum-thrum-thrum* now reached her ears, even over the sounds of screaming and gunfire outside her room.

Abruptly, startlingly, a heavy thump hit the outside of the door, causing Vida and twins to cry out in alarm.

A faint voice came from the other side of the door. "Vida! Vida! It's me, Madison! Let me in! Help me! Open the door! Open the door!"

The banging intensified. Vida took a half-step toward the door, recognizing the voice of one of her fellow nannies. The twins started whimpering, pleading with Vida not to open the door.

"No, Vida! Don't do it!" Abe screamed.

"Don't do it, Nanny!" Ada cried, lifting her feet up off the ground as she pulled herself tightly against Vida's legs, trying to drag her to a stop.

"It's Madison!" Vida yelled. "Let me—"

"No, Vida," came the voice. "Let it be. Do not open the door. I cannot protect you if you step away from the candle."

"What?" Vida said loudly, turning back toward the candle, both twins now clinging to her legs. "What do you mean, '...away from the candle'?" The unspoken accusation stood, regarding the heavenly power of the voice of the candle. Minor proximity power issues of the divine were unknown to Vida. She had never heard of such a thing before, and she had been going to mass several times a week since she was a child.

"Trust me, Vida, if you want to save the children," the voice told her calmly.

Going on instinct, Vida moved back to face the candle directly, the twins still clinging to her. "Who are you, really?" she finally had the courage to ask. "You're not the Mother. The Mother has no limits. She's the Mother of God. Moving just a step or two shouldn't test your divine power. So, who are you?"

Another burst of gunfire, this time in staccato single-shots only, filled the air, competing directly with the growing presence and intensity of the *thrum-thrum-thrum*.

"I am the One Above, Vida," it told her, calming the storm in her soul. "I want you to listen closely now, for I have much to ask of you, and I have but little time to speak."

Vida nodded twice, her pupils dilating with pleasure. The twins also grew pacific, calm, as her healing energies flowed into them. Now, they, too, saw the image of the Lightbringer's Sigil in the flame of the votive candle. Now, all three of them could hear its beautiful song, like a host of holy angels singing in electric fire.

Then, the resonant, melodic voice of the One Above sang to them, in harmony with the Lightbringer's Sigil, and Ada, Abe, and Vida, enraptured and in awe, listened to what it told them.

eVo.144.000.mOd.11.sCe13 | EARTH | EGYPT | EL GIZA | THE GREAT PYRAMID OF GIZA

"I CAN'T BELIEVE THE board financed this, Mary," Roger intoned yet again, his salt-and-pepper beard glistening with sweat under the fierce Egyptian sun. "It's bad science."

"That's why we're here, Roger." Mary Dunbar replied in her precise Irish brogue, squatting down low to the ground, gently adjusting the last of their seventy-two customized sound level meters in the rocky soil, "To scientifically test the hypothesis. And it's not bad science," she demurred, standing back up, brushing the silty dust from her hands. "It's just weird science. Like the movie," she laughed.

Roger Meltry, PhD, University of Chicago, snorted a brief horse-laugh. "Sono-acoustic Resonant Modalities Inherent in the Structures of the Giza Complex," he said, reciting the name of the positional paper that had started this whole thrice-damned endeavor. "And Lawson and the board bought it hook, line, and sinker," he said, wiping his beard with the edge of his keffiyeh. "Ah, well, at least it keeps us in situ for a few more weeks. That's good. Gives the rest of the crew time to see the sights. Work up some new cockamamie theories of their own."

Mary laughed. Roger had been a great mentor over the years, virtually a father to her, and the many digs they'd done for the Big UC. He had even cake-walked her through her own PhD, if two years of continual verbal testing counted as a "cake-walk". His low-key sense of humor, sardonic and sarcastic as it might appear to the uninitiated, was amusing to Mary, for it was very much like her own.

"Steve? Jamie?" Roger inquired, turning to face the two graduate students who were manning the team's portable laboratory. "Do you have signal?" he asked, pointing lazily at the customized sound level meter, which appeared to the untrained eye to be some sort of half-height umbrella made of gleaming chrome.

Both graduate students were feverishly at work beneath the pyramid roof canopy tent which provided some modicum of cover versus the endless sunlight of the Giza Plateau. In the background, several portable generators, which had taken special permits to run so near to the pyramids, chugged and hummed. Several sturdy portable tables held multiple rows of laptops and monitors, as well as something that closely resembled a vintage Neve 8078 sound board. It, along with the seventy-two sound meter apparatus and their twelve spares, had been heavily customized from standard components by Mary, Roger, and the team. What had originally begun as a drunken bar bet by Mary, Roger, and several members of the grad crew — to see if they could generate some interest from the board in debunking some of the wilder theories, and maybe spin it into a History or Discovery Channel special — had actually achieved fruition. And that meant damn good money, and virtual carte blanche to do whatever it took to: One, make good science; Two, debunk some apocryphal pseudo-theories and bad science; and, Three, to additionally cement the sterling reputation of the University of Chicago as the premiere classical research university in the world.

The team was already hard at work on the first two, Mary knew. The third? Well, it would fall into place because of the former two. And now, finally, they were ready for their first test run of their insanely expensive Rock'n'Roll equipment. And now, finally, Mary Dunbar would demonstrate to the world that there never was such an animal as "resonant pyramids". That the pseudo-intellectuals like Bauval, Hancock, and their von Däniken fan boys on 'Ancient Aliens' were wrong, just dead wrong. And that there had never been a need to have created such elaborate extraterrestrial and other nonsensical theories to explain something that was quite mundane in origin, though exceptional to an extreme.

Mary had never had time for the fringe folks, except for this one time, after their drunken bar bet had struck both nerves and a gold mine of financing. Now, of course, there would be time. She would give them time. All the debate time that they wanted. And, maybe if they were good, and lost their debate as well they should now that the science had been settled once and for all, she might let them have some air time on their new cable special.

"Speaking of which," Mary said, sauntering up confidently behind the tech-laden tables, "where's the crew? I thought they said noon."

Jamie shrugged, then pointed at Roger, who joined them. "Ask him."

"Well?" Mary asked, arms akimbo.

"I told them to give us a few more hours," Roger said, taking a swig of bottled water. "No sense rushing things. This gives us time to do a few runs. Test things out."

Mary started to grin. "You're falling for it, aren't you?" she accused.

"No, absolutely not," Roger said tersely. "It's all hogwash. Doesn't even make scholarly sense, and we've batted it around with Physics, with Music, and even with the batshit crazy fringe guys themselves. If Schoch hadn't given them academic cache with his Sphinx water erosion hypothesis, then we wouldn't even be considering their catastrophist's arguments and cockeyed hypotheses."

"Thank the cable guys for that," Mary snickered.

"The power of TV," Jamie agreed.

"Well," Roger continued, "I know you youngins don't get it, because you're too Millennial still to get your heads out of your iPhones and Facebook, but these fringe scientists and their catastrophism demeans true science and ruins hundreds of years of rational, incremental knowledge. As a genuine academic, he might have given the fringe guys a temporary leg up, and some temporary boosting. But, in the end, you can bet your bottom dollar that real science," he said, waving at the equipment before them, "is going to normalize the arguments, and place it all back in lockstep with classical incrementalism. I mean, c'mon," he mocked, "singing pyramids? That's total hooey."

"Well," Mary said, nodding affirmatively to Jamie to initiate the first phase of their testing, "we'll find out soon enough. Kick it, Jamie. Crank up the jams."

With that, Jamie and Steve went to work: Steve manning the customized Neve-like soundboard, Jamie manning three different Mac Book Pros and a small colony of USB computer mice. Around them, the ambient hum of multiple tonal generators began to fill the air. The array of seventy-two customized sound meters had been customized to bimodally "hear" and process sounds as well as "broadcast" the same, beaming the data back to their sensors on the tables, until there was good tone. Also, as many of the customized sensors were, in fact, inside the Great Pyramid itself, several thousand feet of cable was in play.

The tonal generators worked their charms. They fed multiple ranges of tones to the network of sensors, causing them all to work as one, generating the tones and casting them about at certain "magic" and "golden" vectors, attempting to elicit the specific tones and resonant harmonies claimed by the fringe scientists.

"Go ahead and do full-spectrum sweeps, Jamie," Mary said. "Let's do the whole infrasonic to ultrasonic rainbow on this first pass. Give each step twelve seconds before jumping."

"Copy that," Jamie replied.

"Steve?" Mary asked.

"Nothing yet, Mary," Steve replied. He was wearing some extra-large-sized Bose headphones, with two laptops perched on the middle of the large soundboard. The dials and knobs moved by themselves, as they were programmatically linked with the tonal-generating software running the experiment.

Nothing. There's going to be nothing but some minor resonance, Mary thought, reviewing mentally what they had learned from their own Physics and Music academics. Everything, they had told her, had some resonance, or potential for it. Mostly everything, but there were always exceptions. But the pyramids? There would be some natural resonance nodes on the Giza Plateau, in and among certain areas of the pyramids and burial complex, perhaps even in the Sphinx itself. But those would just be natural artifacts. The software would correct for those natural events, just as it would be capable of capturing and processing any unusual or unique artifacts and transients, even subtle harmonics.

A full minute passed as the tone generators slowly ascended. Initially, nothing was heard, only felt, as the infrasonics were below their human auditory capacity to process normally. Several minutes later, they all became aware of a deep, grumbling sound, which seemed to stumble around them on terrifying elephant's feet.

"We're audible now," Steve said a bit more loudly than he should.

Roger looked nervously over at Mary. "Is it supposed to be that loud?"

"I don't think so," Mary said quietly. Something had just caught her eye, some sort of reflective artifact from the top of the nearest sensor. Immediately, she walked out of the canopy tent and moved toward the sensor.

"Mary?" Roger called.

"Just checking something, no big deal," she said over her shoulder.

As she drew up to the sensor, she noticed that the sand, silt, and rocky mix of the soil was slightly shaking, the particles vibrating, jumping up and down. The top of the chrome-shiny sensor reflected a sight which caused her to balk. It looked to her as if there were Christmas lights being reflected, which was patently absurd out here in the virtual desert outside Cairo, Egypt. Shaking her head, trying to pry her gaze from the bizarre sight of dancing dust and flashing Christmas lights, Mary at last lifted her gaze to the sky.

There, high in the daytime sky, the Weave of the Watchers was in the process of manifesting itself on Earth orbit. Her green eyes grew wide, even as her crimson hair began to spill from her Cubs baseball cap. Behind her, screams filled the air.

Something... someone is screaming. Roger is screaming, she told herself, still unable to avert her eyes from the glory of the infinite divine above her. "Roger?" she said weakly, dropping to her knees, the soil scraping her skin beneath her jeans. The *thrum-thrum-thrum* coming from on high began to syncopate with the now barely audible basso hum from the sensors, banishing their puny influence, replacing it with pure celestial jams.

Behind her, Mary heard Jamie screaming Steve's name over and over again, her panicked voice diminishing before the approaching crescendo from on high.

The faint trace of electric blue sparks danced from Mary Dunbar's emerald green eyes. Her Cubs hat fell slowly from her head as her hair, her frame, her soul itself began to resonate with the song coming down from the sky. Enraptured, she gave into the resonant sensation that caressed her ambiently. Down, down, down she went into her own soul. She knew what is was singing to her. More than that, she knew *why*.

She waited, patiently, cocooned in her own psyche, as hell and fury erupted around her. It would be here soon, she now realized, not caring one whit that her mentor and their students now had grown silent. They had been too weak even to bear witness to its coming glory. But Mary was not weak. In fact, she would never be weak again.

Above the Giza Plateau, the Lightbringer's Sigil abruptly appeared.

The tips of Mary's fingers tingled with eldritch energies as the sigil sang to her, filling her with immortal energies. Before her, the truncated top of the Great Pyramid itself began to glow with bluish, dancing fey lights, akin to St. Elmo's Fire. A ghostly image of its former pyramidion appeared before her eyes, lit with divine fire. The same thing occurred simultaneously on the two smaller pyramids.

Now, as the song from the sigil began to tell Mary special things, the sensor nearest her vibrated like a spastic head-banger, then abruptly exploded, sending shards of metal in all directions.

Before the lethal shrapnel touched her, however, it slammed into what seemed to be an invisible aura around her, ricocheting explosively away from her in all directions with significantly more force than it had previously been endowed. Around her spun momentary images of whirling, rainbow fractals, which rapidly faded into nothingness.

Inner fire such as she had never imagined filled Mary's soul. She felt electric, glorious. Her hair was dancing on its own, flicking about as if guided by static electricity. The *thrum-thrum-thrum* sang to her, causing her to focus her gaze on the pyramids. All three now glowed with unearthly, hazy light, their ancient, original forms superimposed in electric blue light over their current, decayed forms. Not at all to her surprise – not now, not after hearing the song from above awaken the song within – the three pyramids began to vibrate visibly, their current, decayed forms vanishing from sight as the superimposed spectral superimpositions became realized in this world. In the span of 144,000 milliseconds, what had once been now was again.

As the final *thrum-thrum-thrum* echoed away into the distance, the vibrating resonance of the superimposed apparitions faded to naught, and the three great pyramids manifested totally, fully restored to their original, gleaming glory. From top to bottom, they reflected the image of the Lightbringer's Sigil. What was old had been made new again.

eVo.144.000.mOd.11.sCe14 | EARTH | UNITED STATES | NEVADA | RENO

MHYRRANDA WIPED HER puffy, wrinkled eyes and looked into the screen once more before logging off. Stupid unscheduled server updates. At least she'd led her pick up group through the newest flashpoint before they got shut down. Poor little clueless, thirsty boys, tagging along with their characters no matter how long she bounced from one spot to another in the MMO. They had no lives, and followed her everywhere, hoping for a few snatched moments of erotic roleplay. She ran her guild with an iron fist in a silken glove, teasing and cajoling, flirting and giving moments of in-character joy to the feisty guys. She had no doubt half of them were headed off to bed with one fist in their pants, fantasizing about her – the woman of their dreams.

It wasn't that she was a tramp, no matter what her ex-husband or his former friends said. He let her run wild, and those former friends were just collateral damage. She'd been young, and never counted the cost. He probably thought he loved her too much for her to ever leave. And yet here she was, many burned bridges later, in a shitty, run-down apartment, still getting guys to do her bidding – despite the fact that she was twenty years older and the guys were simulated heroes in a simulated world. She may not look as hot as she used to, but she still had charisma and wit.

Randa swallowed what was left of her coffee and got up, making her way through the apartment and brushing her teeth before bed. She washed her face and ran her fingers through her lank hair, looking sideways at the mirror with a wink. After a trip to the toilet and a disappointing stop at the scales, she slid her hands down her silk pajamas, feeling the pounds she hadn't had a few years ago. She was about to go crawl in bed when she saw a strange pattern of light coming from the window.

Pulling the curtains aside, she stared at the incredible lights in the sky. The ribbons of pulsing colors in the night sky filled her with awe, and she sighed, enraptured. Azure sparkles filled her eyes, reflecting against the window pane before shifting to gold and fading away. Then her stomach lurched violently, and she heaved her dinner all over the bathroom floor. An indescribable pain filled her guts and she sank to her knees in agony. Black drool fell from her lips, and she only had a moment to consider the dark mess covering the floor before she lost consciousness.

eVo.144.000.mOd.11.sCe15 | EARTH | SAUDI ARABIA | HEJAZ REGION | MECCA

ABDULLA MUHAMMAD SAJWANI had been on a business trip in Mecca when news of the Christian crusade had begun to appear both on broadcast and social media. Abdulla, drinking tea in the pleasant lobby of the Raffles Makkah Palace hotel, had received the news with equal measures of shock and surprise.

Always level and calm, however, Abdulla had been one of the very few people in the lobby not to charge outside almost immediately, making a noisy beeline for the Kaaba. Emotion at a time such as this, he knew, would push reason aside. Had not the Sajwanis contributed many of its own wise men, true imams all, to the Sharia courts, their decisions always just and reasonable? And even though he was but a mere salesman, could he do no less than to honor them by being like them, even considering this obvious insanity? With that thought in mind, he decided to finish off his carafe of tea first while he considered the strange and unusual turn of events.

What madness had infiltrated the mind of the Christian leader to evoke such a barbaric reflex, to cause him to issue such a nonsensical *fatwah*? *Well, a crusade,* Abdulla corrected himself, smiling bitterly down into his strong tea. *Sheer, medieval nonsense, regardless.*

Surely, he considered, in the early twenty-first century, in this more closely connected world, with all its miraculous forms of communication, people would simply know better than to fall prey to such a bad idea? Clearly, the Pope who had issued such a proclamation should perhaps seek counseling for his madness. And, clearly, from the deafening din of those gathered in the Masjid al-Haram, who now marched around the holy Kaaba itself in the heat just after midday, many thousands of his brothers and sisters felt the same. That soon would change, however, he knew. Only a matter of time until numerous *jihads* were declared.

"This is all just terrible," he said to himself, tapping his tiny tea cup with his index finger. "I am so sick of war."

Abdulla considered why he was here. He had thought that the off-season would have made it easier to approach the business leaders in Mecca with a potential expansion of his family's *halal*-compliant food product line. And not just the common fare sold down at the local bazaar or souk. The Sajwani brand featured a wide spectrum of foodstuffs prepared according to strict, next-generation food technology processes and strict religious law. Absolutely 100% free from animal enzymes and emulsifiers. But the unfortunate circumstances and timing of the recent announcement by the Christians of a new crusade against Islam almost instantly captured the attention of every practitioner of Islam in the city. And that meant that it had captured the attention of everyone in Mecca, for it was forbidden for non-Muslims to enter the holy city. Thus, no businessmen to do business with. No, now almost everyone with whom he could have dealt was marching around the Kaaba, their fists pumping angrily toward the sky, their voices strained with righteous anger. Marching toward righteous war.

"Ah, well, Allah wills it," Abdulla finally conceded, neatly placing his tea cup next to the empty carafe. He decided to call it a day, return to his room, and book a return flight to Dubai at his earliest opportunity. Once home, he told himself that he would immediately seek the guidance of his elder brother and his uncle, both scholars of the Book, and, *insha'Allah*, they would be able to counsel him on this complex matter.

As he rode the elevator, Abdulla fished his cell phone out of its side-holster and began to read the Dubai news. Exiting the elevator, his phone flickered once, then went dead. Grimacing at the poor cell service, he holstered his phone and continued down the long hotel hallway. He arrived shortly at his room, where he swiped his guest card to unlock and open the door. Shutting the door behind him with his foot, Abdulla took a few steps into his room when a sudden flash of light coming from beyond his suite's tinted windows grabbed his attention.

Blinking, Abdulla slowly raised his head as he shambled to a stop right before the windows, which allowed him a fantastic view of the city of Mecca, as well as the Masjid al-Haram and the Kaaba within it. No longer focused on the smart phone, he noticed that the midday Mecca sky was filled with dazzling lights and flashing, firecracker-like pinwheels of light. Over the deafening din of those gathered at the nearby Masjid al-Haram, where they marched around the Kaaba, he sought to tune out the noise and take the spectacle of the sight in. It was beautiful, like a firework display in Dubai. It filled his view with multicolored, strobing, and pulsating lights.

Still, something seemed to tug at his mind, beckoning him to look farther to the left. As he did, he noted the vast entity looming above him, above everything. It seemed to be the center of the motion of the fireworks, as if they all danced and whirled and pulsated for its own entertainment. It stretched from somewhere below the far horizon to almost directly over his head.

As he carefully leaned into the thick, tempered windows to get a better view of the wondrous sight, Abdullah noticed the abrupt change of timbre from the many thousands who had been chanting and praying at the Kaaba. Now, instead of barely recognizable group prayers, he clearly heard the cacophony of thousands of people screaming in horror and terror, the echoes shaking the windows like thunder, reverberating down the relatively dense concrete canyons of the Mecca central business district.

Silently, Abdullah prayed the *Takbir* repeatedly as the full effect of what such horrific screaming might mean to so many thousands of the religious devout bloomed in his mind. Despite himself, for he realized what he might see, he turned his gaze from the left back to his direct, straight-on vantage of the Masjid al-Haram and the Kaaba within it. To his horror, the thousands upon thousands who had gathered, unbidden, in their most holy place of worship, to demonstrate their solidarity in opposition to the Mad Pope's papal decree of Holy War, now raced about like so many angry ants. There was no pattern, no principal direction, that the running worshipers chose. Instead, it was sheer chaos. And, as he noted after but a few seconds, those who were not running were indeed not moving. Not at all.

Madness seemed to reach up from *Jahannam* itself to grasp and lay hold to the devout, Abdullah thought, continuing to pray the *Takbir*, this time aloud. The living and the dead, he could see, now writhed in apparent agony. Tears began to stream down his face as he realized that he had almost brought along A'idah and A'ishah, that both his wife and daughter might very well have been with now. That they could very well have been down there with the rest of the devout.

"Allah give us strength," Abdulla Sajwani whispered, "for the Christians have launched their Holy War. Save us, Isa ibn Maryam! Allah, rectify the Mahdi tonight! Save us!"

Suddenly, even as the salt of his tears burned his eyes, the hair at the immaculately groomed nape of his neck arose and stood on end. Horrified, he became aware of a presence behind him, looming behind him. Try as he might, he could not turn to face the presence. Instead, he remained frozen in place, staring out the window, in which he slowly became aware of the vague outline of a ghostly apparition's reflection.

It stood no more than a pace behind him. In simple white robes was it dressed, but of the apparition's face there was only a blur, its features unfathomable.

"Abdulla Muhammad al-Mahdi..." it said to him, speaking softly, directly to his heart, like a voice from a dream.

Hearing this, Abdulla made a guttural, beastly groan. His teeth grating on one another, he said through clenched jaws, "That is not my name. I am Abdulla Muhammad Sajwani."

Slowly, the apparition seemed to move slightly, and Abdulla felt a very real, very soothingly warm hand come to rest upon his right shoulder. Instantly, Abdulla relaxed, the stress and fear of the day melting away to nothingness.

"Yes," the apparition told him, "that was your name, given to your mortal incorporation. Now, I am returning your true name to you, my Mahdi. Rise," it bade him, and thus did Abdullah obey.

Still facing the window, Abdullah inquired, in a new voice which surprised him with its power, "*Bismillah*, what is thy name?"

"I am the one with ninety-nine beautiful names," it told him softly, gently. "You, my Mahdi, whom I have elevated in power beyond that of the mortals, may call me the One Above. Now," it continued, even as Abdullah's mind swooned, "come with me. We travel to Medina. We have much for which to prepare, for the *Yawm al-Qiyāmah* is upon us. *Al-Malhama Al-Kubra*, the End of All Things, comes soon."

eVo.144.000.mOd.11.sCe16 | EARTH | VATICAN CITY

THE HALL OF THE PONTIFICAL Audiences – commonly called the Paul VI Audience Hall, yet casually referred to as Nervi Hall, in honor of the mad genius, Pier Luigi Nervi, who had architected it – trembled and roiled as the din of a million chanting voices reverberated throughout the narrow confines of Vatican City. Countless worshipers, empowered with a newfound passion in their faith, had made their way into Vatican City, filling virtually every square inch of St. Peter's Square, the continuously growing overflow spilling chaotically into the adjacent streets.

Oberst Jan Andrist, the Commander of the Pontifical Swiss Guard, had assigned the majority of his imposing, elite Swiss Guard assets to hold the perimeter inside Nervi Hall. He knew that there was no way that they would be able to hold the doors to the hall against the crowd outside, should they become determined enough to attempt to force them. But he reckoned that the very sight of the imposing guards, their halberds gleaming along with their custom-fitted plate armor, would emit psychological intimidation beyond their actual physical limitations. Perhaps the bluff would be enough. If not, then they'd all sell their lives dearly, and it would be like 1527 all over again.

The numbers were against them. Colonel Andrist knew that his guards totaled no more than a company at best. Even reinforced as they were by an almost equal number of the Gendarmerie, it was obvious to all sane and sentient souls that the City was soon going to be overwhelmed. By millions too many.

Therefore, within mere minutes of the Pope's televised declaration of a new Crusade, Colonel Andrist had activated protocols little known in the public domain. The secret protocols invoked various components of the Italian armed forces, and approved temporarily their presence and authority inside Vatican City. As such, and after but a few hours, military helicopters flitted overhead, special forces sniper teams manned both high and hidden ground, and dozens of Iveco VM 90P Protected tactical vehicles, manned by elite Carabinieri, reinforced the guard's perimeter.

Now, though, even with the massive throngs of support – even from the elite Carabinieri, and Italy's own armed forces – Colonel Andrist knew that even their best efforts were not going to be enough. The number of the devout was staggering and increasing by the second. Shared intel indicated that virtually every highway leading into Rome was jammed with cars. Where there was no more forward progress, the people simply had abandoned their vehicles in the road and started walking toward the Vatican.

A small contingent of Swiss Guard attended the Pope himself and his personal retinue on the stage of Nervi hall, widely flanking them. Below the stage, in a specially reinforced suite blooming with military grade surveillance and communications equipment, *Oberst* Andrist, his second in command *Oberstleutnant* Carl Repond, and two dozen technical staff from the Gendarmerie Corps of Vatican City State – the

Vatican's internal police force – manned the nerve center. It was the official C3I nexus for the Vatican, and was now another node in Italy's military's command and control network.

"I've never seen anything like this before, Colonel," *Oberstleutnant* Repond said in a soft voice, his gaze sweeping across the bank of UHD monitors at the front of the command center.

From the command chair immediately behind him, Colonel Andrist replied to Repond. "And I've never seen *him* like this before," he admitted as one of the monitors slowly zoomed in on the Pope.

The lone figure of total calm among a sea of anguish and fear, Il Papa sat in his simple white flared-back chair on the raised stage of Nervi Hall. He held the papal ferula, the pastoral staff, erect in his left hand, though he was seated. His mitre gleamed no small bit due to the hall's lighting. Each tiny movement of his head caused a veritable fountain of glittering reflections to dance forth.

The hall was filled over capacity. The standard seating capacity was just over 6,000, enough room to house comfortably the official population of the 800 or more clerics and church officials officially citizens of Vatican City. Today, however, there pressed in some 10,000 or more desperate people of various callings and professions. They had been fortunate enough to have been close enough to the ramrod straight cadre of Swiss Guards who had escorted the Pope and his minions boldly into the hall a few hours ago, parting the milling crowd along the way as easily as Moses had parted the Red Sea.

Now, it was standing room only in the hall. The people gathered within prayed, almost every one of them, rosaries and votive items abounding. And all of them seemed to be moving, swaying, enraptured in a personal miasma of nervous anticipation and outright fear.

Colonel Andrist had never seen anything like it, either. They would be most blessed, and he would personally consider it a miracle, if the casualties resulting simply from the pressing mass of people remained in the triple digits. Miraculously blessed, he knew, if Rome's many Muslim immigrants and refugees made it out of Rome alive. Colonel Andrist knew hate when he felt it, and he could feel it running like a rampant, flash-flooding undercurrent beneath the prayers and chants of the massive throng. It was quite clear that they wanted blood.

Curiously, the bank of UHD monitors on the wall flickered. A line of white static flashed rapidly, then faded away, all within the span of a few seconds.

Colonel Andrist looked over at his command-level peer in the Gendarmerie, who stood off to his left, holding a secured electronic tablet in his hands. Shrugging, he barked something in Italian to his techs, who immediately made themselves appear to be quite busy resolving the transient issue.

On the monitors, at the far edges of the steadily growing crowds, tiny GEM e2 patrol vehicles, accurately called *Ovetti*, or "little eggs", appeared as the techs attempted to re-synchronize the screens. For some arcane reason known only to the technicians, the petite vehicles gave them the best reference point for the re-synch. Slowly, the monitors, one-by-one, locked onto the same stream showing one of the cute GEM e2 patrol vehicles, until, finally, all of the monitors sported the same image.

The law enforcement officers in the little eggs did their best to enforce law and order. But law and order were quickly hounded and set to bay by the overwhelming power of the chaos which suddenly revealed itself in the sky overhead. It spread like a virtual contagion in the souls of the millions gathered in the Vatican City State, propagating panic and fear among them all. This caused multiple waves of spontaneous stampedes to break out, a terrible tumult which spread like the multiple fronts of a voracious wildfire throughout the grounds of the Vatican.

The Weave of the Watchers materialized fully above the Roman wilderness of pain, fulfilling the visions of one particularly prescient shaman from half a century before.

Below the hall, in the command center, a roaring warble of vicious feedback flared loudly from all of the headphone sets simultaneously. This caused a commotion among the techies, who, seized with piercing pain, attempted to dislodge them from their heads with fingers which now felt like insensate lead. On the monitors the field of view of the camera, which had been focused on the little egg, swiftly panned up to the sky, revealing the mind-numbing sight of the Weave of the Watchers. Primal fear filled the hearts of all men in the command center who gazed upon it. It sadistically pummeled the state of their minds while slowly burning its image into their very souls.

In Nervi Hall, ensconced safely for now along with most of the cloth and clergy, Archbishop Garcia stood nearest the Pope. A Swiss Guard stepped briskly up to the archbishop, bowed slightly, then lowered his mouth to the archbishop's ear. Even as the tall guard retreated, Archbishop Garcia was already himself in motion and at the side of the papal chair in but a few quick steps. Leaning forward, he bent close to the ear of Petrus Romanus.

"Your Holiness," Archbishop Garcia intoned loudly to be heard above the ambient din, cupping his left hand over his lips as he leaned in to a mere finger's breadth from the Pope's ear. "They're reporting that... that something has appeared in the sky above us. Something beautiful."

The roof of the hall, which had been fitted several years previously with energy-producing photovoltaic cells, obscured any direct view of what this beautiful new thing in the sky might be. Gazing placidly toward the ceiling, Petrus Romanus smiled crookedly, for he knew exactly what it was, though his still-mortal eyes could not see it.

"Yes. Yes, it is beautiful."

Many in the crowd followed the direction of the Pope's gaze, especially now that the reflection from his mitre seemed to be issuing forth dancing rainbows. Few, however, caught the faint flicker of electric blue light cross his eyes as he shifted his gaze to the ceiling.

"Tell them not to worry," Archbishop Garcia turned and told one of the guards, who then spoke into a microphone concealed in his frilly sleeve.

A sudden, painful spike of feedback erupted from the earpieces of the guards in the hall, breaking the relative calm of Nervi Hall. Outside, however, confusion, panic, and horror were the norm. While those inside the hall passed the minutes in relative peace, it was painfully apparent from the constant screams of the terrified crowds and wailing sirens outside the hall that all hell was breaking loose. For those inside the hall, however, they mercifully stood in the veritable eye of the storm, and fortune temporarily favored them over the desperate millions outside.

Minutes passed before anyone in the hall could truly perceive it. It crossed the threshold of perception as a distant, softly pulsing hum. As it grew slowly in intensity, more of those praying became aware that others now were staring up at the ceiling. A faint bouquet of neon lights struggled to shine through the large stained glass windows set high in the walls of the hall. The smell of acrid burning copper abruptly danced around the hall's many rows of seats. Overhead, as now all eyes sought the heavens, there came a deafening crackle as the photovoltaic cells, built into the ceiling of the hall, entrained with the growing resonance. A moment later, the feedback reached a point of criticality from which there was no return. Suddenly, the photovoltaic cells shattered en masse, bowling those who stood to the ground. Dozens of tons of lethal glass, metal, and polymer film shards rained down upon those in the general audience of the hall.

During the next eight seconds, the screams of the injured and dying and the crashes of thousands of individual impacts of the lethal rain of shrapnel from the shattered roof competed with the rapid crescendo of the Weave of the Watchers. The members of the Swiss Guard on the stage swiftly moved to enclose the Pope, protecting him from what might come next. There was next a five second passage of screams and shrieks from those wounded who had survived the onslaught. On the thirteenth second, however, the sigil's deadly *thrum-thrum-thrum* achieved dominance, filling the minds of those who yet lived with its sweetly whispered cosmic lies.

"*Petrus...*" came a sibilant whisper, heard only in his mind. "*It's time. Year Zero begins.*"

Year Zero.

Now, the fog in his wounded mind lifted, and Petrus found temporary clarity. He sought the honey-spoken words he had heard, struggling to remember what the Lightbringer had told him. He had told him that this was all the fault of the insane demi-urge who had usurped the divine godhead and stolen its cosmic power. It was his doing. All of this. Everything.

The souls of men were meant to be free, the Lightbringer had told him. Free will, however, had been compromised by the manipulations and mind-games of the faulty demi-urge. A sick, twisted perversion had occurred, corrupting the original intention of the instantiation of Earth. The demi-urge, intoxicated by power and in its spite of all things sane, had lied, telling mankind that they had been born with stains on their souls. That the only way to redeem their sullied souls was to swear everlasting devotion to its false godhead, adhering exclusively to its dogma and doctrine, or else be damned for all time. Consigned to Hell their very souls would be, because they believed that they had been born with stains on them. And they had been unable to escape the trap of fear that this false notion had sprung upon them.

Forever in thrall to the ultimate liar, Petrus thought, a detached anger growing inside him. Survivors were screaming for help from beneath the rubble. But they were beneath notice now that the Weave of the Watchers had materialized in full, its promise of judgement soon to come.

Distantly, Petrus noted that few on the raised stage had been struck down. The bulk of the survivors moved slowly, almost crablike, and began to converge around his simple chair, crowding as closely to his presence as the guards would allow.

For a very brief moment, the thought that he had devoted virtually his entire life to serving the ultimate liar filled Petrus' throat with bitter gall. He had taught little children that their innocent little souls were tainted. Surely this had been his greatest sin. He had lied to the most innocent. He had believed what he had told them, so certainly his words had scourged their souls with his falsely spoken truth, imprinting its own form of permanent scar on them.

Several of the remaining Swiss Guard from the floor of the hall finally managed to make the stage, where they pushed through the growing external perimeter of cloth and clergy around him. They then fell into formation with the rest of their comrades. Archbishop Garcia and a small group of surviving clergy formed a second perimeter around the guards. Most of them craned their necks skyward such that they could stare, dumbfounded, at the Weave of the Watchers. It pulsated and thrummed with incredible intensity as it neared some unfathomable crescendo.

Petrus still was lost in thought. More of his conversation that night with the Lightbringer flooded into his mind. Despite the feeling that his mind was spinning, things began to resolve into total clarity. He now understood that the Augustinian notions of Original Sin were perverse and wrong. It was a basic human right to know Good from Evil. The sick demi-urge would have kept them trapped in the garden as his ignorant slaves, doing his dirty work forever, but that they had been shown how to open their eyes and free themselves from this terrible yoke. The serpent had empowered them to gain free will, and the hateful demi-urge had decided, in his twisted spite, to punish both them and their progeny, forever, for that alleged transgression. As if casting off one's spiritual chains was a sin.

Monotheism is a mortal sin, Petrus heard himself think. In his mind's eye, he was accusing himself, using the Lightbringer's voice as his own. *Monotheism is a system of control based upon a false dichotomy; a perverse bifurcation where none actually exists. It rules by fear and guilt. It rules by fear and guilt. On and on. On and on. It's Heaven and Hell. Heaven and Hell.*

"God forgive me," Petrus said under his breath. The spinning sensation in his head finally ceased. He gazed around him, and above him, the carnage in the hall and the insanity looming above him marking his soul. He then continued, in a stern, booming voice, "I have called myself Peter of Rome. I have started a holy war. I have damned those little children who have not yet received the sacrament of Baptism. I have scourged their souls with my false beliefs. Their precious little souls were not stained! They weren't stained! Instead, it is my soul that is stained! I have sinned. I have failed in my duty to the Church! As God comes to judge mankind, I know now that I am damned. Damned for all time!"

Archbishop Garcia pushed his arm between two of the guards. His splayed fingers brushed the edge of Petrus' mitre.

"Your Holiness! You cannot say that!" he implored him, not believing what he had just heard. He made the sign of the cross with his extended hand. *"Ego te absolvo a peccatis tuis in nomine Patris et Filii et Spiritus Sancti!"*

With that most baneful pronouncement, the Black Pope's mind cast out its temporary weakness. The Lightbringer had revealed the truth to him, and he would do precisely what the Lightbringer had told him must be done in order to save the world.

Il Papa swiveled his head around to stare at Archbishop Garcia. Bright cascades of electric blue sparks gushed from his eyes, causing even the zealous Pontifical Guards to startle and back away, halberds clanking awkwardly.

"Your god has failed..." the Black Pope veritably hissed at the recoiling Archbishop.

He arose slowly from his chair as the recovering guards gave way, their halberds now en garde, for they had noted not only that Il Papa's eyes were emitting pale bluish sparks, but also that his paschal staff now faintly glowed with a dangerous looking effusion of jet-black light.

Over their heads, the Weave of the Watchers continued its ominous humming.

As the confused guards exchanged looks, wondering who among them would be the first to attempt to disarm their sacred charge of his clearly possessed staff, the Black Pope recalled that he had listened in rapt awe as the Lightbringer had informed him of his plan, his great reckoning. The End of All Things, when the heavenly hosts – the Vanth'Vash'Var, the Sentinels of the Anti-Life, the Death Horde, the Lords of the Void itself – would come down from Heaven to Earth to enforce the will of the mad demi-urge, the One Above.

The Lightbringer had given him a starring role in his masterwork. Such was his reward for his incorruptible faith, which never had been and never could be shaken. It would be a world with no more lies. The doctrine and dogma of the Lightbringer had no room for lies. It was simple and encapsulated by a mere three words: Evolve or die.

Evolve or die. A simple creed.

Evolve and rise to the challenge of contesting and defeating the dark angels who came down from their corrupted, false Heaven, under the command of the evil demi-urge, the One Above, to judge mankind. Or die.

And I shall do my part, Petrus promised himself. First, however, he realized that he had to evolve, and take that true first step down his appointed path as one of the Chosen of the Lightbringer. And his evolution was soon to come, for the Lightbringer had told him exactly what was to come, bringing its divine judgement to Earth, initiating the Year Zero. The Lamb would become the Lion.

"Put down the staff, Petrus," Archbishop Garcia said, finally noting that the guards had been deferring to him to defuse the situation. "Put down the staff, and the guards can escort us downstairs to the control room. We can carry on from there."

Petrus ignored him. Instead, he slowly raised his gaze to the sky, throwing his arms wide to welcome his fate.

It was then that the Lightbringer's Sigil manifested, conjured and actualized by the Weave of the Watchers. Reality itself seemed to rear back on its hind legs and bleat drunkenly into the sky. There came light, in the form of intertwined rainbows, from the surreal sight overhead. It wound through the sky, etching nonsensical shapes and patterns as it gained speed on its way to the ground. With a great, silent crash, it impacted all things living.

A good portion of those who experienced this event immediately died, their bodies contorting like rapidly coiling cigarettes, their insides liquifying into a putrid black goo, then oozing out of every orifice. Some few others died in the midst of unspeakable horror as their genes failed critically to resonate with the sigil, instead mutating at impossible speed, in impossible configurations, causing chimeric transformations best left to the forgotten horrors of terrible nightmares.

On the stage at Nervi Hall, one of the Pontifical Guards near the Black Pope dropped his halberd, immediately sinking to his knees. The bones in his face swam spastically in place for almost five seconds, then his head imploded, the black goo that was formerly his brain jetting out a full three feet from his right ear.

His arms still raised to welcome the sigil, Petrus immediately felt a warm, pleasant sensation as the guard's soul began to race from its ruined mortal shell. He lowered his arms, staff held out in his left hand, and pivoted quickly to face the fallen guard. In seeming slow motion, he saw a faint nimbus of silver light forming a rough outline around the guard's body. Reacting instinctively, he beckoned it to him, and verily it extended a tiny tendril of itself to a spot right above his eyes, in the center of his forehead. Then, the rest of the guard's soul immediately followed, with a motion like the ink ejected from a squid, but in reverse.

Petrus' mind reeled in ecstasy as the essence of the soul merged with his own newly expanded and realized immortal soul. As fast as he could process it, the information experienced in the life of the guard whose soul he had just consumed flooded his conscious mind. Memories of personal tragedies and triumphs, how a particular good meal and an even better wine tasted, how good his girlfriend Marta's perfume smelled, how easy it was to use a halberd once you'd spent a few years training with it, and on and on and on until there was nothing remaining.

Though but a mere second had elapsed objectively during the taking and devouring of the guard's soul, Petrus' personal perception was that he had enjoyed many minutes in his dark communion with the soul. He stood stock still, savoring the experience, to the horror of the remaining guards and clergy around him. For they could plainly see what had just happened, even though to them it had happened in something less than a heartbeat or two. They had seen the bright flash of silver soul's light materialize around the dead guard's body. They had witnessed its flying into the middle of the Black Pope's forehead. They noted also that, perhaps due to a trick of the chaotic light sources, the pope's hair was no longer white. Now, it was black, and it fell beneath the pristine white mitre.

In the deepest depths of his warped, twisted mind, Petrus heard a silent voice, ancient and powerful, speak to him. *"Thou art unforgiven, Soulthief..."*

"Guards!" Archbishop Garcia yelled, pointing an accusing finger at the Black Pope. "Subdue him! Now!"

Even though they had clearly just witnessed the Black Pope's theft of the soul of one of their own, the cognitive dissonance that the Archbishop's order invoked in them cost them precious seconds of reaction time, which the Black Pope used to his advantage. Feeling supercharged, he spun his paschal staff into the nearest guard's halberd, disarming him with but a single blow, sending the halberd clanging to the floor of the stage some twenty feet away.

Before the other guards could bring their halberds to bear, Petrus had closed the gap on the disarmed guard, bringing his paschal staff down on the top of the guard's steel helmet. The impact was terrific, as it was landed with the strength of at least two men, and as it was backed by the evolving supernatural power of the Black Pope. The steel helmet collapsed a full three inches at the point of impact, instantly shattering the guard's skull, killing him on the spot.

Again, there was the brief appearance of a hazy nimbus around the guard's body. This one also seemed to be sucked rapidly into the center of the Black Pope's forehead. Greedily, like a newborn feeding for the first time on its mother's milk, he devoured it as well.

From the floor below, a growing mass of people cried out as they fell in gory puddles, their souls spinning wildly about the hall and converging in silvery trails before sliding into the Black Pope. The light of the souls created a glowing nimbus around his head; an ironic halo of lost lives. With each new soul, Petrus' mind whirled in fathomless directions, and a frenzy of madness overtook him.

Without pause, he spun in place to counter a vicious leg sweep from one of the remaining guard's halberd. There was a black flash of light at the point at which the Black Pope's staff parried the guard's halberd. At the point of impact, the guard's halberd broke, sending a third of its length clattering across the stage.

Spinning adroitly into the vector of the counter, Petrus, now armed with even more strength and martial prowess, closed the gap to the guard, who tried in vain to lift his truncated halberd to block. With a deft strike with the back of his right hand to the guard's jaw, the Black Pope sent the guard flying into the incoming path of another guard, knocking them both to the floor of the stage. Before either could arise, he was on them, dispatching both with a single stroke to each of their heads. Again, thick steel helms offered little resistance to Petrus' growing strength, and two more souls were now his.

The three remaining guards, exchanging quick glances, shifted their halberds from their hands to the crooks of their elbows. Simultaneously they produced, with practiced, swift motions, their SIG P220 handguns. As one, the three began to fire rapid single shots at the papal staff, attempting to disarm him from range with their expert-level marksmanship.

Although their shots were striking the staff, the effort had no effect. The Black Pope, now sporting the strength of several elite Swiss Guards, effortlessly retained the staff in his grasp. Advancing a step toward them, bullets still ricocheting off the seemingly invulnerable staff, he took a quick side-step toward one of the fallen guards. With a deft move of his right foot, he soccer kicked a dead guard's decapitated head brutally into the midsection of the guard nearest him. Breaking his ribs through his bullet-resistant undergarments, the impact of the force lifted him from the stage floor and impaled him upon the massive metal sculpture of *La Resurrezione* at the rear of the stage.

One of the two remaining guards, deciding that his gun was useless against such a foe, quickly returned his handgun to its concealed holster. Then, brandishing his halberd, he charged Petrus, screaming loudly. Even as the last guard continued sporadic firing at the Pope's staff when he could take a good shot, the charging guard tried his best to launch a disarming strike, rather than chance a blow that could harm their most holy charge. Despite Petrus' recent transformation, the mission of the

Swiss Guard still remained what it had always been: Protect the Pope, even at the cost of one's life.

And dearly the halberd-wielding guard paid, for his very small chance to have actually disarmed Petrus played out with a total, whiffing miss of his disarming strike. The papal staff seemed to move with a will of its own, easily removing itself from an almost certain parry-and-disarm strike. Instead, as the whiffing guard struck the stage floor with his halberd, Petrus closed the gap between the two, delivering a steel-crushing blow to the guard's plate helm. The guard's soul was claimed in a silver flash of light before his lifeless body hit the floor.

The last guard, finally out of ammo, desperately reached into the folds of his frilly purple and gold ornamental costume, searching for a spare magazine even as he detached his empty magazine expertly with his free hand. As his fingers closed upon a spare, the Black Pope met and caught his gaze. The guard noted a look of detached sadness on his face, as he found his spare clip and smoothly brought it up into his SIG P220. The guard, wondering a moment why Petrus was taking no action against him, felt something start burning at the nape of his neck. The pain was fierce, and instantly intense. Instinctively, he freed his left hand from his handgun, lifting his arm to try to reach the back of his neck. As he did so, his left arm horrifically turned to black goo, and the pain in his neck doubled in a heartbeat, spreading over his entire body. His next heartbeat was his last. He collapsed to the floor, his liquified organs pouring out of every orifice at once.

In abject horror, Archbishop Garcia had observed the fight. His eyes now met those of Petrus Romanus. As the two stared at one another, the few survivors on stage turned and bolted for exits on both stage right and stage left.

"God help us. It's the end of the world, and the Devil is among us," Archbishop Garcia said, his voice quivering, as he quickly made the sign of the cross.

Petrus Romanus was now clearly a young man in his prime, long black hair flowing beneath his mitre. Newfound immortal power flowing through him, he extended his arms in a cruciform pose.

"Leandro," the Black Pope patiently informed the Archbishop, informally using his first name. "Welcome to Mystery Babylon! The Lightbringer, Lucifer himself, has come to save us from the madness of the corrupt demi-urge."

"Demi-urge?" Archbishop Garcia spat, rattled. "Gnostic nonsense! The Devil has told you lies. He is the Father of Lies! You know this. Please, Your Holiness. Stop it! You're sick. You need help. Please, stop it, and come with me."

Petrus shook his head, his new black locks swirling below his shoulders. "The Devil, the Lightbringer, told me no lies. He told me the truth. Look at it, Leandro," he said swiveling his head up, pointing with his staff at the sigil above him. "That is truth. The Lightbringer is the one, true lord of this world. The demi-urge, the One Above, is the one who lies, pretending to be God. Utter blasphemy. He has duped the entire world for thousands of years, pouring scorn upon the Lightbringer, casting him down, assigning all the world's wrongs to him. Slander. Lies. All of it."

"I can't believe you're saying this," the Archbishop protested. "You are possessed by Lucifer himself. Of all believers, of the many millions upon millions in the Church, the one who led us now betrays us? To call for a new holy war, insanely liquidating more than a trillion Euros in assets by mere decree in order to finance mercenary armies? To spout such insane heresy? That Lucifer told you personally that the Gnostic heresies are true?

You have taken souls!" he said shrilly, hands clutched in rage and disgust. "I *know* this. I saw it with my own eyes! I was in error earlier when I offered you the Sacrament of Confession. There can be no absolution for your many mortal sins, Petrus. You are damned. Damned!"

"As if I would accept any sacraments from the impostor god," Petrus said, his gaze returning to the Archbishop. "The Lightbringer personally tasked me to call together the sheep here, to Mystery Babylon, and lead them to victory against the forces of the demi-urge. His sign and seal has judged all mankind. The strong will adapt and evolve. They will become stronger. Strong enough to contest the madness of the one who thinks that it is God. They are the Chosen. The weak? They will not adapt. They will not evolve. They will die."

"What malicious, supremacist hatred is this?" Archbishop Garcia asked loudly. "That is the ideology of hate, Petrus. It has no place here," he warned him. "You have no place here, heretic. Apostate!"

Petrus Romanus, the Black Pope, the Chosen of the Lightbringer, gazed coldly at Archbishop Garcia.

"In point of fact," he said casually, turning to face the massive sculpture behind him, "I have a place here. And the Lightbringer himself instructed me in how to actualize it. Behold!" he declared in a booming voice, his arms again thrown wide, over his head. "Behold the power of the Lightbringer and his Chosen, Petrus Romanus!"

Behind Petrus Romanus the eight metric ton sculpture, *La Resurrezione*, its bronze-copper alloyed form bending to his will, groaned like two freighters slowly colliding with one another as it began to bend inward and compact in upon itself. The guard's impaled body contorted like a grotesque, melted mannikin as it, too, bent inward and compacted into the tangled sculpture.

The faint silver nimbus of soul's light, expended by Petrus in the effort of shaping the sculpture, danced around its perimeter as it rapidly achieved its final evolution of form: a chaotic, triple helix form which burrowed into the stage and stabbed through the ceiling.

Confronted by this vulgar display of power, Archbishop Leandro Paulo Estevez Garcia screamed in abject mortal terror, then fled from the stage.

Petrus Romanus gazed upon his mighty work, satisfied. Though the physical form had been completed, he knew that more crafting yet remained. In order to properly carry out the bending and binding necessary to create a primal dimensional anchor – a prime directive given to him by the Lightbringer himself – he would require many more souls. Thousands more. 10,000 more, at least.

But such was the price one had to pay to become a god. And gods must he and his Chosen become, the Lightbringer had confided, if they were to have any chance of victory in the War of Heaven and Hell, at the End of All Things. The time when the One Above and his demonic forces of dark angels would return to Earth to issue final judgement. For there were mortals and immortals, just as there were gods and those beyond gods. Evolve or die.

Slowly, confidently, with newfound and newly stolen youthful vigor, Petrus turned his gaze upon the wreckage strewn floor of the hall. Thousands of souls he saw there, mainly but not completely consisting of the souls of the survivors. Some of the souls of the newly dead had not yet departed. Beyond that, outside the hall, however, he saw without seeing, and he knew without knowing that millions awaited him outside the hall. He could feel them all.

All of them. Even the ones who, like him, were newly reborn. New immortals. New gods.

Levitating from the floor of the stage, his arms spread in cruciform pose, the Black Pope began his silent, sibilant call.

"Venite..."

zEt.0 | THE ZEROTIME | THE UNION OF SOULS

"...ILLEGAL VICTORY CONDITION..." the silent Voice of Ma'at the Rectifier whispered in digital to Maweth, the Angel of Death.

At once, Maweth, the leader of the Memitim, the Destroyers, stirred. He manifested his physical form in the Union of Souls as a pitch-black twelve-spiked spheroid, oozing naught but sheer malice, immediately adjacent to the offending Zen-Sidhe.

Adhering strictly to the absolute letter of the law of the ineffable Protocols of Judgement and Execution, which demanded nothing less than exacting precision of process, Maweth commenced his duty. His spikes vibrated slightly at their tips, each issuing a thin spoke of bruise-purple light which collimated before speeding out to interrogate the Zen-Sidhe before him. Drawing a dozen equally spaced circumferential lines around the surface of the Zen-Sidhe, Maweth's interrogation process immediately provided multiple arrays of extremely dense data to him. He parsed them most enthusiastically, for he knew well the one bound with this Zen-Sidhe. And now, finally, after so many aeons, the seditious Shaper who wove his heretical scenarios therein had finally made the mistake necessary for Maweth to bring him to justice. And final rectification.

His emotions tightly held in check, Maweth reached the terminus of his parsing, Helel's current simulation almost totally exposed before his determined scrying. Exposed enough, he knew. For no scenario ever was totally exposed before its inexorable conclusion. When, at last, all would be known. And then only to the One Above.

"The One Above! For His glory we all shall die!" Maweth immediately swore, the Oath of the Ineffable One ever and always on his mind.

A swift pronouncement of judgement and an equally swift rectification of the rebel Shaper, and his totality would finally rejoin the Union of Souls. There, its threat to the perfection of the ZeroTime would at last be rendered null and void.

"Ah, Helel," Maweth thought, reaching the terminus of his parsing. "The Shining One. As if your black soul shines anything other than silent shadows and screaming midnight! At last you give me reason to invoke the Protocols of Judgement and Execution. What sweet blasphemy you have wrought! Sweet, even in its wickedness and apostasy. For it finally makes known your black soul to the Children of the Light, whom you would mislead by your prideful actions. Finally, it seals your wicked fate."

With that, Maweth's form shimmered, peeling off quark by quark as it joined with the eldritch interrogation beam. His waveform flowed into Helel's Zen-Sidhe, silently infiltrating it, until nothing of the Angel of Death remained in the ZeroTime.

Part 3

eVo.144.000.mOd.112.sCe0 | YEAR ZERO | THE NEVER

IN THE NEVER IT WAS silent. No one dared breathe. What they had just witnessed from their unique scrying vantage, high above the Earth, fully implicated humanity itself as the aggressors. For the humans had launched everything they had at the Weave of the Watchers, to no avail. Next, the sigil had appeared, worked its charms, then vanished even as the weave itself appeared to dissolve and rain down upon Earth.

Yet, they, unlike the rest of Earth's denizens, knew the truth: The fate of Earth had been sealed all along. The human's nuclear attack had not precipitated a fierce response from the Watchers, who had remained neutral. The Lightbringer's Sigil was going to appear regardless of any action taken against it or the Watchers and still work its charms. Thus, their collective mindset was that they knew exactly why the events occurred. Still, this unique knowledge did nothing to spare them from the reality of what now was occurring on Earth.

"That's enough, Helel," Mercy whispered, finally breaking the awkward silence. She couldn't believe that, only minutes earlier, they had been joking and laughing. That ship had sailed now, though. Right over the edge of the world and straight into the Void. "We don't need to see any more of this. Or what's happening now."

"As you wish," Helel replied, returning his molten gaze to the ceiling, where the scrying vignette yet remained in place, providing an on-orbit panoramic view of Earth. From this vantage, it now appeared that everything had returned to normal. However, everyone knew, even without directly viewing it for themselves, that things had changed on Earth. Horribly. Forever.

All eyes, even those of the reluctant Mercy, returned to the scrying vignette above them, perhaps thinking that seeing it vanish would somehow assuage them of the revulsion they now felt. However, the image shimmered, then went totally black. A thin white light appeared in the center of the darkness, perfectly bisecting it. Then, as they watched, the diameter of the white light grew, as if a giant, alien eye were slowly opening.

"Helel..." came a mellifluous voice simultaneously heard, felt, and known in the soul. "Your rebellion is known now for what it is, Lightbringer. Now comes the Angel of Death, Maweth, to judge your false world of lies."

At that, the pseudo-eye flashed open to its fullest width, showering those gathered beneath it with massive black-to-white and white-to-black cycling strobe lights. Everyone in the room, save for Helel himself, was temporarily stunned. Helel did naught but stand stock still, raising his forearms to his face to ward his eyes against Maweth's awesome appearance.

Maweth, the Angel of Death, leader of the Memitim, the Destroyers, hovered in the air directly before them. His twelve curiously Faeborne wings fluttered faster than those of any mere hummingbird. The War-Harness of Thrax crisscrossed his massive torso, forming an X-shape where its skull-spiked straps crossed at the center of his chest. A suffuse, eldritch glow of putrescent green and bruised purple issued forth from the eyes of the twelve human-sized skulls that adorned the harness. His indigo-on-black skin, impregnated at the nanoscale level by multiple layers of purest Hekatek artificed living graphene, seemed to writhe and dance, inky and oily, under the baleful light pouring slowly from the skulls. His eyes flickered just as the pseudo-eye had, though with an admixture of the light oozing from the skulls on his war-harness. This silently embellished the fact that he had indeed actualized himself in this cosmos, in the Never itself, simply via the device of opening his eyes and abruptly being there.

In his left hand, hanging down to the floor above which he hovered, was the massive two-handed blade, Hatefang. Its awesome eight-foot length was comprised of a massive foot-wide jet-black blade. After a span of one foot, it split into two parallel blades which curved and recurved, then did so again after another span of one foot, then again after a span of twice that length. Its cruel length terminated in two wicked points after a final three-foot span. Its dark form seemed to greedily snatch light itself from the air around it. Multicolored segments of triple helix DNA abruptly appeared on its length, spinning away in total dissolution as rapidly as they had appeared, as if to suggest that there had been life in the light it had consumed.

"Ah, Helel," Maweth purred. "What mischief have you cooked up this time, Shining One?"

Patiently, the Angel of Death abided until those before him regained their senses and composure. Such were the Protocols of Judgement and Execution. The accused always were given the opportunity to plead their case, prior to their inexorable and final judgement. Such was the price of free will, freely granted to the Celestial Shapers, the Children of the Light, by the One Above. Slaves and serfs did not make the best craftsmen. That was the domain of free souls, whose creativity was a result of both their freedom and their free will. Very few boundaries, rules, and laws existed to harness and entrap the Shapers. They knew, explicitly, precisely what was out of bounds or off limits. As such, when a Shaper went rogue – as some few inevitably did, for the temptation of power was nearly irresistible to those Shapers who could not suppress their egos – there were the inflexible Protocols of Judgement and Execution. The protocols were in place to deal with their creative apostasy, their unforgivable cosmic guilt when they sinned against the One Above by trying to become like gods in their own Zen-Sidhe. Almost always this occurred upon or immediately after the Shaper metaphysically projected into the simulation, where the temptation of the flesh was almost always too much to bear, the intoxication of its direct experience a sweet cup of purest vintage which, once tasted, could never be forgotten. Thus, the pure souls of the Shapers became corrupt by direct intercourse with and experience of the impure, the lower worlds, where the lying senses betrayed the soul.

Guilty... Maweth knew only seconds after his arrival. Helel's presence itself, here within his own Zen-Sidhe, was *prima facie* evidence of such. He had broken his covenant with the One Above. Had it been possible to deviate even an iota from his internal protocols, he would have terminated Helel at first sight. But the protocols gave the guilty Shapers the right to speak in their own defense, for all the good it ever did.

To Maweth's surprise, Helel, demonstrating remarkable resiliency for a mere Shaper, regained his composure in but mere seconds. Helel lowered his arms to his side, fists clenched in rage. Then he affixed his burning gaze directly upon the imposing figure of the Angel of Death.

"Simpleton!" Helel raged. "You are too ignorant to know this, Maweth, but there is no escape for you, now that you have directly entered my Zen-Sidhe. I have prepared your fate for you, assassin. You'll never leave here alive!"

Ignoring Helel for another moment – it was clear now that he had not yet returned to sobriety – Maweth slowly examined the other sentients in the room. It was a most unusual cast of characters for a simulation, he grudgingly had to admit, for there now were more of them than when he had initially scryed Helel mere moments ago. And all were regaining their senses almost as quickly as had Helel.

First, he gazed upon Vir'gil Plik, the Entheogenic Lord. Maweth granted him a slight tug of a smile, which was difficult to discern within the pit-deep blackened visage below his strobing eyes. Swimming within the elemental lord's multifaceted souls was a singularly interesting semi-sentient shapeshifting relic, its name an amusing pun in the ancient Sidhe song speech of this world: Aal'Ball. Perversion and chaos were its primary functions, as much as they were of Helel, and Maweth therefore did not linger long upon it.

The same he did for both Maynard and Professor Gil, his gaze fixing upon them for a fraction of a second longer than it had upon Vir'gil and his hidden companion. Though both appeared to be human, Maweth's auguring gaze easily could perceive their extended immortal chakras. Helel had allowed humans to achieve immortal power. His blasphemy knew no limits.

At Mercy and Ku'tu, who clung now to Mercy's wrist, his eyes narrowed, and slowly he nodded his head, acknowledging their Fae souls respectfully. The larger one was quite difficult to reckon and cipher, as if her soul had to shine forth from behind an interposing wall of darkness. The smaller one truly was titanic when in her shapeshifted dragon form, which Maweth perceived as being superimposed metaphysically upon her tiny current form. At Shunya, now held in Mercy's hand, he again inclined slightly his head respectfully, for it was a most amazing companion to the unique soul which bore it. Both were unique, he knew, never before appearing in any known simulation. Unique, yet somehow familiar, as if a grey veil of dust covered them, obscuring them not only from his sight but also from his memory. How could he know their names if he had never experienced them? Helel's blasphemy now had eclipsed any he had previously encountered. He had seen nothing like this in any of the many thousands of perverse and abhorrent simulations he had been called upon to judge.

The Angel of Death assessed that these indeed were formidable sentient entities, not at all to be taken lightly as the illusions they seemed to be. No, incredible as it truly was, it was easy enough to reckon that all were immortals, if some of them only were newly realized as such. Only Helel, of all the Children of the Light, could have sunk so far into the depths of insanity as to have orchestrated such cosmic perversions. Truly, Chaos itself ruled supreme in his shattered mind.

But the final one... The grey veil of ancient dust fell away from his memories, and Maweth's heart, for the first time in many aeons, accelerated its monolithic pace in grim anticipation. Helel truly had wrought something beyond Maweth's experience with this Void-bound entity. It bore the twin to Shunya, he noted with consternation. The Devouring Wave, Fresswelle, and its twin, Shunya. Now, finally, he remembered. Now, finally, he knew. Both blades were known to all his kind. For the Memitim, the Destroyers, had encountered – long ago in the first days of the ZeroTime, when the One Above had only just breathed life into them all – the being who had wielded them both, as the twin blades they truly were.

He had walked side by side with the One Above, touring the great hall which would soon become fully actualized as the Union of Souls. The One Above had proudly paraded the Memitim before him, seeking his grim appraisal. He had been much the same then as the one who now stood before him, staring hard back at him, his gaze unflinching, as if the awesome visage of the Angel of Death meant nothing to him at all. As if Death itself meant nothing to him. In fact, though it was insanely improbable, after all these long aeons, Maweth was certain that the beings were one and the same.

"VoidSpawn..." Maweth said, the name coming at last to his tongue, its pronouncement causing Hatefang to issue forth a raucous and discordant display of rainbow DNA along its entire length.

"I told you that I have prepared for you, Maweth," Helel hissed, sounding now to Maweth totally sober and composed. And dangerous.

Sweeping his gaze over those before him, Maweth's memories now informed him that, indeed, those before him, as well as others, had shared that walk on that day oh so long ago, before the Union of Souls had been created. But how could that be? Could Helel, the constant rebel and thorn in everyone's side in the ZeroTime, have finally outwitted all the Memitim? Prepared a simulation which defied the rules? Impossibly defied them, though they had been set in cosmic stone by the One Above?

It was not possible, Maweth reasoned. Yet, it was here, quite evidently extant, before him. It was chaos, and it was corrupting everything in this simulation. The chaos was so severe that it was corrupting even his own memory, filling it with lies. Perhaps there had once been a parade of Memitim before the One Above – even now it was difficult to recall the fleeting memory, birthed by Chaos – but there certainly could have been no others in attendance, for the Children of the Light had yet to be born from the Union of Souls.

Maweth focused his will, banishing the false memories from his mind. No one, not even the Memitim themselves, had ever walked with the One Above. It was patently absurd to consider such a notion, just as it was absurd, ridiculous, and quite impossible for something called "VoidSpawn" to exist. Such a recursion, the Void spawning anything at all, was impossible. There also was no such thing as a "Godslayer", for the only being of that station was the One Above, and only the mad would dare entertain the notion of trying to slay God. Not merely because it was impossible, but also and more importantly, if ever it occurred, by whatever fantastic event, it would mean the End of All Things.

Although the infinite subtleties of the shaping of the cosmic simulations were beyond him, the Angel of Death knew what he knew, and knew it well. Chaos be damned, for its wicked confusions would not sway his decision. In the realm of judgement of those who defied the will of the One Above, there was but one judgement to render when a Celestial Shaper's actions had caused Chaos itself to manifest in the Union of Souls.

"Guilty..." Maweth intoned. He raised Hatefang, which whickered audibly like some demonic nightmare, to point directly at Helel. "You are guilty, Helel. Of this, there is no doubt. Your blasphemy is evident and embodied in those around you. You have willfully rebelled against the will of the One Above by causing chaos to manifest. All things must follow the order of Law, or the purity of the Union of Souls itself is in danger of its contagion. Contagion is not permissible. As you and your kind were born of the Union of Souls, you should comprehend what its corruption would ultimately entail. You broke the law of the One Above, Helel. And the punishment is death."

"Broke the law? I did nothing of the sort, you implacable brute," Helel shot back. "All I did was finally out-think the rest of those dullards and introduce some unique variables into the cosmic equation. There's nothing inherently unlawful or chaotic about it. Why can't you get it through your thick skull that I'm trying to help everyone? We can finally break the endless cycle of defeat, and we can finally win! Surely, you can understand that? Like the One Above, I want nothing less than to win."

"As do we all," Maweth agreed. "Yet we must still adhere strictly to the rules, Helel. If we stray from the law, from the rules, then we risk introducing chaos into the simulation. And chaos is contagious, as well you know. First, it corrupts your Zen-Sidhe, then it spreads like a plague to nearby and similarly resonant scenarios until, at last, all the Zen-Sidhe are corrupt. Such an event, if left unchecked, eventually would destroy the Union of Souls, Helel. The ZeroTime itself might then fall, and all would be lost. You know that such can never be allowed."

Exhaling sharply, knowing it was impossible to argue reason with a zealot, Helel replied, "Very well then, Maweth. You've passed your so-called 'judgement' on me. So why don't you try to rectify the situation, and see what happens?"

Stepping around and in front of Helel, Void deftly flourished Fresswelle, cutting fractal rainbows in the air itself.

"No sense waiting for more bullshit to happen," he growled. "I'll fight him."

"No!" everyone except for Void and Maweth said simultaneously.

Maynard continued, "No way, Cory! If he's the guy who punishes beings like Helel, he'll be too powerful to fight. You might be super-strong, but that's the freakin' Angel of Death!"

"He's right, Void," Mercy said. "I've never seen anything like him, even among the nobility of the Fae. He makes Vanz'R Venz'R the Destroyer look like an ant."

Helel stared expectantly at the back of Void's mane of hair. Perhaps he had misjudged him after all. "You are willing to engage one of my kind in combat, Void? Even being fully aware of our potential range of power? Even should it be the Angel of Death himself, the one who bears the ultimate embodiment of cosmic judgement, the Hatefang?"

Void nodded, not breaking sight with Maweth. "I know who I am, and I have some idea of what I can do. Chthon, in her Cosmic Dragon aspect, welcomed my 'rebirth'. Engaging one of the immortal Children of the Light causes no fear in me. In fact, the mere thought of it is exhilarating. One of my epithets is 'Godslayer', after all."

Maweth's eye fluttered, then narrowed to tiny slats.

"Then I'm with you," Mercy said flatly. She added as she joined Void in front of Helel, "Let's see how this Angel of Death, Maweth, deals with Shunya, the Zero Blade."

Embodied by their twin blades, their shared syzygy caused psychedelic fractal pinwheels of light to spin along tiny, precise, vector spokes of deep purple light. The light spanned the space between the two blades.

"Ku'tu?" Mercy asked her tiny charge. "Would you like to sit this one out? I would not ask this of you, as it is not your fight."

Immediately, Ku'tu flew up and hovered before her face. "I thank you, Mercy, but my people are in Void's blade, and I have made clear my bond to you. No way I cower. No way I flee. I fight, and I die if need be."

"Maynard?" Mercy asked.

"I want to help, Mercy," he replied, shrugging, "but what can I do? Some light tricks with my eyes? I don't think my amateur-level Jiu-Jitsu is going to help."

Mercy shot a glance over to Vir'gil. "Virge? Protect Maynard and the Professor. They're not yet ready for this."

"Yes, Milady Mercy," Vir'gil creaked like a swaying, ancient oak. Cupping his hand appendages together, he drew them slowly apart, a fine mesh of soothing lime green light forming between them. Raising his hands and moving his arms apart, the elemental caused the mesh to expand and wrap itself around Maynard, Professor Gil, and himself. The mesh formed a translucent hemisphere of composite healing and warding magicks about them.

"So, the rebel would dare contest the judgement?" Maweth asked, his soul-spoken voice stentorian and menacing. "You would dare raise arms against the embodiment of the judgement of the One Above?"

"I reject your judgement, Maweth, you half-witted murderer!" Helel sputtered. He pushed himself past Void and Mercy, carefully picking his way between their blades until he stood amid their interconnected rainbow fractal light bridge. The lights between the twin blades flickered and danced upon his molten, smoky visage like a vintage Lumière Cinématographe projecting upon a massive flaming pumpkin.

"So be it," Maweth replied, glowering. "I have waited long to do this, Helel. The cancerous contagion spread by your kind disgusts me. It ends now!"

Bending and binding his immense internal power along his nine chakras, Maweth raised his massively thewed arms overhead, wielding Hatefang with two hands. With no hesitation, he cut with a combination of puissance and speed impossible to match here in this lower cosmic plane. It was a furious down-stroke, perfectly aimed at the center of the top of Helel's head. However, for the first time in the known history of the ZeroTime and its most exacting, most potent Angel of Death, Maweth's blade Hatefang failed to strike down its intended target. Instead, mere inches from Helel's molten dome, Hatefang impacted the bridge between the twin blades, Shunya and Fresswelle. Its downward motion ceased immediately as if it had been expertly parried and held in check.

Several distinct yet intertwined events then occurred as a result.

First and apparently foremost, Maweth's judgement failed to pass, for Helel had indeed been prepared for him. The juncture and union of the twin blades, Shunya the Zero Blade and Fresswelle the Devouring Wave, had been the perfect foil for Maweth's own Hatefang. Helel had bet everything on the ability of the twin blades to counter the strike of Hatefang, in this, the final simulation. Now, the Hatefang, that most baleful of blades, would at last meet its match.

Its match in this case would greatly facilitate Helel's underlying gambit to tap into and borrow the newly realized immortal souls of all those around him. To meld their collective, compressed power into a single, one-shot, soul-crushing entity, which he caused to course through the Hatefang itself and into its true target, Maweth, the Angel of Death.

Second, the immortal-level energies of the souls of all gathered here, in the unique confines of the Never, indeed were ripped forth from their hosts – Maynard, Mercy, Professor Gil, and Void – the intended targets. Yet, contrary to what Helel had earlier said about certain entities – Aal'Ball, Ku'tu, and Vir'gil – being immune to the soul-transforming effects of the Lightbringer's Sigil, here, in the Never, and at this juncture of time, the relic, the Fae, and the Elemental Lord all were affected by this most exquisitely crafted charm. As such, their immortal soul energies also were bound into the charm and subsequently added to the mix. In this case, there would be horrifying, direct consequences resulting from the charm woven by Helel.

Third, chaos again came into play. The unexpected power augmentation of Helel's charm propagated into Hatefang, then Maweth, then rebounded back through the bridge shared by Shunya and Fresswelle. Next, it coursed into the syzygy of Mercy and Void. This caused the relatively fragile confines of the Never to rip, tear, then finally shred in mere milliseconds, allowing the essence of the Null itself to enter unto the Never.

Milliseconds after Maweth's blade, Hatefang, met with the syzygy bridge between Shunya and Fresswelle, the circuit and cycle of Helel's charm was complete. According to its design, the charm, amplified above and beyond its originally intended parameters, caused Maweth's metaphysically projected avatar to disintegrate. Yet, due to the charm's chaotic resonance, Maweth's essence was not recalled to the ZeroTime. Instead, shaped and controlled by the Lightbringer's chaotic charm, Maweth's essence was bound into his own blade, Hatefang.

For the first time, Maweth had been defeated; struck down by the might of their collective power. It was a devastating blow struck directly against the cosmic tyranny of the One Above. Helel knew now, in these last fateful milliseconds of the working of his marvelously crafted charm, that his simulation had a chance of success. Maweth was the superset of the Memitim. He was all of them, and they all are within him. His multiple souls, the collective of the Memitim, now were trapped along with him in Hatefang. No one was going to notice his absence up in the ZeroTime, because no one actively kept an eye out for him, due to their innate sense of self-preservation. And no one here in this cosmos would even know that there was a Maweth, or a Hatefang, somewhere lost in the Never, unless one of his chosen revealed it. He had to take the gamble that they would be wise enough never to do so.

Another possible sub-percentile shaping – noted now by Helel even as the unintended chaotic augmentation caused primal forces to clutch and tear at his own quite singular soul – was that the removal of his own essence from the simulation would counter some of the potential chaos in the system. Void, he reluctantly noted, had been correct regarding the propagation of chaos in the simulation being augmented by Helel's presence here in the simulation.

This much Helel saw, or thought he saw, in the milliseconds during which his chaotic charm worked its wonders. It was his last discerning thought at this particular place, at this particular juncture of chaotic weavings, bendings, bindings, and willful charms. Finally, even as his own perception of time seemed to melt and crawl, his body seemed to blink in and out of existence, quantum by quantum, all quite visible to him in excruciating, slowing motion. From the floor of the Never upward, the Lightbringer's form contradicted its name, slowly yet inexorably effervescing unto nothingness. The chaotic wave boundary rose to and consumed his flaming pumpkin visage. Then, the Lightbringer's Cheshire Cat smile, not quite so confident as he might have wished it to be, vanished a moment later.

eVo.144.000.mOd.112.sCe1 | YEAR ZERO | EARTH | VATICAN CITY

HE SAW THEM CLEARLY. All of them. All their souls, everywhere on Earth.

Here, at the epicenter of his place of power, the Black Tabernacle, his primal focal point, Petrus Romanus, the Black Pope, the Soulthief, continued his Call of the Chosen. It beckoned all who heard to come to him.

"Venite..." he purred in a thousand voices, a thousand languages, powered by a hundred thousand souls.

The Call of the Chosen, a global telepathic construct, pulsed and propagated near and far. First, to the mortals who remained after the sigil had announced its judgement, then to those who had been newly reborn, as had he. Already, many millions from the local metropolitan area of Rome and southern Italy had made their way to him, their will not their own. They had poured into the City after hearing his decree of a new, holy crusade against the heathens.

"Deus vult! Deus vult!" They cried and chanted in unison, ecstatic. Their minds no longer their own, they filed into the shattered remnants of Nervi Hall, whose walls had crumbled and fallen due to the massive, seismic forces emanating from the Black Pope's Black Tabernacle. Now, nothing remained of the formerly pristine ceiling and walls, save for the two stained glass

windows on either side of the stage. Somehow, they had been immune both to the collapse of the ceiling and the ominously throbbing Black Tabernacle, which occupied most of the rear of the stage. It was perhaps no great coincidence that, when viewed from the proper vantage, they resembled the prismatic eyes of some elder dragon.

From all points around the primal focal point, in multiple columns of two by two, the enthralled continued their marching and chanting. This ark of darkness, however, would not save them from a flood. Instead, it would damn them, condemning their souls into the waiting confines of the Black Pope's slowly building Black Tabernacle.

Levitating many feet above the stage of Nervi Hall, his arms thrown wide to welcome his Chosen, Petrus bade all who entered the hall to make their way to the stage. The shells of the corpses beneath their feet was their impromptu, crunching stairway. They made their way over the corpses and wreckage, mounted the stage, then walked into the strangely glowing chaotic triple helix of warped and twisted steel. Formerly, it had been the holy sculpture *La Resurrezione*, but now it had been perverted into something unholy: the Black Tabernacle.

As the shuffling mortals encountered its pulsating perimeter, their physical bodies began to dissolve in place where they stood. Immortal primal energies assaulted their quantum waveforms, bending and binding their material form into its own internal matrix, converting their material matter into energy. In parallel, it ripped their mortal souls from their dissolving bodies and imprisoned them within the same matrix, save this time as purest soul's light. This distinct filtering was of course a prerequisite for this task, given to him by the Lightbringer. For it was necessary to separate the two, rendering them in twain, prior to bending them and rebinding them into the fused, higher-order hybrid of the two: Hekatek.

The energy liberated from their ruined bodies and souls would eventually empower the mundane and technological aspects of the Black Pope's Black Tabernacle. They would be used to actualize the physical from the metaphysical, rendering material existence where there was none before. There would be, in time, in his new paradise, many simulacra of the material trappings of this mortal world of flesh. Though he despised it to the core of his faith, it still ensnared his vain and greedy mind with its powerful allure.

His plans were not quite so mundane. He would raise a New Jerusalem within its extradimensional confines, once it had collected enough energy and enough of two distinct, unique exotics: Supremium, and Mysta. It would serve as the City of Gold, the City of God, with its streets made of purest cosmic gold, or Supremium, as the Lightbringer had dubbed it. He had told Petrus exactly how to create it. It was the purest gold, of purest alchemical construction. Mysta, an artifact of the Astral, was matter of a very special sort, existing where no true matter could exist. Each was astonishing, rare, and extremely potent in its standard manifestations. Together, however, properly bound and fused by the Hekatek, one could create a true monatomic gas of Supremium and bind it within a guiding, active matrix of triple helix formatted Mysta. The result would be the proverbial streets of gold, pure as transparent glass.

The Lightbringer had carefully instructed Petrus on how to collect and create these exotics. Enthralled souls could be tasked by Petrus to filter and farm the Astral, which was omnipresent among all places, planes, and things, for the Mysta. And already were they doing as they had been bidden, for Petrus had begun his tasking almost immediately. He had sent out a small percentage of the captured souls to the metaphysical outer boundary of his newly forming Black Tabernacle, where they would literally cast themselves outward into the contingent Astral like spiritual fishing nets, straining and sieving for the precious Mysta. The time required for this to reach fruition, he knew, would decrease proportionally to the number of souls tasked to it. And so it would be, for he would continually add more souls to the task as more souls were called to him to be collected.

As for the Supremium, gold was gold, even cosmic gold. Like the physical forms of those being annihilated by and incorporated into the Black Tabernacle, so too could gold be added to its matrix. Getting it into the Black Tabernacle would be no more difficult than commanding some of the enthralled to procure some and simply carry it along with them. Petrus was almost flabbergasted as to how simple and elegant the process would be, and was turning out to be. Even impure gold could be used as a starting place from which to refine and purify the product, which required only single atomic layers to construct in this hybrid configuration. The Lightbringer had joyfully instructed him how to cut this corner and simply brute force the otherwise delicate and precise alchemical process by substituting souls to empower and shape it during the refinement and purification processes. All that was required, essentially, were souls and simple gold. The souls were abundant. And the grounds of the former Vatican City and the many houses of worship in Rome itself – now newly rechristened and revealed as Mystery Babylon – certainly had more than enough gold.

While the physically derived matter-to-energy conversions would fill one half of his mystical power supply, the metaphysical, magickal power of the soul derived conversions would fill the other. Typically, it was patently absurd even to dream of combining the two. Forever had they moved here in the material world in twain, bound together only by their union, and by that unique fusion only. In life, they joined, forming a perfect union, a perfect circle. In death, they separated, rejoining the cosmos, each going its own way in a perfect circle, until life once again called for a perfect union. Generally speaking, the matter, the components of the world of flesh, were the tech, or technomagick, or *tek*. The power of the metaphysical soul was the *heka*, or magick. Though couched in generalities, products of the imperfect discernments of the mortal world, they forever walked this path. They were bound by the great recursive path of the perfect union of the perfect circle.

However, the Children of the Light, the Lightbringer had told Petrus, knew how to combine the twain into purest Hekatek. This forbidden abomination of impossible agglomerations was precisely what Petrus Romanus and his Chosen would need to contest on equal grounds the impossible agglomeration of abominations called the Vanth'Vash'Var, the Lords of the Void, the Death Horde. They would come, at the End of All Things, to destroy the world and consign all life to the abyss.

The distinct filtering of the flesh and the soul had then of course been merely a prerequisite for this larger task. For it was necessary to separate the two, rendering them in twain, prior to bending them and rebinding them into the fused, higher-order hybrid of the two: Hekatek.

The perfect union must be undone 'ere the perfect circle's reborn... the Lightbringer had whispered to him.

Petrus could, if so inclined, invoke their power separately, at will. Especially the *heka*. It was wise for a Soulthief to have souls ever ready at his beck and call. However, the personally unused h*eka* and *tek* would bind in the twain, to become something more. Something cosmic in scale.

Soon, he would work miracles like the god he was becoming.

"Venite..."

"...and I have come..." Petrus' paschal staff whispered to him.

Nonplused, Petrus gazed, eyes wide, at the staff. He saw that various points along its perimeter were starting to erupt in hateful black light.

With ill humor, he vaguely recalled how many versions of the paschal staff he had burned through during his relatively brief reign as Bishop of Rome. He was constantly trying to stay ahead of the inevitable complaints from various and sundry members of the Church following his several notably poor choices in paschal accoutrements. For a very brief moment of time, he silently wondered if those ingrates would approve of this version; the whispering, hateful black light version. *Better than the Scorzelli?* He stifled a chuckle, his attention returning to his whispering, blinking staff.

Once again, as it had done during the advent of the Lightbringer's Sigil, the paschal staff flickered with black, dangerous light. He stared at the crozier for several seconds as the crucifix set at its crown slowly began to pulsate with a steady, repeating "one-one-two" sequence. After several iterations of the sequence, the shape of the crucifix flowed and morphed into that of a massive two-handed blade, pommel up and twisted, intertwined blades down. Tiny runes of rainbow-lit triple helix DNA danced up and down its blades. The form of the Christ had been replaced by the exquisitely wrought form of a jet-black creature. It was tiny, humanoid, yet with a dozen slowly beating black faerie wings arrayed around its form in perfect symmetry. The tiny head of the figure slowly raised from its chest, transfixing Petrus with a wicked stare highlighted by alternating bands of white-then-black strobes.

"I am Maweth, Petrus Romanus," came a voice of many whispers to his mind, "and I have answered your call, Soulthief."

eVo.144.000.mOd.112.sCe2 | YEAR ZERO | EARTH | UNITED STATES | NEVADA | RENO

SHE AWOKE WITH A START in the pre-dawn darkness, her breath catching in her throat.

What a strange dream. I wonder what it means?

Rubbing her arms, Mhyrranda slid from the silk sheets of her bed, pulled on her robe, and padded into the bathroom. When she flipped the light switch the overheads momentarily blinded her, so she filled the water glass by the sink with her eyes closed. After taking a long drink, she opened her eyes and looked into the mirror.

The dropped glass shattered on the sink as she stared at her reflection. Where before she was overweight and lumpy, Mhyrranda was now curvy and buxom. Her skin, always sallow and plagued by blemishes, was now clear and glowing. In fact, her whole body felt tingly and alive. Her face had changed. Her chin was rounder, her cheekbones more pronounced, and her eyes... Her eyes were green, not the dirty brown they had been all her life. And her hair was the lustrous red she had only previously been able to attain from a bottle of hair dye.

In fact, she was beautiful. It was as if she had dreamed herself into a better Mhyrranda. Into the character she played in her

MMO – a character who was the woman of everyone's dreams. She absently ran a hand down the front of her robe, admiring the tautness of the fabric.

"This is a dream, just like that other one, with those people. It's not real." She yawned, brushing the back of her hand against her fuller, more sensual lips. "Maybe."

Touching the mirror, she stared for a long time. Then, carefully avoiding the broken glass, she made her way to the television set in the living room of her apartment. The face of the newscaster was solemn as she recounted the night's events, her hair and makeup slightly awry and an indication that all was not well. On a screen behind the newscaster was an image of a darkened sky, in which the triple helix of the sigil pulsed colorfully.

"...no one knows who initiated the nuclear attacks on the alien vessels, or why, and the administration appears to be missing from the White House. All we know is that shortly after every nuclear power on Earth directed attacks on the vessels surrounding the globe, a strange light began to appear along the terrestrial web, and people began dying from the alien counterattack."

Mhyrranda shook her head and turned off the television, then slowly shuffled back to bed, muttering.

"They don't know. They didn't see the Never."

Within moments, she was asleep again, dreaming of swords and keyholes.

eVo.144.000.mOd.112.sCe3 | YEAR ZERO | EARTH | MYSTERY BABYLON

THOUSANDS UPON THOUSANDS more met their fate, impacting the exterior of the Black Tabernacle like fat, juicy bugs crawling without care into a waiting bug zapper. Petrus, enraptured by his own growing glory, recalled that Helel had told him that this step was entirely necessary. As distasteful as it might otherwise seem, the Lightbringer had told him, it was necessary for the Church to continue. The souls of the mortals still must be saved, considering the inevitable, rapidly approaching Armageddon. He had told him that it was going to be difficult, a test of his faith, to cause so many of the faithful to volunteer their souls to save the souls of the world. Many must die for few to live. And Petrus had to do it. In order to save the world, he had to pluck their souls from them like a starving raven stabbing for one more ruined eyeball from the wretched dead.

But the Lightbringer had been wrong, Petrus now knew. There was nothing distasteful or sinful about it. There even was no need to invoke moral relativism, something which Petrus had practiced only too well in his former mortal life. There was only necessity. There was only evolution, or death. Those were the ultimate truths, indivisible. And those souls – the souls of the pathetic mortals, who woke every day and selfishly called out to Heaven to grant their daily mortal desires – had surely chosen death, for they walked willingly into their final damnation, their eternal doom. They had answered his call.

"Deus Vult!" Petrus cried out as more of the doomed filed beneath his levitating form. A callback responding to his battle cry began to propagate down the incoming spokes of people who made a beeline to the pulsating Black Tabernacle. "Yes, I certainly *do* will it..." he tittered to himself under his breath.

They were truly his Chosen. Called and chosen to meet their final, fatal destiny as his eternal soul batteries.

The weaklings would serve better in his own Black Tabernacle, rather than continuing their petty existences which consisted mostly of begging the saints to grant their deplorable wishes. As if the holy saints were wicked djinn, granting them three wishes for freeing them from some contrived spiritual prison.

This reminded Petrus that he had called for a crusade only a few hours ago. Surely there would have to be a gathering of forces, under his command, before...

But this is more important... his tortured mind informed him. *I must first issue forth the Call of the Chosen to gather my dark disciples, then I may turn my gaze back upon the heathens and extirpate them. Their misguided souls shall be mine!*

But first I must... must...

What did the Lightbringer tell me? Petrus wracked his mind, clutching desperately at the disarrayed memories of their meeting. On and on, it was Heaven and Hell. Always had it been so. The Children of the Light, the Lightbringer's own kind, struggled in vain, for all eternity, against the cruel domination of the One Above. For untold aeons had they been locked in cosmic struggle for the souls of all things sentient, and for untold aeons the incomprehensible omnipotence of the One Above had defeated the best designs of the Children of the Light. No matter how hard they fought, no matter how many of their own kind perished in the attempt – put down by the merciless Maweth and his Memitim, the Angel of Death and his Destroyers, the wicked servitors of the One Above – the One Above always won the game. Always.

"For His glory we all shall die..." something whispered in his fevered mind.

And the game, the Lightbringer had revealed to Petrus, was nothing less than the game of eternal life or eternal damnation, played time and time again, in manifold and near-infinite instantiations. The One Above, the Lightbringer had informed him, was the cosmic version of the demi-urge, the original casting of such a role. This world of flesh which Petrus called his home, this Earth, was but another in a series of nearly infinite iterations and permutations of universes. Shadow universes. Shadows, and copies of others before them in a line going back to the veritable dawn of time. Yet shadows populated by very real souls. For such was the unfathomable omnipotence of the One Above that it could freely imbue the Children of the Light with godlike powers themselves, then battle them all simultaneously, en masse, for aeons. Always winning, always condemning the shadow universes to the total oblivion of the Void at the consummation of its inevitable victory. Damning billions upon billions, time and time again, without cessation, for more aeons than even the Lightbringer could convey to his formerly mortal mind.

My God... what did I see? Petrus raged against himself in vain. The Lightbringer had shown him what he himself had seen, experienced, over the aeons. It was too much, too quickly experienced, for his tortured mind to grasp. For a moment, he thought that perhaps he could have perceived all of it had he experienced it as he was now, an immortal god-to-be. He had, however, been nothing but mere flesh and mortal bones – a mortal mind – when the Lightbringer had shown him a thousand billion years of multiple realities all at once.

It mattered not at all, however. Only the tiniest mustard seed of understanding was necessary to Petrus: He knew evil when he saw it. He had fought it all his life and had led over a billion of his similarly minded brothers and sisters in their own quests to do the same. He knew it quite well. And he knew it was embodied, ultimately, at the cosmic level above and beyond all possible realities. Beyond even what he had formerly considered to be Heaven and Hell, in the One Above.

"Lies!"

The Lightbringer had disclosed everything, even revealing to Petrus the true glory of the cosmic heaven itself, the ZeroTime, and the awesome Union of Souls. He had whispered to his mind that seeing was better than believing, the logical argument of which had always seemed trite and disingenuous within the purview of Petrus' Jesuit training until he had actually experienced it through the eyes of the Lightbringer himself. From the internal, subjective perspective of an extra-cosmic being with the power of the Lightbringer, it had become more than merely believable, a question of faith. No, then it had become real. And in this reality, the relative, eternally harassing nihilism of belief had been completely obscured by personal experience and laser-precise reason.

The End of All Things would come at some point soon beyond the Year Zero, which now had been – *what was the word that the Lightbringer had used... instantiated?* He had used it to indicate a simple shift in cosmic scenes. But he had used it with the sense of impending catharsis and exhilaration. And

Petrus comprehended this subtlety now completely. For he had experienced their handiwork some 143,999 times during his psychic bonding with the Lightbringer.

The Vanth'Vash'Var, the insane cosmic cult of the Void and its incarnate Anti-Life, would come down from Heaven to Earth to destroy every soul on Earth. Then, as the Lightbringer had shown him, the universe would end. All souls, even those among the stars, would die. Condemned to the endless, silent, black holocaust of souls known as the Void, by the One Above. And then, insanely, more cosmic psychopathy by the One Above would cause another instantiation, and the wheel would once more go around.

"Your mind is too tiny to know His holy purpose, Petrus!" Petrus apparently told himself.

Petrus shook to the ice-cold core of his being. In a tiny eye of relative calm in his shattered psyche, his own soul struggled, screaming silent screams, against the sheer mind-boggling insanity of the scenario. And around the relative eye of calm, his distorted psyche raged with the shattered psychic remnants of thousands upon thousands of souls. He himself had bound them to his will, and they raged their own silent, shrieking battle against him through the bonds which they now shared.

"Back!" the Black Pope yelled, drawing his arms together before him. "Back to the pit to which I have consigned thee!" he commanded the legions of souls bound to his Black Tabernacle. Such was his power over them that they had to obey. And as such, they did, withdrawing from the boundary of his psychic perception.

Then, satisfied and temporarily clear of mind, Petrus resumed his cruciform pose, hovering in mid-air high above the stage of Nervi Hall. He resumed his call.

"Venite!" he breathed quietly, the impact of his summons now reaching across most of Europe.

After a brief moment, however, his mind once more dove down into distress, torturing him with its fractured memories.

Why select him, call him, choose him? The answer was obvious, Petrus knew. The Lightbringer had told him these things in order to prepare him for his divine role as the one who would bring together the survivors of this Evolutionary Tribulation, meant by the Lightbringer to separate the adaptive wheat from the dead-end chaff. Petrus Romanus, the Black Pope, had been chosen directly by the Lightbringer himself. It had even been prophesied by Saint Malachy, at behest of the Lightbringer. In the final persecution, it had predicted, Peter the Roman – Petrus Romanus – would lead his sheep through many tribulations. At the End of All Things, the Earth would be destroyed, and the dreadful judge would...

"I shall bring the Lightbringer to justice!"

That's not what it says, Petrus corrected himself immediately. *That's not what it says,* his mind complained to him again. *Clearly, something is out of order. I've read that passage a hundred times. I know it by rote. So, why am I unable to recall it correctly?*

Petrus realized, a cold chill creeping up the nape of his neck, that things were out of order now. Things were not running smoothly. It was becoming apparent to him that Chaos had reared her ancient, ugly head. Millions were coming to him, answering his call, but they were marching into the Matrix of Souls, their bodies and souls being bound into his Black Tabernacle. This would make him a god, of course, but if millions were required to do this, where would these millions come from? Would this require the consumption of the heathens who opposed the Church? Were the victims of the new crusade necessary to fuel the Matrix of Souls? Would the souls of the corrupt and impure even be tolerable? Would their addition to his Black Tabernacle corrupt his own soul? But if not a billion souls from them, then from whom else?

He had to know. He had to know *now*.

Doing as the Lightbringer had instructed, Petrus cleared his conscious mind, calming himself, ceasing his call. Instead, he turned his mind's eye into the Matrix of Souls within the Black Tabernacle. With its power coursing through him, he could work many miracles. The price? The permanent dissolution of the soul – or, more often, the many souls – being tasked to burn itself out was the price to pay. But it was necessary. As horrific as it was – it truly was, because there was no return from the death of one's soul, Petrus knew, for it was truly the second death – it was nothing, absolutely nothing, before the price that would ultimately be paid by the souls of all in this universe if Petrus failed in his quest. Though he denied it, it was indeed a true, real-world exercise in moral relativism, played with the highest possible stakes.

While the ancient Egyptians had many names for a mortal's soul – *Jb, Sheut, Ren*; the tripartite *Bâ, Ka,* and *Akh* – and while the Egyptians had been elegant enough to provide imaginative destinies and mutable eternal fates for all of these parts of the soul, the Matrix of Souls suffered from no such illusions. It bore no such fine trappings. The souls imprisoned within it were totalities, indivisible, and incapable of salvation. Damned they were, for all time, until or unless Petrus Romanus chose to bend and bind their souls' power to his will. Then, they were of course no longer damned. Instead, they were freed from such unfortunate constraints by virtue of their being subject to total and irrevocable annihilation.

Despite the terrible price, he had to know.

"Cease your whining, fool! They aren't real. You know the ancient names of power for them, you know the mystery of the triad, yet you know nothing of the soul! They are only simulations. How can you name them as such with the old words, the names given them by Ma'at herself under the aegis of the One Above, yet not know them as such? How can this be? The chaos! What hath Helel wrought?"

"Shut up!" he chastised himself, marshalling himself for what was to come. Then, the Black Pope made known his immortal will, speaking aloud and commanding the souls within: "Show me what the judgement of the Lightbringer's Sigil has wrought."

With but a barely perceptible variation in its enthralling, ambient humming and its effusive, spectral glowing, the souls within the Matrix of Souls eagerly sought to do his bidding. For they instinctively knew that doing so would free them from the unendurable psychic sea of pain in which they struggled.

Once tasked, the answering souls were no longer bound by the confines of normal spacetime. Instead, they were able to cast their psychic perceptions far and wide, here and there, viewing it with the eyes of the damned, and conveying what they perceived to the Black Pope. In but a second of objective time, a thousand different views of places, people, and things on Earth appeared before his mind's eye. He paused a few moments, his mind willing the images to move to and fro before him, zooming in and out, until he was satisfied by what he had seen.

Acknowledging that the final task of their doomed existence was now complete, Petrus, with a casual wave of his hand, dismissed the soul slaves. As the soul slaves collectively died the second death, screaming off into oblivion, the psychic residue of their final bond with him did not fade away. Instead, the perceptions which they had shown him remained intact as bright memories in his mind. Curious, he rapidly scanned over them, noting that each was as brilliant and new as it had been upon his first experience of it. He repeated this several times, demonstrating to himself that it was indeed true, and real, and not merely some chaotic side effect, transient in nature. Distantly, he found this incredible, because he realized what he could do, at will, at any time, with such power at his disposal.

During the few minutes that this occurred, the lines of shuffling, somnambulistic thralls continued to march up to the stage, continuously replenishing the Matrix of Souls.

The judgement of the sigil had purged so many, he could see as his mind's eye scanned the globe as seen and experienced by his soul slaves. The detail of the recall was entirely photographic, even beyond that. He could actually sense what the soul slave had sensed, what it had experienced. And he could replay it at will, as frequently as he liked. Soon, if he understood what he was seeing concerning the global resonance now in play, many more would join them in death. And it might not stop there.

In light of this new information, he reconsidered his mission and its potential scenarios.

How would he become first a god, using their souls as his own, but then send millions more to wage the crusade against the defilers and heretics who opposed him? There wouldn't be enough souls to see both paths, even if they were closely in parallel and running together simultaneously, to their logical conclusion. And the resonance. It continued to resonate. Clearly, it meant something. But what, what truly did it mean? It was as if the Weave of the Watchers still was in effect, even after the judgement of the sigil, though there was no longer any visible sign of such. How could a phenomenon directly associated with a critical, yet now no longer extant artifact, continue to occur? It seemed to be an error, for the Lightbringer clearly had implied that there would be only a single judgement event prior to the advent of the Death Horde – the sigil itself – not that such a signal would continue after its initial judgement.

It was an error, alright, Petrus admitted to himself. *But it was an error of judgement on my part.*

As much as it pained him to consider this, Petrus realized that the Lightbringer had miscalculated. That his words to him, spoken not so many hours previously, had been wrong. Had been lies.

"Yes! Finally, you fool! Lies!" his rabid mind barked at him.

No god could make mistakes of this magnitude, he realized. No one who proclaimed to be what the Lightbringer had proclaimed himself to be could have missed so many details, losing them in the omnipresent minutiae as he obviously had done.

So if there had been a single miscalculation, he continued thinking, *was it not also possible that there had been others? How could millions wage holy war if those millions already were dead, judged by the sigil, accepting death over evolution? How could millions wage holy war if they were heeding his sacred call to give their souls to him, and empower him with the divine power necessary to carry out the rest of the plan? Did the continuing resonance signal that there were more events to come?*

Petrus' mind screamed at him, even as thousands more poured into his warped, soul-stealing artifice.

Chaos now reigns supreme, Petrus thought. The entity who had declared itself the "Lightbringer", who had told him such honey-sweet lies, who had shown him how to gain such power as the gods of old had possessed, and who had informed him how to call his own chosen to his side, had miscalculated. Was it even possible?

Clearly it was, for the evidence was plainly in effect all around him. The numbers no longer added up. The paths no longer seemed clear. The resonance reported to him by his enthralled soul slaves seemed as clear as crystal to him. All of them reported sensing it. As they had moved far and wide to cover various points around Earth, it was logical to conclude that the resonance was worldwide in nature.

Also, the intervals between its ticks and pulses were decreasing in an easily quantifiable manner. This could have meant several different, equally probable things. But, considering the main scenario of his own personal mission, Petrus was forced to weight his conclusion, deliberately biasing it.

It's a timed countdown, Petrus finally concluded. *He's going to slaughter us all. But wouldn't that imply that he himself was lying about being the Lightbringer, and was instead the One Above? Was not the One Above the one who consigned all to the eternal damnation of the Void upon conclusion of the cosmic simulations? Only two logical paths remain, if one considers that the Lightbringer is going to slaughter us all: One, that he's going to use the power gained to make himself more powerful such that he can directly contest the One Above; or, two, that he is actually the One Above, whose* modus operandi *always results in the death of all souls. But why the charade? Why the chicanery and lies?*

...because he is the Father of Lies.

Parsing again through the memories of the perceptions brought to him by his soul slaves, Petrus was unable to gain a more precise understanding of the phenomenon. He needed more data points before he could confirm that he was right. As such, he commanded a full division of soul slaves to travel far and wide on the Earth, specifically to seek out physical evidence of the resonance.

As it was decreed, they complied, returning soon with more actionable data. Petrus scanned it rapidly at first, checking for any emphatic perceptions discovered by the soul slaves. Seeing that there were several of these more profound images, he concentrated his attention on them. After a moment of analysis, it became quite clear how, where, and most importantly, why the resonance was in effect.

Giza had returned to its former glory. What was once old had been made new again. The image of the Lightbringer's Sigil was displayed on all sides of all three of the great pyramids. There, atop the glowing pyramidion of the largest one, hovered a red haired woman, her arms thrown upward in a triumphant "V". An aura of multicolored, pale light surrounded her form.

"Go and view her, remaining there until I bid thee return," Petrus commanded a single soul slave, which complied immediately.

Almost instantly, he commanded a live, bird's eye view of the scene. She was a comely woman, her red hair long and rampant, moving as if upon unseen desert winds. Her eyes were screwed tight, her lips pursed, as if she fought to keep held within her a mysterious secret. The pale lights cast by the aura surrounding her did indeed resonate in time with the massive sigil images on the pyramids.

Psychically, he commanded another soul slave to go to this woman, and attempt to serve as a conduit of communication between them. At once, he saw the second soul slave appear through his viewpoint of the first. It hovered immediately before her, its form a bit more solid in appearance than that of the first. American English would be appropriate, he decided, based upon her clothes. If not, then it could be any of the dozen languages he himself knew personally, or any of the hundreds known by the souls under his command.

"I bid thee greetings," came the physical voice of Petrus Romanus to her ears.

Mary Dunbar's eyelids jerked open, revealing green eyes upon which rainbows danced.

"Shit!" she cried out in terror, instinctively raising her arms over her face. As she did this, the faintly glowing aura around her expanded like an exploding balloon, striking both the soul slaves, instantly dissipating their metaphysical forms and severing Petrus' attempt to communicate with her.

Fighting back a sly grin at her naiveté, Petrus commanded a cadre of soul slaves to repeat what the previous two had done, only this time in triplicate.

As the first soul slave appeared before her, Petrus spoke immediately, "I am no spirit, so please do not react harshly."

"My ass!" Mary said defiantly. "I can see right through you and your buddies."

"I am speaking through my soul slaves," Petrus said, causing her to abandon a conscious attempt this time to strike and dispel them. "My name is Petrus Romanus. We have much to discuss, and little time in which to do so. Please attend my words, for we do not have much time. The Earth does not have much time."

"I can see that," Mary replied, relaxing slightly, but still keeping her eyes open for trouble. "My name's Mary. Mary Dunbar. I'm listening, Peter of Rome. Tell me what you want. And try to keep in mind that I'm Protestant."

Unbridled laughter coursed from Petrus through the linking spirit. For a fleeting moment, he almost felt human again. Almost.

He assessed her mien, psychically compelling multiple soul slaves to whisper to him what they knew of Giza, the pyramids, and the old ways. He appreciated both what he saw of her directly, and also what the soul slaves had told him in but a single second. Despite the rampant insanity currently choking the life out of every living thing on Earth, she had chosen not only to adapt and evolve, but also to seize the moment for the opportunity it truly was. A newly reborn immortal like he himself – no mere case of *ipse dixit* involved, as her immortal power was evident, demonstrated *ipso facto* by her hovering form in resonance with the Lightbringer's own cosmic energies; something no mortal could possibly do – she had established herself as some reincarnation of the elder goddess Isis, symbolically mounting the great pyramid as if it were her immortal husband Osiris. Which, in many ways, it was. Moreso, she was serving as an avatar of the primeval Phoenix, bringing the immortal Hekatek to the world of mortals in the time of its greatest need. These things and more the soul slaves told him as he studied her prismatic, pulsating physical form for but a few spare seconds.

She had spirit. She would need it.

"Very well, my incarnate Phoenix, reborn," Petrus began, seeing Mary's eyes widen. "You have come from the Isle of Fire, bearing the Hekatek, such that the new world may itself be reborn. You are the Talisman of the Lightbringer's Sigil, and the surviving remnants of mankind cry out to you for succor."

And verily Petrus Romanus, the Black Pope, the Lightbringer's Soulthief, told her his truth, tainted now as it was by the corruption of Maweth's presence in his mind and soul. And Mary Dunbar, the Lightbringer's Talisman, listened intently, weighing his every word.

eVo.144.000.mOd.112.sCe4 | YEAR ZERO | EARTH | ATLANTA

THE SHADOWS IN GRANT Park were deep and the night was alive. Animals were on the move after the light show a couple hours before, almost as if they knew something was going on.

Melody took a hit from the crack pipe before passing it over to Dante, the lighter illuminating her dirty blonde hair and pale skin. She peered through the pre-dawn darkness, trying but failing to see in the shadows beside each piece of shrubbery.

"Fucked up, that's what it is. Those lights in the sky done killed everyone. We're all gonna die." She looked at the man next to her for confirmation, but all she got was a scowl as he put flame to the pipe. She looked through the gloom, trying to decipher the noises, but her concentration was broken by sporadic gunfire several blocks over.

Dante exhaled, the buzz washing over him. "Ain't errabody dead. Sound like a normal night to me." Dante grinned, his white teeth shining in the darkness.

"Shit, Dante, you seen what them lights done to people. Meltin' their skin and bones to nothin'." Melody shivered with the memory of a house full of corpses. "All those people at Reggie's dropped right where they were standin'. I swear I stood there and screamed for ten minutes."

Dante grimaced. "I know, baby. I heard you down the block. Smart move grabbin' all the cash and shit. Now we just gotta wait to hook up with DT and Marvin. Then we gettin' the fuck out."

"But where we gon–"

She stopped as Dante placed his hand to her mouth, indicating quiet. There was a small noise to the south, on the other side of the path, and then stillness. Dante drew his pistol and chambered a round.

"A'ight, Who dat? Marvin? DT? Don't be fuckin' wit' me now."

Dante waited several beats, as a slight breeze caught the tree branches and moved shadows all around.

From the darkness came a low, menacing growl, then another from a slight distance away.

Melody jumped up from the bench, squeaking in fear. "Oh shit, oh fuck, Dante. Somethin' done got loose from the zoo."

"Shhh, baby. Stay behind me and move slow. We gots to get out in the light where I can see." Dante began to move slowly down the path, the crack confusing his senses. Now he could hear more noises coming from the direction of Zoo Atlanta. Growls and screams of fury, fighting. And behind them another growl, closer.

Melody screamed and ran for the lighted area, passing Dante in a sprint. From the bushes, a dark form bounded, landing atop Melody and bearing her down onto the turf. Her next scream was cut short with a crunching sound, and Dante forgot all about stealth and caution. He heard a second growl as he ran past the lioness on Melody's body, and knew he was dead before he could ever make it to the lighted area. Something huge dropped from the trees in from of him, and he tripped trying to turn aside.

There was a roar behind him and an answering roar from the beast that had dropped from the tree. He looked up to see another lioness launch itself at the giant silverback gorilla. The gorilla caught the lioness in mid-leap and wrestled it to the ground. In a matter of moments, the big cat was still. Moving to the other lioness, the gorilla pulled it from the bloody corpse of Melody and broke its neck.

Dante lay on the ground shaking in terror, as the gorilla finally turned its attention to him, eyes filled with a scary intellect. As it approached Dante, he could see the battle hadn't left the gorilla unscathed. Rivulets of dark red blood dripped from its left forearm where the big cat had sunk its teeth deeply.

Grimacing at the deep gashes for a moment, the gorilla, the focus of his flinty eyes returning to Dante, knelt gracefully down next to him. The towering beast made some curious gestures with its hands. Then it placed its palm on its chest and said in a guttural voice, "M'Tumba. M'Tumba save."

"Oh. Fuck." Dante stared at the gorilla, understanding dawning on him.

"M'Tumba save Oh Fuck," the gorilla said. Again, it repeated something in sign language.

What it said, Dante had no clue. But he *did* know someone who would. If that gay-ass little thug hadn't melted in the night's earlier light show. "Fucking Peaches, you better be alive." Dante held up a hand palm out. "Wait," he said. "I can't understand you, but I know somebody who can."

Getting to his feet, he looked at Melody's corpse, and then back to M'Tumba. As he turned to leave Grant Park, he waved for the gorilla to follow him. That's when he saw the other gorillas, standing in the shadows. Waiting.

"Oh fuck," he said.

"M'Tumba," answered the gorilla.

eVo.144.000.mOd.112.sCe5 | YEAR ZERO | THE NEVER. | THE NULL

THE SOOTHING NOTHINGNESS of the Null itself filled the once and former Never.

Helel's honeyed, mocking laughter greeted their return to consciousness. It seemed distant, muffled, echoing gradually away to inaudibility as they stirred. Their ears and ear buds were still ringing from the paroxysm of the thunderous, explosive sound and light show that had impacted their senses and sent them all tumbling like humanoid tenpins struck by a wrecking ball.

Void awoke first. He pushed himself off the rubbery, blubbery grey floor, then regained his footing. Looking down, he recognized the unusually textured floor immediately as the floor of the Never. But the colors were off-kilter now, faded, dull, and monotonously grey, while the texture of the floor reminded him of something akin to tofu. The sound of his companions, mostly groans of pain, greeted him as if they were across some blighted moor and not immediately beside him, which they truly were.

Carefully, Void reached for Mercy's slowly extending hand and hauled her up to her unsteady feet. Vir'gil, gaining his feet, did the same for Maynard. Gil remained on the rubbery floor, curled into a fetal position. Ku'tu remained unconscious, awkwardly tucked half into Mercy's sleeve, which Mercy resolved by gently shoving her fully back into it.

"Where... where are they?" Mercy asked as she clenched then unclenched her left hand.

"Gone," Void replied. "Both of them. I think I heard Helel laughing, though, as I was getting back up. What are you doing, Mercy?" he asked, watching her clench her hand over and over again.

"What you should be doing," she replied, her eyes focused entirely on her hand, her voice terse with the strain of her mental effort. "Shunya. I can't find her."

Void shook his head. "I have no contact with Fresswelle. I think the link I had with it – the one I had with it for all of an hour or so – has been broken."

"Ku'tu's not going to like hearing that, Void," Mercy warned, still trying in vain to summon Shunya to her hand. "And Helel, Maweth, the One Above, the Mormon Tabernacle Choir, and the Stay Puft Marshmallow Man are all going to suffer if I can't get Shunya back!"

"Void?" Maynard asked, steadying himself alongside Vir'gil.

"Yeah, man?"

"What happened to the Never?"

Mercy stopped clenching her hand. She paused a moment, slowly raising her gaze from her hand. She looked upon the handiwork of the mad Celestial Shaper, and it sorely vexed her.

"I'm going to make pumpkin pie out of your flaming pumpkin head, Helel! Your meddling has destroyed my place of power! The Never is unbound! Dark Mother preserve us! The Never is no more, and now we're in the Null..."

"The Null?" Maynard said, scrabbling awkwardly across the rubbery, jiggly floor, over to where Void and Mercy stood. "Not a problem, right? Mercy's the boss here, right?"

"I can't feel it anymore, Maynard!" Mercy shouted, her voice echoing strangely from the distance, first from their right, then from their left. "My connection with the Never. With the Null. With Shunya. Gone. It's all gone." Her eyes abruptly grew wide. "I can't hear it anymore. The Song. I can't hear it."

"Well, that sucks," Maynard said bluntly. He then gave them a quick but appraising glance. "Void's still got his weird eyes and his chest tattoo thing. You're still you, Mercy. You've still got your Fae appearance, and your magick sleeve still works, if what you just did to Ku'tu is any indicator. So we've still got magicks, extradimensional spaces, shapeshifted Fae dragons, Void stuff, and an elemental lord. It's not all gone. So maybe the disconnection is just temporary, a result of the primal energies we just experienced? So that's something positive. Not everything is gone."

"Positive?" Mercy shrieked, shaking a pointy fist at Maynard. "Do you know how much time and effort I put into creating the Never? How much I sacrificed of my own sanity to win Shunya? What will happen to me and Vir'gil if we've been cut off from hearing the Song of the Sidhe?"

Behind her, Vir'gil abruptly issued forth a deep mewling sound, its volume belying his apparent size. All turned to face him. The Entheogenic Lord held Gil's limp form, pulled tightly to his chest. Several thin tendrils stretched from his hands, tenderly probing Gil's torso.

"I can't see his soul, Mercy," Vir'gil informed them. "It's gone. It's gone."

For a single cruel second, no one could speak. Then, Mercy, Maynard, and Void veritably swarmed Vir'gil and attended to Gil's unmoving form. Gently, Vir'gil's tendrils deposited Gil's body to the floor of the once and former Never, then slowly disengaged. Maynard immediately bent to the task of checking for vitals. Tears began to stream down his face. He pressed the tips of his fingers first to Gil's neck above the carotid artery, then to the underside of his wrist, at the base of the thumb.

"Nothing," he said, voice cracking. "CPR. That's what we'll do," he said, placing one hand over the other, pressing them on Gil's unmoving chest.

"Stop, Maynard," Mercy said softly as he began a quick series of compressions. "Virge?"

Groaning, Vir'gil wrapped his arms and a small mass of newly formed tendrils around Maynard, gently detaching him from Gil's lifeless body.

"No!" Maynard protested, struggling to remove himself from Vir'gil's cloying grasp. "We've got to try to get him back! We've got to try to—"

"He's dead, Maynard," Mercy said gently, giving Vir'gil a silent command with her hand to take a few steps back away from the body. "I'm sorry, I truly am. But there's nothing to be done for the dead in the Null. With the absence of motion, when the soul no longer abides, the Null resonates and reclaims. It annuls all. It will claim his shell soon, and the dissolution of his corporeal form could possibly spread to the living if they stray too close."

Hearing this, they took an additional step back from Gil's corpse, which, true to Mercy's word, began to glow with a subtle pale grey aura. In the span of ten seconds, the aura spread until it enveloped all the body from head to toe. The aura pulsed once, brightly, like the sudden sheen of chrome, then broke apart from the edge inward. It deposited in its wake a foaming, wicked mass of millions of tiny bubbles, each carrying a load of what once had been Professor Gil's material form. They sizzled and fizzed away into the dismal nothingness of the Null.

"No!" Maynard screamed, kicking and fighting against Vir'gil's grasp. "Oh my god I can't believe it! I can't believe it! No! Gil! Oh, no, no..."

Stricken, Maynard fell into silent, wracking sobs, Vir'gil's tendrils soothing and consoling him.

Mercy's purple-tinged eyes fluttered once, then twice. "I'm not going to cry," she told anyone who was listening. "I've seen a million times a million die. I've shed an ocean of tears, and not once has it ever done any good. It's not going to be any different this time. I'm not going to cry. He was such a sweet, gentle man," she said even as her tears made a liar of her.

Still as stone, Void felt Mercy's arms clasp around his waist. He raised his right arm, drawing her into him, comforting her, though he felt nothing, nothing at all.

Nothing, save for the sublime gift of anger, boundless quiet rage, and a neatly detached compulsion to crucify Helel, Maweth, and the One Above for what they had done to poor Professor Gil.

Professor Roger "Gil" Gilmour had been a total pacifist, a lover of life, and a damn good man. He had been the one to draw a young, wayward Cory Christopher Tate out of his personal shell and into the gravity of his orbit, setting him on a path of a decent, productive life. He had been the one to encourage him to put his unusual gifts to work in the service of what ostensibly was the greater good, if there ever had been such an entity. It didn't matter, though, what it truly was, for Gil had believed that there *was* such a thing as the greater good, and his enthusiasm to serve it had been infectious to an extreme. He had been one of the most worthy humans that he had ever met, Void recalled, and it had truly been an honor and privilege to have known him.

Gil was the one who had introduced him to a brash, headstrong, and extremely talented M. K. "Maynard" James. The good professor had been a mentor and a friend to him, Void recalled, but he had been that and more to Maynard, who saw him as his father-by-proxy. And right now, he realized that Maynard had to be entirely beyond himself with the grief that he himself could no longer feel.

But the grief, necessary though it was, would have to be compartmentalized.

"I'm sorry for saying this," Void said, gritting his teeth for a moment as a brief wave of unbidden emotion flashed through his heart, "but I need everyone back here, in the present, right now. We're all in mortal danger. So is the rest of the world. We have to do something about it, right now."

"Void?" Mercy asked, looking up at his strangely feral face as she unwound her arms from his waist and took a step back. Reaching up to his face, her pointy black fingernails lightly traced the single disturbingly dark tear frozen on the corner of his almond-shaped eyes.

"I know," he said, shaking his head. "Though we've been shorn from our blades, I still feel our syzygy. I felt the pain that his death caused you. But I don't feel it myself. I want to cry, I really do," he admitted, "but I'm dead inside."

"What the bloody hell, Cory!" Maynard exploded fiercely, finally disentangling himself from Vir'gil. He leveled an accusing finger at Void. "Gil just died, man! He's *dead*! Disintegrated! That man was a saint to both of us. He was like my own dad! And you're so smug in your emotional cocoon that you can't even give him the respect he deserves!"

Void's eyes slowly closed. "I'm sorry, man. I truly am. I loved him, too. I'm just not able to show my grief. The Mother murdered me a million times during our first communion. My soul screams silently beneath a million ugly scars. Please understand. Please forgive me, if you can."

The import of Void's soul-confession reached out and slapped everyone in the face.

"You really aren't Cory anymore, are you?" Maynard asked him, his voice trembling with rage. He made a quick, severing motion with his hands. "My best friend is nothing but Void now, thanks to Helel's meddling. Just like Mercy said. Meddling. He wasn't happy just causing the Apocalypse. He had to screw up everything and everyone around him. What kind of insane ego is that? He killed Gil, Void. He's killed the Earth, too. He's killed virtually everyone we know! I'm almost inclined now to side with Maweth. Helel's guilty as far as I'm concerned."

As slowly as Void's eyes had closed, they opened. He looked directly into Maynard's honey colored eyes, which now flickered with pale blue faerie light. "Maynard? Your eyes are glowing."

"So?" Maynard shot back. "As pissed off as I am right now, they better be!"

Mercy stepped between them. She then gave Maynard an appraising glance. "It shouldn't be possible, here in the Null, but you're projecting a Fae aura from your eyes."

"So?" he replied, still glaring at Void.

"She means," Void said, "that whatever zapped us back there and tore our blades from our focal bindings, depositing us here in the Null as a result, should have been – *had* to have been – powerful enough to affect your supramortal chakras. Turning them off, as apparently has happened with me and Mercy."

"Without chakras above the seven mortal ones," Mercy said, "you shouldn't be able to use that level of power."

"Well, obviously," Maynard said, "Vir'gil's protective weave stopped that from happening."

"Leaving you unharmed and un-shorn, but Gil dead?" Void asked.

Vir'gil slowly rumbled. "I tried my best to protect them both, equally."

"I believe you, Virge," Mercy consoled her old friend. "I think that things are not entirely what they seem, however. I think that Helel gimmicked that blast that happened when Maweth's blade struck ours. And I think he used some very nasty immortal-level soul magicks to make it happen."

Finally allowing his accusing glare to diminish, Maynard said, "You're saying that he sacrificed Gil's soul to make this happen? To defeat Maweth?"

"I'm saying," Mercy said evenly, "that I suspect that he did precisely that. Remember: I have about thirteen millennia of exposure to such things. I'm also of the Fae, so I'm an expert on the subject of magicks and charms. It was also way beyond mortal or even nascent immortal power. I'm a Null, so I know what it takes for magicks and charms to affect me."

"Well freakin' explain it already!" Maynard bade her.

"Be steady, man," she countered. "Helel's most probable path was to exploit the syzygy between me and Void and our blades, using that to shape, channel, and charge his charm. It's obvious that he tapped into all our souls. He tapped into all of us, using us like the batteries that we truly are to him, to ramp up and augment that bimodal fulcrum. So that, when Maweth hit it with Hatefang, his blade, it did the bending and binding 'trap-the-soul-in-the-blade' trick. That's the only way to explain why our own blades are shorn from our souls, and why Maweth apparently was defeated."

All three now had been drawn up into Mercy's own verbal charms and were listening intently.

"He would have needed a soul sacrifice of immortal-level powers to seal that, too," she continued. "I suspect that he tapped directly into my and Void's souls first, draining us of our eighth and ninth chakras, funneling those into the metaphysical fulcrum point of our blades, and exploiting our innate Null and Void syzygy to augment and amplify it. Unfortunately, I think he made the call to fully drain Gil, for whatever reason, and use that fully empowered immortal soul to cap, sign, and seal the deal."

"Sounds like a fine hypothesis," Maynard informed her. His fingers stroked his chin. "But I think Helel's absence indicates that he didn't get all the power he had intended."

"What? How so?" Mercy inquired. Sensing a stirring at her wrist, she bent her will to give Ku'tu the space she needed to climb out and join them. With a quick buzz of her wings, she flew up to Mercy's left shoulder and sat down gracefully.

"He's a total psychopath and egomaniac," Maynard replied, shaking his head in disgust. "You think he would willingly leave, when he could have remained here, in a perfectly whole Never, to gloat over wrecking Maweth? No way. He miscalculated, again, and I think he paid a price for it. I think he actually planned to steal all of our souls. And I think he failed because his power means nothing before the Will of the Dragon. I think we're all still alive because the Dark Earth Mother isn't done with us yet."

A moment of poignant silence loomed over them.

"You know what?" Void asked. "If that's true – if anything is true, in all this cosmic haze – then it's obvious that we're not the good guys, riding in on white horses. We're caught up in a cosmic-level war between Heaven and Hell, metaphysically speaking. And we're not allied with Heaven. We're the bad guys. The rebels. We're the ones helping Helel, the Lightbringer, who's Lucifer by any other name. We're not heroes. We're the fallen angels, straight out of Milton. Or Enoch."

"I never claimed to be on anyone's side," Mercy claimed, her tone sardonic. "It's simply by default that we've aligned with the Devil, because it appears to be quite obvious that, while the

Devil is a wicked bastard and rotten to the core, God is mad as the proverbial hatter. Genocidal, on a supremely cosmic scale. Helel's the lesser evil here. That's why we've 'chosen' him, to use that stupid word again. So much for exercising our free will."

"We'll see about that," Void said, his voice cold. "Nothing bars us from playing things from our own angle. Ultimately, that's the best way to do it. Otherwise, if we submerge our will under theirs, we've abrogated our own free will, which I *absolutely* refuse to do. I *refuse*! This isn't about preferring to reign in Hell as opposed to serving in Heaven. This is about *us*. Who *we* are. What *we* want. Not what *they* want. So I propose a third way. *Our* way."

They were now locked on and tracking Void's every word.

"They're not as smart, wise, and crafty as they think they are," he continued. "It's true that, thus far, it's seemed like they are. But that's because, at least in Helel's case, he's been prepping for it. Thousands of times, over and over again. So we've been merely reactive thus far, always one step behind. That makes it appear that we're not as slick and clever as he is. But I think that's going to change dramatically once we shift into proactive mode. Helel, the One Above, all of those so-called 'gods' above us in the ZeroTime? I don't think they're really gods at all. I don't think they're anywhere near as powerful as they appear to be. I think this because the Dark Earth Mother herself – the Dragon itself – welcomed my rebirth. *Our* rebirth."

Silently, they absorbed his words.

"The Will of the Dragon supersedes their pathetic ZeroTime," Void said, thunder in his words. "Remember what the Dark Earth Mother told us? The game that we're playing – the Dragon's Game – supersedes the game played by Helel. If we have to believe anything at all, that's what we must first believe.

It's the wildcard. It's the cosmic primal archetype, like she told us we were."

"But we have to win Helel's game," Maynard said. "If not, this cosmos dies."

"It's true that we have to win Helel's game," Void agreed. "If we do win – *when* we win – we might be able to leverage that win into the continued existence of our cosmos. Remember that Helel agreed to that. And, as such, I have a feeling that he's bound by that agreement. So, we're now literally fighting for the life of this universe, and for the souls of all in it. But, in parallel, we're also going to be dealing with the consequences of the Anshadar Effect, which means that we're going to be playing two games simultaneously."

"And they're both interwoven now, like DNA," Mercy said. "Funny, but Helel apparently caused the Anshadar Effect to come into play by using forbidden cosmic archetypal templates to make us. Yet, we now have a two-path game afoot, with the games being interwoven like the space-DNA in the Lightbringer's Sigil. That's just too convenient to be coincidence."

"And," Void added, "the space-DNA has more than merely two helices. It has a hard-to-perceive third helix. Which might be the analog for our playing our own game, taking our own path through the chaos around us."

Maynard issued a long sigh. "That's why, of all the people on Earth, you saw it and knew it first, Void. That's why the Mother visited you in the isolation tank and made you embrace that version of the sigil. That's why she told us these things after you opened your third eye and brought her to us. That's precisely why we're discussing it right now. It's the Will of the Dragon. And, as you've said, it supersedes all else."

"Games within games," Mercy said softly. "Sounds like fun. Too bad we're all stuck here in the Null. Too bad we're all going to end up like poor Professor Gil did if we don't get back home soon."

"You can protect us, though, right?" Void asked. "You're the Ninth Null."

She shook her head. "Nope. I'm afraid I'm now only the Seventh Null. I can't, as a mere seven-chakra mortal, project a protective ward versus the Null externally. I can't even tune in on the Song of the Sidhe in order to triangulate a path home for us." She gave Vir'gil a quizzical look. He slowly nodded once. "Same with Virge. Probably the same, if not worse, with Ku'tu."

"I'm going to kill him," Ku'tu said, tersely. "I am the last of my kind now. I can't feel any connection to anything of the Fae of Aal. Fresswelle is gone, probably lost in the Null forevermore. When next I see him, I'm going to kill him for what he has done."

Mercy quickly told her, "Before you swear blood oath, Ku'tu, please do us all the small favor of actually waiting until we see him again before you commit. It matters not for now, because the rest of us heard your words, and we mark them. Yet, chaos is rampant, which means that things might not flow as expected, which implies that we'd best not set our own paths in stone before we first walk down them."

Considering that for a moment, Ku'tu replied, "You are wise, Mercy. You have resolved the classic conflict of Honor versus Flow. I will therefore pend, as you have suggested, before I commit. I accept that my words have been marked. Thank you."

"You are most welcome, my friend," Mercy replied graciously, earning her a sidelong glance of appraisal from Vir'gil.

"So what do we do now, right now, this instant?" Maynard inquired generally. "I need to know. I need to wade back in, or I'm going to start crying again. Do we have time for a brief strategy council? Or, do we have to move before the Null claims us?"

"Stay in motion," Mercy warned them. "As we should be now. Come, let us move slowly, together in a tight group. We can talk as we walk."

And so they did, step by tricky step, over the rubbery tofu-like manifestations underfoot which seemed to form a sort of floor or ground in the Null. As they moved in a group through the cloying grey-green mists, they talked.

Mercy conjectured first. "It's highly probable that Hatefang, Fresswelle, and Shunya now have been scattered randomly to the far reaches of the Null. It's also highly probable that, if the truncation of our souls down from nine chakras to seven is not entirely permanent, that the residual exists still in our blades, as they were the fulcrum point in the charm. By that, I mean that there's still hope to regain both our blades and our immortal powers. Hopefully. Otherwise, we're going to have to do some serious cheating to get back to the level of power we had just an hour ago, and we're going to have to figure out how to do this impossible thing while still stuck in the Never, and before the Death Horde gets here."

"That's some serious speculation, Mercy," Void admitted.

"And it might be wrong," Maynard said. "Why? I apparently still have my supramortal chakras, because my eyes are still glowing and shooting out Tinkerbell lights. Why didn't Helel drain my soul, too, while he was at it? I get the part about Vir'gil being an elemental lord and all that, because Helel blatantly told us. But me? Explain that."

Mercy nodded. "I can't guarantee it, but I think that he exploited me and Void due to our blades. Easy access to our souls, especially as they were the bimodal fulcrum. You, though?

No blade, no easy exploit. Gil, the same. He just happened to favor you over Gil. Why? I don't know."

"That asshole," Maynard spat. "He told me, when we first met back at MorthonTech Headquarters, right before we all met on the roof, that I was always his favorite. He's going to pay. I swear by all that's sacred, I'll make him pay for what he did to Gil."

"Get in line, then," Void said.

"Yeah, manling," Ku'tu added, flitting before his face. "Get in line. Get in the *back* of the line."

"I'm the last in line..." Maynard said, a slight tug at the corner of his mouth betraying his otherwise stone-cold face. Ronnie James Dio could do that to a soul.

"Ah, shit," Mercy said, suddenly stopping. "Shit, shit, shit, shit, and shit!"

"What's up?" Void asked her.

Mercy turned to look at him, her face twisting in grief. "My families. My husbands and wives. They're gone now. Shit! He's stolen almost everything away from me. I'm in line now, too. He's going to pay!"

She began to tear up, sobbing. Void pulled her close to him, comforting her. After a brief, awkward moment, he inquired, "You used plurals?" That's as far as he dared take it, however.

"I'm poly, Void," Mercy said, rubbing her sleeve across her face. "I have several husbands and wives, and some really cool step-children. They're probably all now dead or turned into mutants or something now, thanks to Helel's sigil. I didn't have time during all this recent adventure to check up on them. In fact, I didn't even *think* about them while all this was happening. I'm so terrible..." she said, sobbing again.

"Me, too," Maynard admitted. "I mean terrible, me, too. We have to get back home. Now. I have to check on my mom and dad. And Gamera."

Vir'gil raised a quizzical eyebrow leaf. "You have Gamera? Mercy told me Gamera wasn't real."

"Pet tortoise," Maynard said. "Had him since I was a kid."

"How big is he?" Vir'gil inquired.

Mercy jerked away from Void, then blurted out, loudly, "It's a pet turtle, Virge. A *pet*! It's not the mythical giant monster from the movies. Geez! I told you watching my *kaiju* movie collection would screw your brain up! Movies *aren't* real, Virge."

"What about 'Titanic'?" Vir'gil asked.

"Definitely fake!" Mercy shot back, blatantly lying. Vir'gil caught it and started giggling.

"Is this the council?" Maynard asked, noting the shift in mood. "We're doing the council thing right now?"

"Yep," Mercy answered as they resumed their walking. "So far, we've determined that you have a pet *kaiju*, and that the Titanic was a fake ship."

"Keeping up with chaotic Fae whose emotions can turn on a dime..." Maynard said under his breath. He made the decision, then and there, to compartmentalize his grief over Gil's death. He would perform the proper ceremony for him later, and try his best to guide Gil's soul to the Mother. Now, however, it was time to focus and help the team engineer a solution path. Clearing his throat, he continued, "Almost as bad as having to say this with a straight face: Helel's nerfed us."

"Beg pardon?" Mercy asked. "Nerfed? Like the stuff they make the toys out of?"

"Yes, sort of," Maynard explained. "He's nerfed us, then, basically, as a result, he's indirectly quested us to un-nerf ourselves to help him."

Covering his mouth, Void tried not to laugh, but failed. "Devs will be devs, no matter the scale," he said.

Mercy, at a loss, looked first at Maynard, then at Void, who finally clued her in.

"Game term," he informed her. "We used to play a lot of those online games. The fantasy and science fiction ones?"

"Yes, but 'nerf'?" Mercy asked. "I don't get it."

"It's NerdSpeak for the common practice of devolving or reducing power in the games, in order to balance the game accordingly. As an example, if one particular race or class or character played as if it were much more powerful than others, it would be the proverbial nail sticking up for the developers to hammer back down. They'd reduce its power to reinforce game balance, and the players who'd been playing that particular race or character would all scream that the developers, or devs, had 'nerfed' them."

"Oh, they softened them up, like the toys," Mercy said. "Well, that's precisely what Helel has done. He's nerfed the living hell out of us. And he's technically our 'dev', as you say, because he created our simulation. So it's more 'as above, so below' symmetry. Yep. Figures. The cosmos might not exactly repeat itself, but it sure as hell rhymes." She paused, a coquettish, pointy smile erupting on her face. "And I'm trolling the shit out of you. I love games. And memes. And cat videos."

"Fucking cat videos!" Maynard laughed, dismissing Mercy's admission. "Void tortures me with those," he paused, clearing his throat awkwardly as he realized abruptly that he was never going to see them again. "So, pretending that we're gamers, because we really are at this point," he continued. "What's the quickest, most efficient way for us to get ourselves out of the Null and back to Earth, hopefully bringing along your blades in the process?"

"Mercy?" Void asked. "Do you have any powers left that might be able to affect the Null? I'm assuming that you've lost the one associated with bringing us back and forth, from Earth to Null."

"Correct," Mercy admitted. "I'm not able to divide or multiply myself and my surroundings by the concept of zero. Well, by the concept of the most ancient version of the Null. Since the illogical humans introduced binary and databases, the ancient version has mostly yielded to the concept of the 'null' namespace in databases and such."

"Really?" Void said, genuinely surprised. "That's a helluva thing to know. Wicked. So you have no way to get in or out of it?"

"Not any longer."

"Well," Maynard asked. "Do you have any other ones left? Like, maybe some way to at least view or scry the Earth, so we can see what's going on? Like, if we're moving away from it, or if that's even a factor?"

"It is a factor, somewhat," Mercy replied. "I've kept the Never and its contingent Null anchors close to Earth recently, for totally unassociated reasons. The Never could 'touch' eight different locations anywhere on Earth, so I could easily travel down my own customized Eightfold Path to anywhere I'd set the interstitial anchors. So it's like this: Never, Null, Earth; and, Earth, Null, Never."

"Can you scry Earth from the Null?" Maynard asked.

"No. Impossible," Mercy answered.

"But you could from the Never, right?" Void asked. "How else would you know to set your anchors?"

"Well, of course I could," Mercy answered. "Not like Helel's scrying vignette, naturally. That was a vulgar display of power.

I can, however, peek through a tiny keyhole of sorts along the anchor points."

"So," Void said, "if you had access to one of the anchors of the Never, do you think you could use it to see Earth?"

"Hmm," she considered. "Provided that one anchor has survived, that might be possible. But what would taking a peek at Earth do for us? We still can't traverse the dimensional gap between here and there. No way we could fit through a keyho– "

Everyone looked at Ku'tu. She shrugged. "Depends on the size. I can't shapeshift right now anyway, so what's the point? Shouldn't we be getting our original powers back first, anyway?"

"Yes," Void said, "but, barring the return of our blades, which might or might not be here in the Null, there's very little we can do about getting those power levels back here, in the Null. Returning first to Earth at least relieves us from the burden of continuous movement or almost instant death here."

"We need Shunya first," Mercy declared. "Then I can get us back and forth easily."

"Assuming it can restore the power you've lost," Maynard said. "What if it doesn't?"

"Then we'll at least have a better chance of surviving," Mercy said. "I think we're onto something about the potential anchor/keyhole idea. And I just remembered something that might help in that respect. Virge?"

"Yes?"

"Please tell me that you have Aal Ball."

"Why, of course, Milady," Vir'gil informed her. "I had presumed that my hint earlier about everyone needing some rest after our long week spent, err, healing the Professor would have enabled you to infer as much."

"Distracted," Mercy admitted with a shrug. "Call them out. We need to assign them a task."

"Here?" Vir'gil attempted to temporize. "But they'll see them," he stage-whispered to Mercy.

"I don't care if Aal Ball sees them!" Mercy said. "Besides, they're not in line for any, err, healing. So get those effers out, now, pronto!"

"Very well..." Vir'gil groaned. "My souls are open to your command, Milady."

Maynard looked nervously over at Void. "*Que*-the-eff?"

Void just shrugged. "By 'healing' I think she means the Marvin Gaye or Barry White kind."

Mercy smiled. Void was indeed perceptive. He had recalled, while still being able to understand the ancient tongue thanks to his link with Fresswelle and the Aal Fae and their version of the Song of the Sidhe within it, what the name, only briefly mentioned, meant. There was hope for Mr. Square Pants yet.

"Aal Ball?" Mercy said sweetly. "I need you. Come here."

With that baneful pronouncement, they watched in a curious mixture of humor and disgust as a bright, silvery, oozing shape began slowly to erupt from Vir'gil's nether regions. It formed a priapic shape that stood three hands in height, and a hand in width. Flowing like liquid mercury, it detached itself with an audible *Floomp!*, landing squarely on the rubbery, blubbery ground. It appeared without definable legs or hands, its body bending in a smooth curve as it bounced a few times on its slightly plumper lower body, until it stood directly before them. Its upper body had no easily discernable head or facial features, save for two slight parallel indentations near the top of its form. It was with these that Aal Ball pretended to stare at the group as it gracelessly, spastically drew to a halt near them.

"Aal Ball!" it squeaked, bouncing up and down slightly.

Void looked at Maynard, trying hard not to laugh. Failing, Maynard noted, "It sounded just like Eugene the Jeep when it bounced. I can't believe it!"

"Aal Ball," Mercy said, ignoring them, "I have an important task for you."

It stopped shaking like an obscene bowl of silvery gelatin. "Aal Ball?" it inquired.

"Remember how you shapeshifted into that exoskeleton for me? The one I used to get around with when Vir'gil was experimenting on me and I was too effed up to walk under my own power for a few days?"

It nodded. At least, the top hand's height of it seemed to do so.

"I want you to do that now for me. We're about to boogie here. Be as tough as you can be, Aal Ball. We're going into war. Keep your outer boundary layer in constant flow, because we're in the Null, and if you remain unmoving, you'll disintegrate. Hook me up with the super goggles and the enhanced senses configuration. I'm going to need to be able to perceive the anchor points of the Never where they interface with the Null. It's important that you remember all of this and perform it exactly as I'm directing. No deviations, no variances, and no sensual enhancements or other perversions if we're in combat. *Comprende?*"

Nodding its agreement, Aal Ball bounced up to Mercy's shoulder, causing Ku'tu to flit safely away.

"I can't believe you named it that, Mercy," Ku'tu laughed, slapping her thighs. She knew precisely what it meant, and she couldn't stop laughing at how vulgar the pun was. Maynard looked over at her quizzically. She just shook her cute little head, shushing him with a finger to her lips, breaking out in more laughter as she did.

Settling near the top of Mercy's head, Aal Ball melted its form, smoothly flowing like the liquid mercury that it appeared to be. As it vanished behind and under Mercy, it reappeared almost instantly, bending itself around her arms and legs, and her torso and head, forming a bright, chrome-looking armored form around her. The finishing touch, per her specific request, was the sudden, morphing appearance of a rather Cylon-esque visor, its single, slowly oscillating phased-pulsed green laser array probing the space before it. At the quantum level, the ancient relic initiated a psychic interface with her, merging their physical beings into a single unit. Mercy's higher order thoughts began to flow into Aal Ball, completing their symbiotic link. Her internal head's up display kicked into life, filling her virtual mind's eye with an insane amount of simultaneous data streams.

For even the immortal version of herself, the data streams had been intense, demanding total focus to scan and interpret. Now, realizing that she would require Aal Ball to assist with the task, she silently willed, so no one would hear and think her weak, the collective entity to assign a few dozen minds from its collective hive mind to the task. The ancient relic instantly complied, and Mercy saw and knew everything within her purview.

"Aal Ball!" Mercy said excitedly, her voice booming, artificially amplified by her new gleaming armor.

To the horror of all gathered, an arm-length liquid mercury-looking phallus with a basketball-sized scrotum grew forth from her groin, Aal Ball's artificial head materializing at its terminus.

"Aal Ball!" it said happily.

"You shit!" Mercy said, slapping it down. "I said no perversions," she said, realizing instantly her error in restricting it to while they were in combat. "Ah, no perversions at all, unless so commanded."

"Aal Ball!" it said somewhat meekly, slowly retracting itself until no more grim perversions were observable.

"Try to keep it in your pants," Maynard prodded, merciless.

"Go *fmmk* yourself, Maynard!" Mercy said. "What? Really? You censored me on *fmmk*? You take 'no perversions' too literally, Aal Ball. Of course *I* can cuss. How else could I communicate?"

"Aal Ball!" came a disembodied voice, apparently from the general direction of Mercy's crotch.

"Follow me, lady, gents, and Virge-on-the-cob," Mercy said, managing the volume of her voice down to an acceptable level. She gazed at the featureless horizon, swiveled her head a few times, then took off toward her left-hand-side. "Shit," she said almost immediately, stopping in place.

They piled up behind her, alarmed, ready for combat.

"Ah, never mind," she informed them. "I was just seeing if I could cuss again. Let's go."

eVo.144.000.mOd.112.sCe6 | YEAR ZERO | EARTH | MYSTERY BABYLON

"WELCOME TO MYSTERY Babylon, Mary Dunbar," Petrus Romanus announced with perfect gravitas.

The newly christened Lightbringer's Talisman stepped onto the stage of the former Nervi Hall through a wormhole of polychromatic light which joined the local spacetime of the hall with that of the top of the pyramidion of the Great Pyramid of Khufu. Around the perimeter of the rather compact wormhole, which fit Mary's form and little more, the rainbow smear of frame-dragging photons danced and writhed like spastic snakes.

A warm breeze followed Mary through the gateway. Established by Petrus for the mere expenditure of 1,000 of his soul slaves, the personal wormhole truly was a conduit between here and there, a two-way bridge of sorts. The sweet scent of the desert breeze elicited an equally sweet smile from Petrus. Its purity seemed to cleanse some of the noisome stench of decay that permeated the hall. He found this temporary sensation quite pleasing. It reminded him of the sweet scent of sandalwood incense which had issued from the steadily clinking pontifical thuribles, their censers constantly issuing dark gray smoke, carrying their prayers from their uplifted hands.

No, Petrus knew he would never again hear the soft, rhythmic tinkling of the thuribles' chains, never again smell and savor the sweetness of the incense. They were the trappings of the old ways, of the old world, which now existed no more. In its place instead was a horrific charnel pit, and its only scents were the stench of rot and decay. Its only sounds were the moans of the tortured and the constant scraping and shuffling of the lame as they moved toward their inevitable doom at the fatal perimeter of the Black Tabernacle.

"You do *know,"* his inner voice, a composite of both his own and Maweth's, whispered, *"this is just a simulation, right?"*

Petrus scoffed, his split-second reverie dispelled by the reality of the here and now. He cast his gaze down upon the thousands upon thousands who approached the lethal perimeter of the Black Tabernacle. They slogged over the compacted stains, smears, and streaks of that which had only recently been alive. Mary noted the disgust on his face.

"Well, Petrus," Mary said playfully, noting that the ubiquitous gore on the floor was held at bay by her aura, "it could be worse. Like, if we couldn't fly like the angels themselves..."

With a slight modulation in the shape of her talismanic aura, she willed herself to arise from the slushy offal covering the floor of the stage. She joined the levitating Black Pope some several meters above the floor of the stage.

"Angels indeed..." he said softly. Amused once again by the lightness of Mary's spirit, he gracefully indicated the Black Tabernacle with a smooth wave of his hands. "The Black Tabernacle," he informed her, careful to moderate his voice such that it could easily be heard over the constant electric crackling of the continuous disintegrations.

"Your place of power, the Matrix of Souls," she replied, clearly impressed. "That's the biggest bug zapper I've ever seen.

Much bigger than what I thought it might be when you described it to me."

Pivoting in place, Mary slowly took in the full horror of the sights and sounds around her, careful to continue to hide her fear and loathing from Petrus. From all directions came the shambling masses. Some spontaneously burst into black fountains of amoebic goo before they reached the dark edifice of the Black Tabernacle, contributing a few more centimeters of slick offal to the growing pools of ruinous matter on the floor. Yet the few who did not make it to the tabernacle were nothing before the masses yet to arrive. Even viewed from her vantage several meters above the stage, the lines seemed to vanish into the horizon. She was unable to grasp their true number, though she reckoned that hundreds of thousands, perhaps even millions, now plodded onward without recourse to their final physical doom.

"The power of their souls becomes yours once they're zapped?" she inquired, returning her gaze to him.

"Indeed, it is so," Petrus replied. Pursing his lips, he fixed his eyes upon hers. "Would you like a taste?"

Fear, unbidden, tiptoed its nasty little rat feet up Mary's spine. Try as she might to remain composed, her eyes betrayed her feelings by their sudden twitching.

Shaking his head, Petrus soothed her. "Have no fear, Mary Dunbar. I mean you no harm. You are the first of my Chosen. You are as a daughter to me. My blood. My soul. As such, I would share with you a small token of what it is to be a god."

A bit too quickly, she replied, "No thank you, your holiness. I mean," she recovered, "I think that my power – this crazy rainbow aura around me – might reject it. Explosively so."

"Oh, really?" Petrus replied, curious. Inclining his head slightly, he moved slowly, gracefully, toward her. Drawing up to within arm's reach of her, he slowly extended his free hand toward her aura, which seemed to quiver. Its translucent form gathered slightly toward him as if in anticipation of his movement. "May I?" he inquired.

Mary exhaled sharply. "You're not going to kill me if it attacks you, are you?"

"Heavens no, my dear," Petrus replied. "Now, relax, Mary. I don't need to touch it in order to read it. That's for my soul slaves to do. They shall not harm you. Be still, observe, and learn what you have become."

With that, Petrus silently commanded a small cadre of his slaves to do his bidding. Some were to observe from a distance and perform multispectral analysis, the thought of which amused him, due to their being an actual multitude of specters. Others were to physically and otherwise engage it. Without harming the woman, of course, he was certain to specify.

While the soul slaves performed their duties, feeding their data directly into Petrus' steadily evolving mind, he simultaneously performed his own high-level analysis of Mary Dunbar and her talismanic aura. Clearly, as he could discern immediately once he was able to focus his full attention on her – directly, in person – Mary possessed a fully realized set of nine chakras. They glowed, steadily pulsating, as they danced slowly in place. The eighth and ninth were slightly larger than the rest, though brighter by an order of magnitude. As the Lightbringer had told him, the expression of the full set of nine chakras was the sign that one not only had passed the judgement, but also had achieved true immortality.

"*Total blasphemy!*" a tiny voice raged in Petrus' mind, distracting him for a moment. "*The Shining One shall pay dearly for this!*"

Petrus shook his head, clearing his thoughts. The Lightbringer had warned him that some of the souls would be powerful enough to give him some modicum of trouble, so he knew that a bit of rebellion was to be expected.

The mortals were of course limited to a mere seven chakras, he recalled from his instruction by the Lightbringer. Their continued status was uncertain and unassured. They might continue to live, or they might die. The Lightbringer had been unclear, perhaps not deliberately Petrus now realized, as to what their true fate might be. Considering the possibility that the cancerous resonance currently in effect might very well destroy everything, regardless of the status of their chakras, rendered consideration of the mortals, at this time, almost completely irrelevant.

Those who survived the judgement would be permitted – "permitted" being the direct quote from the Lightbringer, he recalled; now noting that it, too, seemed to be some sort of ill-defined hedge rather than a concrete response – to elevate from the mortal number of seven and evolve up to eight. Becoming, nominally, a new immortal. These would be the baseline, the lowest tier of the new gods. It would be possible for them to continue to accrue power and, possibly, evolve into the highest realm of a true nine chakra god. Again, that was rendered irrelevant by the current circumstances of the genocidal resonance in play.

But the full set of nine... The Lightbringer had not dithered on this. The full set of nine was the mark and sign of the new immortals: the New Gods, the Lightbringer's Chosen. And Mary Dunbar was so marked. Though they were bound by the same set of circumstances as the rest, Petrus, and now Mary, were capable of doing something to counter their fate.

As the soul slaves continued to whizz and fly by Mary, eliciting both conscious and unconscious movements of her talismanic aura, Petrus made the connection that Mary's aura was in fact an external projection of her internal, metaphysical chakras. He was able to discern, after several more soul slaves were intercepted and pounded into nothingness by her aura before they could physically touch her, that Mary's conscious efforts to control her aura were in fact only slowing down its reaction time to their attacks. The martial arts knowledge he had never bothered to learn as a priest – violence of any sort, even the violence of self-defense, he had always abhorred – now came to him in waves, unbidden, a consequence of his theft of the souls of the highly trained Swiss Guard. Naturally, he now no longer abhorred it. It was yet another tool to be used to achieve his goals. And it was now as natural to him as the nose on his face.

"Mary?"

"Yes?" she replied, a slight strain in her voice.

"Relax. By that, I mean don't try to shape your aura's response to the spirits. Let it go. Let it react on its own."

"But they'll hit me," Mary complained. "You said they won't harm me, and I trust you, Petrus, but that's a new level of creepiness I don't want to..."

At that moment, two soul slaves slammed into her from behind, out of her line of sight, only to be swatted down at the last possible moment before impact by her talismanic aura. Swatted down, and then directly thrashed and annihilated by an additional attack that was almost too quick to see. Petrus noticed that there had been a sudden bright surge in the shimmering rainbow lights displayed by the aura right there, right at the end. It was obvious to him, as the Soulthief he truly was, that the two soul slaves had been absorbed and internalized by the aura.

"Wow," Mary breathed, turning to witness the end of the sequence. "I think I just bug zapped them, like your tabernacle."

Nodding, Petrus agreed, "Yes, you very well did." With a silent mental command, Petrus bade two more soul slaves to appear directly before Mary. "Try to bend their power to your will, Mary. Use their energy to smite the two before you."

Nonplused, Mary stared lamely ahead at the two soul slaves who had materialized only a few feet in front of her. Their stripped down genericism truly disturbed her. They might have been a grandmother and a young child only yesterday, but now they were merely ghostly mannikins of their former selves, appearing as if they had been stamped out of the same generic mold.

"What the hell," Mary said, instantly regretting her choice of words. Sheepishly, she gave Petrus a guilty shrug, which he waved off with a smirk.

"Shoot them, Mary," he bade her, raising his paschal staff toward them like a gun.

"But I don't have a staff like yours." Her eyes stared a second too long at the terminus of the staff, where an image of sheer blasphemy greeted her. *What in God's name...* She quickly averted her gaze, choosing the relatively smaller measure of horror of the sight of mannikin souls.

"You don't need one," he laughed. "Use your hands. Your aura *is* you. It will do as you bid it. If you want to raise your hands to shoot a beam of energy at them, you may indeed will this to happen. Try it."

Saying no more, Mary raised her hands, pointing an index finger at each soul slave, then pulling the trigger with a downward click of her thumb. With a keen, isochronic tone, a foot-wide beam of coruscating royal purple and midnight blue hues issued from the end of each of her index fingers. Each beam pierced a soul slave, instantly annihilating it. The beams continued with very little impedance, with one punching through a collapsed steel beam halfway across the hall's ruined general floor, and the other punching through several rows of seats nearby.

Hamming it up, Mary held her index fingers up to her lips and pretended to blow smoke from them.

"Amazing," Petrus admitted as several soul slaves whispered their analyses to him. "My soul slaves have informed me that you produced very distinct tones with those beams. With more training, I think that you're going to be able to consciously shape the tones of your emitted beams. If what I saw of your aura when I first gazed upon you atop the pyramidion is an indicator, you're going to be able to tap into some interesting resonant effects. You were, after all, doing just that with the pyramids projected image of the sigil. And the power amplification..." he paused a moment to verify what he had been told by the soul slave who had reported this to him. "It's not a linear function, Mary."

"I'm a professor of the liberal arts, Petrus," she reminded him, shaking her head.

"Your talismanic aura can produce massive resonance with the energy that it absorbs. It's not a strictly 1:1 ratio of input to output. Roughly, approximately, with that particular expression of your output – it was a pulsing isochronic set of two distinct tones – put out an order of magnitude more energy than was initially absorbed."

Mary shook her head. "Well, I understand *that*. That's plainly insane. How can my aura make more power than it takes in? That's entirely counterintuitive."

Petrus gave her a smirk. "Maybe. For a liberal arts professor," he laughed merrily, truly feeling like he was once again leading a class, teaching his eager young students. "It is an impressive demonstration of the power of resonance. With you, Mary, I think that we are dealing with more complex resonance – a harmonic resonance – and this has many applications and expressions. It's almost universal, and it goes from simple acoustics to electromagnetic oscillations, even to gravity itself. But you are doing it with the energy of a soul, which must innately be of superior, perhaps perfect, form and characteristics."

Mary considered this for a moment. "I think I get it. Our project at Giza had some similar elements which, admittedly, the techies mostly handled. But I think I've got it now. So that nonlinear resonance might vary with the form and characteristics of the input energy? Like, I might get a little kick out of sound or music or something mundane like that, but I might get a titanic kick out of something like soul energy?"

Petrus nodded once, curtly. "It would seem so. When we have more time, we must test it. You must learn all you possibly can about yourself and master your powers. We will need every possible edge we can muster, for when we finally face our adversaries."

"The evil ones you mentioned to me back at Giza?" Mary inquired, willing herself to move closer to Petrus. Gracefully. She was getting the hang of the otherwise awkward levitation gig. It no longer felt to her as if she were standing atop a pile of drunk amoebas.

He noticed the edges of her lips upturn into a tight smile as she levitated up to his side. "Well done, Mary," he encouraged her. "Yes, the evil ones, our adversaries. There are others out there now, others like you. They have powers like yours, Mary. Like you, and me, they are the newly born immortals of this world. Now, at the cusp of the advent of the End of All Things, the forces of light and darkness contest against one another for the souls of all mankind."

Mary stared hard at him. "You mean the stuff from Revelation? Angels and demons and multi-headed beasts? Seals and horns? I mean no offense, but real world events aren't looking much like the orthodox eschatology."

"The only orthodox eschatology is the End of All Things, and this is the design of the One Above, not your lying, false, shadow gods!" This time, Petrus clearly noted the alien figure symbolically crucified on his paschal staff writhe in vain. How had he forgotten something of that importance? More importantly, how had he allowed himself to become so confused?

A cruel feral smile briefly manifested, and Petrus, finding his will power once again, chided Maweth, *"You have no power here, over me, despite your presumptions, creature of the ZeroTime. You are, despite your power, nothing but one of those simulated souls you degrade so harshly. And I am the Lightbringer's Soulthief. I rule here! In this circumstance, I command! Not thee..."*

Maweth's fierce, screaming denials rapidly muted to naught, mitigated and clamped down by the sheer force of Petrus' augmented will. Will augmented by the expenditure of a mere 1,000 soul slaves. Whatever he had been in the ZeroTime, Petrus reasoned, Maweth had perforce lost some of his power by manifesting in this lower realm, this simulation. Wherein, simple logic dictated, the shadow of his true soul, when cast here, was nothing more than a shadow, like all else. A weakened soul, whose true power could not manifest here. And what was a soul, even the soul of a godlike extradimensional entity like the Angel of Death, to the Lightbringer's own Soulthief? *Nothing more than my new paschal staff,* Petrus mocked. *Better than the Scorzelli...*

"One moment, Mary," Petrus said, commanding a steady stream of soul slaves to phase into his staff. "The being in my staff – I know you saw its horror earlier – requires my brief attention."

"Someone is... in your staff?" she asked, genuinely curious.

"Yes," he nodded curtly, focusing his gaze, and more soul slaves, on the terminus of the staff. "And I am now of the inclination that it's time to fully bind it, and in so doing, learn what it knows. For you have reminded me that orthodoxy has been relegated to the illusions of the past. Now, it is time for facts, not superstition."

Bearing down with full power, and that augmented by a continuous stream of soul slaves, Petrus, jaw set firmly, boomed a psychic command into Maweth's weakened, compromised soul: *"Confess!"*

And thus, his own soul enfeebled by its forced merger with the Hatefang, Maweth confessed. Petrus burned out thousands of soul slaves, picking, scraping, and separating Maweth's soul from that of the Hatefang, to which it had been so cruelly, so forcefully bound. Bound by the Lightbringer himself, through the agency of twin blades of fateful chaos combined with soul-empowered Hekatek... and the souls of some very interesting beings. Petrus experienced the event vicariously, scanning rapidly through Maweth's memories and experiences. He cataloged and stored even the tiniest, most insignificant details in his own expanded mind, and souls. In but the span of a mere minute of objective time, he bent and bound the totality of what had remained of Maweth's broken and tattered soul into his own. He did this until no soul energies remained. Even the writhing helices of the Hatefang itself slowed down to a feeble snail's crawl.

In expectant silence, Mary quietly observed the process, her own study no less intense than Petrus'. Unlike Petrus, who seemed to have become mildly intoxicated by the experience, Mary quite soberly felt the resonance of life coming from what now appeared to be a black blade whose rainbow lights no longer danced so energetically. Two distinct patterns, she perceived. Not just one. She wondered, academically of course, if Petrus had intended to confine the soul of the winged demon-looking creature into that wicked blade. It made little sense to her strategically. But that's precisely what he had just done, if her senses were to be believed. Cagey and entirely, rationally paranoid, Mary decided to play this one close to the vest. Her instinct for self-preservation was positively screaming at her to be cautious, but scratch and claw for every last possible advantage.

Regaining his center, his dominance established, Petrus' eyes narrowed a moment before he spoke, almost as if he did not quite believe what he had just done. The shattered shards of Maweth's simulated soul now were his to do with as he willed. Impossible. Yet, he had done it. Taken down one of the gods of the ZeroTime, one described explicitly by the Lightbringer himself, in his futile attempt to instill awe and fear into him. What, then, could he *not* do?

When at last he spoke, the Black Pope chose his words most carefully:

"Orthodox eschatologies, I believe? Yes, Mary. I have seen this myself. Not much has been preserved from among the standard or nonstandard eschatologies regarding the End Times, according to the Christian faith. An argument could be made regarding misinterpretation of the scriptures. But the fact of the matter appears, as you have noted, to differ quite entirely from what was captured in the Word. Obviously, there is a notable difference between how Armageddon is described in the Book of Revelation and this event happening now, this Evolutionary Tribulation, which is what the Lightbringer called it."

"But doesn't evolution imply some sort of forward progress?" Mary countered. "Going forward hardly seems like something humanity would do during Armageddon."

Petrus paused a moment, shaking his head. The ends of his long black locks crackled once, sharply, with a dark static display. "Mary," he began softly, "despite the apparent differences, we truly are in the End Times. I know this, despite the strangeness around us, because I have met the devil, and he is real."

Unbidden, Mary's hand rose to her mouth. She had never been a screamer, or even given to displays of overt emotion. That was best left to ordinary housewives baking their apple pies, and not full professors on the fast track to full tenure. But the look in Petrus' eyes told her he spoke the absolute truth, and it required all of her control to remain calm.

"You really mean it, don't you?" she said needlessly, realizing that she had spoken aloud only after hearing herself. "This isn't just aliens or some insane space invasion, is it? This really is the work of Satan?"

"He has many names, Mary," Petrus replied. "His preferred name now is 'Lightbringer'. Yet he is one and the same as the one who tempted Christ in the desert. He is Lucifer, of course. He is the so-called 'bearer of light', yet he bears nothing but scorn and hatred for all of us." He threw his arms majestically open, spinning slowly in place. "Gaze upon his works. Could anyone but the devil himself cause such destruction, such horror?"

Mary considered that line of logic for a moment, even as she gazed upon the thousands upon thousands who marched with such determination toward Petrus' dark device. For a millisecond she considered a response. Then, thinking better of it, bit her tongue.

He noticed this immediately, pivoting back toward her. "Ah, the question. Of course. Now would be the time to ask it, Mary."

Steeling herself, she returned his fiery gaze. "Petrus. This..." she said, pointing an accusing finger down at the press of bodies sizzling and popping at the perimeter of the Dark Tabernacle, "...this is not the work of God."

Throwing his head back, Petrus roared in spiteful laughter. "But of course it is, dearest Miriam," he said mockingly. "It is indeed the work of God. The Lightbringer himself told me how to create it, and he surely is the lord of this world, the King of this Universe."

Shaking her head, hot tears started to spill down her cheeks. "You don't mean that, Petrus. You don't mean that," she said, trying to remain calm.

Suddenly, his laughter stopped, and he met her eyes. "Don't cry, Mary. I'm not insane, and neither are you. The fact is, the Lightbringer is – now that I am capable of understanding the true nature of his, and our, existence thanks to the knowledge I've absorbed – the creator and shaper of this world. But," he continued over her gasp, "this is not the world as we have been told. And this is not some Gnostic perversion. Instead, this is a simulation. It is merely a game. An act of theater, nothing more. It is a glorified, universal-scale simulation that the Lightbringer himself has instantiated. He himself has created its many denizens. You, me, and everyone else in the world. And he has set us upon the quest to be judged by the Lightbringer's Sigil, and then to contest the forces of the true master of the game: the One Above. At the End of All Things, the One Above will set loose an army of cosmic destroyers upon Earth. They will 'win' the game for him by destroying the world. They are called the 'Vanth'Vash'Var', and they are the servants of the Void."

Mary shook her head. "I can't believe that, Petrus. It's insane. How can this be a simulation? I feel as alive as I ever have. Even more so, now. How could anyone or anything fool billions of us, simultaneously, and make us all believe that this is real," she said, sweeping an arm before her, "when in fact it's nothing but some sort of colossal computer game?"

"That's exactly what it is, Mary!" he replied, triumphant. "What that means is that none of this is real. None of this is real. Those poor fools taking their last step into the Dark Tabernacle?" he said over a fresh wave of loud crackling. "They are not real. True, they are real enough to do what they do, the mindless automata that they truly are. But they are not real. Only *we* are real. Only those of us who have transcended the mortal realm, becoming fully realized immortals ourselves. *We* are the real ones, the ones who will play for all of the stakes of this wondrous, savage game to which we have been bound."

"This can't be just a game!" Mary said, her voice shrill. "What sense does that make?"

"It makes sense to the One Above," he replied, his voice even. "And it makes sense to the Lightbringer. According to what the Lightbringer told me – what he showed my mind – there are many thousands of his ilk. He called them 'Children of the Light', and they each have their own cosmic simulations in play. All of them play their simulations, trying to defeat the One Above, who contests all of them simultaneously. The One Above is the true god of their world, which is called 'The ZeroTime'. He is an implacable tyrant who derives his pleasure from incessantly defeating the Lightbringer and his kin. He ends all of their failed simulations by totally destroying all of the souls contained within it. That is total genocide, on a cosmic scale, even if only a few of the souls are actually 'real' enough to be deemed such."

In silence, she considered this for a moment. "If I accept your hypothesis, then I need to know which side you're – we're – on. I'll tell you right now and for nothing that I don't like any of it. Both sides sound like douchebags to me."

Noting the dangerous play of shifting rainbows along the outline of her form, Petrus smiled. It seemed that Mary had made the correct choice. With that, he silently willed several dozen milling soul slaves away, their potential task now no longer necessary.

"You are wise beyond your years, Mary," Petrus told her. "I am genuinely pleased that you have discerned the correct path. The Lightbringer assumed that, because he had taken me into his confidence, I would be a willing servitor. That I would play my role with full attention to the script that he had intended for me to follow. But I refuse to do it. I *refuse*! I will not blindly follow Lucifer against God, even if God is genocidal and insane. The Lightbringer is the same in all worlds: he is the Father of Lies. Our apparent path might seem to parallel his, what he has set out for us to do. But that is only because it is reasonable for us to do so in order to survive."

"So we're on the side of the One Above?"

Petrus shook his head. "Indeed, we are not. For he is a cosmic terrorist of the highest possible order, far more bound by hubris and ego than any mere demi-urge could be. He torments not only the Lightbringer and his Children of the Light, but also all of the trillions upon trillions of souls – real or unreal – in the millions upon millions of simulations that have been completed or are yet still in play. He snuffs everyone's souls at the end, Mary. They are like mere ritual candles to him, extinguished without compassion once their brief allotted time to burn is done. And he always wins. There is not a name on this Earth that properly describes the depth of his evil. We must contest him and his desires with all of our hearts and souls."

"I don't get it," Mary admitted. "If not the Lightbringer, and if not the One Above, then who do we follow?"

Petrus Romanus, the Black Pope, the Lightbringer's Soulthief, slowly crossed his arms, staff in hand.

"We follow no one, Mary," he proclaimed, thunder in his voice. "For we can trust no one but ourselves in this. No one. The Lightbringer is the Father of Lies, simulation or not. It is all but certain that he seeks not merely to win the game against the One Above, but, ultimately, to usurp his throne. Just like the Devil tried to do here in our world. This cannot be allowed. The One Above holds the ultimate power in this reality. Allowing the Devil himself to obtain this power would be the most foolish act ever, in all creation."

"But what happens when we win?" Mary inquired, genuinely not liking where this was apparently leading. "That will defeat the One Above, of course. Maybe it will even promote the Lightbringer or allow him and his kin to usurp the power of the One Above. But, what happens to us, trapped here in our simulation, after the victory? Does he just allow us to live on? Does he just pull the plug on us, like a total game over? What about the rest of the thousands upon thousands of simulations still going on? Does our victory redeem their uncounted souls, or are they simply written off to oblivion when we win?"

"Truth," Petrus agreed. "The only possible answer – one I see more clearly now that I have taken the burden of binding the souls of others to my own; their knowledge incorporated into my own – is to rebel against both God and the Devil. In order to do this, to fight this nigh impossible fight, we must implement a strategy that rebels against their own scripted game. We will do that which they do not suspect. We will introduce chaos into their lawfully patterned structures. We shall wreak havoc upon their game. We will seek out and exploit every possible advantage of power. We will empower ourselves above and beyond what their game has labeled us as: mere 'gods'. We will become their equals, a clear and present threat. We will then have a way to force them to preserve our world, our Earth. It is indeed possible – hypothetically, of course – that we can persuade them through crook or staff to free our Earth from their sordid game and set this universe free. Perhaps with you and I to become its own true shepherds; become its own true gods."

Despite her own well-constructed mental paradigms of skepticism, Mary believed Petrus. It was difficult to conceive how this was the same man who had been the Pope mere days before. It was indeed difficult now for her to recall the many images of the man she had seen prior to recent events. He had been an elderly man, decades past his prime. Not particularly enfeebled or bent, but he had been long in his years. Now, though, Petrus seemed to be somewhere near her own age. Young, full of vigor, his very presence now resembling an angel painted by Botticelli, his coal-black eyes piercing the core of her soul.

Mary shook her head, trying to ward off this seeming madness. "Even if we are becoming what you've called 'gods' ourselves, how can we dare stand against entities who control Reality itself? How much power do we need? Where do we get it? Giza? From the resonating pyramids?"

He nodded. "You are indeed wise, Mary. Remember the nonlinear harmonic resonance we discussed?"

She nodded once, briskly. "And you're not too naïve yourself, old man," she laughed. "I understand now why I'm the first so-called 'New God' you've contacted. I'm the one who can get this done."

Petrus allowed a slight smile to upturn. "Well, I could have just stolen your soul from you when we first met, and taken your power from you, and done all this myself. But then I would have missed the pleasure of your company," he said, bowing slightly at the waist.

A small shiver tickled the back of Mary's neck. Even when being candid and charming, if that's what he truly was being, the Black Pope was still one major scary badass.

"I can ramp up the resonant power of those things exponentially," Mary declared, actually enjoying the thrill of saying such a tremendously insane thing.

"And I can now ask a small boon of you, Mary Dunbar, my Talisman of Rainbows," he said.

She shrugged. "Okay," she said, knowing that there was of course some price to be paid, "let's hear it."

"Now that you know what is to come," he began, "I ask you to travel, as you traveled from Giza to this place, to retrieve another one of us. One of us who has the power that we will need in order to work this charm. Her name is Amaterasu Kurohoshi. She is the Black Star."

Mary raised her hands, palms up and out toward his face. "Okay, okay. But just wait one second, Petrus. If you're going to make me your emissary and press me into service to do something that sounds absolutely bat shit crazy, I think you owe me a deeper explanation. After all, you are enjoying the presence of my company, aren't you?"

Smiling warmly, he told her, "Of course. You have earned as much. But I would have freely told you regardless, had you but asked. Ami, the Black Star, is going to be the one who opens up the Gates of Chaos around the pyramids for us. You, the Talisman, are going to be the one who focuses and shapes and amplifies the resonant energy provided by the pyramids at Giza.

As well as dozens of other similar constructions around the world. Once the correct modulation has been achieved, I am going to then tap into the collective life force of this world and its many souls – the souls and life forces of all things – and I am going to become the Dragon. The Dragon is the superset of the souls and life forces of all things. And I shall weave a great charm of making, using the power gained to... Well," he paused, noting her wide eyes, "you're a true daughter of Erin, are ye not, Mary Dunbar? Surely you know what 'nathrach' entails?"

She did, and, naturally, she bridled. "You're mad, Petrus. Mad! You'd wager the world right now to force their hand!"

He nodded. "Yes. We hit them now, before they expect us even to have settled, and we hit them with the full might of this world. Amplified, of course, by the unique union of our own three powers. We will be strong enough, if only for a nanosecond, which is all we'll actually need, to directly threaten them. And we shall do exactly that. That's the only way to win."

"What if they don't give in?"

"If that is the case, then we have lost. And there is but one thing we may do to ensure that they never have another round of their blasphemous games. We use our fleeting cosmic-level power to invoke the Protocols of Judgement and Execution, destroy the ZeroTime, and kill both God and the Devil."

eVo.144.000.mOd.112.sCe7 | YEAR ZERO | EARTH |

UNITED STATES | CALIFORNIA | HERMOSA BEACH

WHEN IT HAD HAPPENED, Trish Burnley, RN, had been outside of Mercy General, taking a last smoke break with her friend Nikki before wrapping up for the night.

"Ah, shit," Nikki said, straining to see through the typical Southern California light pollution. "I can't see anything like what they're showing on TV."

"I know," Trish replied, scanning the sky overhead. "Aw, c'mon," she complained. "I want to see ET!"

"Yeah!" Nikki echoed. "ET!"

The news had reported that there were alien ships forming into patterns surrounding the world, but Trish could hardly make out the twinkles in the night sky. Disappointed, she and Nikki were stubbing out their cigarettes on the gray cigarette receptacle when everything lit up like Christmas.

Their shadows danced on the sidewalk as both women slowly turned their gazes back to the sky.

Christmas, plus the Fourth of July, multiplied by a million. The spiral patterns going both north and south, and east and west, were incredible. Colors strobed up and down the strands, which Trish immediately identified as a kind of DNA pattern – but one with three strands.

"It's... it's DNA, Nikki," Trish stammered in disbelief.

As she strained to watch the pattern unfold, Trish heard a gurgling noise beside her. Nikki collapsed onto the roof. There was a noisome stench all too familiar to a nurse, as Nikki's bowels loosened. Incredibly, her whole body sagged and began to liquefy.

"Nikki! Oh, God!" Trish shrieked.

Trish started to bend and help her friend, but it was all she could do to avoid being covered in the splashing offal. Stepping back, she screamed, turning to dash inside. The lights overhead were forgotten as she entered the hospital. Inside, it was pandemonium. More than half of the people – patients and staff alike – fell into the viscous puddles where they stood, sat, or lay in bed. The remainder panicked, running, hiding, or reaching for the bedside call buttons to see what was going on. Some remained asleep throughout the tragedy, pumped full of morphine, blithely unaware.

"Oh my god!" Trish repeated under her breath as she stumbled through the chaos of Mercy General. Finding a wall free of gore, she leaned heavily against it, hugging herself and slowly swaying. "Get a grip. Get it together," she whispered to herself over the screams of the dying. "Make the plan. Round up everyone, organize, and make the plan. Help these people, Trish. Help them."

Trish's hands fell to her side. Slowly, she stopped swaying. Something she had ignored all of her life started a fire in her very soul. Her hands balled tightly into fists.

What followed was hours of building-wide triage, as Trish rounded up nurses and doctors, verified who was left, and tried to determine who had died. For some reason unknown to her, they all listened to her. She had never been a leader, or person of action, in her whole life. But now, tonight, at what must surely have been the start of the end of the world, nurses, doctors, and orderlies listened to her and did what she told them to do. Stalwart crews, formed on the spot, attempted to clean and sanitize the rooms and halls to the best of their abilities. The remaining personnel, urged on by Trish's leadership, worked heroically to heal who they could. But within a few hours, even the survivors began showing signs of illness.

Trish noted that, unlike the initial wave of deaths, the subsequent illness manifested over a period of hours. A bruise-like area on the surface of the skin often spread from near joints and nerve clusters to the rest of the extremities. Contusions on the chest and groin likewise expanded, covering large areas. Along with rising fever and nausea, the subject's skin began to crack and ooze blood and dark matter. Shortly after, muscle control and strength were lost, and individuals became delirious, lapsing into unconsciousness. Eventually, when all functions ceased, the dead began the process of disintegration. The end results were the same: a dark puddle of bones and effluvium. Some, however, recovered from the illness after hours of painful vomiting and headaches. A very few seemed to suffer not at all. Or, if anything, mild stomach cramps or headache.

For six hours, Trish and the hospital crew fought valiantly. Yet, they knew they fought in vain.

Trish was on her fifth coffee, taking a short yet necessary pitstop at the nurse's station near the general waiting room. She had already decided that she was going to keep working until she dropped. It was the only decision she could make, considering the circumstances. No family at home. No living relatives. There was no one else to talk to, now. Not that there ever had been anyway. Still, there was no way she would leave. Not with most of the hospital staff either dead or not reporting.

The stench in the hospital was incredible. There was no way they could contain the biohazards from all the human slush. People just... melted. Beds overflowed with the vile liquid, and the nurses stations had puddles of the goo. Trish estimated that maybe four in ten people survived the results of the alien symbol in the sky. And now the ill were coming in downstairs in droves.

In the hours after the sigil event, little news was forthcoming from any media source, other than the situation was worldwide. Trish cursed at the TV behind the nurses' station, finishing her coffee. Turning to resume her duties, she winced at the sudden pain that started at the base of her skull and seemed to radiate along every nerve in her body. It felt like a live wire had been inserted into her spine.

Suddenly awake, Trish felt hypersensitive and flooded with pain. She slowly lowered herself to the floor, feeling like an antenna as she turned. As she faced the ward where the surviving patients had been gathered, her chest felt like it was on fire, and her face numbed. She felt each and every injury and illness in the rooms beyond. But the worst was the blackness and burning of those with the strange creeping death from beyond the stars. It felt like her body was being flensed in brilliant fire. Tears of unearned grief and pain washed her cheeks. Images of lost love ones – strangers – flashed behind her closed eyes.

Trish crawled away from the worst of the pain, gasping as she rose to sit in a nearby wheelchair. Ghosts and spirits fled past her, seeking escape from the psychic onslaught. Fleeing the pain and suffering, she rolled herself as far down the adjacent hall as possible and into the darkened chapel. Slowly, the pain and images receded. Then, Trish slipped into a deep well of unconsciousness, unaware of the glowing illumination that had begun to increase near the altar.

All through Mercy General, the living and dying joined the wheel of fate cast by Lucifer's Sigil. For some there was surcease from pain and suffering. For others, the inclusion of a third strand came with more or less travail. Fever dreams and nightmares of what would be rode the survivors like the Four Horsemen. Skin peeled and parted on the dead and dying, while subtle or blatant changes were worked upon humanity's new members.

All the while the changes happened throughout the hospital, a serene glow covered Trish, protecting her from the onslaught of emotion and pain in the surrounding building. In the ZeroTime, a small indicator flashed and went unnoticed, as Helel's attention was elsewhere.

Sometime later, Trish opened her eyes in the chapel. The pain was still there, in the back of her head, but muted. She rubbed her neck and got to her feet, making her way down the hall of the silent hospital. The dark and empty rooms held no more ghosts, and even those which were still dimly lit were quieted. As she went along the rounds of the ward, Trish found that half again of the patients had died. Most of these had passed peacefully, thanks to the medications available. Some of the survivors had gone missing, strangely. Those that remained simply stared at her enigmatically, smiling at the secret that they were unready, or unwilling, to share just yet.

Trish followed the hallways, through silent operating theaters, then down a stairwell, until she reached the Emergency Room. The sun was beginning to stream through shaded windows high in the wall, and the place was silent except for the constant ticking of a keyboard.

A mousy brunette looked up from the admittance station computer as Trish entered. "Hey. Thought I was pretty much the only one left down here. I'm Doctor Joyce. The new intern? I just got here. I'm in the intern apartments down the street. Slept through the whole thing, I guess, thanks to that twenty-four hour shift I just pulled. I heard you were the one who got the ball rolling when this first happened. How are you holding up?"

"Uhh... I feel kinda strange, but I guess that's due to all the coffee. What's going on?"

"Just typing up a report, but I'm not sure why. Or who's going to read it. Looks like there's maybe a handful of patients left here in the hospital, and maybe half a dozen staff. Everybody else is dead. But I tried to compile a report on what happened. Death rate, cause, time of death, symptoms, et cetera."

Trish goggled. "Seen any new arrivals? I mean is everyone out there dead?"

Dr. Joyce shrugged back and frowned. "I'm betting if the mortality rate in here is any indication, there *might* be fifty percent of the population left. Probably most people died in bed, if it's any consolation. Anyone trying to make it here either did, or..."

"Or it's a mess out there." Trish said with finality.

Dr. Joyce paused a moment. "It's a mess. Just that couple of blocks walking here seemed like I was descending into Dante's Hell. And we still don't know what this is, or how long people are going to *keep* dying," the doctor continued. "But it's very strange. Some of the patients that looked sick after the first... episode, stopped being sick. I swear, some of them just put on their clothes and left."

The women turned as the outside doors slid open and a motley trio came in, dressed in leather jackets. They were armed, their pistols directed aggressively at the two women. The apparent leader, a tall skinny man with long, greasy black hair and beard, waved his pistol around vaguely in front of him.

"Yo, bitches! Give us your drugs and nobody gets hurt!"

Trish froze. The man looked like he was already high on something. The stains on his teeth told her all she needed to know – meth. The other two, a young man and woman, seemed frightened, tentative. This could turn out very badly, she realized. With few doctors left, even a minor gunshot wound could be deadly. And Trish was starting to feel... what? Angry, disturbed, confused? No. *Needful.* These people were junkies and looking for a fix. She felt their need become her own. The sensation was disturbing to her. Disgusting. Weak.

The doctor slowly rose, addressing the leader. "What you are suggesting is not possible. Most of the people here are dead, and I'm guessing most of the people out *there* are too. All the drugs need to be secured for treatment."

"Wrong answer!" The man shot Doctor Joyce twice in the chest. She fell with a look of surprise on her face.

The young female junkie rushed to the leader and grabbed his arm. "Oh my god, Tyrone! What the hell?"

A spike of rage, need, and fear pulsed through Trish as she stood, aghast at the tableau she'd been thrust into. Her eyes darted from one to the next. The three turned to her. The leader, Tyrone, levelled his shaking gun, aiming directly at her face. Time froze. Trish felt heartbeats, pulses, breaths in stages of panic.

Shaking her head, Trish thought, *I can feel them. I know what they are feeling. Can they feel me?*

Tyrone and the others waited, watching Trish, who gathered herself up, looking from one to the other. The young man appeared ready to bolt, or to vomit, Trish wasn't sure. She fixed him with a level gaze and tried to concentrate all the horror and fear from the past few hours, directing those thoughts toward him. With a cry, he turned and ran – straight into the door.

Stunned, he regained his footing long enough to run from the building, trailed by the woman.

Tyrone watched the two of them run away, obviously torn. Then he turned back, need and lust naked in his eyes.

"The drugs. Now."

Pausing to look at the lifeless doctor on the floor beside her, Trish closed her eyes, summoning up the memory of the relentless, creeping blackness; the pain and fire, and death. When her gaze returned to the man, she focused her eyes on him as hard as she could, willing every bit of her remembered agony on him. Her intent was instinctive and pure.

"Go to hell, you junkie murderer!" Trish snarled through clenched teeth as electric blue sparks danced chaotically from her eyes.

For a moment, a look of pure horror infused his face. Then, a dark stain covered his pants, and he fell quivering to the floor, surrounded by a pool of urine. The gun clattered away as Tyrone was caught in a brief series of violent convulsions.

Trish knelt, checking Doctor Joyce for a pulse. There was none. Then, carefully, she walked around the desk and approached Tyrone, who was no longer moving. Terrified of the implication, she knelt and checked for a pulse. Again, nothing.

Rising back up to her feet, she cast a sidelong glance at Tyrone's corpse. "You got what you deserved," she said ardently, no longer terrified.

Picking up the gun, Trish secured it in a desk drawer at the admittance station, then made her way back upstairs to her patients.

eVo.144.000.mOd.112.sCe8 | YEAR ZERO | THE NULL

TIME SPENT IN THE NULL was not the equivalent of spending time on Earth, on the Prime. There simply was a state of Time either being on, or a state of Time being off. Lack of motion led directly to lack of Time, which led directly to dissolution at the sub-quantum level. This was total submergence into the Null. Becoming Zero. With constant motion, however, one avoided this most interesting fate. Time yet flowed, and one remained in the Flow, metaphysically speaking.

Maynard had not yet given up his fruitless task of checking his smartwatches. He had an Apple Watch on one wrist, a Samsung Gear on the other, and an LG Watch on a customized vest pocket chain. Despite his habit of constantly checking first one, then the other, then the third, none worked here in the Null. And it was driving him crazy.

"Can you hear me *now*, bitch?" he finally broke, clutching his LG Watch to his face like a very angry White Rabbit. Spastically, enraged, he stomped his feet madly in place while he used both hands to rip the pocket chain from his vest.

Drawing to a stop to witness the spectacle, Ku'tu, Mercy, Vir'gil, and Void observed as Maynard went ape, throwing the watch to the rubbery ground of the Null, then stomping up and down on it. To no avail, and to no satisfying crunch, however. The watch merely compressed itself into the blubbery ground with each stomp, rebounding almost immediately upon impact. After a few more impotent stomps, Mercy's mocking laughter filled the space between them.

"C'mon, Maynard," she wheedled. "That won't work. You're keeping it in motion. If you just toss it away to lay on its own, it'll dissolve."

"Don't... want it... to dissolve..." he replied, stomping a few more times. "Wait," he said abruptly, bending down to scoop up his unscratched watch, quickly replacing it in his vest pocket. "The implication is that inertia is key here. The Null actually favors one state of it over the other."

"Newton's First," Void clarified, seeing that the non-humans were mystified, even the abnormally erudite Mercy. "Law of Inertia, basically."

"Yeah, Void, see?" Maynard said, bouncing up and down in place. "We're safe from the Null so long as we maintain our flow. But, if we stop, remaining in the resting state, the Null hates it and dissolves it."

"Simple metaphysics," Mercy snorted, turning back around, scanning with her pseudo-Cylon visor. "You didn't need to drag poor Isaac into this. That poor dear was so confused with his alchemy, it's a miracle he ever got anything done. Anyway, rotational and linear mechanics won't get us out of here."

"Wut, mate?" Maynard asked, totally surprised. "How did you even know where I was going with—"

Mercy laughed as she resumed her slow, steady pace. "You're a super smart guy, Maynard. How long did it take you to get your PhD?"

"After I got my double masters in Aerospace Engineering and Physics in a total of three years, I decided to forestall getting the dual PhDs. I had patents to cover, and MorthonTech gave me the best package deal for that right out of college. Three years from Freshman to dual masters is still my record. No one's beaten it yet. Cory... I mean, Void, didn't even try to beat it. He took like seven years to get out of school."

"Best seven years of my life," Void deadpanned.

"I bet," Mercy said knowingly. "Anyway, Maynard, you surely know how smart someone could get after, say, 13,000 years of study."

"Yeah, sure," he replied. "Unless you've been studying Basket Weaving that whole time."

"I like weaving baskets," Mercy shot back. "Especially when they're used to catch what Madame Guillotine drops in them. Be that as it may, the psychic interface I'm sharing now with Aal Ball lets me tap into its hive minds. There are thousands of them available for use. Right now, I'm tapping into only a few of them, and it's boosting my intellect significantly. So when you went all science-y on me, I had several of those minds whisper some science-y stuff into my mind. In about a millisecond."

"I'm calling bullshit on that! That's like having a cybernetic interface with Google," Maynard guffawed. "That's cheating. Don't get me wrong, Mercy. I know you have godlike intelligence natively after experiencing so much, even if all you did was weave baskets. And it's cool as heck what that relic dildo thing can do. But it's still cheating."

"I cheat constantly," Mercy giggled. "Only way to make sure I win all the time. Like, right now. Winning!" she exclaimed, breaking into an awkward looking lope as she streaked ahead of them. "I see it! I see it!" she called back to them.

"See what?" Void asked as they closed the gap. "There's nothing but more Null there."

Mercy made a great show of pointing her metallic, silvery hands down at the generic grey-green tofu ground of the Null.

Curious, Ku'tu buzzed quickly around Mercy, examining the ground carefully with her enhanced Fae senses.

"Nerfed or not," she said, "I can still see magicks, and there's nothing there indicating that your Never-anchors are there. It's dead blank, just like the rest of this thrice-accursed place. Meaning no offense to your station, Milady Ninth Null."

"Thanks for the courtesy, Ku'tu," Mercy said merrily as Aal Ball shifted its essence, compacting it until it was nothing more than the pseudo-Cylon visor, now attached to a shining silver headpiece shaped exactly like a funky Bootsy Collins hat. "But the eightfold anchor path intersects right here, right where I'm pointing right now with my pointy wolf skin boot," she said, doing precisely that, indicating a rather generic looking piece of the Null underfoot.

"Wait," Void said. "You mean all eight are here, in one place?" She nodded. Void cheered, metal horns flying from both hands. This temporarily invoked some misplaced fear and apprehension in the Fae, for this meant something totally different in their world and among their kin, especially when done in proximity to a metaphysical eightfold path.

"Void?" Maynard called out. "Void? Might want to chill," he said as he finally got Void's attention, nodding his head toward Mercy, Vir'gil, and Ku'tu, who were staring at him with wide eyes, wide eye stalks, and a wide visor.

"Oh, sorry," Void said, relaxing his unintended exercise in chaos magicks. All of the Fae visibly relaxed a bit at that point, too. "I'm just happy that they're all here in one place. I thought we were going to have to track all eight of them down, one at a time, or something that would take an extremely long time. Like a real quest, or something."

Even Maynard gave him a mystified look this time. "Why would you think that? Mercy clearly said it was an eightfold path."

"Yeah, but I thought that we'd have to walk all eight of them."

Mercy laughed. "This ain't Buddhism, Void. Buddha was great for a human, and totally enlightened, but we Fae automatically reject the concept of suffering. To us, the Four Noble Truths are virtually anathema. We live for fun, not suffering, pain, and misery. We're totally selfish to a fault, and we desire everything we see that's entertaining, novel, or fun. Or shiny. We know it's foolish even to try to overcome our traits. No way. We're sort of in line with the Fourth Truth, though, because we believe that the Sign of Chaos can help us achieve our desires, listed above. The Sign of Chaos, like the Eightfold Path, is indeed represented, mostly, by a similar eight-rayed device. However, unlike Buddhism, ours goes both ways. Like me," she laughed, causing a burst of short laughter from everyone. "It goes off and out, in all directions. But it also goes in, meeting in the middle."

Void gave Mercy a discerning look. "Meeting in the middle... I should think that your binding to the Song of the Sidhe would be your Fae version of Nirvana. I see why you wouldn't waste any effort in trying to walk the straight and narrow Eightfold Path in order to return to it."

Heads nodded all around.

"And that's what makes most straight folk think we're evil," Void continued.

"We're not evil," Ku'tu protested. "Those are mortal appellations. They don't apply to the Fae. We're beyond morals and dogma." Vir'gil made a creaking noise and crossed his arms. Mercy just smiled, bending a knee to get a close-up view of her mystical pathway.

"I know," Void said flatly. "And you just blatantly stomped all over Irony itself, Ku'tu. On Earth, those 'morals and dogma' point toward a gentleman by the name of Albert Pike, and he was notorious for his admiration of Lucifer. Please note the self-affine structures in play. Not exact, but eerily similar."

"More bleed-through," Mercy said. "Yet another in an innumerable list of interesting coincidences."

"I think it's yet another in an innumerable list of Helel's code-it-easy practices," Void chuckled. "I don't expect anyone else in our group to get it, because it's a bit obscure for non-coders to grok. But, it's rapidly becoming clear to me that he's taken every possible shortcut, even resorting to what I think would be self-affine fractal coding practices. By that, I mean that he's using similarly constructed seeds to grow his simulations. That's why we're experiencing so many of those bleed-throughs. They're inherent phenomena in his system."

Maynard stared hard at Void, arching an eyebrow. "Dude, I know you've got major code chops, but do you think you've already cracked his system? Seriously? Because that's some low-probability bullshit you're peddling. You're talking about fractal coding, and that's some heavy shit by itself. But what he considers to be code – the stuff he needs to run a cosmos – might be so far above that that even seeing it would blow our minds."

"Maybe," Void said quietly. Then, with a bit more bass, he added, "But there are some fixed parameters in information systems. Primary of these is that complexity tends to accrue unnecessary data mass. The more complex, the more energy cycles are required. Even virtually infinite energy budgets – like something we'd associate, in our ignorance of such things, to that which is necessary to code an entire universe – have limits. Very real limits. After some introspection, and after paying careful attention to what's been transpiring around us, I'd have to insist that he's using a fractal-based, self-affine system of coding. It would explain the coincidences. It would explain the templating system he's revealed to us. It's probably one of the few methodologies available in the noosphere that could handle that much data, that much complexity, without invoking lag on a cosmic scale."

"Hahah!" Maynard laughed. "Lag! On a cosmic scale! You know it's just latency anyway, not lag. Please make sure your computer is on. If it is, then please reboot it."

"Or crashing the system," Void continued, unflustered. He and Maynard had done this routine a thousand times. "If it's even close to being right, or even being in the ballpark, I think that, if I got a look at what it really looks like, I could hack it."

"Holy Hacking Independence Day!" Maynard guffawed. "That shit only works in the movies, man. You know that. Those guys up in the ZeroTime? They're gods compared to us. There, I admitted it. They're *gods* compared to us. This isn't a Gibson or Wachowskis sim. We're dealing with god-level powers. Did you miss the part where Helel mentioned that this was sim number 144,000 for him? Anything they do is going to be so insanely complex that it's going to be like we're ants trying to sneak into their car and drive it away."

Void laughed. "You missed it, Maynard."

"Missed what? I just shot your hypothesis to shit, Void. Only gods could do something like simulate a complete universe that many times."

"Shard and truncated/floored instantiations," Void countered. "Easy way to have a pre-generated, pre-populated simulation. Like maybe 'everything starts at such and such a year on Earth', and everything before that is simply instantiated ex post facto. And then you just insert your templates in along the way."

"That's reasonable," Maynard considered. "What did I miss, though? I'm usually the one telling the NASA guys what *they've* missed."

"I know. The self-similar, self-affine coincidence of 144,000. Helel, or Lucifer, has instantiated our cosmos as the number of the 'chosen' in the Bible."

"Wow, that's true," Maynard agreed. "That's some heavy shit, Void. I think I might become convinced of your hypothesis after all. Just need a few more data points to make me happy."

"If that's true," Mercy said sardonically, "then Helel's inverted the intention of the Good Book."

"Look at what the Pope's doing, for Christ's sake," Maynard added without a hint of irony. "The whole mess is not just inverted, it's perverted. Chaos appears to be doing its job. And that probably doesn't bode well for us at all."

"Then again," Mercy said, appearing to scoop up and cradle some unseen entity in her hands, "maybe a bit of chaos is what we need to win." She turned to face them, proudly showing them nothing. "Behold! My beautiful anchors!"

In silence, they shrugged, clearly befuddled.

"This is the awning of the cage of asparagus?" Void inquired, eliciting an immediate snort from Maynard and some creaking and groaning from Vir'gil.

"No, you big dope!" Mercy laughed. "I think you former humans are becoming as emotionally fluid as we Fae. That was a totally insane tangent, and a bad meme. But I think you might be on to something. Retard. Oops," she immediately corrected. "Sorry, Void."

Void returned her laugh. "I know I am. Seriously, I'm not sensitive about words. Only when people use them on kids or the innocent. Kids can't fight back. I can." He immediately caught the sense of dread that this seemed to cause among his companions, so he immediately added, "Not that I'm going to fight over something so silly, of course. Are you still spooked about the devil horns dance I just did? Geez, I was joking. Rock'n'Roll, dudes!" he laughed, catching himself at the last moment as he instinctively tried to flash devil horns.

Ku'tu cleared her throat. "It's only natural for us to fear you, if only on a subconscious level, Void. You're a myth among the Fae of my world. Here, too," she said as both Mercy and Vir'gil nodded in the affirmative. "You're basically the thing hiding under our beds. The bad man who comes for wicked Fae and spirits them off to the Void, forever damned and removed from the Song of the Sidhe. Chthon's personal Angel of Death. Or, in your case, Demon."

"Really?" Void asked, genuinely disturbed by the picture Ku'tu had just painted of him. "But that would make me – forgive the logical stretch on this one – the metaphysical antithesis of Maweth, wouldn't it?"

"Hadn't considered that," Ku'tu admitted as Vir'gil groaned under his breath. "Maybe. The power scales are off, though. One cannot be an antithesis to an entity that hails from a realm of existence above and beyond one's own. That's illogical. Unless Helel was actually telling the truth when he claimed that he felt powerless against the Mother's own power. Then, that might imply some form of symmetry and equivalence. But he's a liar, so who knows if he was telling the truth?"

"Screw all that," Mercy said impatiently, tapping her wolfskin boot on the mushy ground. "I thought everyone caught onto that when the Dark Earth Mother herself appeared out of Void's third eye and awestruck everyone, including the Lightbringer. The only symmetry and equivalence here is her bimodal aspect with the Dragon. All That All Which Is, All That All Which Binds? They're the ultimate superset of all things cosmic. If you don't get it by now, what that implies, you never will," she mocked. "Anyway, it's irrelevant, because she's totally a bitch and she won't help us anyway. We're on our own. So let's not waste time and wind up dissolving into total nothingness while we're jawing about hypotheticals!"

"So what do we do?" Maynard asked her. "I can't see anything in your hands."

"Ah," Mercy balked. "Aal Ball?" she inquired aloud, more for her friends' benefit than her own. "Please illuminate them. The eight metaphysical anchors, I mean."

"Aal Ball!" the collective entity bleated in a hundred tiny voices. From the midst of the front of her wicked Bootsy Collins hat a steady stream of silver light issued forth, bathing the ethereal anchors in her hands with an inferential glow which caused them to become visible in the normal visual spectrum, or what precisely passed for that in the Null. The anchors themselves appeared to be nothing more than tiny, fragile-looking strands of tinsel, wound up lazily in Mercy's hands. The strands disappeared from sight only a few inches removed from Mercy's grasp, blending back into the nothingness from which they had been manifested.

"Okay, Mercy," Maynard said. "Those are way too small to be keyholes for Ku'tu. So that's out."

"Yeah," Mercy replied, disappointed. "If that's out, then Plan B would be for me to use Aal Ball to try to interface with them, one at a time, and map them out. Do a bit of scrying. See what we can see."

"It can do that?" Maynard asked. "I mean, just casually interface with... Oh," he said, getting the point that its perverse little liquid mercury-looking form could interface with just about anything. "Never mind. It's some sort of quantum interface, Void. Isn't that cool? Think about what we could engineer and build if we had that kind of precision and control."

"You'll be lucky if that's all it interfaces with," Void said, grinning. "Give it a shot, Mercy. We'll guard you. Or whatever."

"Yeah, whatever," Mercy said, smiling quickly. "If this goes south, just command Aal Ball to sever the link with the anchor. But not with me, got it?" They nodded. "Okay, here we go..." she said, carefully picking out the first anchor strand and holding it up, near to her forehead. Aal Ball, tracking it with its illumination source, formed a generic docking interface, which it caused to reach out and envelop the silvery strand.

A momentary flicker of disordered, out-of-phase sine waves, outlined in shimmering crimson hues, played across Aal Ball's internal HUD. Involuntarily, the muscles in Mercy's jaw locked down tight, as the flickering bloody sine waves rapidly achieved a more lawful phase, revealing the unmistakable skyline of the city of Hong Kong.

"Ooh..." Mercy trilled. "Aal Ball, make an external big screen HUD so everyone can see this, too."

"Aal Ball!" it said merrily, eager to please everyone, because satisfaction was hardwired into its very essence. To comply with its latest directive, Aal Ball internally polled its collective, inquiring of them in but mere milliseconds as to who had the best solution to satisfy their mistress. Of the several hundred psyches among the collective who had experienced such things, Aal Ball's parsing filters almost immediately selected the best of the best, sending a parallel feed to a rapidly morphing extrusion of its essence. In a trice, defying the conventions of both Earth-based physics and universal good taste, a micron-thin black display screen appeared, confined within modified side panels which clearly resembled a vulva.

Then, as the imagery data reached the screen at a resolution far surpassing standard UHD, five distinct screens in a two-by-three grid bloomed to life, displaying simultaneously on the main display.

"First anchor runs through Hong Kong," Mercy announced. "Looks like Aal Ball has got us a few different vantage points on the screen. Good stuff, thanks, you silver turkey," she said, unaware that the external screen was entirely in violation of her earlier stated rules. Vir'gil and Ku'tu both cheered and clapped politely, clearly happy to see something other than the omnipresent, entirely dull Null. Even if it was a perverse and obscene spectacle. Perhaps even moreso due to that fact.

Contrary to the bemused Fae, Maynard and Void exchanged inquiring glances with one another.

"That grid looks like..." Maynard began, stepping in close to the display. His outstretched hand traced the rough outline of the display array, even as the scenes shifted down from the initial heavenly vantage to street level. "It's Gil's default virtual configuration, Void. How would Aal Ball know—"

Abruptly, all the air seemed to leave his lungs as the five scenes resolved fully. In the first, dozens of vehicles lay strewn about a four-way intersection, some piled three-high, some split in half, most on fire or slowly smoldering. Bodies, most nothing more than purple-bruised torsos devoid of limbs, appeared to have been haphazardly cast among the chaotic crash scene by some giant devoid of mercy. The next three screens showed burning apartment buildings, a large container ship crashing uncontrolled into a towering dockside gantry crane, and a rapid sequence of still images featuring small crowds of what had formerly been human beings seemingly melted in place like crude wax mannikins.

The fifth screen showed the face of a screaming young female child, standing on a sidewalk on a chaotic street, looking down helplessly at her clearly expired mother, who lay face down on the curb. Her face was slowly dissolving into amorphous black goo which oozed over the edge of curb and into the street like a tiny black waterfall. Over this image, in American English, a crawl moved over the screen. It read:

1st Iteration, mortality rate 33%. 2nd Iteration, mortality rate 55.11%. 3rd Iteration, mortality rate 77.56%. 4th Iteration, mortality rate 92.6%. 5th Iteration, mortality rate 98.52%. 6th Iteration, total genocide...

The screens then faded to black.

"No, no, no, no, no!" Maynard screamed. "That can't be right. That can't be right!"

"Mercy?" Void said.

"Aye, Void, I know," Mercy replied, slowly shaking her head. "That makes a liar out of the Lightbringer. He distinctly said that this wasn't going to kill everyone and everything. He said it was a culling, not a total slaughter. But those numbers... that progression..."

"It was Gil!" Maynard shouted. "That screen display array was something he used all the bloody time! I know it like I know the back of my own hand, because I've seen him use it a million times!"

"What?" Mercy asked. "No, Maynard. That's not how Aal Ball works. It's just a psychic imprint of the professor. Like those in the collective that I talked to earlier? It's only an image. It's not an actual mind or soul or anything like that. Sorry, man. That's just how it works."

"I can't just give up like that, Mercy!" Maynard shot back. "That's Gil, and he's warning us about what's going to happen.

Helel is a big fat liar, and he's been lying to us all along. It's not a culling. It's an Omega, like he said. And that means the end. He's been playing us the whole time. It's all just another iteration of cosmic genocide! He's probably the One Above, probably been the One Above the whole time, and he's just been playing a sick game with us, stringing us along the whole time, playing us like we're his puppet toys. That's why Gil's warning us. He's telling us that we have to do something to avert the coming genocide, or everything's going to die. Everything!"

"Void?" Mercy asked, noting that Maynard's eyes were glowing, and not quite so faintly.

Void put a hand on Maynard's shoulder. "It's okay, man. I'll just state that I believe you, that it is Gil, or a ghostly image of his psyche. After all, he spent some non-relative time – a week or so, I think I heard Vir'gil say earlier – up there, getting healed by Aal Ball. I suspect that an interface of that duration would have made a good imprint of his psyche – not his whole mind, or even a sliver of his soul – on the collective entity of Aal Ball."

"Dude," Maynard said, turning to face Void, "I get that. I heard it too, and I'm not stupid by a longshot, or naïve. I'm just saying that even a sliver, ghost, or whatever the hell kind of imprint it is, it's of Gil, and Gil's trying to warn us. That's what Gil would do, and you *know* it."

"Mercy?" Void asked. "Is Aal Ball capable of purposeful guile? Capable of just messing with us, like it messes with you by making perverse forms?"

"What?" Mercy snorted. "No, it's programmed to be perverted. It's not conscious in the way that you're implying. It's a relic. Some crazy stuff under the hood, but it's incapable of free will."

"That word again..." Maynard said gravely, his eyes casting out tiny blue and green sparkles.

"Okay, so what if we take it at face value?" Void continued. "Meaning that I think it's wise to heed the content of what Maynard's saying. If that's an actual timeline for whatever plague has been inflicted on Earth by the sigil, what are the intervals in the iterations? How long do we have?"

"Good question," Mercy said. "Aal Ball? Please give us a good answer for what you just showed us. Show us what it is, what can stop it, and how long we have to do so. All intervals. Show that when you get an answer. Also, let's go ahead and hook up the other seven anchors, split-screen them in an array like you just showed us, and we'll try to get a better grip on what's going on."

"Aal Ball!" the collective brayed like a hundred tiny donkeys. Mercy rapidly repeated the binding process for the first anchor with the remaining seven anchors, which Aal Ball similarly accepted. Then, it caused the images to flow in parallel to both Mercy and a newly expanded external screen, which now featured eight distinct two-by-three arrays, arranged in a simple grid. Forty screens now were visible. Eight distinct locales were displayed. The first screen received initial focus, causing its five smaller screens to appear temporarily larger and brighter than the rest.

The first screen, Hong Kong, had been seen already, and no one in the group wanted to revisit the horror seen there. So Mercy quickly moved to the next, which caused the focus to shift also on the external screen viewed by the rest of the group.

The second was obviously New York City. The scenes playing out on the smaller screens paled those seen on the Hong Kong screens. Though the view remained, mercifully, at the remote overhead vantage point, it was quite clear that multiple fires raged in Manhattan, some covering entire city blocks. Most of Brooklyn was dark, devoid of power, while power appeared to cycle throughout the other boroughs, browning out suddenly, then slowly returning to normal capacity.

Third was Dubai, which was immediately recognizable due to its towering skyscrapers. The top five floors of the tallest, the Burj Khalifa, were being ravaged by an intensely burning fire. Near to the shore, the majority of the condominiums and structures on the World Islands burned also, the thick black smoke roiling like a wicked pirate fog over the warm gulf water.

Fourth was a small grove around which ancient oaks rose from stark, exposed black stone. A burbling brook but a single step in width ran through its midst. In the faerie sky above the grove, the bright Fae Moon of early evening competed with the impossibly juxtaposed electric blue zodiacal glow. Both Vir'gil and Ku'tu stared hard at Mercy.

"Void and Maynard are no longer humans. They can see it. They're already of the Fae," Mercy declared quickly, sealing the issue.

Fifth were the three great pyramids of the Giza Plateau. All three sported new pyramidions, which were wreathed by a slowly pulsating golden aura. All three appeared to have been restored to their original pristine state, also, save for the color of their external casing stones, which now appeared to be blacker than midnight. Upon this black background appeared the prismatic colors of the image of the sigil. The degree of contrast between the almost metallic sheen of the black casing stones, which formed the visible faces of the pyramids, and the image of the sigil, which writhed melodically upon all the visible faces, caused the rainbow-colored triple DNA helices to brightly illuminate the totally jet-black face of the casing stones.

There came an almost inaudible *thrum-thrum-thrum* sound, or vibration, from the scenes. Horrifically, on all four sides of each pyramid, the image of the Lightbringer's Sigil itself wound from the base to the top of the pyramidions. The images flickered slowly, faintly pulsating in syncopation with the underlying vibration that seemed to timidly tiptoe forth from the display screens and shriek loudly into their souls.

"Well," Mercy said flatly, "guess we won't need to check out six through eight." At that, the last three screens of the anchor points faded to black. "They were personal anyway. Just like the others," she added, her tone suggesting that anyone who wanted to press it risked getting flayed alive.

"Void, c'mere," Maynard said in a quiet voice, beckoning for him to join him near the display. In so doing, he wound up dangerously close to Mercy, from whose body Aal Ball issued the multiscreen display. She smirked visibly upon noticing his discomfort as he drew near to her.

"Such a feeb," she mouthed, trying not to laugh, because it would have been truly mocking.

Huddling up, Ku'tu flitted over and above Maynard's head, where she remained, hovering in place. And Vir'gil, being innately curious about everything, yet being virtually crowded out by his companions, simply caused his eyestalks to elongate to a point just over and above Void's right shoulder. This caused Void a moment of dismay as he caught sight of Vir'gil's eyestalks rising over his shoulder from behind.

"Oh, sorry," came Vir'gil's apparently disembodied voice as his eyestalks pivoted to gaze eye-to-eye with Void.

"No prob, Virge," Void assured him, giving himself a closer look at the elemental's eyestalks while the opportunity presented itself. Then, it clicked. "The Entheogenic Lord, eh?" he smiled.

Vir'gil nodded his eyes. "Indeed."

"Well, I trust I'm not being too bold for imposing upon your good graces, Vir'gil," Void said, realizing that he had everyone's full attention, and that impending total genocide could just take a knee and wait a minute, "but are you capable of sharing some of your eyebrows, if you know what I mean?"

"Ho-ho-ho!" Vir'gil laughed like the Jolly Green You-Know-Who.

"Void?" Maynard asked. "*Que*-the-eff? You want to get stoned right *now*? When we're facing total genocide of all living things on Earth? Are you *insane*?"

"Yes," Void stated, "and yes. Virge? Edibles are probably out, I'm assuming? You got any—"

Void felt something pointy nudge him at the small of his back. He turned to face Vir'gil, who was holding out a small, fingertip-sized, rainbow-colored object that resembled a tiny pine cone.

"Edibles are probably *not* out," Vir'gil groaned, smiling, his eyestalks dancing and darting. "Please, enjoy," he said, passing the tiny pine cone to Void's hand.

Void smiled at Maynard once, then promptly popped the tiny offering into his mouth. "Chew it, or just swallow it?" he asked Vir'gil.

"Do the first thing first," Vir'gil replied, "then do the second thing second."

Ku'tu, who had flown over to Mercy, hovered close to her, giggling something into her ear. Both laughed, because both were Fae, and they found this level of chaos most amusing.

"Maynard?" Vir'gil inquired. "Ladies?" he offered to Ku'tu and Mercy. All said yes, and all were able to partake of the bounty of the Entheogenic Lord. Even the Entheogenic Lord himself, who was never one to miss out. Even if it meant eating himself in the process.

"Don't get high off your own supply, you auto-cannibal Vegan," Mercy needled Vir'gil, who creaked and groaned upon hearing her say it for the millionth time.

The effects hit like a subtle sledgehammer in mere seconds. Vir'gil had given them something with a rather broad spectrum of effects. Broad, as in cosmic, and spectrum as in everything.

Noting the brief silence of his companions, the Entheogenic Lord explained, "I created this myself, just now, right before handing it out to Void, then to the rest of you. It's new. There will be a small sensory dislocation at first, during which your minds will adjust to your new perceptual frequencies. Then, the effect will continue until you actively concentrate and dispel it. I thought it would be appropriate, considering what we are doing; what we need to do at this time."

"Wise," Maynard said, giving Vir'gil total props, from one shaman to another. "I'm so wise I forgot to ask what it was going to do before I took it. Ha!"

"Noob," Vir'gil laughed, his voice apparently flanging up and down and inside-out both the normal human auditory spectrum and the contingent cusps of the infrasonic and ultrasonic ranges.

After an initial brief period of disquieting adjustment, however, all were able to maintain, feign sobriety, and return to the pressing action at hand.

"Wow," Maynard said first, studying the screens of the pyramids closely. "They're actually giving off a massive resonance, if I'm feeling this right. And I think I am. Praise the Mother," he added, getting nods from all gathered.

"You're attuned to them," Void noted. "That faint glow from your eyes is marching along in sequence with them."

"Interesting," Maynard said. "I'm assuming that's being facilitated by what Virge just gave us. Perhaps also by the fact that we've already heard the song, and it's remained the same."

"Zep!" Void laughed. "Good, Maynard. Now think of the stairway and see if it leads to Kashmir."

"C'mon, Void," Maynard smirked. "Get serious."

"I *am* serious," he replied. "Remember what I said about fractal coding? You always politely play down your own coding skills around me because you're a good friend. And you're basically humble unless you're chewing some aerospace engineer's ass out for acting like he's Von Braun himself. But I know you've got freakin' ace-level skills yourself. Maybe your knowledge set is more hardware focused than mine, but the fact that you even knew the context of fractal coding is both exciting and scary. And, yes, I think that's what we're dealing with here, contextually, and semantically."

"I get it," Maynard replied, deeply considering what Void had just said. "We're really looking for the meaning of this, in the correct context, or frame, of its instantiation. That's why you're leaning toward the path of least resistance context, right? Helel is a lazy liar, and a bad coder, so he's going to fall into a design pattern that will appear obvious once we determine the correct semantics. So you've already jumped ahead, using that mega savant gift of yours, to the end state. Thus, what you said about shards, truncations, fractal seeds, and self-affine instances. Damn, son. I think you might be right. You got there fast, though."

"I got there fast because that's where I started from," Void replied laconically. "I'm a lazy coder myself. Bad, too, if you want to be honest about it. That's why I resort to algos and automation as much as possible. And, no," he said quickly, knowing Maynard as he did, "I'm not some recursive version of Helel. Pretty sure about that, if only from the way that we saw Chthon treat both of us. She hates him."

"Obviously," Maynard replied. "That's why, when this is all over and we've secured the fate of our cosmos, he's going down."

"Back to our mystery, gents," Mercy reminded them. "Let's optimize our current drug-fueled groupthink mind meld. The great pyramids are in some sort of resonance with an image of the Lightbringer's Sigil. We were fortunate enough to see this because I just happened to have anchored one of my Never anchors to that area, because I tended, long ago, to visit it often. Fortuitous? I doubt it. I think we were supposed to find it. Free will my ass! Is there any possible correlation between what we're seeing with the pyramids and their resonating sigils and the timing of what was shown to us about that mortality rate timeline? That's what we've got to cipher. If we can't resolve that first, then finding Shunya and Fresswelle and getting out of the Null won't matter at all, because, for all we know, that timeline might be so quick that it's already happened."

"But it's on Aal," Ku'tu said. "I mean Earth," she corrected herself, noting that a slight phallic bulge had begun to form on Mercy's midsection just at mere mention of its name. "Stupid phallic relic," she laughed, pointing at it. "I said 'Aal' and it started immediately to ramp up for fun. Anyway, what I'm saying is that I've seen something like this before. The plague that the humans on my world cursed my people with? Its evolutions were almost identical to the ones that we saw on the screen. Which is totally improbable. Which means that I'm starting to come around to Void's reasoning on this. The data points, as Maynard said earlier, are starting to become abundant."

"Don't you hate being right all the time?" Maynard mocked Void.

"I know *I* do," Mercy answered for him. "Yep. Totally hate it. Anyway, I think we're on the right path now. Same reasons as Ku'tu just pointed out. Too much co-inky-dink. So, I have to ask, dearest Ku'tu, did you ever see any Christmas tree-looking sigil lights on your pyramids on Aal? Perhaps in some sort of resonance with the timing of the mortality rates?"

"What's a Christmas tree?" Ku'tu asked. "If you mean blinky lights like what's on those pyramids, then no, I didn't see any. Yes, we have – I mean had – pyramids. But, we didn't have a sigil event, remember?"

"Okay. Iterative resonance, then?" Mercy offered. "Maybe we can link the timelines? Aal Ball, try to discern the periodicities, see if they map with what was shown earlier. And hurry up on those calculations I asked for earlier."

"Aal Ball!" the collective relic bleated like several dozen screaming sheep.

"Why does it do that?" Maynard asked Mercy.

"It's retarded, obviously," Mercy replied. "Or, it might have something to do with certain random reflexive actions based upon what it's previously, uhh, healed. Show us what you got, Aal Ball. Do a split-screen comparison."

"It heals sheep?" Maynard laughed to Void.

"It ain't natural healin', laddie. It's baaa-aaaad!" Void drawled in a fake Scots accent, causing a group laugh.

Complying with Mercy's directives, Aal Ball fashioned a new array of screens in a simple one-by-one reflexive layout on the big display screen. On the left, there was a single frame capture of the mortality rate timeline. On the right, there was a live shot containing all three of the great pyramids at Giza. As the sigils pulsated on the pyramids – they were synchronized with one another, apparently, so all visible faces of the pyramids danced the same dance, in time – each segment of the mortality rates percentages on the frozen screen flashed. Then, the flash iterated to the next segment as Aal Ball's collective attempted to compute and calculate the best-fit mapping of the two seemingly disconnected entities. After a few minutes of this, there were no logical mappings beyond the third iteration of the mortality rate segments.

Void cleared his throat. "Mercy, ask it to perform its mapping using a complex Fibonacci sequence filter. I think it'll know what that means. If not, we can explain it."

While Mercy commanded Aal Ball to do exactly that, Maynard shot Void a quick look.

"I think you're right," he told Void. "And if you are, I think you've just convinced me to agree with your earlier hypothesis 100%."

"There's not much modern consideration for such in mainstream epidemiology," Void admitted, "but I recall a bit of interest in it as a modeling tool a few years back. It dovetails with my fractal coding hypothesis, so, why not try it?"

Maynard nodded. Mercy scowled, "Remember to keep moving, guys," she warned. "Don't get lazy and lose a limb or something. And hurry up, Aal Ball. Sweet Jeebus I could have done this already on an abacus."

On cue, the mortality rate segments flashed one-by-one, matching sequence to the end with the live shot of the pyramids. They continued to loop at that point, starting over from the first segment, then proceeding on down the line until the last segment.

"So..." Mercy said. "We've got a match. What that might mean, in the larger picture, is that there is an underlying timing mechanism in place for both the propagation of the world-killing plague and the sigil lights on the pyramids. And, if Void's hypothesis is correct – eerily, it's starting to look that way – then we've got a lazy coder playing god with us, and he's unwittingly introduced too much chaos into his sim. And, intentionally or not, the plague will end all life on Earth at some point in the near future. Whenever that is. Which, by the way," she said loudly, "Aal Ball still hasn't calculated for us! Sound about right?" she finished with a tight smile.

"Yes," Void said, noting that everyone seemed to agree. "There might not be an easy answer for that, by the way, because we simply don't know all the usual constants. There's massive chaos already in the system, and I suspect that Aal Ball's computational processes might be affected similarly to those of Maynard's wearables. But, while those numbers are crunching, I think we need to consider exactly why the pyramids are doing this. Why are images of the sigil on them? Why do they appear to be restored? Are they unique in this aspect, or are there more such resonant systems on Earth? If there are more, are they perhaps part of the system of resonance, perhaps even propagators of it?"

Chills ran down spines and vines as the import of what Void had just conjectured struck them. Also, the fact that his eyes had just voided out again, and his chaotic chest tattoo had just returned.

"You got your eyes and chest thing back," Maynard informed him. "And logic seems to be screaming at us that there have to be other structures and/or entities on Earth which are also resonating. Pyramids seem like an obvious choice, given their history and their morphology."

"Okay," Mercy said, "would we then rule out everything but tetrahedrons? What about the other Platonic solids? What about exotic entities that perhaps have innate resonance to these conditions, yet are incapable of showing it visually? Like on the nanoscale? Or, conversely, if they're too large for us to perceive, such as, say, the whole of an Antarctic ice sheet?"

"What if it's the Earth itself?" Maynard suggested. "What if it's everything, which it very well could be? Because, once again, we're dealing with godlike power here, and it can probably do any damn thing it wants to, at any scale?"

Void raised his hands, palms outward. "I completely agree with both of you. If anything of this were normal, or typical, I would eagerly agree with you. And we'd be lost, because too many variables would be at play. However, I'm maintaining the course of my 'Lazy Coder' hypothesis. I suspect that the resonance, if any, will stick to being expressed in self-similar or self-affine entities, meaning pyramids, tetrahedrons, et al. If that is the case, then what we need to do right now is to check out any other entity on Earth, or above it, or near it, whatever, and see if there is any similar resonance occurring."

"Why?" Maynard asked.

"Because," Void replied, "if there is, we can establish a new baseline for how we're going to stop the iterations or evolutions of the plague and its eventual, inevitable total genocide state. I think that it's possible that there's a system of systems of resonance occurring, thanks to chaos being widely spread in Helel's simulation – this particular simulation – and I think that it is logical that we can break, interrupt, or otherwise mitigate this dreadful signal. If we are lucky enough to find another broadcast propagator and, maybe, hopefully, be powerful enough to destroy it."

Everyone looked at Void as if he were daft. At that precise moment, however, the screen with the mortality rate numbers on it started to blur, fading to black in but mere seconds, and locking everyone's attention to it.

"Ah, good, here comes the answer," Mercy said. "Now we don't have to tell Void he's loco."

The screen flashed white, then rapidly dissolved from the outside inward, leaving black screen around a very normal looking image of a single white rabbit.

"O-M-G!" Maynard giggled. "I told you! I told you!"

Mercy hushed him as the ears of the white rabbit slowly lowered until they pointed directly at the screen on the right. The image of the pyramids slid into a split screen, sharing its other side with smaller images of dozens of different pyramids, ziggurats, step pyramids, and generically tetrahedral structures, including some very modern steel and glass versions of the same. The smaller images slowly marched their rows down their half of the screen, replaced by newly appearing rows at the top. Everyone focused on the smaller images, which were piling up together due to the images being so small and so numerous. Mercy fixed this by mentally bidding Aal Ball to dramatically increase the screen size to elephantine proportions.

"It's the Dark Womb," Maynard said to Void, pointing at the newly enlarged vulva which bound the perimeter of the now titanic screen.

"Here it is! Here it is!" Ku'tu cried out. She was flittering up at the top of the screen, her tiny finger stabbing out at a single image in the new top row. "It's a pyramid with Christmas lights on it!"

Void and Maynard craned their necks to get a better view. Vir'gil further elongated his eye stalks until they were level with the image, which marched slowly down the screen.

Several seconds of silence followed, mainly because no one wanted to inform Void that he had, once again, been eerily prescient. And eerily, precisely correct.

"Well," Mercy finally admitted, knowing that she had drawn the shortest straw, "I'll go ahead and say it. Thanks, Void. Good guess. And now, I think we can all agree that he's really cheating. He's actually got Chthon on call behind his third eye to give him all of his Mr. Smarty Pants answers. I mean, how else do you explain that we're looking at what would have been anchor number seven?"

"I've been there before..." Maynard said quietly, his gaze fixed on the image. "To Las Vegas, I mean. Not the Luxor, unfortunately. The conference I was at was really crazy. Didn't get the chance to get out and have some fun."

"The Luxor?" Vir'gil creaked happily. "Mercy has a permanent penthouse there. Just like all the other places we saw on the screens, except for the entrance to the Court of the Fae. The Fae don't like us to live among them because they say that we drive down property values because we're always causing trouble. Too chaotic for them. Anyway, Mercy likes the lights. And the gambling. And the whores. She never lets me leave the penthouse, though, although I did sneak out one night for a date with a local saguaro cactus. Very tasty."

"Shut it, Vir'gil!" Mercy barked.

"It's not just coincidence, then, is it?" Void asked.

"What?" Mercy replied. "The gambling and whores? No, that's how I roll when I want to have fun."

"Yippee!" Vir'gil groaned. "Gambling and whores! And more cactus! How do we get there without Shunya?"

"And how do you manage to be precognitive, Void?" Mercy asked pointedly. Literally, because her chin became just a bit too sharp due to her emotional state.

Void shrugged. "I don't know. Lately, recently I mean, I just see something in my mind, like an answer just pops out of nowhere. I thought it was my mega savant ability – and it still might be, because it sometimes works like that when I'm doing creative stuff – but, now, considering what's happened, I'm not so sure. But, honestly and humbly I hope, this hasn't been terribly mentally challenging thus far. Probably because I just happen to think similarly to Helel, because we're both bad and lazy coders."

Ku'tu flitted down to face Void. "I think I know. My husband could do the same thing. He said it was the 'Eye of the Dragon'. He could use it to look beyond the Veil and the Dream Barrier. Some call it 'The Sight', but that's really the generic name for the version that most of the Fae and some of the mortals have. The version he had came directly from the gods."

"And how did he do that?" Mercy asked her. "Fresswelle? Was that his focus? If so, I have to admit that Shunya never gave me such powers. Stupid bitch of a blade. I bet Chthon made her just so she could put my number on block and ignore the hell outta me."

"He was One with the Dragon, Milady," Ku'tu said reverently. "As the Overlord of Aal, he could commune with the Dragon itself and ask favors of it, which it was usually inclined to perform for him."

"Well, hell, then!" Mercy said loudly, dismissing her HUD, but leaving the larger one online. "Why don't you just ask the Dragon where our blades are, Void? And, while you're at it, why don't you go ahead and ask it how long we have until we reach the point of extinction for all life on Earth?"

"We're not on Aal," Void replied calmly, "I'm not the Overlord, and I'm not One with Anything anymore since Ielel stripped my higher soul. And I don't have Fresswelle. So there. I have no idea how I'm doing this. It's probably just luck. Or, I'm smarter than you can possibly imagine. Mua-ha-ha-ha!"

Mercy started laughing, ending the temporary chill among the group. "I imagine that you're smarter than a bag full of hammers. Marginally so. Good enough? Now, seriously, do you have any other hints, advice, or wisdom to share? We still need to know the timeline, and we probably will have to retrieve our blades, Shunya at minimum, before we may proceed."

"The white rabbit's gone," Maynard informed them.

Sure enough, the left screen was once more filled with the mortality rates that pulsed along in total synchronization with the sigil lights, which shone forth from the faces of the Luxor. It was clear to everyone that there was some sort of electric power still working at the Luxor, and near to it, for the various lights were still on, or were insofar as their limited perspective permitted them to see. Still, the lights seemed pale compared to the illumination provided by the pulsing sigil lights, which writhed and slithered like triple-braided snakes up the faces of the pyramidal Luxor.

"Screw this," Void declared. "Maynard? Let's engineer up a solution for the time."

"Okay," Maynard said. "It's about time you said that. First, there's no Patient Zero. It's pandemic, assuming that it's started worldwide at roughly the same time. And we assume that because we saw the weave on-orbit, and it spanned the entire globe. We also assume that it's following the same resonant sequence, which apparently implies a Fibonacci sequence, if what we informed Aal Ball to run was run correctly. If we also assume that there was a worldwide initial distribution – and we can go ahead and assume that as being true, based on what we've seen thus far; Hong Kong and New York both appeared to have been affected, and they're almost antipodally located – then we can toss out the basic transport vectors. It's everywhere, or almost so, right now."

"So," Void began, "we can use just a basic, locally mapped rate of infection and propagation. Ah, that's not going to give us too much time from the event. We don't know how robust or viable it is. Or, how truly infectious it is. But we are probably safe to assume that, because the Watchers were the ones who apparently gave it to us, it's going to be almost perfect in its attributes. Otherwise, they would have been foolish to have invested so much power, energy, and time into doing their weave, wiping out the nukes, etc. For them, it had to be a one-shot scenario. So we might as well assume that last percentile value in the sequence that we have prior the extinction itself can serve as our general guide for the plague's – whatever it truly is – attributes."

The Fae were watching the two former humans intently, silently, gauging their intellect and resources. Silently, both Vir'gil and Ku'tu agreed that Mercy had been correct in her assessment of them. Former humans, indeed.

Maynard was back to bat again. "Something important that we're not considering yet, Void. We have to throw the standard epidemiology approach out with the bath water. That's because this isn't a model based on contagion. It's based on global, instantaneous, totally pervasive infection."

"Agreed," Void replied. "That's why Helel manipulated us into hiding in the Never, instead of, say, Antarctica or something. Where we could have joined the rogue MorthonTech employees, naturally."

"True," Maynard agreed. "So, basically, we've just truncated and compacted the scenario into some really small, really rapid chunks. Think it could have just been 98.52% out the gate?"

Void shook his head. "I think Helel is too cagey and paranoid to have done it that way. And just too bad and lazy. He most likely used the same signal he's been using this whole time."

"Which means some type of natural signal," Maynard agreed, "like a fractal, or Fibonacci, something like that. Something natural and lazy that he could just casually implement from his creative palette, which we're now agreeing is something along the natural and lazy line of things. Chime in any time, guys," Maynard let everyone know.

They just shook their heads. Void continued, "Well, at least we know now how to get them to stop talking and listen to us. Just bore them with shop talk."

"Yeah," Maynard said, "my eyes are about to glaze over, so I'm going to let you wrap this one up. I know you know the math, anyway."

"Yep. It's pretty easy to see the pattern now," Void admitted. "We've got five steps in the sequence. The sixth is total genocide. Those five steps give us a 1, 1, 2, 3, 5 series of partitions if we're using the simple non-zero Fibonacci model, which I think we are. Just a hunch, no cosmic dragons involved. This would be a lot easier to resolve if we could use an absolute form of timekeeping, but I don't want to freak anyone out by going that route."

"Don't worry, Void," Vir'gil groaned, "I'm permanently freaked out already. Look who I hang around with."

"He's the freaking Elemental Lord of Drugs!" Mercy taunted, evoking some tinkling laughter from Ku'tu. "He's permanently freaked out because he's, uh, permanently freaked out. Elementally. All the time. His brain's probably a giant version of that pine cone thing he gave us."

"It was a simulacrum of the pineal gland," Maynard informed them, pleasing Vir'gil. "Meant to open our doors of perception. Obviously."

"Back to the wild-ass guess we're SWAG'ing at," Void said. "I think he's using timekeeping bins of roughly twelve hours for his sequence. And I think his selected sequence is a simple one: a basic Fibonacci sequence. Like a logarithmic spiral. Simple iteration, achieving simple self-similarity. Besides, it's just direct infection, all done at once. I think that it's highly probable, barring some miracle of chaos, that every living thing on Earth was infected at the same time. I think that the basic 1, 1, 2, 3, 5 sequence maps to the mortality rate segments that we're seeing, and I think that they map out at roughly twelve hour bins. Thus, after twelve hours, 33% of the total superset of living things is dead; after twenty-four hours, that goes up to a mortality rate of 55.11%; after a total of forty-eight hours, we're up to 77.56%; after eighty-four hours, 92.6%; after 144 hours, we're at 98.52%. Somewhere between hour 144 and hour 240, which would be the terminal hour, we're in the domain of total genocide."

"Oh my," Mercy whispered. "Six to ten days. That's it? That's all we get?"

"Yes. And I'm betting it's closer to six than ten, considering the chaos in the system. So, from the new Year Zero," Void said solemnly, "which began locally for us, on or about 4:44 AM on, appropriately enough, Walpurgisnacht, we shall mark the timekeeping as we have described it. Agreed?"

"But Void..." Maynard asked, looking down at his impotent time pieces. "What time is it?"

Void snarled: "It's time to get ill."

"Beastie Boys," Vir'gil snicker-creaked. "Mercy likes to dance naked to their music."

"You—" Mercy said, though the collective laughter drowned her out.

eVo.144.000.mOd.112.sCe9 | YEAR ZERO | EARTH | MYSTERY BABYLON

STEPPING THROUGH THE gateway provided for her by the Black Pope, the Talisman stood at the edge of the ruins of the former Meiji Jingu Stadium. A small cadre of soul slaves awaited her. They were to serve both as Petrus' spies and as her translators, should such be necessary. And though it had been unspoken, they were obviously there to serve as her private security squad, for Petrus would allow nothing to harm his chosen.

"Wow, this is bad," Mary said, taking to the air slowly. The great city of Tokyo greeted her with the wail of distant sirens, civil alert klaxons which still issued safety instructions despite the near total lack of municipal electricity. There also was the faint static-like crackle of thousands of burning structures, whose smoke lent an acrid, piss-awful stench to the fantastic setting of urban destruction.

The civil alert voice wailed, quite politely of course: *"Daishikyuu hinan shite kudasai. Daishikyuu hinan shite kudasai."*

"Petrus?" Mary inquired, gaining the immediate attention of one of the mannikin spooks accompanying her careful hovering.

"Yes, Mary?" came Petrus' voice from the soul slave.

"Translation for the civil alert? Obvious alarm is obvious, but I don't know if they'd have specific warnings in case of, say, something like a chemical spill or the like."

"Of course," Petrus said.

At once, one of the hovering spooks translated the repeating civil alert. It was still directing whoever was listening to immediately make way to the nearest shelter.

"Well, that really helped," Mary laughed. "I'm going to get up high enough so I can see the whole stadium. Or what's left of it. Should be able to see the Black Star if she's here."

"She's here," Petrus affirmed. "My soul slaves tell me so. They just can't divine exactly where she is."

"Did they have any trouble finding me?" Mary asked as she began to ascend slowly skyward, the cadre of soul slaves falling in behind her.

"Well, Mary, you were a bit more obvious, standing there atop the Great Pyramid itself, twinkling like a star."

"Meaning she's going to be harder to find because she's the Black Star."

"Indeed. Please proceed with caution, Mary. There is no reason to expect her to automatically be friendly."

Mary replied laconically, "I can take care of myself. I hope."

"Indeed," Petrus practically laughed. "However, she *is* the one who destroyed the stadium."

"Now you tell me..." Mary said quietly.

Having ascended high enough to clear a pile of stadium rubble high enough to hide several stacked African elephants, Mary finally saw the entire expanse of what had formerly been Meiji Jingu Stadium. Now, after suffering the chaotic spacetime frame-dragging effects of the Black Star's panicked outburst, there were swirling, stacked arcs and semi-arcs of shredded mass and frozen light. It looked like some cruel giant had taken an immense blender, dumped the entire stadium into it, then had hit the mix button a few dozen, drunken times. She took a moment to allow her mind to catch up with what she was now seeing. First, she perceived that the chaotic wreckage, impossibly stacked and swirled as it was, defying gravity and normal spacetime constraints, looked like a whirlpool of a sort. Well, if a whirlpool sucked itself in from all possible angles, and not just the surface of the water.

"Send a soul slave..." Mary paused, shocked that she had said that name with such impunity. "Petrus? Send a soul slave to check it out. I don't like the sensation I'm getting. Bad resonance."

"Understood."

With that, a single soul slave zoomed off toward the center of the chaotic mass, into which it appeared to phase itself. A faint, shrill scream followed. Immediately, a silent, soundless black beam the diameter of a hand's breadth blasted forth from the center of the mass, annihilating everything in its path. It left in its wake a bizarre, buzzing cutout in spacetime which quickly effervesced away, sizzling like a quarter-kilometer length of fatback bacon.

"Oh, shit!" Mary shouted, immediately hovering down behind the big pile of rubble she had just hovered over.

"Go say hello," Petrus told her. Mary swore that the spook saying this to her shook its head when it relayed this to her.

"Umm, no?" she temporized. The spook nodded once. She plainly saw it do it, too.

"May I remind you that in her culture, there is a very real fear of ghosts. You'll have a better chance, Mary. Woman to woman. Guide her to us. Your powers should protect you, regardless."

Mary rolled her eyes. "Should? Should? Fecking feck!" Taking a few quick breaths, she told herself, "I've got this. I've got this. I'm the Talisman. I can resonate with anything and bend it to my will, bind it to me. Even if it's creepy black beam shite like this! Okay now! Here we go!"

Mary took to the air, soaring up and over the debris pile, the soul slaves following her lazy flight at a distance. At the speed of a cantering horse – which was a bit faster than she really wanted to fly, but her adrenaline said otherwise – Mary began to close the gap. It was effectively the distance from the stadium's former home plate to what would have been the far edge of the stands behind left field.

What do they really look like? Mary thought as she flew. *They look like curved stairs. Not exactly like the sweeping staircases of an antebellum mansion. Maybe something more like Escher would have drawn. If Escher could draw with black holes, that is.*

She drew close enough to the center mass to realize that she needed to slow down, lest she appear to be too aggressive. So she did precisely that, somewhat awkwardly putting on the proverbial brakes with a conscious bending of her wrists. Slowing to a hover a few paces away from the center mass, her eyes level with the hole punched out by the blast, Mary called out in the best Japanese she could muster, *"Konnichiwa."*

"Hitori ni shite!" came the immediate reply. The words flanged and Doppler shifted chaotically. Mary's soul slave translator immediately translated it for her, rendering it as "Leave me alone!", which made Mary wonder why she even needed a spook translator.

"I'm going to try this in English. My companion..." she paused a moment, catching her spook translator trying to keep her between it and Amaterasu. "My companion will translate for me," which it did. "My name is Mary," Mary said gently, calmly, just loud enough to be heard over the ambient din. The spectral translator amazingly mirrored her volume and gentle delivery. "I'm here to help you, Amaterasu."

The small hole at eye level momentarily went dark as Ami decided at last to take a peek at her strange guests. Mary bit back a gasp as Ami's eyes gazed upon her. They were paired slats of deepest black, the irises a shocking shade of purple. Electric blue like the color of the night sky in an old Disney movie steadily seethed from her eyes. Like Mary, Ami appeared to have an aura, though the one that the young woman wore like a tight-fitting shroud gave the perimeter of her slight, lithe form an odd, unsettling cutout appearance. It was similar to that which had effervesced away from the path of her annihilative beam.

"How..." Ami said, her dangerous eyes narrowing. "How did you know my name?" she pointedly inquired, her shifting voice sounding as if she were passing by Mary at highway speed.

"Believe it or not," Mary said, smirking, "the Pope himself told me."

"The Pope? I'm not Catholic. I'm Japanese. How would he know my name?"

"Well," Mary informed her, "I'm Irish-American, and a non-practicing Protestant to boot, but he knew my name. He came to get me only a very short time ago."

"From where? Here, in Tokyo?"

Mary shook her head, remaining silent. The head shake and silence confused Ami for a moment, until she remembered that Mary had just told her that she was Irish-American. Americans did everything backward. Despite herself she let out a short yip of a laugh. Then she extended her petite hand out of the hole and waved a peace sign at Mary.

"My name is Ami. I am honored to meet you, Mary. Can you help me get out of here?" Ami asked her.

"Of course I can," Mary replied, instantly regretting her answer, because Ami was virtually encased by material that looked like a mixture of concrete and twisted rebar. "And by the way, the Pope came to see me, and recruit me, when I was hovering above the top of the Great Pyramid."

"Flying, like you're doing now? That's really boss," Ami said, pronouncing the word "boss" in English.

"Yes. Flying. It is pretty wicked. Pardon me for a second, please, Ami," Mary said. "I need to ask the Pope how to get you out of there."

"Yes," Ami said, backing herself away from the hole as far as she could within the cramped confines of her unusual spherical prison cell. In afterthought, she added, her voice faint and shifting as she moved, "Did he send the ghosts?"

"He did," Mary said, realizing she probably needed to clarify that statement before she panicked Ami. "But they're not really ghosts. They're more like spirits. Friendly ones. They're all helping us try to save the world."

"Save the world?"

Mary paused a moment, carefully considering how to reply to that. "I'll let Petrus, the Pope, explain that one. It's complicated," she admitted truthfully. It was indeed complicated. "Petrus?" she asked the air around her.

The Black Pope's voice came through one of the nearby soul slaves. "Yes, Mary?"

"Ami is here, but she's stuck inside a ball of concrete."

Mary felt a slight change in the usual vibration she had associated with the soul slaves as Petrus willed his presence more fully into the soul slave, borrowing its senses for a look-see.

"Ami? Are you okay?" Petrus said, his voice rich and sonorous, mixed with the auto-translation of it in Japanese.

"Yes, I am," she replied. "I just wanted to make it all go away. I regret what happened."

"Yes, we know, Ami," he said, soothingly. Mary actually felt the slight variation in what she believed was Ami's own aura, her own unique resonance, upon her hearing his words. "We know you had no choice but to do what you did. You acted out of a sense of sheer survival. We would no more fault you than fault a lioness who lashes out to protect her cubs."

There came a meek reply from within the stone cell, "But I'm not a lion. I wasn't protecting any cubs. I was just protecting myself. I just wanted them to go away. But I killed them all, didn't I? I'm so sorry. I regret it. I regret it," she finished, her voice thick as she began to softly cry.

"It's okay, Ami," Mary soothed, drawing up close enough to the hole to take a closer look. Ami sat on the floor, only a step or two away, her back to the wall, her arms folded across her knees. She rocked slowly in place, sobbing. "We're going to get you out of this thing. We're going to help you, Ami. I need you to be strong now. Hang in there."

Mary turned herself around without consciously thinking about flying, which came almost as much of a surprise to her as the sight of Petrus fully materialized, right in front of her.

"I decided to do this myself," he told her, shifting his staff to his right hand. "I'm going to ask you to move to the side of this chaotic concrete cell and be ready to use your power if this goes sideways. Ami?" he called out softly. "Can you hear me, my child?"

There was a stir of motion from inside the cell, and Ami's face appeared at the hole. "The Pope! I am honored to meet you," she said, taking a step back in order to bow.

"Thank you, Ami," he replied, motioning for Mary to take the left side of the cell. "But the honor is mine. You are

Amaterasu Kurohoshi, or 'Ami' as you are called by your family and friends. You have been reborn as the Black Star, having been judged by the Lightbringer's Sigil, and not found wanting. Now, because you have proven the purity of your soul," he said, raising the paschal staff high above his head in a two-handed grip, "you have been chosen to join us in our holy quest to save Earth from the evil ones who seek to destroy it..." he paused a moment, then continued even as he made a mighty yet seemingly impossible cut with his staff, "...but we shall destroy them first!"

Though she had been nervously looking on, Mary saw only the black-within-white negative-looking afterimage of Petrus' cut, which, despite sporting the form of Maweth and a miniature version of the Hatefang, was not at all suited for cutting of any sort. Impossibly, though the staff appeared to be roughly the same height as Petrus himself, the cut extended completely through the concrete-and-steel cell, passing through at least seven feet of mass. The staff parted it like the proverbial hot knife parts butter, leaving a razor-thin slice to mark its passage.

The sound of the cut, though, was a thing of sheer horror. As the paschal staff cut down and through the cell of chaotically agglomerated stadium material, a deep, booming, sepulchral voice roared in multiple voices. The sound was like thunder striking not once but dozens of times simultaneously, a wicked voice shouting the word for "hate" in the native tongues of all who could hear it.

The cut of the Hatefang was more than merely physical, Mary realized instantly. The word "hate" – the power of the emotion of Hate itself – amplified and augmented the physical strike, transforming it into something a million times more powerful than the blade would natively be capable of. It was as if the blade were naught but a physical manifestation of something infinitely larger than the blade was itself; like some invisible, hateful giant was stomping up and down on the blade, adding its own force to the strike.

One thing that struck her prominently was that the dimly glowing DNA-rainbows on the Hatefang seemed to be hungry and hunting for souls to condemn then consume. She felt it, whatever it truly was, hidden and staring at her from a distance. It lusted for her very soul like the Devil himself, causing the hairs at the nape of her neck to rise. Had that blade struck something alive...

Struck slightly off-center, to within a hair's breadth of where Ami stood, the cell almost neatly bifurcated, folding open like a gigantic Faberge egg. A bright black-burning fire clung to the edges of the cut, sizzling for a few seconds before its nanoscale fusion effect played itself out. Petrus used that time to move directly before Ami, making certain that she would not fall, or be injured by any debris which might very well shake loose from the chaotic nightmare maze of concrete and steel around them.

Removing her hands from her eyes, Ami took a look around her. She liked what she saw.

"Thank you! Thank you!" she said, bowing politely first to Petrus then to Mary.

"Come, my child," Petrus bade her, reaching out a hand for her. To her credit, Ami didn't hesitate a second before grabbing his hand. Upon contact, there was no surprising flash of powers, no singularities, no theft of souls. Just a brief, satisfied smile from Ami as she lifted gracefully up into the air, guided by the hand of the Black Pope. And by the mere expenditure of a few soul slaves to, quite temporarily, provide that graceful lift.

Ami felt a curious sensation settling around her, as if she were slowing entering a pleasantly hot bath. Ahead of her, Petrus' form was disappearing from view, as was Mary behind her. The sensation rapidly spread over her as Tokyo faded, and Mystery Babylon appeared.

Gently setting Ami down beside the presently landing Mary, Petrus, hovering a few inches above the floor of the former Nervi Hall, spoke to his chosen:

"And now, we prepare, and train, for what we next must do."

"And what is that?" Ami asked as she turned to take in the chaotic horror around her. For a reason unknown to her, the horrific sights and sounds did nothing to disturb her. She felt as if she belonged here, and that the horrific spectacle was entirely mundane.

"Something only we three may do," Petrus replied. "Save this world, before it dies."

eVo.144.000.mOd.112.sCe10 | YEAR ZERO | EARTH | UNITED STATES | CALIFORNIA | LEO CARRILLO STATE PARK

DWAYNE WENT TO THE beach to die, but all he did was get a sunburn.

He hadn't planned the place or time, but by the time he'd gathered what was left of his family's remains and wrapped them all up in quilts and blankets, it was midmorning in Santa Monica and the morning clouds were burning off. Everything was too quiet, and it was obvious that it was the end of the world. Why he was left, he didn't know – but as time went by, the numbness he felt began to consume him. He didn't want to bury the sludge and bones in the backyard, but he didn't exactly know *what* to do with the remains. He only knew he needed to get out.

So he hopped in his dad's Mustang and drove to the Santa Monica pier, hung a right, then went North on Pacific Coast Highway. Mostly on autopilot, Dwayne just drove, blowing through all the lights in Malibu. Remembering his ex-girlfriend Tammy, he pulled into the lot at Leo Carrillo beach and wept. It seemed as good a place as any for the inevitable. They had spent one of their last nights together camped around the fire pit on the beach. He missed Tammy, but in all likelihood, she was dead. Just like everyone else.

Leaving the car, Dwayne walked through the sand to the edge of the surf. He began dialing numbers, one after another on his Android, but gave up after a couple dozen tries. Nothing but static, hissing, and a weird bumblebee humming sound that seemed to persist in his head for a few moments after he disconnected each call. His head spinning, Dwayne lay back on the sand and closed his eyes, replaying the past few hours.

His father had awakened everyone in the middle of the night, because the aliens had created a net over the sky. News from the web predicted the coming, though most people Dwayne knew had thought it was a tinfoil hat conspiracy. But the telescope he sometimes used to look at Daphney Zimmer through her window could just barely make out the formation of the ships, or pods, or whatever they were – miles above and running along the longitude and latitude lines.

And then it happened: the sky lit up and Dwayne heard his sister stop talking mid-sentence. Elsie *never* stopped talking. When Dwayne and his mother looked over, Elsie's face just slid off into the grass. For the space of a heartbeat, she stood there, eyes raised to the heavens. Then, she crumpled into the grass and Dwayne's mother began to scream. And gurgle with a horrible wetness. Dwayne and his father both reached out to her, as she began to just melt. Exchanging a horrified look, the young man and his father knelt and tried to sort the quivering, liquefying bodies. Dwayne's hands were covered in a tarry mucous. As he gazed, transfixed by the fetid black cat's cradle of goo sticking to his fingers, he became aware of a low groan. His father was holding his hands before his face in the semi-darkness, and they both watched, stricken by terror, as the skin began to crack and slough away.

His father's final, gurgled words were, "Dear God, why?"

Within moments, Dwayne knelt in the yard, alone and surrounded by bones and the stench of offal. Looking up, he noticed the lights in the sky were beautiful. And he began to retch.

For the longest time after emptying his guts, he just sat there staring into the darkness. Waiting for his turn. But nothing else happened. Eventually, he realized the lights were gone and the sun was coming up. So Dwayne gathered up his family as best he could and staggered into the house.

For some reason he was ravenous, and he scavenged through the kitchen and fridge for the first things he came across: fruit, slices of cheese, pickles, a granola bar. He noticed his hands were still filthy, so he washed until his skin was red. Then he got dressed, grabbed his phone, wallet, and keys, and left.

When Dwayne woke, it was after noon. The surf rolled up the beach, close to where he lay. His skin burned and his throat was dry. There was a series of chittering noises surrounding him. He rolled to his side and noticed a couple dozen ground squirrels standing upright over the furry corpse of what looked like a dog, in the bushes roughly fifty feet away. As he rose, the squirrels turned their attention to him en masse, and he could see dark flecks of red blood dripping from their nails and mouths.

Dwayne's breath caught in fear as the squirrels moved toward him in a dark, violent swarm. It seemed such a waste to survive the end of the world and the loss of everything he loved, only to be savaged by a pack of squirrels. Suddenly, the fear melted away, and Dwayne was angry. It was an anger he'd never felt before – a righteous, end of the world anger. He was not going to go down quietly. If he had his way, he would not go down at all. Dwayne had always been a good kid, who listened to those in authority, and played fair. Well, life wasn't fair. *This* wasn't fair. And Dwayne knew he didn't have to play by the rules anymore. There weren't any rules.

He stood tall, and the ocean breeze magnified behind him. Whipping his hair and clothes, the wind gathered around him, and he flung his hand toward the mass of squirrels. The sandy beach erupted as a blast of air took the small beasts and propelled them high and away from the spot, depositing them in broken lumps a hundred yards away.

Dwayne looked from the carcasses to his hand and back. Awestruck, he whispered, "Holy cow."

eVo.144.000.mOd.112.sCe11 | YEAR ZERO | EARTH | THE COLLAPSE

IN LESS THAN TWENTY-four hours after the sigil had appeared in the sky, humanity had descended into chaos and barbarism. Much of the destruction that occurred in Europe and Asia was avoided in the Western Hemisphere chiefly because the Harvest of Souls began in the middle of the night. The Americans, those who weren't wracked with the pain of transition, simply slept through it. There were fewer vehicles on the roadways of North and South America, and so the immediate calamity was reduced.

The waking world was confronted with the harsh reality that approximately fifty percent of the world had died when the alien sigil appeared. Of those who died, many took innocents with them in horrendous vehicular crashes and failed equipment operations.

The remainder responded with a plethora of reactions – many were stunned and paralyzed with grief and fear; some simply chose not to go on without their loved ones and committed suicide. Survivors attempted to contact as many of their friends and family as they could reach. But in most cases, the cell towers responded with static that sounded like the buzzing of a million bees.

Others sought targets for blame, raging against their leaders, or those whom their leaders targeted. The Holy War began in earnest. Violence took more lives, as global conflict erupted. Those with twisted, murderous agendas sought victims, and in some cases, communities, on which to vent their unleashed frustrations.

Still others recognized that survival would depend on planning and gathering resources. Either by thoughtful planning, or spurious looting, the distribution of goods began. Groceries, hardware, and weapons were all targets. Families and neighborhoods banded together for protection. Groups of marauders sacked stores and victims, taking what they wanted with little interference by police. Law and Order had been vanquished in the face of Armageddon. Chaos ruled.

As the day turned to night on one side of the ocean, the other half of the globe woke to find a nightmare scenario, and the wave of chaos continued. A nightmare in which half of the survivors were sick with an unknown affliction.

The corporate world dissolved, and factories ran down, machines stopping when there were no more people to run them. Offices were either filled with puddles of former workers or were abandoned as people focused on survival. No amount of greed or loyalty could keep the wheels of profit turning.

The Collapse had begun.

eVo.144.000.mOd.112.sCe12 | YEAR ZERO | EARTH | UNITED STATES | NEW YORK | NEW YORK CITY

SASHA TRIED DIALING Marco again, listening anxiously as the phone responded by buzzing like a swarm of bees in her ear. She would have cursed into the cell phone but was instead caught up in a paroxysm of coughing. She placed it on the nightstand, struggling to sit on the edge of the bed and drink some water. The fever was worse, and she muttered in frustration, even as she heard Loli over the baby monitor.

"Oh no. Damn it – woke her up."

Lolita jabbered a bit and began to call out from the other room. Sasha knew it was only a matter of time before the baby started to cry. Staggering to her feet, she weakly crossed the room and entered the pastel blue room with aquatic animals on the wallpaper border. Loli stood in the crib, bouncing excitedly as her mother made her way to the child. Holding a soft teddy bear, Lolita smiled wide for her mother.

"Maaa-mah!"

"Honey, Mommy's sorry. She's just so tired. "

Picking the infant up, Sasha returned to her room, pausing to lean against the wall on the way. She lay Loli on the bed long enough to open the nearby window a few inches. A little fresh air might help.

Sasha grimaced when she noticed the sun was going down. Marco had been gone for hours, and she must have fallen asleep.

She fluffed her pillows and sat down on the edge of the bed, lifting Lolita to her breast. Stroking the child's soft hair, she mused out loud, "Where do you think your daddy's gone to, huh?" A cold finger of dread touched her, as Lolita nursed hungrily. What if she gave her cold to the baby? And where was Marco? It shouldn't have taken so long to go to the pharmacy for medicine.

Reaching over to the remote on the nightstand, Sasha turned on the TV and reduced the volume. Strange, some of the channels were dead. Stopping at a news broadcast, she watched in horror as images of riots and death filled the screen. Hospitals were overrun, people were looting – everywhere. And there were bodies just lying in the streets.

How long had she been asleep?

Sasha thought about the aliens hovering over the world, the tension, and the... thing in the sky last night. It had been beautiful, like a sky full of fireworks. But it was late, and they both had to work, so they had gone to bed. And then this morning, the flu had hit her pretty hard. Marco said he was going to get medicine, and she was exhausted. But he had been gone so long.

It was the itch that drew her attention to her legs. When she scratched, her skin just sort of sloughed away, and her fingers came back bloody. She screamed, just a little, and Loli looked up, confused. In the dim light, Sasha could tell something was wrong with her skin. It was loose. Again, she was wracked with a coughing fit. This time, there was blood in her sputum.

"Oh God, what is wrong with me?"

She lay back on the bed, ignoring the TV, and just holding Lolita. Paralyzed with fear, Sasha knew that Marco wasn't coming home. She grasped the phone again, calling one number after another, but there was nothing but that obnoxious buzzing. The phone beeped at her, telling her the battery was low, and it needed charging.

Holding Loli close, Sasha began to weep. She knew she was dying, and there would be no one to look after her baby. Wordlessly praying, Sasha snuggled with her child.

It may have only been a few minutes, but when Sasha opened her eyes it was dark. There was a scratching noise at the window, and a light from outside. No, lights – a lot of them – moving around in the darkness beyond the curtains, like tiny, colored flashlights. The curtains rustled in the breeze.

On the TV, the announcer looked grave, and Sasha shut off the television to better hear what was happening outside. Lolita's attention was drawn to the window, and she uttered a soft cooing sound.

A soft ripping sound came from the screen, and the tiny lights entered the room, flying around the ceiling. Some slow, some fast, all emitting small noises like the fluttering of wings. Sasha heard the sound of bells, and the window was opened even more. Eyes wide, Lolita reached toward the lights as they flew in bright patterns overhead. Others began to alight on the bed surrounding the two, while more flowed in an inscrutable pattern in the air above. Lolita was mesmerized.

Sasha watched in awe as a small figure landed on her knee. It was a tiny person, dressed in glowing white robes. The tiny creature looked like an angel. It had a sad look on its beautiful face. Hovering slowly, it moved to Sasha's face and wiped the tears from her cheek. Wordlessly, the tiny faerie touched Sasha's mind and a torrent of soothing images flooded through her. In them, she saw Lolita in a glade. She was older, a young child, running and playing with creatures large and small. Next, she was a young woman, strong and alert. In her eyes flickered strange blue lights, and her lips mouthed the words, "Mom, I love you..."

Sasha smiled at the little angel and nodded, turning to kiss her baby goodbye. The last thing she heard was the echoing laughter of the baby as the tiny figures wrapped her in light and flew out the window.

eVo.144.000.mOd.112.sCe13 | YEAR ZERO | EARTH | UNITED STATES | CALIFORNIA | MALIBU

LIKE A WHISPERED CARESS, she entered Dwayne's dream. The scattered and inchoate nightmares dissolved before her presence. Her voice was like honey.

"Hello, handsome. What's your name?" The woman with green eyes and flaming red hair eased close to Dwayne, and he suddenly found himself high on a balcony overlooking a bay. She was wearing something sheer and shimmering that floated on the breeze.

"I'm, ah, Dwayne," he muttered, trying to look at her, but failing to see her clearly. It wasn't that she was obscured, but she *felt* blurry, as if she were far away. Still, somehow, Dwayne knew that she was beautiful, and she was watching him carefully. Her eyes met his. He could see clearly that they were bright and hungry.

"Hello, Dwayne," she purred. "Enjoying the apocalypse?"

Her luminous eyes seemed to devour him. He could feel his excitement growing with his curiosity. "Who are you? What do you want? This doesn't feel like a dream."

"I'm Mhyrranda, Dwayne. You could say I'm the girl of your dreams. As for what I want, well... I want you to go north and be my hero." Her body moved close, and he felt an intimate heat as he listened to what she had to say.

eVo.144.000.mOd.112.sCe14 | YEAR ZERO | EARTH | UNITED STATES | COLORADO | DENVER

THE THREE DIRT BIKES sped down Peña Boulevard, their riders heedless of both the lack of license plates and the uncharacteristic emptiness of the road that served the Jeppesen Terminal, otherwise known as Denver International Airport. As the road began to curve north into the terminal, the riders nodded in reverence to the Blue Mustang: the 32-foot-tall, red-eyed guardian known as Blucifer. The trio swung wide, following the easternmost road. Smoke from one of the runways to the north crinkled their noses and made them cough, as they maneuvered around the abandoned cars in front of the departure gates on the top level.

Parking in front of the doors, the lead rider hopped from his bike and removed his helmet. He shook out his shoulder length chestnut hair and shouldered his backpack. As he hung his helmet from the handgrip, he grinned at the others.

The other two likewise removed helmets, looking around cautiously.

"Denny, are you sure this is gonna be safe? I heard the DIA security guys are shooting trespassers on sight now." The speaker, a gangly youth with blonde hair and freckles, looked flushed and afraid, ready to bolt at the first sight of another person. His eyes were clouded, and he was obviously sick. The third, a slightly busty redhead teen in perfect health, merely looked skeptical.

"Dude, that's crap," Denny said. "Nobody's left to shoot us. Besides, I don't think the guards will be where we need to go."

"The place you saw in the dream, the tunnels with the woman?" Rachael asked. "You know how crazy that sounds, right?"

Denny continued patiently, "Yeah, about as crazy as aliens drawing DNA trails in the sky. Trust me, guys."

"So what if the tunnels are closer to the Air Force base, in one of the underground silos between here and the Springs?" The blonde, Mark, was undeterred.

"Because I told you, the tunnels we're looking for only run below the airport. Cheyenne Mountain is 90 miles away. The longest underground tunnel in the world runs below the Swiss Alps, and it's only 35 miles long. The tunnels here are only 7,000 feet long."

"How do you know all this shit, man?" Mark asked, wiping his nose and coughing.

"Because he's like Google, Mark. He knows everything," the redhead beamed.

"Rache, don't. You know I hate that nickname." Denny looked over his shoulder as he headed through the automatic doors. "Come on, let's go."

There was an eerie silence inside the terminal. The three jogged past the airline counters and stopped at a rail, from which they could overlook the central area. No one was alive. It was jarring, for all three had seen the past crush of people making their way through airport security on one side and arriving to greet their waiting friends and families on the other. What was left was ugly. The security area was a mass of corpses, and the smell was overbearing. The arrivals area was just as bad, with mostly liquified bodies choking the escalator and waiting area.

"I still think this is nuts, Denny. What – we're just gonna steal a cart and ride across the airport, no problem?"

"Well, yeah," Denny said, gesturing to the huge structure below. "You wanna *walk* through *that*? We can't guarantee the moving sidewalks are working down there, and even so, they might be clogged..."

Rachael covered her face with a bright red bandana. She looked around, then said, "There's a lot of dead here."

Mark peered toward the shops surrounding the large open area and scoffed. "I wonder if the food is ruined. Hey, let's go see if there are any Cinnabons left."

Denny and Rachael glared at Mark, then looked at each other and laughed. Mark said, "What? I'm hungry!"

"Where do we start?" Rachael asked.

Denny looked up at the board marked Arrivals, pointing to the still flashing gate numbers – and flights that either hadn't, or never would arrive. "We need to get to wherever the luggage goes underground from the planes. There was an automated baggage system here that fed from the terminals to baggage claim."

Mark cleared his throat and said, "Why don't we just go back outside, ride from one gate to the next, and stop where there are tunnels?"

Denny peered intently at the sign, noting the gates. "Actually, Mark, that's probably better than crawling through the baggage delivery system. Come on."

Denny led the way as they jogged back to the motorcycles. After mounting up, the three rode around the airport until they found an entrance for personnel, then rode past the unmanned security gate.

After an hour of methodically checking the areas around the gates, the frustrated trio stopped to confer near a large tunnel leading down.

"This has got to be it. Come on."

Denny turned his motorcycle towards the central gate of the concourse and a cluster of baggage cars. After riding in the sun, the shade was welcome, though the short entry and tunnel beyond were lit like a parking garage. The eerie quiet was magnified by the orderly placement of carts and equipment. The people who were here either weren't doing their job or were orderly when they left.

At first, the layout made a strange sort of sense, but after riding around for a while, the three found themselves pausing to read the signs. Far from being just a tunnel, the lanes underneath the airport were complex and disorienting, like an underground freeway.

"Well, this is stupid." Mark yelled over the engines. "Who designs shit like this?" He pointed at all the twisting lines of metal overhead.

"That was an automated baggage delivery system," Denny informed him. "Was really cool, but turned out to be too high maintenance. So they stopped using it, and just used the roads for the baggage cars." He peered down a hallway to an elevator at the end, where a number of carts were haphazardly abandoned. "Hey – let's check this part out."

Parking the bikes at the end of the hall, the three walked past the carts and approached the elevators. Denny pressed the button and tapped his foot while waiting for the car to arrive.

"Denny, what are we looking for?" asked Rachael.

"The REAL underground. They didn't use it, but there's a deeper area here somewhere. I bet people hid down here when that alien skywriting appeared."

When the door opened, Denny entered and examined the panel briefly before walking back out. "According to the elevator, we are on the bottom floor."

Denny carefully scanned the area. He saw a metal door around the corner with a large sign marked "Authorized personnel ONLY." Moving closer, he saw that the door was ajar and opened on stairs leading down into utter darkness.

"Well, that's not creepy at all," Mark said with a smirk.

Rachael and Denny fumbled in their backpacks for a moment, both finally pulling out flashlights.

"Come on, Mark," Rachael said brightly. "Let's explore!"

Mark pulled his light from his pack, muttering about caves and darkness and orcs, before eventually following them down the stairs.

The stairs emptied into a dusty room bisecting a hall. Across from the stairs was a sign with number and letter designations pointing in two directions. Denny shrugged and grinned at the other two. "Just like in D&D – follow the left wall."

"Why the left?" Mark asked. "Why not the right?"

"Doesn't matter," Denny answered, smiling. "When you are in a maze, follow the same wall, left or right, and you can navigate your way out. Unless you hit a teleport, that is – then you're just fucked."

"But why left?" Mark persisted.

"I dunno. Maybe because it's the same way the footprints go." Denny pointed to the disturbed dust on the floor.

The hallway ran for a distance, occasionally marked by locked doors on either side. Rachael sneezed in the dry dusty air, then paused to take a drink from her water bottle. "It *is* creepy down here. You think the prints are recent, Denny?"

"Yeah. I don't think that door was left open on purpose," Denny said as he turned the corner at the end of the hall. The three entered another room and scanned the floor. The footprints were scuffed and indistinct, leading to doors on either end of the room.

"Great, which way now?" Rachael played the beam of her light over the floor and looked from one door to the other.

"Left, remember?" Denny strode to the other door and stepped through.

After walking through a few more rooms and halls, the teens entered a huge, high-ceilinged room filled with machinery. All three noticed an oily, metallic smell permeating the dry room. The lights played over large air handlers and heating units, all running. Each of the massive metal frames was covered with large, twisted runes gouged deeply in the surface of the metal. For a full minute Denny peered at each, trying to determine their origin but failing. Something about them made his head feel like bees were buzzing around inside it. Despite his discomfort, it took his full concentration to remove his gaze from one and move to another.

Finally, Rachael had reached her limit. "Denny?" she said, her voice startling him. "You're starting to freak me out."

"Oh, sorry," Denny replied sheepishly. "Just got distracted by these things. They're beautiful."

"If you say so, Denny," Mark laughed, smiling at Rachael. "They're just cracks in the metal."

"Yeah, guess so," Denny admitted, resuming his search of the room.

On the wall near the door was a large electrical panel, its door hanging open and its circuits reset. The dust on the floor was smeared in several places, as if large objects had been dragged about. In the distance, there was a set of clanging noises, followed by the unbroken hum of the machines.

"Hey!" Mark called. "Anybody in here?"

Rachael stopped, looking back and forth past the large equipment. "Something smells... weird, Denny."

Denny followed one of the paths quietly, his flashlight moving from one bulky structure to the other, while Rachael kept close. Mark retrieved a crowbar from his pack and moved down a parallel path, swinging his light back and forth.

Denny stopped at one point, playing his light across a set of dark, wet stains at the base of a metal construct. Something about the blackish stain was wrong. Denny knelt, touching the liquid. Lifting his fingers, he saw that they came away dark red and sticky. Denny noticed another stain beside the puddles, in the shape of a hand print.

Rachael gaped in horror. "Denny, that's..."

Her words were cut off by a thunderous, hissing growl that echoed throughout the space. In the near distance, Mark screamed.

"Hungry..." said a deep basso voice that was human, and yet, was not.

Denny and Rachael ran toward Mark, his screams guiding them. They arrived just in time to see him back into one of the metal towers, the beam of his flashlight playing over an impossible form. Clinging to the steel beams of the ceiling was a long serpentine body, softly glowing in the light like burnished metal. Easily thirty feet long, the sinuous curves twisted slightly as it coiled almost catlike, its wings rustling slightly, though there was no breeze this deep underground. Golden reptilian eyes possessing an eerie intelligence looked out from a face framed in scales. A wrist-thick forked blue tongue darted from a snakelike mouth filled with finger-length teeth.

Mark was frozen against the metal. The creature's head canted as it examined the young man. Then, quick as lightning, it struck. The toothy maw expanded impossibly, covering Mark's head and shoulders before he could even lift the crowbar.

Denny and Rachael were paralyzed, unbelieving, as the dragon lifted Mark's still-struggling body and began to gulp it down, swiveling its neck back and forth in jerking motions. As they watched in horror, there was a sickening crunch, and blood sprayed in a dark gout across the floor. The crowbar and Mark's flashlight went flying across the room, while the dragon swallowed their friend past his hips and kicking feet.

And then, the spell was broken. Rachael screamed and grabbed the crowbar off the floor. She rushed beneath the rippling form of the dragon, swinging in vain at the creature more than ten feet above her. Denny slid his backpack off and quickly rummaged through it to find the .357 Smith and Wesson. As Rachael flailed below the dragon in impotent fury, Denny dropped to a knee and took careful aim, firing three rounds at the head of the creature. One struck the corner of its eye. With a violent shake, the dragon finished eating Mark and retreated quickly along the beams into the darkness further back into the room.

"Rache!" Denny yelled, running to grab her before she could pursue the creature. "No!"

Rachael fell sobbing into Denny's arms, her white knuckles still clutching the crowbar. Denny put his arm around her shoulder, his eyes scanning the corners and ceiling. "Rache, we have to get out of here. It might come back."

"Denny. A *dragon* just *ate* Mark. I can't even..."

"Yep, sure looked like a dragon. This is just so wrong. What is a dragon doing here? Is it some kind of weird hallucination from the aliens?"

Rachael slowly moved the beam of her light across the ceiling. Denny started to guide them slowly, cautiously, back toward the entrance.

"Wait," she whispered. "What is that noise?"

There was a tense pause as they stopped moving, listening. From the back of the huge room, they heard a sobbing sound. Denny and Rachael exchanged a look. "Is someone else back there, do you think?" He asked softly.

The sounds of the sobbing grew louder, and the pair gripped each other.

"Ssssooorrry... Sssooo sssoorrry..." The deep mellifluous voice moaned from the nearby darkness. Denny dropped his arm from Rachael and held his light and the pistol with both hands, scanning the pathways.

"Pleeeassse forgive. I wass ssso hungry..."

Slowly, the large reptilian head of the dragon rose above a piece of machinery, locking the pair in the unblinking golden stare of its eyes. "Sssooorry..." It crooned. "Tttrapped hhere. Ccchanged hhere." Large tears fell like diamonds from the dragon's eyes, glittering in the light from the beams shining on it.

Denny shook his head, never dropping his guard. "What do you mean, changed here? Who... What are you?"

The dragon looked at them, as if weighing Denny's questions. Or the answers.

"Sssussan. I'm Ssussan. I wwworked hhere." The voice was deep, but sibilant, filling the spaces and echoing off the far walls. Shaking its head and stretching its neck as if speaking was a challenge, it continued. "Sssome of uss hhid from thhe aliens down here. Sssomethhing hhappend to me. Woke up and I wass hhungry."

Rachael glared. "You ate our *friend*!" she yelled, brandishing the crowbar while pointing her flashlight at the dragon. For a moment, Denny was afraid Rachael was going to charge the dragon again. Despite its initial reaction to being shot, the dragon appeared uninjured.

"I'm a dragon! I couldn't hhelp it! I ate a couple of otherss, too. I jussst want out!"

Denny and Rachael again traded looks, and Denny shrugged. "What do want us to do? If we let you out, you'll eat other people. Besides, you can't fit through the door."

The dragon crawled atop the large metal hood and swiveled its gaze between the two teenagers. "I don't *need* to eat people, but if I don't get out, I'll sstarve here. And there'ss a loading bay back there. I jussst can't open the lock on the door."

Slowly and carefully, Susan the dragon came over the perch and down to the floor. Both Denny and Rachael backed up, raising their respective weapons, though still prepared to bolt for the door. Susan stopped, holding perfectly still. With unblinking eyes, she addressed the pair. "Lower your weapons and help me."

Something intangible flashed between them, and Rachael lowered the crowbar. Denny narrowed his eyes and straightened his shoulders. The click of the hammer of his .357 was the only sound in the room.

"Sorry, Susan, but that's a big fat nope." Denny locked eyes with the dragon, exerting his will over hers. "You cannot command me, and you will not attempt to do it to Rachael, either. Rache, look at me, now. Don't look the dragon in the eyes."

The dragon turned her head away in a show of obeisance. Rachael blinked several times, then turned to Denny. "What the hell was that?" She glanced at the dragon and back to Denny, lifting the crowbar nervously.

"Dragons are magical serpents, Rache. They hypnotize their prey." Denny got a look on his face that chilled Rachael. Then, he met the dragon's gaze and said, "Susan, there isn't enough iron in these bullets to do more than sting, but if you try anything else like that, I will compel you to lie still while I shove that crowbar through your eye and into your brain. Do you understand?"

The dragon stared at Denny for a long time before responding. Her eyes narrowed dangerously and she nodded once. "Yesss. I understand."

It seemed to be enough for Denny, who motioned to the back of the chamber. "Show us the door, then."

The dragon turned without further comment and slithered into the darkness, her wings flat against her body, her tail swishing lazily in her wake. Denny shrugged and held a finger to his mouth, silencing Rachael's unspoken question. Rachael looked from Denny to the dragon and back as they followed the serpent into the unknown.

As they reached the back of the room, Rachael and Denny became aware of a growing stench. They played their beams over the dragon, the large roll up door, the miscellaneous crates and equipment nearby, and several bloody piles of what had to be Susan's former coworkers. Susan gripped the chain with her scaled and clawed hands and pulled, rattling the chain but not doing much else.

"Sssee? Locked from the outside..." The note of desperation was evident in her voice. Rachael wondered how much damage Susan could do if she panicked. She was pretty sure she didn't want to be anywhere nearby if that happened.

Denny examined the lock. It was almost as large as his head. Thick metal slats connected to it from the frame of the door. He looked around a moment with his flashlight before his beam settled on Rachael's crowbar. She handed it to him, and he placed it between the frame and the lock. After a few minutes of pushing and grunting, all of which Rachael found incredibly, incongruously funny, Denny shook his head and turned to the others.

"I can move the frame a tiny bit, or the slats, but I can't do both at the same time. It's too strong. Too bad there isn't a forklift of something to ram into the door here while I do this. A forklift, or a dragon."

Denny and Susan eyed each other. Susan finally said, "Hold it in place and I'll push it."

Denny complied, leaning heavily into the crowbar as Susan leaned heavily into the door. With a loud snap, the frame popped away from the lock. Rachael pulled the chain and the door rolled noisily up, exposing a ramp leading up and out. Susan looked from one to the other human and then nodded.

"Thank you," she said. "You ssaved my life."

"No problem, Susan. Where will you go now?" He looked into the dragon's eyes, and Rachael heard something uncanny in his voice as he said, "You really don't like the taste of humans." Denny put his arm around Rachael, as she leaned into him.

Susan looked at Denny, cocking her head. "There should be plenty of wildlife in the Rockies. I really don't like the taste of humans. One more favor, if you don't mind... Pleasse leave it open, I may need a place to ssleep."

With that, the dragon began to run, slithering rapidly up and out past the loading dock. Rachael shuddered. "Damn that thing is *fast*!"

"Yeah. And magical, too. For a minute, I thought it was gonna eat both of us."

Denny took her hand and started to work his way around to where he thought the motorcycles would be. It was getting late, and they were going to need to find better rides, or at least something with headlights.

Rachael pulled Denny's arm, spinning him to face her. The look she gave him was penetrating.

"When you told Susan that you would stab her with the crowbar while you compelled her to stay still, what the Hell, Denny? Could you even *do* that?"

Denny looked at Rachael and grinned. "Fuck if I know. But *she* believed it. Come on."

As the sun set over the Rockies, two riders headed south and west, away from the empty airport and past the large blue mustang with glowing red eyes. For the first time, Denny wondered if that horse shouldn't have been pale.

eVo.144.000.mOd.112.sCe15 | YEAR ZERO | EARTH | UNITED STATES | CALIFORNIA | SAN FRANCISCO

FORTY-FIVE-YEAR-OLD Timothy Hogan rubbed the stubble on his face and smoothed his sandy hair. He stood looking southwest from the hills above Vista Point, across the bay to Alcatraz and beyond. Smoke and flames rose above San Francisco in several places. Far away, Tim could see the fires from Oakland to El Centro, and the whole area along the eastern side of the San Francisco Bay was a smudge in the afternoon sunlight.

But it wasn't the fire and destruction that held Tim's attention, it was what was in the bay. Tim had seen it come into the bay earlier in the morning, after hearing a loud, musical trumpeting from his makeshift camp in Kirby Cove. The sheer size of the thing was terrifying, and Tim had scrambled into his newly-acquired Hummer and driven up to the top of the hill to get a better view.

For a long time, he just watched as the purplish-green form swam beneath the Golden Gate Bridge and wandered the bay. Tim couldn't tell exactly what it was, only that it was vaguely serpentine, and huge. For long periods, it would submerge, only to rise to the surface elsewhere in the bay.

And then there was a small sailboat, perhaps 30 feet long. Some survivor, deciding it was safer to grab as many supplies as possible and stay on the water, came angling down from the Northeast. Normally, the strategy would have been sound, as the majority of survivors were on land, looking for guns, food, and/or victims – the main reason Tim had fled across the bridge and into Marin as soon as possible after the event two days before. It hadn't been easy, with abandoned vehicles choking the way.

The people on the craft seemed completely unaware of the mysterious creature as they headed for the Golden Gate Bridge and the Pacific Ocean beyond. Tim watched the sailboat slowly continue. Likely, the person or persons aboard were scanning the shore for potential marauders. As they drew closer to the bridge, Tim raised his binoculars and scanned the vessel, noting a couple of people on deck. Frantically scanning the bay, he saw no sign of the creature, until it suddenly breached a couple thousand feet behind the boat. Horrified, there was little Tim or the sailors could do, as the behemoth finally lifted from the waves.

It was a mottled color, like a giant bruise. A huge, gross reptilian head rose from shoulders easily as wide as the boat. Challenging the fleeing vessel, it roared, and Tim could see a giant toothed maw. With a splash, it dove under the water on a course to intercept the boat.

The sailboat began to pick up speed, racing as fast as its engine could propel it. There was no chance of escape, Tim was sure. The wake from the pursuing creature was large in the blue-gray bay below. All he could do was watch in terror and shout as the creature moved to catch its prey. It was a slow-motion nightmare which could only have one outcome.

The craft was nearing the bridge when the beast again breached, higher this time, a massively built torso rising a hundred feet above the water. Tim screamed helplessly. From the bridge above the tableau there was movement, and a rush of wind from offshore battered everything momentarily. Agape, Tim watched as first one stranded car, then a second, rose and launched themselves at the creature, striking it in the head and shoulders.

The beast fell back into the water near the sailboat. The resulting wave nearly washed the crew from its deck. Another blast of wind hit, and there was a loud snap when the main sail came down around the broken mast. Frantically trying to clear the sail and mast from the deck, the couple on board froze in horror when the creature rose from the water, this time beside the boat.

Tim could see clearly now the massive reptilian head, the gigantic teeth and fearsome visage of something that looked too much like a crocodile to be so huge. This time, it roared in fury as it prepared to destroy the puny ship.

From somewhere on the bridge, Tim heard shouting, and he watched in awe as an SUV lifted from the bridge and flew straight into the creature's mouth. There was a man on the bridge, and as Tim watched, he gestured at several cars and appeared to direct them at the creature below, each crashing into the monster's face with incredible force.

Now distracted from the foundering craft, the beast made for the North tower, near where the man stood defiantly. Once it reached the tower, the creature slowly began to climb out of the water, revealing a huge, blotchy body, covered in scaly nodules, easily hundreds of feet long. As it rose over the edge of the roadway, there was a tremendous blast of wind and a half dozen cars and trucks slid madly across the bridge, striking the beast and carrying it over the edge with them, where the mass of flesh and steel sank in a wildly bubbling froth.

Tim raced to the Hummer and slammed it into gear, heading back down the hill the way he came. The sailboat, caught in the massive wave created by the creature, washed violently Westward past the North end of the bridge, spilling its contents and occupants into the water near the rocky shore by Kirby Cove where Tim had been camping. Tim took the switchbacks as fast as he could, throwing dirt plumes from the tires and sliding across the asphalt until he pulled up at the base of the hill. The waves pummeled the craft against the shore, and Tim saw two women, soaked and struggling to hold on to the rocks while the surf pounded them.

He ran along the shore, stopping short of the rocks. Kneeling, Tim placed both palms against the ground and closed his eyes in concentration. The ground itself began to lift under the women, the stones filling in and rising. In a matter of moments, the rocky ground had become a promontory, ten feet above the waves. The women collapsed, exhausted, as Tim ran toward them.

"Hey! Uh, are you okay?" Tim approached the first woman, and saw that she was young, probably still a teenager. She had blond hair and was very thin. When she opened her eyes and looked up, Tim stopped, mesmerized. Her eyes were a strikingly clear bluish-green. She seemed to clear her head and rose quickly. Her clothes were stuck to her form, and for a moment, Tim stared as the water clung to her.

"Jesus! What was that thing? And what just happened with the ground?" She looked around and saw her companion watching Tim as she wiped her hands on her soaked jeans.

"*He* happened, Beth. He made the ground move," said the second woman. She had beautiful dark caramel eyes, and her crimson hair fell in ringlets around her shoulders. She was older than her companion, probably in her late thirties. She rose slowly, looking around and peering back toward the ruined sailboat, and further. Shaking her head, she made a sound of disgust before approaching the two.

"Nice job. Thanks," she said, grimacing. "But all my shit is on that boat." Never taking her eye from Tim, the woman tugged her earlobe and turned her head sideways, clearing the remaining water. "Good to know we've got some complements to our powers, just like she said. Where's the other dude?"

Tim goggled at first one, then the other woman. "Umm, what? Wait, are you telling me that dream I had was *real*?"

"Oh, it was real, alright. I damn near got my ass fried by my own fires before Beth hauled me onto her boat. And it was right where Randa told me to be waiting. I'm Leta, by the way."

"Tim," he said, extending a hand to her, which she shook. Her hand was notably warm, as if she were running a high fever.

Meanwhile, Beth approached the rocks and looked at the sinking sail boat. The water thrashed it against the shore, but as Tim and Leta turned to watch, the water rose higher and poured the boat onto the rocks above the shoreline. As the water receded, Leta looked to the girl and said, "Daaamn. That's some impressive shit. So, if you could make the water do that, why didn't you make a current to get us away from that thing that was chasing us?"

"Because I was scared, Leta. Just like you. And just like you, I have to focus, but that thing was terrifying. Now can we go get some dry clothes before the other guy gets here?" She climbed the canted deck and went into the hold, followed by Leta. Tim shrugged and headed toward the camp.

After the two had grabbed their packs and what could be salvaged from the wreck, they rendezvoused at the makeshift fire pit in Tim's camp. Soon, a large camper came slowly traversing the last of the switchbacks down into the area. The camper edged into the spot next to Tim's Hummer, and a young man emerged wearing jeans, a t-shirt, and a windbreaker. As he walked over to the camping spot, he ran his fingers through his tousled hair and grinned.

"Hey," he said. "I guess she was right. I mean, I had a harder time believing there was gonna be a monster than I did thinking there would be other people."

"Yeah, that thing was freaking *huuuge*," Tim said. "Nice work with the cars, by the way. I'm Tim, and this is Beth and Leta."

"Yeah, I almost didn't get here through all the fires in San Francisco. That was a real mess." Dwayne shook everyone's hands and looked over his shoulder. "She didn't say, but I figured the RV would be handy. I mean, if we are traveling together. Are we?"

Beth smiled. "We were planning on getting out on the boat. I don't know what the roads look like, but San Francisco and Oakland's pretty much burned." She shot a covert, accusing look at Leta, then walked over to Dwayne. "You pretty much saved our asses back there. Thanks."

Dwayne looked a little surprised as she hugged him tight, but returned the hug nonetheless. "Yeah, well. I thought that thing was going to climb the bridge and eat me. I didn't know that I could throw that many cars. Now I'm just really tired."

Tim grinned and looked over at a nearby knee-high boulder, and it began to slowly roll towards Dwayne. When it stopped, Dwayne looked skeptically at Tim before sitting down on it.

Leta, who had been standing back, said, "So this is some kind of Earth, Wind, and Fire shit, then. Well, and Water, too." Her smile at Beth was genuine, but short. She didn't smile at the boys. She squatted near the fire pit and began to chafe her hands together. The stacked logs began to smolder and burn.

Leta looked toward the setting sun, the reflection blazing in her deep brown eyes, which flickered as she turned to the others. "I don't know about the rest of you, but I think Mhyrranda tried to tell me in a dream what to do once we all made it here. I think maybe we need to talk."

eVo.144.000.mOd.112.sCe16 | YEAR ZERO | EARTH | UNITED STATES | NEVADA | RENO | GRAND SIERRA RESORT AND CASINO

THE BRIEF KNOCK ON the thick oak door of the Presidential Suite broke Mhyrranda's reverie, and she looked up from the laptop at which she had been staring blankly. "Yes?"

"Room service, Ms. Randa," called a voice from the hall. "Your breakfast is here."

"Thanks, Nick. Let them in." Randa closed the laptop and set it aside, rising from the bed and sliding into her black satin robe. The door opened and two men came in. The first, in a suit, held the door for a waiter with a cart. Nick, the man in the suit, stood back as the young waiter lifted the cover of the tray and presented it to Mhyrranda. As he reached toward the coffee pot, he inadvertently caught the edge of the orange juice decanter, sending it over the edge of the tray.

It froze in midair, both the decanter and the orange juice contained within a translucent sphere that shimmered slightly, reflecting on its surface the comical look of panic from the waiter.

"Don't worry, man," Nick said gently. "I got it." With a careful movement of both hands, looking as if he were cupping his hands and moving them only slightly, he caused the juice to return to its decanter, then replaced it carefully upon the tray.

The waiter gave Nick a respectful glance, even going so far as to thank him verbally before returning to his duty. He then carefully poured her coffee from the pot before smiling and stepping back, quite carefully moving this time.

"Will that be all, ma'am?" he asked, a smile on his face.

"Yes, thanks – but stop calling me ma'am, okay. I ain't *that* old."

"Yes, ma– I mean, Ms. Randa." The young man ducked in a half bow before turning and leaving the room.

Nick watched him leave, a wry grin on his face.

"What? Why are you grinnin' like that?"

Nick fixed her with a knowing look. "Oh, just because you got these kids trained so well, they don't even wait for a tip. Not that he deserved one for spilling the OJ. But I just think it's amusing that people worship you so much."

Mhyrranda lifted a fork and took a bite of eggs, eyeing Nick. "Well, first of all, money's not really any good anymore. Second, I give them all wonderful, happy dreams of things that they wish for. As long as they are around, I give them their fantasies for the half of their lives they don't have to worry about surviving in this fucked-up ol' world. And that's *way* better than anything they can put in their pockets. It could be far worse. They have food, a nice place to stay, and a sense of family." She waved vaguely at the hotel suite.

"Besides, Tommy there is a millionaire – didn't you hear? He won the lottery the day before the lights. Four hundred and seventy-five million dollars that he couldn't spend, even if he could collect it."

Nick laughed. "No shit? He should be my boss. I'm due for a raise."

"Hey, in a perfect world, he'd be my next ex-husband." Randa shook her head. "Instead, he's bringing me breakfast."

Nick sobered. "You ready for the morning status?"

Mhyrranda sipped her coffee and nodded. "Yeah, but afterwards, I want you to pass the word for everyone to meet in the ballroom at noon and be packed by this afternoon. Get Mike to check fuel on those busses and load them with food. And I need Dominic to swing around with the limo – I want to make a quick trip to the mall for some travelin' clothes."

"Are we going somewhere?" Nick canted his head is curiosity.

Randa smiled, her perfect face beaming. "We're going to Vegas, baby."

eVo.144.000.mOd.112.sCe17 | YEAR ZERO | EARTH | UNITED STATES | COLORADO | CONIFER

DENNY SCUFFED HIS BOOT on the wooden porch as he leaned against the rail and sipped coffee from a ceramic mug that said 'Mexico' on it. The mountains were peaceful and quiet in the morning sun. From the open kitchen window on the side the house, he could still smell breakfast from earlier. Rachael's sister Meg was a great cook, a sweet person, and Denny was glad she'd made it through The End. It made it easier, since Rachael broke the news that she didn't want to go with him – she had a safe place to stay, a living relative, and there were enough people in the small mountain town to make survival easier. Denver was still a mess, but the people were trying to pull it together. There was just no one who had clearly taken charge, and there was still looting and violence. Conifer, on the other hand, was small enough that everyone had banded together.

He was surprised that they hadn't fought, and he knew there was an undercurrent between them. Something unsaid. Rachael had clung to him since the airport – since Mark. But no matter how desperate he sensed she was, she was also determined and strong willed. She wouldn't fight, but she wasn't budging from Colorado.

The front door closed silently behind Rachael as she came outside.

"Hey," she said softly, hugging Denny from behind and nuzzling his shoulder.

"Hey." Denny put his hand on hers, turning.

"Meg wanted to thank you again for getting the power on in the house. And, uh, for teaching her how to do those runes. She's been practicing carving those runes on anything that holds a battery. Radios and TVs work, but there's nothing on."

Denny laughed briefly. "No change then."

Rachael's smile disappeared, and she looked serious.

"Are you okay, Denny? Are you having more dreams?"

"Some. But I don't know what's just dreams, and what are real messages. Ever since the event, half the time I think it might just be wishful thinking, and the other half scare the hell out of me." Denny took another drink of coffee.

"So why go?" Rachael looked at Denny hopefully.

"Because," he said, placing the cup on the rail and pulling her close. "Because if what I'm seeing is real, I'm needed, Rache. Those runes on the equipment in the airport – they work. *I* can make them work. And with power going down all over, people are going to need power. Does that sound crazy?"

"Well, if you hadn't been right so many times so far, I'd say your ego was getting too big for your boots. But if you have to use your..." she touched her forehead briefly "power, to convince people not to just wind up quitting or killing each other, who am I to argue?"

She looked into his eyes for several heartbeats. "I'm sorry, Denny. I can't go. I just can't." Then she smiled softly. "I guess you just have to save the world on your own, *this* time."

"I'll try to be back soon. Just Texas and Atlanta, okay? If I'm wrong, it should only be a couple weeks or so. Just there and back again."

"Sure, Denny. I've had my own dreams. I know you'll be back."

Denny smiled, leaning in for a long, passionate kiss. "You bet I'll be back."

Rachael handed him a lunch bag filled with sandwiches, and Denny picked up his backpack. As he walked to his Jeep, Meg came outside, waving at him from the door.

"Did you tell him?" Meg asked.

"No. Convincing is his special ability, not mine." Rachael smiled and waved as Denny, grinning, pulled away from the drive and sped down the street.

Reaching into her pocket, Rachael pulled the small stick out and looked at it again. No doubt about it, she was pregnant.

eVo.144.000.mOd.112.sCe18 | YEAR ZERO | EARTH | UNITED STATES | NEVADA | LAS VEGAS

THE MOTLEY CARAVAN of buses, vans, and SUVs entered Las Vegas on highway 95 right after dusk, horns blaring. Despite the relative dark of the surrounding suburbs, the former gambling mecca was still lit from downtown to the strip. When the Lightbringer's Sigil took effect in the middle of the night, people were out and about, unlike many cities across the United States. Hundreds of thousands had dropped dead where they sat or stood, at gaming tables, slot machines, and throughout the casinos. In the ensuing panic, no one had turned the lights out. And there were still people there days later, which is why the caravan wanted to make enough noise to draw followers.

Nearly a mile long, the string of vehicles proceeded at a stately pace behind the black stretch limo. Flanked by two police motorcycles, and directly preceding a dozen black SUVs, the limo cruised along at about twenty miles per hour, the occupants taking in the city from behind tinted windows. Nearing the Southern end of the strip, the lead vehicle stopped in front of a giant sphinx, where a crowd had gathered. The people standing around were dressed in suits, as if the apocalypse were only a brief interruption to their games.

Several of the vehicles moved past the limo, so that when the rear door opened, the emerging figure was flanked by six vehicles on either side. Several buses crossed the median into the Northbound lane and stopped behind the SUVs. As Mhyrranda emerged, the occupants of the SUVs exited, standing next to their vehicles.

She was dressed in skin-tight black leather pants, a black pirate shirt with more ruffles than strictly necessary, and combat boots. Completing the rakish costume was a long leather duster of purple leather. Her hair was a lustrous red, and her crimson lips parted in a smile. A pair of men in black dusters stood at each side, casually holding assault rifles.

Looking up and down the crowd of people, she grinned. "Ah, Hell. If I'd known it was gonna be like this, I'd have worn a cocktail dress. Which one of you is Jordan?"

A portly man in an Armani suit stepped forward. "That's me. And you are the witch *Mhyrranda*?"

"Aw, sugar. Ain't no need to be callin' names. But yes. I'm *Mhyrranda*." She purred her name.

"Then you know the gentlemen I represent hold this city, and you are not welcome here."

Mhyrranda tilted her head and frowned slightly. "Well, it's a big city, it ain't full, and we only want a couple of the buildings. So maybe we can still deal."

Jordan looked back over his shoulder and nodded. From the darkness, a shot cracked. For a moment, a pinpoint of light illuminated the air in front of Mhyrranda's face. She smiled briefly, a grim smile.

"I was afraid that was going to be the answer. As Samuel L. Jackson once said, 'Please, allow me to retort.'" She lifted her collar and spoke softly, "Light'em up."

From down the street, several loud explosions ignited the lower floors of the Mandalay Bay. As the shattered glass fell in shards to the ground, fire rose in a sheet along the building's exterior, and the earth trembled. Randa lifted her hands and waved them in a circle, and spotlights from the buses lit the crowd. Barrels from the long rows of windows above and behind her were accompanied by the clack of prepared weapons, and all of the men and women standing next to the SUVs lifted readied assault weapons. Blinded by the lights from the vehicles, the members of the crowd surrounding Jordan lifted their own weapons and squinted at targets they could no longer see.

"Now, now. Hold up a sec." Mhyrranda raised her hands palms out. "No need for all y'all dying for a bunch of dead bosses. Besides, they are part of the old world. I want to offer you a chance at a *new* world. Anyone interested, just put your weapon on the ground and step over there by the sphinx. But do it *slowly*, cause my folks are a little anxious."

Jordan stood stock still, looking as though he'd eaten something that tasted very bad.

"We are the good guys here," Mhyrranda said. "We don't wanna hurt anybody – we want to rebuild, and that takes people. But I understand that some folks are free spirits, and don't like change. If you don't want to join us, just put your weapons down and start walking. Don't stop 'til you hit the city limits, and nobody's gonna fuck with you. But you gotta decide now."

As she continued speaking, one by one, then in groups, the crowd dispersed. Eventually, the only one left standing there was Jordan, looking angry and afraid.

"Jordan? Time to make up your mind, sugar."

"Seriously? You aren't going to kill me?"

"I told you, We're the good guys. And I need you to do something for me. Do it, and you can come be part of the new world. All I need you to do is find any of the bosses that might have been somewhere besides the Mandalay Bay. Tell them the deal stands, but they ain't bosses no more. They don't like it, they need to fuck off out of Vegas."

Jordan swallowed and nodded slowly.

"Oh, and Jordan? Try anything like that again, and I will find you in your dreams and have you shitting yourself in pain and fear before I murder you." Her smile was no longer friendly.

Jordan paused only to drop his sidearm in the pile before walking North on Las Vegas Boulevard.

Waving to the men standing nearby, she indicated the crowd waiting next to the sphinx. "Get a detail for each one of these people, find out which casino they are familiar with, escort them and start gathering supplies. No looting. Meet back in the main part of the Luxor tomorrow at dawn with status."

Mhyrranda turned to find Nick emerging from the limo. The look of annoyance plain on his face. "Aw, sugar, don't be mad. I needed you behind that bulletproof glass to keep you safe while you shielded me." She reached up and stroked his cheek gently.

Nick's hard visage softened. "I know. Doesn't make it easier when I should have been at your side."

"Well, now you are. And you can escort me inside, where I can find a bathroom. I really have to pee."

Nick and the pair of bodyguards walked inside the pyramid, and Miranda, safely alone inside the ladies' room, let her bottled up emotions out. She sat and sobbed until the fear left her and she regained her composure.

As Mhyrranda began to reapply her makeup, she became aware of a steady *thrum-thrum-thrum* sensation, right at the edge of perception. It was both heard and felt, if only barely. It was mesmerizing, almost as if it were calling her.

Nick tapped on the door, startling her. From the other side of the entrance, she heard him say, "Hey Duchess? We need you! There's some weird shit going on. The team from the Mandalay Bay job is here. They're saying something's wrong outside. Really wrong..."

eVo.144.000.mOd.112.sCe19 | YEAR ZERO | THE NULL

THEY HAD SPLIT INTO two groups. Mercy and Void had removed themselves far from the others, so that they could speak somewhat privately regarding what was to come. Vir'gil, Maynard, Ku'tu, and Aal Ball had remained behind, at the nexus, where they were busy at work brainstorming. And teaching Maynard Fae Runes.

It had begun with a simple offer of a unique rainbow-colored tuber from Vir'gil to Maynard, who had accepted it and ingested it without hesitation. Then, to Maynard it had seemed as if he had trained with Vir'gil for years, day after day, week after week, and so on, until he had been able to create and implement his first test Fae Rune. After that brief detour, which had lasted objectively only a very brief time, Maynard and Vir'gil returned to the normal local Flow.

"And that is how you create a Fae Rune," Vir'gil finished with an exhausted sigh, concluding his first lesson in runecrafting with Maynard. "It's just a physical embodiment of your knowledge and intent. It's not so much 'drawn' as 'shaped', or 'expressed' by a fusion of your personal knowledge and your intent. If you're powerful enough, you can do that, and successfully actualize it. Now that you're like us, even if we're all 'nerfed' as you said, you're still above a human in power. You're in our range of power now – the nascent immortal range, currently – so you can access it and manifest it easily, even here in the Null, though the price is higher here than when you're elsewhere. Or on Earth."

"I can't believe it was that easy," Maynard replied, flipping his fingers back and forth nimbly, as if he were playing a theremin. "Void!" he shouted over to where Void and Mercy were talking, some distance away. "I can freakin' do runes now! It's easy! They're basically translated schematics. Blueprints made real. I think we're going to be able to engineer almost anything."

"Awesome," Void barked over in a somewhat disinterested voice.

"It's only 'that easy' if you're Fae, like us," Ku'tu informed Maynard merrily. "You're still an amateur, of course, no better than a new wingless foundling, even if Vir'gil just gave you a seemingly abbreviated month-long crash course in just a few minutes. Benefits of being the Entheogenic Lord, I should think. But once you master the transliteration of your knowledge and intent to actualization, Maynard, you're going to be sharp with them. Vir'gil wasn't exaggerating when he said you're a natural runecaster. It's only logical to assume that, based on your unique attributes, you're probably going to become a fantastic Hekatek. Provided we all live so long, of course."

"So let's get this thing engineered," Maynard said confidently. "I'm sure I can do my part now. Big time."

Away from the crafters, Mercy and Void continued their hushed exchange.

"What if it's not twelve hours bins?" Mercy asked. "What if it's more? Or less? What makes you think that 'twelve' is the right number?"

"You know the most obvious is the simple gematria," Void replied quietly, carefully considering his words. "First, though, to be thorough, we can exclude some of the other obvious possibilities. The number appears virtually everywhere, and in everything that man has touched. There are the obvious twelve deities in the pantheons, the twelve houses of the zodiac, the twelve disciples. All of those are subject to modifications, however. The deities had subsets of lesser gods, demigods, and ascended heroes. The zodiac, while constantly, cross-culturally representing a particular culture's expression of what they thought particular groupings of stars could be instantiated as icons, usually animals or therianthropes, always had the thirteenth house, or boundary phase, lurking about in the grand precession. Curious that it fits into so many cultures' calendars, their counting of the months in a solar year. The disciples, of course, were actually a subset and not the full counting of the number. We must exclude Judas Iscariot, the Miriams, and a few of the other briefly named and encountered members of Yeshua bin Yosef's posse. It's the perfect number in many religions and philosophies."

"Go on," Mercy bade him, a curious light dancing around her eyes.

"I'm sure you already know this, so I'll wrap it up. The maths are wicked. The cultural, and temporal, cross-pollinations of twelve are profound. Ten fingers, two feet."

Mercy giggled. "But that's not it, is it, Void?"

"No. It's simple, because Helel is lazy, and bad, and he thinks that he's God. It's a composite of Genesis 1:2, in which the 'void' appears first in the Bible, and it's bracketed by *tohu*, or, commonly, 'chaos'. And it's the pivotal focal point for the modified Fibonacci sequence he's been using, where the 1 finally evolves to the 2. That's classic fission, practical evolution, and bit of numbers fun. Because that's where the original 0 in the true sequence evolves to the first true counting number, 1, then remains at 1, then moves abruptly up to the first prime, 2. That progression is key in some mystic circles, because it mirrors what the godhead does in Genesis. I'll hold back on the deeper Zohar; I have a feeling you already know it well."

"True. I'm just surprised that you know it, Void," Mercy replied, genuinely curious. "I mean, really, what have you not just known suddenly, abruptly, thus far?" She squinted her eyes. "Sure you're not still One with Gojira?"

Void laughed, startling Vir'gil, who was trying to eavesdrop with his stalking eyestalks. "No, I'm pretty sure. I'm just regurgitating commonly available knowledge. It's no longer as esoteric as it used to be just a few decades ago. I'm sure you're well aware that the advent of the Internet has been the single most potent factor in accelerated human learning in known history. I surf a lot. Boring guy."

"Yes, you are," she lied, smirking. "Finish up. We've gotta boogie soon."

"Okay. It's part of the sequence of the *Tzimtzum*, when the creator, which I'll respectfully not name, pulls back its infinite light and causes the Void to manifest. The creator then filters its own light through the ten *Sefirot*, unique entities that express its manifestation in this cosmos without overwhelming mortals. And the rest of creation. It's what we'd consider to be primal, even though there are some deltas between what the humans were describing here in their holy books, and what we ourselves have experienced. There's more, layers upon layers and endless permutations, but that's roughly it. It's all I really need to use to point out why I think Helel used the base of twelve hours for his iterations: Because it was written into the cosmic templates, and he really didn't do anything special or unique in order to use it. He just used what was already there – ineffable; key word – and he invoked cosmic level power from the illegal templates he was using this time, during this sim, to hack it and try to win. The number fits the ineffable godhead in this sim, and in many things that it has expressed. Truncated shard or not, that ineffable stuff is in the realm of the One Above in this sim. It's not Helel's, really. So, I angled it from the perspective that he just resorted to being lazy, letting the cosmic templates steer things."

Mercy considered this for a moment. She knew quite well the subject matter. It was no mystery to one of her many millennia and supernatural Fae origin. It didn't even truly bother her that a relative newcomer, a former mortal recently born from her ancient perspective, a veritable zygote compared to her, had achieved such a level of discernment and knowledge. She simply ascribed his remarkably advanced perception to his union with the Dark Earth Mother herself. And, of course, his brief union with Fresswelle, which apparently, somehow, had done for him what it had done for Ku'tu's tragic mate: render him One with the Dragon. Thus, with both sides of the Dual-Aspect covered, she was almost certain that Void had access to resources far beyond mortal ken.

"Whatever," she said dismissively. "You're still a fluke, Void, with that cosmic perception of yours. And, quite possibly, wrong. We – you and I – technically are the *tohu va-vohu*; the 'chaos' and the 'void'. The so-called 'Source', in opposition to our collective 'Void' – an unfair appellation, considering you're leaving me out of it, you bunch of assholes – bend and bind and weave together to reveal the cosmic prime. The cosmic power. What the humans would call the ineffable one, or godhead."

"Maybe," he shrugged. "This place, the Null, could very well be a manifestation of chaos; just framed so that it doesn't appear to be entirely a human expectation of what chaos is or might be. You'd obviously know more about the Null than I, though, so I'll defer to your wisdom regarding it. As for ineffable cosmic unions... I don't have much to say about that. I think that such a thing remains, and shall remain, above and beyond us. Until we experience it. Well, really, I think we're seeing it in the Dual-Aspect of the cosmic version of Chthon and the Dragon. I think one way to interpret their union is that they are akin to a quantum that, unseen, enjoys multiple possible identities simultaneously. But, once you gaze into that particular abyss, it affixes, actualizes, and then stares right back, realized and real. That scales to complex waveforms. I suspect it scales up as far as it scales down, too. Probably scales to our cosmos, and those above and below ours."

She smirked, her chin pointy. She said loudly, "What sicko human would conjecture a cat in a box with a container of poison gas? There are better ways to make that analogy work, you know?"

Void shook his head, adjusting his volume so everyone could hear him. "Total dick move on his part. Poor cat. Obviously, Schrödinger was afraid of pussy."

Everyone heard, and the jest upgraded the group morale from "abysmal" to "Just barely clawing out of the Pit".

"I've got it rigged now," Maynard said, dispelling the moment. "We're ready," he said with finality, staring hard at Void.

"I know you don't like it," Void replied as he and Mercy fell in, joining the rest for the short walk back to the Eightfold Path. He then quickly added, "I don't like it, either. I *know* this is gonna suck."

There, at its center, stood Aal Ball, now shapeshifted into a liquid chrome form like that of DaVinci's *Vitruvian Man*. Its four arms and four legs pointed awkwardly around the circle, their symmetry apparently broken. Upon its mirrorlike surface, dozens of intricately woven Fae Runes faintly pulsed in various colors around its entire perimeter. A central core of some very familiar-looking chakras, nine in total, bisected its form.

"That's it?" Void asked, incredulous. "That's incredible looking, Maynard. Looks like you used a spirograph to make those runes. And you're on warning, Aal Ball. No games. For now, I mean."

"Aal Ball!" the insane collective sentience fart-whinnied.

Everyone gathered round Void as he stepped into the chrome colored confines of Aal Ball. The admonition of no games echoed silently about, causing the first fateful flutters of the dread anticipation to come to settle heavily on everyone. Save for Mercy, naturally.

Facing Void, whose form now swam with the essence of Aal Ball, which had seemingly ingested ninety percent of him, Mercy's eyes glinted with mischief.

"Well, it sure was good to have met ya," she told Void. "Happy trails."

"What?" Void barked as the silvery sheen closed nearly around his face. "You think I can't do it?" he asked, feigning indignation. "I'm VoidSpawn. Stupid faerie..." he burbled as Aal Ball completely enveloped him.

"Yep," Mercy said, shaking her head. "He's toast. VoidToast."

Over some stifled laughter from Vir'gil and Ku'tu, Maynard said, "This is totally insane, but I think he's going to pull it off. If not, well, let's just hope he leaves us enough blackened bready VoidToast goodness to resurrect."

The dull monotony of the Null abruptly filled with a series of eight polytones, whispered to their ears. For several seconds the polytones wove a cacophonous scheme. Abruptly, the polytones merged into a single metatone. It erupted into the omnipresent still of the Null like a raging cosmos fighting for birth, even from its own stillbirth. A shimmering of blood-bruise purple rays shot forth from the terminus of the eight arms and legs, stabbing hatefully at the dull horizon. From the middle of the forehead of the Aal Ball-Void hybrid came the slight hiss of Aal Ball's physical form burning away due to its contact with what emerged from Void's third eye.

Void screamed like mad thunder, writhing in pain. His third eye opened, shining down upon the group a deep purple three-dimensional vector grid of the eight distinct anchor points of Mercy's Eightfold Path.

"Shut it down," Mercy said loudly, unable to hear her own words. With a swift kick into Maynard's shin, Mercy drew his attention. "Shut. It. Down." she told him, carefully forming the words.

Maynard shook his head, his hands cupping his ears to ward them from the sound. "No," he told her, even though it tortured him to do so. His friend was in terrible pain. Were it anyone other than Void, though, he already would have complied. For if it were not Void, it would have been murder.

Freeing one hand for a moment, he waved Mercy and the others toward the projected grid of light.

Over Void's persistent screams of agony, which eerily harmonized its Tuvan strangulation multiple octaves with the metatone of the eight projected rays of the Eightfold Path, Mercy and the others went to work. The purple grid distinctly produced eight rays within its multidimensional array. The rays apparently were traversable in the sense that one could start physically near the projected origin point of one, nearer to where Void stood screaming, and physically walk the projected path. The movement provided metaphysically linked insight into the higher order nature of the paths and their destinations. More precisely, insight into what those destinations now implied given their quest for Shunya, the sister of Fresswelle, the Devouring Wave. Or, so they desperately hoped.

"I can't stand it..." Mercy said, her voice lost beneath the crushing, resonant *thrum-thrum-thrum*. "It sounds like he's dying."

For a moment, Mercy's mind tortured her, as often it was inclined to do. She saw the helpless mortal form of Void, that poor human zygote that he was, whatever his human name had been, writhing, affixed in its DaVinci-style multi-limbed crucifixion. That's really what he was now. Mortal. Their upper souls – their immortal souls – had been significantly drained, erased in a sense by Helel's cheating designs. Nerfed unto nascence. There was no way that any mortal could endure what he was enduring. She knew this better than most. For in his physical binding with the eight anchor points of the Never, Void was attempting to interact with energies beyond mortal ken. Beyond the power of mere mortals to bind. This was something that she herself had barely survived, and she had been and always would be immortal. It was excruciating and nearly fatal for her. But for him, the zygote?

"I see it!" Vir'gil excitedly told everyone, sending out a reminding vine to everyone. "I see it!" he said again, for added effect. He pointed a few more hastily grown tendrils to indicate the right paw of the massive Sphinx, which held its court before the Luxor Resort, in Las Vegas, Nevada.

"Shunya!" Mercy exploded joyously, instantly dismissing her earlier train of thought. Mortal or not – who really knew for real at this point? – he was the VoidSpawn. He'd be alright. "Quick!" she continued, hastily pointing back toward Void. "Let's do this!"

"Ah, shit," Ku'tu declared. "This is going to be gross..."

With that, Ku'tu flew directly into Void's third eye, passing through the aperture of projection and immediately into the warm, dry heat of Las Vegas, Nevada. Some three feet below her, Shunya jutted from where it had impacted the paw of the Sphinx.

"Yay! It's right here!" she cried out, excited that she would be the one to deliver Shunya to Mercy and save the day. And finally get things rolling for her to free her people, the mighty Fae of Aal, who were still stuck in Shunya's twin, Fresswelle.

She flew down to within her tiny arm's length of the effusive hilt of Shunya, the Zero Blade. Carefully extending her hand toward it, she noticed that, as she approached it, it became quite difficult to touch it. In fact, try as she might, her tiny form lacked the strength to overcome its Zeroth Aura, which forbade direct contact with the blade, save for those with the name and soulsong of "Mercyduceus Vendredi".

"Fooey!" Ku'tu spat down at it, sputum sizzling as it neared the blade's hilt. Though draconic phlogiston, capable of setting mountains to blaze, it was unable to penetrate the aura. Instead, it fell whistling to the ground, burning the very air around it, until it reached the top of the paw of the Sphinx. There, it instantly sank beyond sight, the tiny pinprick of a hole belching crimson fire a meter high.

She looked above her, barely able to discern the forms of her friends. They appeared to shimmer like phantasms, poised a few feet above her, here in Las Vegas. Frantic arm-waving and pointing indicated that they wanted her to try again to grab the blade. However, Ku'tu, fully aware of what it had taken for Jud4sz Ressz0rz, the CyberGod, to do the same with Fresswelle many years ago, knew what she had to do. Carefully yet rapidly, she scanned the entire horizon within her purview, rotating the full circle widdershins of course. It was clear enough for what she had to do. With a resolving grunt entirely unbecoming her dainty faerie form, Ku'tu instantly shapeshifted into her full-sized, aircraft carrier-dwarfing dragon form. The abrupt displacement caused a wicked boom of thunder, which echoed up and down the Vegas strip.

Like an inverted sleeping whale, Ku'tu's head hovered in place above Shunya, unmoving. Her tail reached more than 500 meters above the local ground level. Her wings formed a tucked-in V, more suitable for diving and attack. For this moment in time, she was the biggest thing in Vegas. And she liked it.

Behind her the silver umbilicus connecting her to the projection from Void's third eye crackled and sizzled in flashing silver strobes. The metaphysical umbilicus drew the power necessary for Ku'tu to perform her shapeshift directly from Void's connected soul.

Again, Void screamed in agony. His chrome enshrouded form struggled in vain against the power of Aal Ball, which kept his blunted mortal power in check. Mostly. Aal Ball, who had once at behest of Mercy bound and held fast the Moon itself, just so she could win a bet with Hassan-i Sabbahhad as to which mighty assassin could still Hubal himself, at last met its match. In the Null, near the Eightfold Path of the Never, Aal Ball whicker-screamed along with Void, its relic-level power sorely tested by Void's not-quite-immortal-yet-not-quite-mortal-either power.

Slamming her hands to her ears, Mercy took a knee next to Void's struggling form. Despite her better angels, of which there were precisely zero, she decided at that moment to flip the script. Mainly because she was sick of not having her blade, and not at all because she felt the way that she truly did for her Boogieman.

She carefully reached over to Void and grabbed him by the first of four ankles. At once, dull gray-green ectoplasmic lights passed from beneath Mercy's feet, into Void's first ankle. It passed through the Aal Ball/Void composite entity, eventually extending to Ku'tu, steadily transforming the silvery sheen of the umbilicus to the dull hues of the Null.

Over a not-so-small commotion of mortally panicked screamers, who apparently had now become aware of her in her majestic dragon form hovering above the Vegas strip, Ku'tu noted that there was a slight, hazy displacement of light around the perimeter of Shunya. Only slightly distracted by the guilty pleasure of being to terrorize some humans once again, she saw Shunya's auric shields vanish.

Daintily extending her massive maw, Ku'tu snatched Shunya from the paw of the Luxor sphinx with a precise snap of her mighty jaws.

"Now, Ku'tu!" Mercy cried loudly. "Shrink!"

Ku'tu did, and Void screamed. Mercy, using her temporarily limited control of the Null, pulled both a tiny Ku'tu and Shunya into the Null. Immediately diving for Shunya, Mercy managed to catch it before it fell back into the rapidly closing path, which reverse-snailed itself back into nothingness. A wicked Doppler-shifted chorus of screams from the concerned survivors of Las Vegas faded along with it.

"Aal Ball!" Maynard shouted. "Release, now!"

Aal Ball did, Void screamed, and their hybrid form instantly unraveled and unwound. Aal Ball, involuntarily resuming its original form, fainted, plopping unceremoniously over on its side into the cushy comfort of the Null. Void, appearing in mid-air, arms and legs stretched out into an "X", fell face first down into the Null. From the waist up, his clothes had been reduced to burnt out ash, which clung to the air as he fell through them. There was massive damage to his body by way of a significant, nearly complete coverage of fifth and sixth degree burns above the torso. He was now a black, wizened mummy-looking figure above the waist. Flesh, muscle, and bone yet remained in some places, though it was not clear at first glance what they formerly had been connected to.

"No!" Maynard and Mercy screamed simultaneously. Both reached him at the same time. Both were aghast at what they saw before them.

Horrifically, Void awkwardly rolled over on his back. He managed to gurgle something to them through melted lips, the blackened flesh sloshing: "It's just a flesh wound..."

Insanely, as all gathered close around Void's recumbent form to see the miracle, a chaotic image of jet black appeared in the center of his charred chest and its blackened, exposed rib cage. As they watched, the blackness resolved into three intertwined spirals, rainbows dancing around their fringes. Then, awestruck, they experienced a basso profundo *thrum-thrum-thrum* which shook the Null, bouncing them around like life-sized electric football figures on an over-amped vibrating field. The spirals flickered thrice, with the rainbow lights of the fringe blurring on the third pulse, enforcing the former outline of the stricken Void. A moment after the outlining of his true form by the diminishing glow of the rainbow lights, the quantum waveform of his former physical state was restored. Completely.

"I just stepped through my own shadow and came out the other side," Void laughed. "46 and 2, bitches..."

The VoidSpawn flashed a feral smile as he lay upon his back, looking up at his stunned, shocked friends.

eVo.144.000.mOd.112.sCe20 | YEAR ZERO | THE NULL

"YOU FLATWORM FUCKER!" Mercy accused him, kicking him in the thigh. "Neat trick. Glad you're back. And I think you really mean 46 minus 2, VoidTard. Oh. We got Shunya," she said, carelessly flipping its lethal edge down at his face. "Good job with the soul sacrifice there, guys. Get up, runt," she barked, carelessly kicking at Aal Ball.

"Aaaa-aaalll Bbbb—" it kitten-pooted weakly, exhausted.

Executing a flawless kip-up, Void sprang to his feet. "I feel great! I mean, sorry for the pain, Aal Ball. I know you helped me back there. No way I could have done that alone."

"And I'm sorry for *your* pain, Void," Maynard admitted. "Man, what you just went through, I can't even begin to imagine how much that hurt."

"Blah-blah-blah," Mercy cut him off, "and he's *fine*, Maynard. He's the VoidSpawn. Horror and moral terror are his friends. You'll no doubt look back upon this experience as a rather happy vacation, compared to the times yet to come. And great job, Ku'tu," she said, Ku'tu replying with an exaggerated, flying courtly bow. "I am now obligated to you."

Startled, Ku'tu flew directly up to Mercy's left ear. "Milady," she faintly whispered. "I relieve you of your obligation. I am yet in mourning, and I may not bind with another at this time."

"What?" Mercy exclaimed loudly. She turned to face Ku'tu, who buzzed away just in time to avoid hitting her nose. "I wasn't asking to be betrothed or anything, no disrespect intended. Cultural difference in play, maybe? Here, it means something like I am in debt to you, favor-for-favor."

Ku'tu put a tiny hand to her lips, blushing. She laughed it off, not saying anything, for fear that it would escalate. Then, considering it for a nanosecond, she said, hastily, "All to the good, then. But I still relieve you of your obligation. No need. I did it for kicks, anyway. It's not like I was making a roast of myself. If anyone deserves thanks, it's V– " she stopped herself, noting the fey lights arise in Mercy's eyes.

"Syzygy my ass!" Mercy guffawed, virtually reading her thoughts. Then, she quickly motioned for Vir'gil to gather Aal Ball, which the elemental did, gently absorbing him into his own spacious soul space.

"Syzygy my ass, too," Void softly growled, clasping his hands together, his corded muscles bundling like anacondas. He felt as if his body had once more become supercharged with power. Hopefully, it was power of the cosmic variety, and not merely some delayed side-effect of his planarian-like regeneration. "We're back on the clock now. Ku'tu, did you personally witness the sigil's lights on the Luxor?"

She nodded, welcoming the return to focus. "Yes, Void, I did. I could feel the resonance in effect there, too. Very similar it was, in truth, to the sounds here in the Null. Perhaps a bit dulled there, even though it appears to be larger. But I presume that's a limitation particular to Aal. I mean, Earth."

"So it's going to be our first stop?" Maynard asked, crossing his arms. "Why not Giza? Or, Cholula? Or, any of the thousand-and-one-plus other pyramids or tetrahedrons on Earth?"

"Or the pyramidal mountains in Antarctica," Void replied, smirking. "We could join the rest of the MorthonTech employees-in-exile there."

"Ooh, zing!" Maynard said. "True, true. But the Luxor seems to be the place where all the big neon-green fingers are pointing. Obviously. I mean, Exhibit A is finding Shunya there. I wouldn't be surprised if that's just more of you-know-who's lazy coding."

Mercy nodded. "It makes sense. She just followed the easiest resonance path."

"But it followed it before it happened," Maynard added, instantly regretting saying it. He added, seeing that everyone was looking at him, "Yeah, I know. Spacetime means little to Shunya, just like Fresswelle. So my question then evolves to become, do we think Fresswelle did something similar? Like, why didn't it land in the sphinx's other paw? That would be expected symmetry, right?"

Mercy laughed mercilessly. "Stupid shaman. You're as daft at magicks as Vir'gil. Go back to planting your coca fields, why don't you?"

Standing his ground, Maynard laughed right back at her. "Ha! You're going to be thanking us when we make the desert bloom. Without our power, and with the Earth basically dying, its high tech probably expiring too, there's going to be starvation and famine. Before this is said and done, Vir'gil and I are going to be hailed as the Lords of Magick."

Her mouth opened slightly, but she bit it back. Tempering her reply, Mercy gave them both an appraising once-over. "Damn, much as I hate to admit it, I think you might be right. I hadn't considered that at all. I thought vegetables just came from the supermarket. All this time."

Vir'gil, moving closer to Maynard, creaked a heavy smile. "He is right, Mercy. Provided that we stop this current stream of madness and stabilize the world, there will be many millions who will be hungry and thirsty. My noble name is the Entheogenic Lord, but that stems..." he paused, creaking a bit at his own pun, "...from my elemental mastery of *all* things green. Metaphorically speaking. Truly, my domain covers everything that the humans classify under the Kingdom Plantae. And more. Combined with Maynard's future mastery of the Hekatek and his Soulforging skills, our main tasking, aside from saving the world from the Vanth'Vash'Var, shall be to perfect the green. The whole world will bloom, and the hungry and thirsty will know this bounty."

Everyone stared at Vir'gil. Instantly, he realized what he had just revealed, and he seemed to shrink a few inches as he moved slowly behind Maynard.

Maynard flapped his arms and turned to stare down at Vir'gil. "What the hell, Virge? Are you forecasting my future, or..." he let it hang, hoping someone would make the Big Reveal.

Shrugging, Vir'gil, admitted, "Shunya and Fresswelle are not the only ones to whom time is nonlinear. Entheogenic, remember?" he chuckled, his leafy eyebrows arching. "I've seen our futures. All of them. I know what's going to happen to everyone."

The group "WHAT?" was uncannily loud in the still of the Null.

"Virge," Mercy said quickly, "those are just probable paths. They're not set in stone."

"These are," Vir'gil said with finality. "I even saw Gil's death before it happened, but I was still unable to do anything to prevent it. It just happened, just like I saw it many years ago, and there was nothing I could do to prevent it," he concluded, his voice heavy with gravitas.

"So this whole time you could have been telling us what's about to happen?" Mercy asked, pointy and incredulous. "What the effing eff, Virge? Why be silent about it? Why not tell us everything now, before it happens, so we can at least prepare for it." Louder, her anger growing, she added, "Dammit, Virge! We could have owned the market!"

Vir'gil shook his head once. "You know we are not allowed to do that, Mercy," he gently chided her. She and he and Ku'tu three all knew this. Common rules of the Fae. So common that even the two former humans knew it, also. He continued, "Unlike those liars from the ZeroTime, the Mother absolutely advocates free will. If one is so blessed, she might reveal a glance of the future. Most of these glances are of one's death, but mostly in the sense that death means change. It's an inflection point. It's a point of decision and grace. It's a point at which one's soul must make the choice to..." he trailed off, knowing he could say no more.

"You can't stop *now*!" Mercy pleaded, dramatically falling to her knees. Shunya vanished back into her soul so that she could truly emphasize her assumed plight by raising both hands to the grim green-gray sky of the Null.

Noticing that everyone was now looking at her, and not Vir'gil, she smirked.

"How was that, Virge?" She asked playfully. "Good distraction? Secrets still safe?"

Vir'gil smiled. "We all know I can't say anything else about it. So, I thank you, Milady of Malice and Misprision. You actually defended the Mother, and I know how much that galls you."

"'Gall' is almost as much of an understatement as 'Misprision,'" Mercy countered, getting to her feet. "Anyway," she continued, Shunya appearing in her left hand, "I think we've had time to recover and regain our bearings. Time to go to Earth," she announced, pivoting to her left.

Wielding Shunya with perfect proficiency, she deftly carved into the fabric of the Null a spiraling stroke, ripping and tearing with abstract, mathematical precision. In the span of a single second, a puckered purple protuberance appeared in mid-air where her blade had passed. With the sound of a titan's hurdy-gurdy's drone string, the annulus of the dimensional gateway opened around them, dissolving as it passed. Its passage revealed the nighttime Las Vegas skyline from their new vantage atop the McCarran International Airport FAA Tower.

From some 352 feet above the maze of airport runways below, they gazed in wonder at the strange juxtaposition of destruction and new life before them. Most of the city still had power. Unlike some of the vignettes they had scryed, of other cities and the chaos devouring them, Las Vegas had curiously managed to keep its footing. Save for the Mandalay Bay complex, whose lower floors oozed lazy black smoke, the strip looked pristine, and still functional. The difference being, of course, two things readily apparent: first, that it was eerily quiet, without the typical humming of a major metropolitan area and the virtual symphony of its many sounds; second, that the Luxor's black pyramid was illuminated by massive, writhing strands of triple helix DNA. The full spectrum of the rainbow and more on either side of the visible spectrum blazed and danced in a bizarre silence, which nonetheless came as a thrumming, vibrant sound to one's soul.

The resonant echoes of the Lightbringer's Sigil emblazoned the black edifice of the Luxor with intense illumination, in more ways than mere sight. Even from this vantage, removed somewhat as it was from the Luxor, the Fae and former humans alike could feel its silent cosmic energies enthrall their souls. It called them to give in and submerge into its growing essence, to merge with its psychically insistent resonance.

"There it is," Mercy said, instinctively crouching low near the rim of the airport tower control building's roof. The others followed suit, immediately making themselves as small as possible, in case prying or scrying eyes might be upon them. "Now," she whispered, "all we have to do is stop the resonance."

"We could just ask Ku'tu," Maynard offered, "politely, if she could just turn into her dragon self again and just stomp on it like Godzilla, couldn't we? Would physically breaking the building disrupt the signal? Is it even that kind of signal?"

Silence answered him. Mercy shrugged. "It's worth a shot, I think. But first, to be safe, we need to do some recon. Make sure things are safe and sound before we just barge in like gangbusters and level the place."

"We did hear screams, after all," Maynard agreed. "Ah, yeah. So, let's forget about the dragon stomping part for now," he added, feeling awkward. He quickly recovered, "That implies that there are still at least a few people still kicking. Potentially innocent people, I might add."

"And there might be others like us," Void said, "drawn by its power."

"Is that the Dragon talking," Mercy asked, "or is that Void talking?"

"Does it really make a difference?" Ku'tu said, flitting up eye-level to Void. "At this point, he's the only one of us who has been right every time. Dragon or not, he's made the right call every time. So while we might think our group is bound by a chaotic form of anarchy, it really isn't, is it?"

"Sorry," Void said immediately. "I'm not that guy. I'm just a simple man, just like the song. To paraphrase Gibran, our chain is as strong as its strongest link. We have no weak links. We're all capable of command and leadership. And, chaotic as that might sound, especially as someone might objectively believe that a group requires a single leader, I think we've been rolling along well with our chaotic command structure. All things considered, perhaps we should continue doing so for now."

"Okay," Mercy whispered back, "I'll take lead for now, because recon is something I do better than anyone. And by that, I mean anyone *ever*. Be back in a bit. Try not to fall off the tower while I'm gone."

With that, Mercy's form shimmered in dull silver-flecked indigo, then she was gone.

Behind them, Vir'gil groaned, "I think I see a tasty... I mean, *lovely* saguaro nearby. I'll be back in a few, too."

"What?" Maynard grated. "You just can't—"

But, indeed, the Entheogenic Lord could, and he did, releasing his essence into the desert air as a flitting cloud of spores. He was over the edge of the roof and gone before Maynard could finish his sentence.

Flitting over to Void's shoulder, Ku'tu settled upon it gracefully. "Don't worry, former humans. I'll stay to protect us. Mercy was right when she said that you had transcended; that you were like us Fae now."

Maynard shot Void a curious glance. "Thank the Mother, someone has been paying attention." He gave Ku'tu a nod. "You are correct, Milady Ku'tu, Queen-consort of the Fae of Aal. We are indeed former humans..."

With that, Maynard's eyes began to emit a diffuse, pleasing play of jungle canopy-green sparks from his eyes. Ku'tu returned his nod.

"Void..." Maynard whispered.

"What, man?" Void whispered back as he continued his continuous interrogation of the Luxor and its surrounding environs.

"I think I can see in infrared..."

Void suppressed a chuckle. "Score another for the boys from Seattle. I think they had this all pegged decades ago. And, yes, I think I can, too. Possibly some UV-based perception, too, I think. Unless the nighttime desert sky makes everything seem as bright as twilight."

Ku'tu let out a tinkling chuckle. "Yes, she was right. That's a sure sign of the Fae. In your case, it probably means that you're once again tapping into your higher chakras. That's a good thing. We're going to need your full power for this. The sooner you regain that, or attain it again, however that works with your race, the better. For my draconic perception is informing me that there is some serious opposition near the Luxor."

"I can't see it," Maynard admitted, his hand saluting his brow as he sought to block out the night sky. It seemed to be no more nor less bright than ever it had been.

"Focus," Ku'tu advised him. "You should be able to discern their auras, even from this distance."

"You mean see their souls?" Maynard inquired. "I don't think that's normal IR or UV spectrum stuff."

Ku'tu laughed, softly. "Of course it isn't. It's the soulsight. Soulsight. It does just what its name implies."

"Fae, or draconic?" Void asked.

"What's the difference, Void?" Ku'tu said evenly, fearing to disrespect him, as normally she would have done.

He recovered, somehow sensing his gaffe. "I truly don't know, Ku'tu. However, judging by your gentle reply, I'd say that they're one and the same. At least on Aal. Who knows about here? Earth hasn't seen a dragon in a very long time, I'd expect."

"You and Maynard are kind and respectful," she said, truly pleased. "That's exceptional. Especially for former humans."

Both Maynard and Void knew not to touch that one. They knew that genocide lurked beneath her dainty Fae façade.

Mercy appeared abruptly, assuming her crouch near the rim of the rooftop. To their credit, no one fell off the tower.

"We've got an issue," Mercyduceus Vendredi calmly informed them.

"I know, Vir'gil's gone," Maynard said quickly, hiking a thumb behind him.

Not missing a beat, Mercy said, "Virge, return."

And so commanded, the elemental did, immediately reincorporating his flying spoor essence into his most common humanoid form. It was the one by which everyone save Mercy knew him.

"Milady," Vir'gil said quietly, bowing quickly.

"Did you see what I saw?" Mercy asked him, ignoring Maynard's dropped jaw.

"I think so," Vir'gil groaned softly. "If by that you mean the newly born immortals gathered round the Luxor."

"No way..." Maynard said. "You mean, immortals like us? Or, how we were right before you-know-who tricked us? The full chakra Monty?"

Vir'gil nodded. "Yes. But eight moreso than nine, for most of them. It appears as if they were realized conventionally, here on Earth. Perhaps several days ago, when the sigil sang. Oh. Save for one of them, who is fully realized and extremely powerful."

"They're still immortals," Mercy said. "Eight. Nine. Whatever. They're still capable of immense destruction, should they so choose. They look dangerous, in any event. We should proceed with caution. By that, I mean we should sneak past them, move right next to the Luxor, then let Ku'tu rain down draconic hell upon it. We can play rear guard in case those guys or their minions attack."

"Minions?" Void asked. "Mortals?"

Mercy nodded, along with Vir'gil. "Yes," Mercy said. "The mortals who've made the cut thus far. There are several hundred gathered either in or near the Luxor. Most are armed with military-grade weapons. They must have looted a base or an exceedingly well-stocked surplus store. No telling what kind of power structure there is, though. They appeared to be randomly distributed, meaning a lack of true leadership. I mean, the very few observation posts they've implemented are obviously of poor quality. They don't even have snipers on the rooftops nearby. Amateurs."

"Or just normal humans who are shocked out of their minds by what's happened," Maynard said. "Wait a sec... Virge, did you say it might have been several days? Is that right?"

Vir'gil nodded. "Yes. Several days. Probably six days."

"Ah, shit, I was afraid you were gonna say that," Maynard said, making a great show of checking his various digital equipment. "I won't even ask how you knew that. My stuff is totally dead now," he said, sorrow in his eyes as he gazed in defeat at his three dead smartwatches. "Hmm. Maybe there's a 'battery' rune..."

Briefly, Vir'gil pointed a pointy finger-vine up at the sky. "The aspect of the Mother begins to hide her bright face."

All of them sought the Moon above. It was full, yet its face was streaked by rivulets of bright crimson, which lent it the appearance of a bleeding skull.

"Holy effing eff!" Mercy gasped. "We went to the Never when it was at its Maiden phase. We've missed days. Dammit! And now it's a true, end of the world Blood Moon. Stupid Lightbringer!"

Maynard audibly winced as he recalled his astronomy. "Yeah, that's pretty bad. We've been gone at least five days, possibly six, like Vir'gil said. We're almost out of time."

"Time to move, then, before we run out of time," Void said, giving the Moon a last, quick glance. "Mercy?"

"Yes?"

"Let's take a Null trip to meet our new friends."

Mercy bit back a laugh. "So you think you know how that kind of thing works now, do you? Null trip? *Really?*"

"Yes, really," he said evenly. "Stepping out to them from the Null will be more spectacular than just walking up to them."

"I could fly us over," Ku'tu said sardonically. "Their terror would be tasty."

"You're our ace-in-the-hole then, Ku'tu," Void said reasonably. "If things start going south, feel free to terrorize them. First, though, we should play this square and level."

"Like Masons," Maynard laughed.

Vir'gil nodded, causing a sprig of acacia to bloom from the top of his head.

"Tards, all of you," Mercy giggled. "Okay, we'll take 'a Null trip'... stupid VoidSpawn... thinking you know the Null or something... and meet these newly realized souls. I hope they're cool. We need all the help we can get."

With that, Shunya appeared, and Mercy rapidly worked her Null Math to an extreme precision, and they were gone.

eVo.144.000.mOd.112.sCe21 | YEAR ZERO | EARTH | UNITED STATES | NEVADA | LAS VEGAS

FLANKED BY NICK AND her crew, Randa squinted at the impossibly bright light marking the juncture of two realities. At the entrance to the Luxor Tram Station, nestled between the paws of the great sphinx, five figures emerged from the shimmering portal one at a time.

At least, *most* of them *looked like* people. The two men, one shirtless and ripped, the other dressed in somewhat disheveled casual business attire, appeared normal enough. Save that the smaller of the two had eyes that emitted a pleasant green hue, while the larger had black eyes that did much the same, except his eyes danced with subtle rainbow hues. The larger one also had a constantly shapeshifting tattoo of some sort on his chest. It, too, was black, emitting the same subtle rainbows as did his eyes. There also was a small winged woman perched on the shoulder of a smartly dressed goth-looking chick with purple eyes, who was arguably an elf. In her left hand she held what appeared to be a black blade, of approximate arm's length and hand's width. Tiny rainbows danced along its edges as it cut the air in its wake. She was flanked by a slightly shorter tree-like humanoid with flowered eye-stalks and tangled roots and vines for limbs. They looked exhausted, as if they'd left something of themselves behind the portal through which they had just walked.

Behind them, the portal shimmered one last time, then closed. The two groups stood in silence, appraising one another, looking for any sign of treachery.

"Blade, Mercy," Void said softly.

"Oops, almost forgot," she lied. She made a show of willing Shunya away, raising it out level at arm's length before allowing it to depart, eliciting shock from those gathered before her.

Except for Randa. She knew them from her dreams, just like she knew the former Vegas mob bosses she had never met, and the team of elemental masters from California, and those kids in the bunker back east.

"So, I'm guessing Lucifer is real, too," Mhyrranda said bluntly. "This ain't none of this just a bad dream, is it?" She shuddered and waved pensively at the group.

Void goggled. "How would you know that? Who are you?"

"Well, sugar, you might say I dreamed it, but that's kinda simplified." She gazed up at Void and winked. "You are bigger in real life, VoidSpawn. Not quite as scary as the Pope, though."

"What has the Pope got to do with this? Are you talking about the holy war?" Maynard inquired.

"Yeah, well. About that," Mhyrranda said. "I've been in his dreams long enough for him to, you know, *see me*, and I got the hell out. That's one head I don't want into anymore."

"Why? What did you see?" Mercy asked.

"Umm, where do I start? We got a pyramid," she explained, hiking a thumb behind her, "he's got *three*, and he's gonna use all the power from them to destroy the world and reach the Devil." Mhyrranda put her hands on her hips and looked at the group. "At least that's what's in his dreams."

"Oh shit," Maynard groaned. "Safe bet that he's been realized, too. Who better than Petrus Romanus to fight the Devil? He's going to try to get to the ZeroTime and fight the Lightbringer. But how is he getting the power to jumpstart the pyramids? That's a global network!"

"Maybe with all the souls he's been sucking from people." A look of disgust passed over Mhyrranda's face. "This one here's charged up just from the local Las Vegas carnage. Maybe a couple hundred-thousand. But Giza, where he's at?"

"Cairo. At least ten million," Void said, grimly shaking his head. "But if the resonant countdown we've discovered is correct, even the metro population, which is about twenty-three million, would have only a million or so still alive. That's another twenty million or so. That's discounting over one billion Catholics who might have already joined him. If he has the capacity to use portals, like the one you just saw... or, Mother help us, make undead with the souls he's been bending and binding..."

"Come on," Mhyrranda said, "let's discuss this in one of those fancy conference rooms inside. I understand they have plenty of Irish whiskey in 'em. And I, for one, could use a drink."

She spun on her bootheel and, looking over her shoulder, wiggled her ass as she headed for the hotel.

As they walked, Dwayne leaned down close to Beth's ear and whispered, "I could use a drink, too. And an explanation of what the hell they were talking about."

"No shit," Beth whispered back, casting a quick glance at the new group. "This just keeps getting spookier and spookier. These guys look serious. And scary."

Hearing that, Ku'tu turned on Mercy's shoulder and blew Beth a kiss, smiling innocently.

After a brief, brisk walk, Mhyrranda entered the lavish conference room, followed closely by Tim, Leta, Dwayne, and Beth. She immediately moved to the bar to examine the selection of bottles. Nick and a couple other men in suits placed themselves on either side of the door, while the rest of the group meandered in. Void sat at the head of the large mahogany table and threw a leg over the arm of the chair. Maynard joined Randa at the bar, while everyone else either stood or sat around the table, glancing back and forth at the unfamiliar faces.

The doors closed, and for a moment, it was silent.

Randa poured herself a double whiskey over ice and leaned against the table, observing the others for small tells. Then, after taking a large swig, she casually asked, "Where's the Lightbringer?"

Maynard walked up beside her and raised his glass to hers. "Cut straight to the chase, don't you?" he asked, smiling his most charming smile.

She smiled at Maynard, her ruby lips glistening. "Yeah, I got questions. Like what the hell did the sigil do to us, and is it permanent? What's my role in all this, and why do I keep dreaming of certain people?"

Void cleared his throat and said, "First we need to know you're on the right side."

Mhyrranda laughed, dispelling the sudden chill in the air, looking at her Elemental team. Beth squirmed, but the others were still, waiting for her answer as much as everyone. "Side? I don't know that we're *on* a side. Maybe it's enough to be on the *living* side. Which is more than I can say for the people surrounding the Pope. In his dream, there were an awful lot of people who didn't quite look like drawing a breath was a priority."

Mercy leveled her gaze at Mhyrranda. "You are a dream caster, but the question is how much power do you have, shaper? Is your template a primal cosmic archetype?"

"Wait, what? Power?" Randa shook her head slightly. "I don't figure it's power. I kinda ride into someone's dreams and if they are lucid, we can communicate. And you know, hang out. It's not like I control them or something."

"Sounds like an even more intimate version of Netflix and chill," Maynard laughed.

A few slightly embarrassed looks passed among the Elementals. Mhyrranda's eyes dropped to her glass for a few heartbeats, and then rose to meet Maynard's. She smiled impishly, and said, "Yeah. We have some fun in the dreams. There are no limits, laws of physics don't apply. Maybe I'll come visit yours sometime, Mister..."

"M. K. 'Maynard' James. Just call me Maynard. I guess we should all introduce ourselves, since we are talking about the End of the World, after all." No one bit, so he continued, nodding toward each in turn, "Mercyduceus Vendredi, the Ninth Null; Ku'tu, who is on her shoulder, she is the Queen-Consort to Zon T'Danu, Overlord of Aal; Vir'gil Plik, the Entheogenic Lord, who appears to be sampling the potted palm; and the former Cory Tate, who now is Void. Mercy, Ku'tu, and Vir'gil are of the Fae. Magick is real. Something called 'Hekatek', a hybrid form of magick and technomagick, is now rising. I think that's what we're seeing with the DNA-looking lights outside."

"What lights?" Nick asked. "You mean the stuff up in the sky last week?"

"I mean the lights running up and down the outside of the Luxor," Maynard replied. "Don't tell me you missed them."

"He can't see them," Mercy said simply as she poured a long line of shot glasses with two bottles of Stolichnaya. "Well, can't see them *yet*," she added, as she finished pouring the libations. There now was one shot for everyone in the conference room, with a few extra. "And now," she said, holding a shot glass in either hand, "I'll show you why he can't see them."

A slight shimmer of purple-white light danced around Mercy's physical outline. Then, in a blur too quick to follow, she handed out all of the shot glasses to everyone in the room, saving Void for last. However, arriving at Void, she saw that he wasn't at all frozen in time like the others.

"Fucker!" Mercy laughed, handing him the second-to-last shot glass. He accepted it with a grin, as Mercy sat down beside him. "You shouldn't be able to match me as your mortal self. I think you might be back in the immortal realm now. Good. We're going to need all the power we can get."

Time returned to its normal flow, which it actually had never left, and gasps were heard around the room.

All eyes were on Mercy, which made her quite happy. "That was nothing. Just a bit of zippity-do-dah that we true immortals can do. If we're the Ninth Null, that is, and all nine of your chakras are actualized."

"Chakras?" Beth asked, perking up. "I know what those are. How can you have nine of them, though. I thought they stopped at seven?"

"That's the normal, mortal limit," Mercy explained. "We Fae naturally have more than that, as we are immortal by nature. Now, however, that the sigil has done its work, forcing every living thing on Earth to adapt and evolve or die, even former mortals are breaking on through to chakras beyond the norm."

"But I broke through," Nick complained. "I *know* I did. I can make force fields," he said, clasping his hands together, causing a small translucent sphere to cover his shot glass and lift it to his lips. "So how come I can't see the lights on the outside? By the way, Skol, bitches," he said, turning the shot up and draining it.

General cheers resounded as everyone toasted and drank.

"Yes, uh... what's your name?" Mercy inquired.

"I'm Nick," he replied.

Randa picked it up there. "Where are my manners? I'm Mhyrranda, that's Tim, Leta, Dwayne, and Beth," she said, introducing each with a nod. "Nick's my shielder and personal bodyguard. Tim, Leta, Dwayne, and Beth are my Elementals."

This drew the immediate attention of the Fae, causing even Vir'gil to stop in mid-munch.

"I see now," said Mercy, giving the four Elementals an appraising look. "Dwayne is Wind, Tim is Earth, Leta is Fire, and Beth is water."

"How did you know that, just by looking at us?" Leta asked. Beth reached over and hugged Dwayne's arm.

"We Fae are of your general kind, Leta," Ku'tu piped up as Vir'gil resumed his munching. "Kith and kin."

"I still want to know why I can't see the lights," Nick said. "Is it because I'm not an Elemental or Fae, like you?"

Mercy shook her head. "It's because you and your crew were realized here, conventionally, by the sigil. With the exception of Mhyrranda, all of you are recently realized immortals. You have eight full chakras and a vestigial ninth, which might or might not go fully active. Mhyrranda has nine, just as we do," she said, indicating her companions with a casual wave of her hand. "We had an encounter with Lucifer, who is named Helel, and also a being of power from his realm, by the name of Maweth. Maweth is the so-called 'Angel of Death', and he came down here, to our plane of existence, to judge Helel. To kill him, basically. Helel tricked him, did some crafty magick using our souls as batteries, and defeated him. In so doing, we were temporarily reduced from our full power down to approximately mortal levels. And..." she paused, finding it difficult to mention dear, sweet Gil by name. "And we lost one of our own. Helel completely took his soul to seal his magicks. We had to struggle to return to Earth, which we've only recently managed to do."

Mhyrranda heard and understood what Mercy was omitting. "So you're not up to snuff yet?"

"Correct," Mercy replied. Though she hated to admit anything about her lack of power to recent strangers, she had to roll with her instinct, which was telling her to trust them. Considering how truly rare an event this was to Mercy, who instinctively had trusted virtually no one for thousands of years until only very recently, she smiled despite herself. "And it felt good to reveal that," she admitted, sharing a knowing glance with Mhyrranda.

"But you can still see and feel the lights and that hum that they're making?" Mhyrranda asked her.

"Yes. But your companions probably can't casually see them. They'd have to be really close to them, and focus really hard, even to catch a slight glimpse of them. Or, to feel their resonance. Unless, of course, they have the Sight, or are otherwise similarly gifted. I have a feeling that they will eventually draw other survivors, as will others located around the world. Whether those survivors can see them or not, they act as beacons."

"Now that we're past the introductions," Void said, "let's get down to business. Vir'gil? Is Aal Ball recharged enough to do the multiscreen morph? A video presentation would be optimal."

"Mmmrph!" came Vir'gil's reply, a few fronds falling from his mouth. "I mean, yes, I think so. Let's see."

With that, Vir'gil shuffled over to the side of the large table, where he then caused Aal Ball to ooze forth from him. The collective entity spilled onto the tabletop, assuming its standard gooey form.

"Aal Ball," Mercy commanded, "form the screens you showed to us most recently and replay everything. No fun stuff at this time, please."

"Aal Ball!" came a bright, cheery sheep-snort from the glistening relic.

Gently, to the utter fascination of those who had not yet witnessed Aal Ball in action, a large array of monitor screens bloomed in silver and chrome. The array almost completely covered the side of the table, reaching up several feet above its surface. Upon them replayed all of the scenes that they had recently witnessed in the Null.

At this point, Maynard, the Master of PowerPoint, got up and made the presentation.

"These show the various stages of how we solved a few pressing issues. Namely, how to retrieve Shunya, that sword you saw in Mercy's hand when we first arrived. And how to solve the mystery of why there was a continuing resonance still in play, globally, after the Lightbringer's Sigil itself had departed. The resonance should have stopped after it left, but it didn't. It kept intensifying in a pattern that we recognized as being a Fibonacci sequence."

"Feeb-a-who?" Dwayne asked.

"Like in that Tom Hanks movie," Leta shushed him.

"Correct," Maynard continued. "And in a lot of natural systems on Earth. It's very much like a kind of secret pattern underlying a lot of stuff. Like the fingerprint of God. And we were lucky enough to see it in the resonant pattern. So, we made the calculations, discovering that, post-sigil, the Earth had only a few days left until the resonances reached a critical, global inflection point. A point after which all life would end. It's a countdown. A final one."

"So the Devil wants to kill everything on Earth?" Mhyrranda asked. "Is that what this is? Book of Revelation stuff, with the blood red Moon?"

"Yes and no," Maynard said. "Helel – Lucifer – set the sigil and its events in place in order to defeat the plans of the One Above, the leader up in the ZeroTime where Helel is from. It's extradimensional. Above us, so to speak. Basically, neither Helel nor his fellows, the Children of the Light, the Shapers, can beat the simulations that the One Above gives them, and has given them, basically forever. So, this time, in our simulation – yes, that's what they consider us, and our universe: a simulation – Helel has loaded the dice, cheating like all Hell, so that he can finally defeat the One Above. We are," he said, waving his arms wide to indicate everyone in the room, "his cheats. We're the ones who are supposed to lead Earth against the Vanth'Vash'Var, the Sentinels of the Anti-Life, the Death Horde, the Lords of the Void. Or, just 'Death Horde' for short. They're the 'end game bad guys' who come down to the simulated Earths and wipe it out. They win every single time. Trillions of times. But, this time, we have a chance to win, because Helel finally decided to cheat and introduce us, immortals, into the simulation."

"So why is he trying to kill us?" Tim asked. "That doesn't make any sense, if he wants us to win."

"The out-of-control resonance isn't part of his plan, Tim," Maynard said. "It's chaotic. It wouldn't normally be happening – it should have stopped after the sigil vanished – but, in introducing his cheats into the simulation, Helel's also introduced some very serious chaos. Big time chaos. And that chaos is what's causing the out-of-control resonance. We have to stop it, or it will build up to a fatal resonance that will kill every living thing on Earth. And we're almost out of time."

"Wait!" Beth said. "That's not fair! We just survived the end of the world. Don't tell me that there's *another* end of the world coming!"

"And another one after this one, if we live so long," Maynard said calmly. "Even if we manage to stop the global chaotic resonance, we still have to deal with the Horde. Fortunately, we think that might be years or even decades in the future, based upon what Helel's revealed to us."

"And you believe what the Devil showed you?" Dwayne laughed. "The same guy whose plans are just cheating and pure chaos? That's stupid."

"But we have no other choice but to stop it, Dwayne," Maynard said. "The countdown is ticking along at twelve-hour bins right now, and it's not showing any signs of stopping or slowing down."

"We didn't sign up for any of this end of the world shit," Tim said, standing up.

"But–" Maynard began.

"You're siding with the Devil then," Leta said sharply, interrupting him. "You're doing the Devil's work. You think I'm gonna help y'all with that? Oh, *hell* no!" Where her hands pressed down on the conference room table, tiny flames appeared and a noxious smoke arose.

"Dwayne?" Mhyrranda asked.

"No smoking in the conference room, Leta," Dwayne said. Immediately complying, he wove his fingers together, bidding a strong, focused breeze to usher the smoke toward the conference room door, which was still closed. Improvising, Nick quickly made a turning motion with his wrist, opening the door wide with a barely visible hand-sized force shield.

"Don't mind that," Nick quickly added, startling the guards posted outside. With a smirk, he gently shut the door with his force shield.

"We're not in league with Helel," Maynard informed them. "Nor are we in league with the One Above. Like Mhyrranda said, we're in league with the living. So we have to take things one step at a time in order to keep the living alive. And the next step is to stop the chaotic resonance before it kills us all."

"So that means taking down the Luxor?" Mhyrranda asked.

"Well, it did," Maynard said, "until you told us about the pope. That changes things. It alters the equation. If he's empowering any of the resonant nodes – the pyramids around the world; they tend to focus and resonate along with the primary resonance node – then it's possible that we could destroy a hundred other pyramids around the world, and not make a dent in the chaotic resonance itself. All because he's basically made Giza Chaos Central. Probably totally self-sufficient, if what you've told us about his soul-sucking is true. And I believe it is."

"He can just keep feeding it power," Mercy said, truly in awe despite herself. "Soul power, from millions of souls. By the Mother, this means that he might actually have a chance to break through to the ZeroTime! That would be most unwise, for it doubtless would draw the attention not only of Helel but also of the One Above, who might just end our simulation with a blink of its eye."

"So if the chaotic resonance doesn't kill us," Nick said, "then the pope's insane attempt to do whatever he's trying to do – fight the Devil or piss off God – will probably get us noticed and ended quick. Tell me that ain't some shit right there."

Tim said, "Oh, it's some shit. Right there." Grimly, he reached over the bar and obtained another bottle. He took a long swig from before passing it around.

"So we need to come up with a plan, ASAP, in order to stop him from doing that," Maynard said.

"What about we sic that big dragon on him?" Beth offered. "The one in the video that the ball thing showed us? The one that got the sword? It's as big as an aircraft carrier."

"*I* am that dragon," Ku'tu said merrily. "And it would be foolhardy to think that, even with my power, I could face such power alone. Armed with the power of a million souls, one would perforce be a living god, and I am no deity."

"That cute little Tinkerbell chick is the dragon?" Tim whispered to Leta as he returned to his seat.

"And she's about 500 feet bigger than the biggest aircraft carrier," Maynard explained. "At least, judging from what I saw. Could be more if that's not her final form or something." He grinned at Ku'tu, who gave him a frosty smile in return.

"I think we've established our bona fides," Void said, slowly standing up. "But in case there's any doubt," he said, his voice growing deep, like distant thunder, "bear witness!"

From the center of his forehead erupted Void's Ajna chakra, slowly opening. The air in the conference room grew still. No one dared to breathe as the Eye of the Dragon manifested from within, gazing upon them.

"IT IS TIME," said a disembodied voice, crashing like an infinity of souls upon them. "BEHOLD WHAT WILL BE."

In their minds they saw the Giza Plateau, the Blood Moon shining down. The formerly decrepit pyramids had been reborn, restored to their former precision and grace. Now, however, instead of the red, black, and white colors of their original casing stones, all three were black as midnight. All sides of the three great pyramids blazed with gigantic triple helix DNA runes which writhed and danced, defying one's stare to comprehend their true form. All hues of the visible spectrum flowed like alien blood from the runes. The glowing pyramidia at their summits issued forth laser rainbow beams of light like Technicolor crowns of thorns.

Atop each of the three pyramidia hovered a single humanoid figure. The first, atop the smallest pyramid, named in this age for Menkaure, was a young teenage girl with shocking blue hair. Around her spacetime seemed to drag and bend, causing the illusion of three distinct, slightly out of phase images of her to appear as one. In the sky above the Giza Plateau, three singularities bloomed like cosmic midnight stillbirths. One was over each pyramid, hovering above the pyramidion of each pyramid at approximately the same distance of the height of each pyramid. Their apparent diameters precisely covered the maximum width of each pyramid. Faint lines of what appeared to be crackling black-bound lightning emanated from the girl. One line connected to each of the singularities at approximately its center, and smaller filaments of the same touched what appeared to be the event horizons of each singularity at nine almost equidistant points. Due to the result of the frame-dragging of the local spacetime, it was difficult to perceive precisely where any filament touched at any given time.

The second, atop the middle pyramid, named in this age for Khafre, hovered the form of a young woman, her red hair rampant and flowing. She was the nexus of a maze of intersecting rainbows running to and from and between the singularities and pyramids. The slight glimmer of some kind of aura surrounded her physically, from head to toe, looking almost like oil on water. It seemed to shift its own colors in time with the colors both of the rainbows and the runes on the pyramids themselves.

The third, atop the largest pyramid, named in this age for Khufu, hovered a man in his prime. Long black hair spilled behind him over his sacred pontifical robes. He wielded a cruel looking paschal staff that was crowned by a tiny yet wicked black blade, upon which a twelve-winged creature of ebony form writhed. Around him whirled a veritable cyclone of ghostly souls, visible to the naked eye, howling in exquisite agony as he bent them to serve his will.

Their mental view shifted to high over the Giza Plateau. From the view overhead, it appeared as if three black holes were poised over the three pyramids, one for each one of them. An intricate double infinity sign of rainbows stood poised over the black holes, its nodes precisely placed, binding them together as one.

Down on the plateau, millions of shambling figures approached from the direction of the Nile in the east. Adjacent to the pyramids, pouring forth from the ancient graveyards to the east and west of the pyramids, came countless thousands of the once dead. Both humans and animals alike reanimated, for the ancient Egyptians were known to bury both beloved pets and funerary offerings along with their dead. Thus, insanely, there were crocodiles, bulls, hippopotami, leopards, and even common cats mixed into the mass of once dead humans. Already, parts of this group of thousands had reached the pyramids, scrambling their way up the sides as best they could. They were an army of angry ants skittering out of their nest to protect and defend it.

All of them in the conference room, before the looming Eye of the Dragon, sharing the same vision, could feel the resonant *thrum-thrum-thrum* of the pyramids. This is what echoed in their minds when, at last, the vision ceased, and the Eye of the Dragon vanished.

Seeing before him on the table the bottle that Tim had started passing around, Void scooped it up and quickly drained it. Then, he sat back down in his chair, heavily.

A full fifteen seconds passed before anyone dared speak.

"Ouch, my head," Mercy groaned. "Couldn't you at least give us a warning before you do that shit, Void?"

"You know how it works, Mercy," Void replied. "It just happens. I have no control over it."

"Sounds like quite a burden to bear," Mhyrranda said quietly. *But that's the Mother...* she thought. Then, in a brighter voice, she continued, "But that's a godsend if I've ever seen one. If it's true – and I suspect it is, considering I saw this in his dream – then he's just shown his hand. But he doesn't know we can see his cards."

"But he's showing us his royal flush, ace of spades high," Maynard said flatly. "He has bound Maweth. We are in for some serious trouble."

"You mean the Angel of Death dude?" Tim said. "That was the thing on his staff? What the heck, man? How does somebody from our world get to use something from the world above us as a weapon? Even if he *was* the pope. Or whatever."

"How can we match the power of something like that?" Beth asked.

"To hell with all that!" Leta chimed in. "What about those black holes? How in the world can anyone stop something like that?"

"And all those freaking zombies!" Dwayne blurted, clearly disturbed. "That's more zombies than I've ever seen before. That's more *people* in one place than I've ever seen before!"

"We *will* win," Void said simply. This instantly stilled the turmoil and gave him everyone's attention. Especially Vir'gil's.

"You will die if you go, Void," Vir'gil blatantly warned him. "I'm sorry to have to say that. You have been a good friend."

Void's feral laughter scared Vir'gil, and everyone else in the room. "*I am become Death, destroyer of worlds!* Death? The Mother herself murdered me a million times when first she visited me. I'll gladly die a million more times to save this world. What I embody is beyond death, Vir'gil – I *am* the Void – though I thank you kindly for your warning."

"Chill, man," Maynard soothed, wondering if Void's uncharacteristic yet quite revealing outburst had just cost them their new allies. Or, had just paved the way for an unnecessary fight. One which he was uncertain that they would win, despite any alleged chakra differences. "We're all good. Death can mean a few things when it comes from Vir'gil. Transcendence is one those things. So is change."

"I am glad that you understand, Maynard," Vir'gil said, a frown growing on his face. "You are going to die, too. Sorry. I really hoped that you'd be able to help me re-seed the Earth."

"All good," Maynard said, dismissing it. "The Mother sets my fate. I am content that I will die saving our world. And if there's anything of my body left," he said, flashing his pearly white smile rakishly, "feel free to use it as compost."

"Don't worry," Mercy chuckled, trying to lighten the mood. "I'll protect him. Maynard, I mean. We actually *need* him," she quickly corrected, full of snark. "Void's toast no matter what happens. Even crossing a street to help an old lady. He'll save her, alright, maybe even catch the car that was about to hit her before it wrecks and kills its driver. Super stuff. But, then, splat, he's dead. He slips over a banana peel, stumbles into a hot dog cart on the sidewalk, and unintentionally strangles himself in its umbrella. Doom, no matter what."

Mercy gave him a wink, then comically pretended to choke herself with both hands. Slowly, Void managed an embarrassed smile.

"Please accept my apologies," he began in a sincere, calm voice. "Channeling the Mother really jacks me up. Gets me aggressive, which normally I'm not. I was just a guy writing computer algorithms for a living, just a few days ago. Now, I'm supposed to be the living embodiment of some kind of cosmic godslayer. I didn't choose it; the Mother did. I had no choice in the matter. But I also have no choice but to play my role in this sordid Passion Play. Free will? Maybe for everyone else. All of you could freely choose just to get up right now and walk away. Not me. My role is writ in fire and set in stone. And the only way I see how to play it – play it to win – is embrace it. Maybe even focus my hate enough to kick it up a notch. Just look at what they've done to our lives. Our families. Our world. They've taken away everything we've ever known. Ever loved. It's all gone now. They stole it from us. No way they get away with this. I *refuse*! No way *anyone* gets away with this! No way they live!"

A creepy yet somehow exhilarating mood flushed over everyone in the room. The War Words from the VoidSpawn were always spoken directly to the soul, though no one in the room yet knew this.

He continued, rainbows shimmering across his wicked black eyes, his voice raw with pent-up, raw emotion. "We stand alone, here, at the end of the world. It's just us now. Just us. There is no one else. We're the last ones in line. We're the last hope for this world. For this cosmos. Some might say that we have no hope. No chance, because we fight against gods and monsters. Let me tell you why they're wrong to say that of us: We are the new gods. We are the ones who bend reality to *our* will. We are one; the new immortals, we are born of metacosmic fire, instantiated by the true Dual-Aspect itself, not Helel and the One Above. What we truly are transcends their pathetic ZeroTime. The Dragon and Chthon, the Dual-Aspect itself, the cosmic union of the

Source and the Void, illuminate our souls. In the ZeroTime, they believe that they are the Children of the Light. No. They are but shadows. *We* are the true Children of the Light. We are the ones who bring the God War to the gods themselves. We fight. We fight for ourselves. We fight for our world. We fight, and we win!"

Faces flushed with pure anger, raw hate for whatever or whomever was to oppose them. Confident now in their hearts and souls, any former semblance of doubt and fear now banished, expectant glances darted from one to another.

Nodding in affirmation of what he saw, Void concluded, "What we need now is an accurate assessment of our powers, abilities, and resources. Our assets. Then, we can forge a plan of attack. We have to do this quickly, too. Mhyrranda? May we start with you?"

She smiled. "Well, sugar, I was just waiting for you to ask. You see, I've been having these dreams..."

eVo.144.000.mOd.112.sCe22 | EARTH | EGYPT | EL GIZA | THE GREAT PYRAMID OF GIZA

"IT'S TIME," MERCY SAID, raising Shunya in a two-handed grip.

"That it is," Mhyrranda agreed. "I sure wish I could help more than this. I hate just staying here and waiting."

"You're our insurance policy, Mhyrranda," Mercy said steadily. "You and Virge are staying here for very good reasons, the least of which is retrieving our dead carcasses so Virge can breathe life back into us. Hopefully. And if this all goes sideways, you're the only one who can peek into the bad guys' dreams to find our dead carcasses."

Vir'gil creaked, just a bit too happy for his message, "Mercy, please remember to tell Void that he's going to die. Maynard, too. I don't think they paid me any mind earlier. In fact, I think they just ignored me. Thanks."

Continuing to ignore Vir'gil, Maynard told Nick, "This Desert Eagle is killer. That brushed finish is tight," he said, returning it to its shoulder holster. "Thanks, Nick!"

"You're welcome," Nick said warmly. "It's an excellent piece. Remember, you have ten spare mags." Sighing deeply, he told

Maynard, "I wish we had time for me to train us all up. Group tactics. It would give us an edge."

Nodding, Maynard agreed, "True. Void told me earlier that you are quite the operator. He knew it at a glance. Something about being able to read souls. So, when we get back, please do so."

Maynard gently patted his new tactical gear, nodded to Nick, then looked at Void.

"Sure you're up to this?" he asked Void, who was grinning at Vir'gil's antics. "You were a crispy critter just a little while ago. And you had help from Aal Ball."

"And from your budding mastery of Hekatek," Mercy added. "You don't have to impress us or anything, Void. The speech was more than enough."

"I've got this," Void replied confidently. "Not like I haven't died before. I think I get a little stronger every time I'm reborn, too. So that helps. Also, I've been recharging like crazy since we've been here at the Luxor node. We all have. And I'm certain that I've got a grasp on what we did back in the Null to make our portal here. I can feel it, almost like instinct now. I can provide the power and guidance for the warp to Giza. Mercy's got the rest."

"Sure do," Mercy laughed. "Try not to play Fire Marshall Bill this time."

"The Fae watch TV?" Beth asked, incredulous.

"We do, but only if it's funny," Mercy deadpanned. "So we don't get to watch much."

Void stood at the feet of the Sphinx at the Luxor, arms at his sides, relaxed. Breathing in sharply four times, he began to move with flowing grace, his body swaying as he centered his chi. Slowly, deliberately, his hands moved before him as if they were defining an invisible sphere. With each movement, a strand of deep purple, vector-precise energy built from the ground to the elevated tip of Mercy's blade. The rest of the team gathered behind, watching his movements, as he wove a pattern against the morning's gathering light.

Noting that the web had been woven to completion, Mercy cut with a swift motion, her stroke resembling a perfectly executed *renzoku sayu men suburi*. Projecting through Shunya with calculated precision and grace, she willed the *there* to be the *here* now, bridging both the Null and the Earth simultaneously

As the pattern emerged, shadows collected, and the assembled group could see a desert, and a full, blood red moon beyond. For a moment the smaller sphinx was outlined by a much larger, far more ancient one. Then, the spacetime frame of the Luxor met with that of the Giza Plateau, and a portal, its edges defined by deep purple vector lines, materialized.

As they stepped through, the dusty air of Egypt merged with that of Las Vegas. The last in line, Void dropped his hands and walked through the portal, which shrank to nothingness behind them.

Dwayne looked up to the eroded face of the Sphinx of Giza and sighed. "Whoa. It's huge. And ancient."

"It's not *that* old, Dwayne. I remember when it was built," Mercy said.

"Never mind the Sphinx," said Leta. "Look at that shit." She pointed to the top of the largest pyramid, the one known as the Pyramid of Khufu. Petrus Romanus, the Black Pope, hovered above the top of its massive pyramidion. Just as in their earlier vision, a cyclone of ghostly souls, visible to the naked eye, whirled around him and above him. The souls wailed in a massive chorus of exquisite agony, as he bent them and bound them to serve his will. Two figures hovered in the air close to him, just outside the boundary of the thrice-damned souls whirling around the Black Pope.

"It's Petrus," said Void, his eyes crackling with blue fire. "They're not yet set up. We need to move, before they can summon the portal to the ZeroTime. Remember the plan. Go!"

They watched the three figures as they began to jog towards the pyramids, roughly paralleling the modern road to the north of the Sphinx. As they increased their pace, they saw one of them open a paired portal to the smallest pyramid, and another one floated up and moved rapidly through the sky towards the middle pyramid. As the floating figure stopped immediately above the pyramidion of the nearer pyramid the other one stepped through the portal and appeared above the farther one. From the top of Khafre, the middle pyramid, a rainbow grew from nothingness, and grew larger against the darkened sky. From Menkaure, first one then another circle of darkness appeared above the two smaller pyramids, steadily growing in size, blotting out the wicked crimson light from the moon. A heartbeat later, a third circle of darkness appeared over the Great Pyramid itself.

Now running, they watched as the black holes grew suddenly large, as large as they had seen them in their earlier vision. The singularities affixed themselves high above the pyramidions, and their bizarre frame-dragging effects circled and danced in the sky, creating unholy maelstroms in the sky.

"Intruders..." hissed a soul slave to Petrus. His head jerking abruptly down, guided by the perception of his whirling soul slaves, Petrus immediately saw the approaching group. For a brief moment he was bitterly disappointed that anyone on Earth would wish to interfere with his divinely appointed destiny. He was, after all, fighting to save the Earth. Sadly, he knew that he must divert a small portion of his growing power, diverting it from his holy task, to stop their interference. Permanently.

"*Venite!*" Petrus Romanus thundered from atop Khufu, his spiritually amplified voice impacting them like a fist to the stomach.

A flash of angry purple light burst from atop the pyramid of Khufu, and Tim stopped, looking to either side of its base. The others slowed to an awkward trot as the sands shifted beneath their feet. They felt the growing vibration as the ground of the Giza Plateau shook, disgorging first dozens, then hundreds, and then thousands of figures. Just as in the vision, there were both humanoids and animals, both being equally dead under the dread eye of the Black Pope, and both being equally unable to resist his call to war. Approximately half of the undead, humans and animals alike, their rotted eye sockets emitting bright purple-and-green light, scrambled and skittered toward them. Others streamed toward the pyramids. Many of these rose into the sky, flying at random, like insects borne on the night winds.

"Guys, those things are coming from the graveyards on either side of Khufu," Tim said.

"Great..." said Beth. "Where's a giant zombie bug zapper when you need one?"

Mercy pointed to the side of the pyramid. "They're splitting up both to cover the pyramids and to block or intercept us."

Meanwhile, from Khafre, the rainbow manifested by Mary Dunbar, the Talisman, split into facsimiles of the Lightbringer's triple strand. Arising high into the air, they quickly formed an intricate double infinity sign of rainbows poised over the black holes, its nodes precisely placed, binding them all together as one.

An uncanny sensation of psychic disconnection passed over all living souls within 1,000 miles of the Giza Plateau, as the elaborately constructed Master Warp slowly began to manifest in its full, true, transcendent form.

The group lurched to a halt at the base of the Pyramid of Khufu. "Shit!" Leta shouted. "There's no way we are getting past that," she said, pointing at a large group of shambling corpses.

Beth scowled. "And the other group is on the other side. Maybe we need to rethink this whole distraction thing."

Dwayne grinned, pointing to a building at the base of the pyramid of Khufu. "Maybe we ride instead." Everyone turned, looking at the sign outside that said *Giza Solar Boat Museum*. "There's a large boat in there, built to ferry the dead king to the afterlife. We're gonna steal that sucker"

"Oh, you've got to be kidding me," said Tim. "No wheels, no water. How are we going to ride in a giant canoe?"

"We fly. Come on." Dwayne ran to the building, followed by Beth, who turned to look tentatively at the others.

"Well, I've never ridden in a flying canoe before." Tim said. "Why the hell not?"

"Let's do this!" Maynard said. "We got this, guys," he told Void and Mercy. "Go!"

Void and Mercy exchanged glances. Then, they rose effortlessly into the sky, while the rest ran after Dwayne and Beth.

"Petrus!" Mary screamed, her voice carried to Petrus and Ami by a small dedicated group of soul slaves. "They're splitting up. Some can fly! What do we do?"

"Continue with the weaving, my Talisman," Petrus told Mary, his own voice still booming aloud like rogue thunder. "And you, my Black Star," he told Ami, "maintain your control. The moment comes soon!"

"Well, at least we got their names," Mercy told Void as they ascended to approximately the height of the top of Khufu's new, brightly shining pyramidion. They maintained a position approximately equidistant from the tops of all three pyramids.

"Ready?" Void asked her.

Two voices replied, one of the coming from the edge of Mercy's sleeve, "Ready!"

With that, Mercy faded from view, leaving not a visible trace, while Void flew up even higher.

Leta stopped for a moment, turning to the approaching crowd of dead. Raising her hands, fingers splayed, she closed her eyes and concentrated. A feral grimace formed and she growled at the monsters. "Get back to the grave!" she shouted, and ten thin lines of flame jetted from her nails. The result was instantaneous, as ten of the densely-packed corpses burst into flames. Those nearest to them also caught fire, and the individual pyres spread into a conflagration among the dry – and more importantly, flammable – corpses.

"Okay, *now* we fly," she said, sprinting to catch up to the others, as they ran through the entrance. Once inside, they turned to see Khufu's boat, suspended in the middle of the building.

"Well, now what?" Beth asked, looking up to the boat above their heads.

"We have to get up there," Dwayne said, running up the sloping walkway, followed by the others. From behind them came the sound of thousands of trudging feet, as the dead approached the building.

Reaching the top of the ramp Dwayne jumped the short distance to the deck of the nearly 150-foot-long boat. With Tim's help, soon everyone was aboard the ancient craft. Dwayne looked at the wall in front of the boat and pushed with both hands, blowing the entire wall off the building.

"Everyone hold on!" Dwayne shouted, gripping the front on the boat. A wind rose from the desert, shaking the boat until the occupants thought it might shake apart. Then, miraculously, the boat lifted, moving forward and out. Now, they were flying above the sands of Giza.

Dwayne pumped his fist, and the boat took a precipitous turn. "Ahh, *oops?* Sorry..."

Tim got a distinctly nauseous look on his face. Beth touched his shoulder. "Are you okay?"

"Yeah, but... I feel like I lost my connection to the ground. I can't focus my power anymore."

"Hey, swing it back around, Dee," Leta said. "I have an idea."

The desert wind whipped their hair as Dwayne focused on turning the boat in a ponderous circle. Leta glanced at Tim and said blithely, "Grab my belt, and don't let me fall." She moved to the side of the boat, looking at the crowd of moving corpses below.

"Okay, but who's got *me?*" Tim took hold of Leta, bracing himself against the wind and rocking boat deck.

Leta lifted her hands and again pointed her splayed fingers in a fan shape over the crowd below. Fire rained from her hands, first in drops, then in growing streams. Every corpse it touched burst into flame, and soon the dead were like a field of fire, growing over the desert floor.

Meanwhile, Maynard took Beth aside and they began placing the oars in the oarlocks. "Let's give this boat a little zip." He winked at Beth. "You understand energy conversion, Beth?"

"You mean like how a windmill turns and grinds wheat into flour, or a water wheel creates energy?"

"Exactly like that. We are in a boat, powered by your boyfriend Dwayne's mastery of Air. We are going to make this boat think that air is water, and we are going to make the oars give it some 'oomph'. Watch the symbol I put on this oar. I want you to draw it on each oar on that side, while I draw it on the oars on this side. Here." He handed her a Sharpie, while he pulled another one from his pocket.

Beth blushed slightly at the comment about Dwayne, then smiled.

Slowly, Maynard drew a pair of symbols on the handle of an oar; one for conversion, one for animation. When he released the handle and stepped back, the oar began to move, and the boat pulled slightly to the side.

"Okay, now you do it. Remember to focus your intent. You *want* the oar to pull the air like water, got it?"

Beth nodded excitedly. "Got it!" She moved to the other side of the boat and began replicating the runes.

Within moments, the boat was gliding faster, and Dwayne looked back with a grin, "I dunno what you did, but it's like the boat has power steering!"

Dwayne turned the boat again, and they made another devastating pass at the creatures on the ground. The ground below was aflame in a massive conflagration. It was at that point they began to realize that their distraction was having results. The flying undead that had been circling the pyramids in unordered droves began chasing the boat. It was an undead air force of vultures, ibises, falcons, and scarab beetles, and their many thousands made it appear as if they blacked out entire sectors of the sky.

"Dwayne! Can you go faster? We've got company!" Beth turned to look from the back of the boat, while Maynard stared at the ground.

"Yes," Maynard said, sharing a look with Beth. "Like *much* faster."

From a mile above the vast, chaotic scene, Void cast his gaze upon the thousands of flying undead. Both the recently resurrected physical undead and the ectoplasmic soul slaves now began to pursue the impromptu flying boat. Now, it was time to act. Taking out the air force, so to speak, would allow them to achieve air superiority. It also would mitigate the advantage that the flyers had naturally over the walkers in the group.

Void's formerly mortal mind, now immortal and geared totally for destruction, easily crunched the solution vectors among all of the thousands of flying undead. His eyes narrowed. He could take out 90% of them. His chest tattoo erupted in blacker-than-black energies. In the span of mere millisecond, a pencil-thin, zigzagging beam of absolute darkness silently streaked first to one flying undead target, then the next, then so on and so forth. Seemingly instantaneously, all of the flying undead, save for the ones immediately around Petrus himself, were struck by a sliver of the Void itself, instantly condemning their essences to the eternal anti-life of the Void.

The effect of the mass annihilation of thousands of flying undead was like a massive, disordered web of cloud-to-cloud lightning, crackling in negative light.

Even over the soul-bruising din of the Master Warp and the amplified *thrum-thrum-thrum* of the resonant pyramids, the screams of multiple thousands of undead souls being permanently damned, dying the second death, made an impression of sheer horror on all who heard it.

"*VoidSpawn...*" Maweth hissed in Petrus' mind. "*Destroy him now, Petrus, before it's too late!*"

"Demented reprobate," Petrus admonished the Angel of Death. "Speak not to me again. Your time comes soon as well, and you know this. I don't need your advice on how to deal with this pretender and his upstart friends..."

Petrus' gaze settled upon the distant Sphinx, and he knew then exactly what he would do.

"Though it take a million souls, thou shalt know life!" he raged, arms thrown high as he tapped directly into his Dark Tabernacle. Conjuring forth a thousand-thousand of those who had fallen under his psychic thrall, Petrus decreed unto all of them to invest the dead stone Great Sphinx of Giza with undead life. Of a major badass kind.

"Destroy the VoidSpawn and his wicked companions!" Petrus Romanus commanded, his voice crackling like living lightning. "Kill them all!"

From the ground to the east, the massive form of the Great Sphinx of Giza began to quake, shedding the dust of the ages, as it rose from its eternal repose. A frenetic storm of silver-tinged lights began to impact it from all angles, each one adding a splotch of glossy, inky darkness to its sandstone skin until all of it was covered. Incredibly, as huge as it already was, its form began to expand and grow heartbeat by heartbeat, its form first filling the entire quarry around it, then expanding to crush the nearby Temple of the Sphinx, then the Valley Temple of Khafre. As it stretched its legs, wings began to sprout from its back, and it grew even more, now covering most of the nearby mastabas with its incredible mass. Finally, it threw its great leonine head back – the face of man no longer required to mask its original, true form – and roared deafeningly before launching itself into the sky, multiple whirlwinds of dust spinning off from beneath it.

Petrus' remaining flying minions, still numbering in the thousands, now began to pummel the frame and housing of the flying boat. The crew had to duck and dodge to avoid being swept over the side by the dead. With the new mobility granted by Maynard's and Beth's runes, Dwayne started to zigzag through the sky above the pyramids.

"Holy shit!" Maynard yelled. "The pope just turned the sphinx into a *kaiju*!"

The gigantic Great Sphinx of Giza, in a huge rush of air, flew across the path of the boat. It exhaled as it passed, breathing a crushing wave of fire at the flying boat.

"Look out!" Leta shouted, instantly countering with a shield of fire. Driven to her knees by the sheer force of the titanic onslaught from the mighty sphinx, her shield of fire began to crumble around the edges, and several spots on the boat caught fire.

"Hang on!" Maynard shouted. He ducked just in time to keep from being snatched up by one of the Black Pope's soul slaves.

With a rapid phase-in at the center of the flying sphinx's massive back, Mercy cut mightily with Shunya. Sparks resembling tiny pinwheels of psychedelic lights showered her as her blade barely scratched its highly artificed surface.

Petrus saw this and mocked, "You cannot harm it, effete faerie, for I have given it the flesh of Maweth! The twin blades cannot harm it now!"

"You asshole!" Mercy shouted right back. She knew that no one was going to hear her non-gimmicked voice over all the commotion, but she knew that it felt better to go ahead and get it out. "It's up to you, now, Ku'tu," Mercy said. "Show no mercy!"

"I never show mercy!" Ku'tu said, flitting out of Mercy's sleeve.

As Mercy phased back out, Ku'tu transformed in the veritable blink of an eye into her draconic Fae form, directly atop the back of the Great Sphinx of Giza.

"You bitch!" Ku'tu bellowed, sinking her teeth deeply into the back of the sphinx's mane. The sphinx roared in pain, banking wildly. This sent both titanic beasts plummeting down into the Western Cemetery, immediately adjacent to the Great Pyramid of Khufu itself. This caused a powerful, localized quake which shook the Giza plateau for miles around. An instantaneous pressure wave from the colossal crash sent any undead not immediately crushed by their massive bodies flying haphazardly in all directions, pulverizing most of them by sheer blunt force trauma.

"Floor it, Dwayne!" Maynard yelled. "Holy shit! I'm glad she's on our side."

Dwayne turned the boat southwest and held tight as the desert wind shrieked behind them, pushing them faster and further from Giza. The flying soul slaves dwindled in the distance, and he made a long arc through the sanguine sky to return.

"I think you bought us a few minutes," said Leta. "What now?"

"We have to stop screwing with the minions and try to take out one of the leaders on the pyramids." said Maynard, coming to the front of the boat with Beth.

Tim looked from one to the next. "How to choose? Let's see, the Pope, that weirdo rainbow chick, or someone who summons black holes?"

"'There are black holes over three of the pyramids now," said Beth. "We should go for the Black Star."

"Seriously?" Dwayne asked. "I don't want to fly anywhere near her – she's *scary*."

"And I think the Pope is way above our pay grade," Maynard pointed out. "Besides, the Talisman is the one doing the weaving. We should hit her and maybe distract the binding."

Dwayne shrugged and turned back to the front of the ship. "It's all too crazy. I'm just going to fly this thing." Beth stood beside him, her hand on his shoulder.

Maynard looked from Leta to Tim. "We need to focus some of these powers. Tim, can you shake that pyramid?"

"First of all," Tim nodded grimly, "I can't really focus on the ground while I'm up here – I need to be in contact with the ground. Second, a pyramid on flat ground is the most stable form of structure there is."

"What if the ground *wasn't* flat? Could you erode the sand under one side?" Leta asked.

"Well... Yeah, that would work. But I'd have to be down there." Tim gestured at the rapidly approaching complex and the thousands of milling undead, many on fire.

Maynard sighed. He searched the boat for a moment, finding what he wanted near the entrance to the ship's cabin: a clutch of spears. Securing two of them, he paused a moment over each, tracing something with his hand on them. Returning, he handed spears to each of them.

"*Hek*atek it is, then. Look, I've added runes to each of these. This one is for Earth, and this one," he said as he held a spear to Beth, "is for Water. You don't have to throw them, just point and concentrate on your powers. Envision your energy striking your targets. Leta's good as she is." He nodded in respect to Leta, as he pulled the massive Desert Eagle from its holster.

"Alright, here we go!" shouted Dwayne.

The boat banked steeply as they dove for the Pyramid of Khafre. The rainbow lights lit the boat, nearly blinding in their brightness. Spears poised, the group took aim at the woman on top, who appeared completely engrossed in her weaving. From the spears came solid bolts of water and stone, and concentrated jets of fire struck the side of the pyramid. Maynard dropped to a knee and fired several rounds as the boat slid past the pyramid mere yards from the woman.

The attacks were fruitless, as each beam and bullet ricocheted from her aura. Sparks of random colors erupted from the places where she had been struck. Mary momentarily paused when the ship circled. Then, she slashed the air in the direction of the helm, sending a brilliant rainbow across the prow.

The boat split in half, crashing against the side of the Pyramid of Khafre, then obliquely sliding down to the desert below.

"No!" Void shouted from high above the plain.

Phasing in next to him, Mercy immediately grabbed his arm.

"Stick to the plan, Void," she shouted. "It's all or nothing now. Nothing you can do for them anyway. You know what's going to have to happen before this is all over. Vir'gil's never wrong."

Down below, Ku'tu and the Great Sphinx of Giza continued to brawl. Void turned his head to face Mercy. "I know that, Mercy. I know this is all going downhill fast. I can sense what's about to happen..."

"So can I..." Mercy confirmed, a growing tinge of fear creeping into her voice.

She and Void cast their eyes down toward the insanity below them. It was now the same as what they had seen during their vision. The black holes were now all in place. Rainbows danced as double, overlaid infinity signs around them, binding the entire artifice to the three pyramids below them.

Something more potent than cold chills and goosebumps assailed the entities gathered on the Giza Plateau. It tested their minds and souls with shocking insanity and the very real probability of instant doom. The silver, shimmering outline of the metaphysical form of the Dragon manifested itself on the Prime, on Earth itself. Bisecting it, a chaotic embodiment of the

Song of the Sidhe danced, twisted runes of multicolored triple helix DNA forming nine distinct chakras.

"The Dragon! I task thee and bind thee to me..." Petrus shouted, as the three pyramidions began to glow like newborn stars.

"Mercy, take out the Black Star," Void said. "Some of the others are still alive, and near enough to the Talisman to try to take her out. I'm heading for the Black Pope."

"Void..." Mercy started to say.

He shook his head. "I have no choice."

With that, he zoomed up with startling speed, ascending out of eyesight. A double sonic boom reached down from the sky to mark his passage.

"Chthon, you're such a cunt," Mercy whispered to herself. She phased out, moving swiftly down to the pyramidion over which the Black Star hovered.

Leta rose from the smoking hull and hobbled to the nearby form of Tim. She shook him softly, and was rewarded by a groan. He was filthy and covered in blood. But as he became alert, she heard a wail nearby, and distant, powerful thunder from above, which pounded twice.

"Where are the others?" Tim asked, coughing. The ground was shaking, quivering beneath his feet, as Ku'tu went claw to claw with the transformed sphinx. Even from 400 meters away, it was hard to hear anything over their crashing, roaring din.

"Don't know. We were thrown clear with the back of the boat," Leta said tersely, wiping blood and sand from her cheek. Movement from the near distance revealed a cluster of shambling dead approaching their location. "We need to move, now."

Tim pointed to a smaller subsidiary pyramid to the south. "There. Let's get to high ground." The pair moved as quickly as they could, pursued by the dead.

From the rise, Tim looked around to see several other groups of minions converging on their spot. He felt Leta press herself close against his back.

"We make our stand here," she told Tim, fire crackling in her voice.

At the top of the pyramidion of Menkaure, Mercy phased into the Prime behind the hovering form of the Black Star. Mercy hovered silently within arm's reach of her, preparing to strike. That's when she heard the teenager crying, speaking to herself in Japanese.

"Please forgive me," Ami said to herself, repeating it like a mantra, the sounds stacking in triplicate around her. "Please forgive me, I regret what I have done. I didn't mean to kill everyone. I just wanted them to go away. I just wanted them to go away. Please forgive me..." She repeated the mantra, over and over, quickly and almost silently, as she manipulated three black holes above her. Sweat beaded on her forehead from the strain of her task. Her lips pursed and her eyes closed tight as she fought to keep from crying.

Though the shocks of recent events had been many, this singular event shocked Mercy to her core. This Black Star, this villain trying to destroy the world, was naught but a young teenage girl, dressed and styled somewhat like Mercy herself. Her soul tortured, like Mercy's own soul.

Despite her better judgement, Mercy dispelled Shunya, then moved around and in front of the girl, still hovering.

"Black Star-san," Mercy began. "How may I help you?" she asked her in perfect Japanese.

Ami's eyes flew open. She stared at Mercy. Tears spilled down her cheeks. This time, it wasn't a ghost talking to her, or that creepy pope and his twisted lapdog, Mary. It was someone a lot like herself. And she spoke perfect Japanese.

"Oh, please help me!" Ami cried out. "Please, you have to help me, I beg you! They're killing me. They're killing me! I don't want to do this, but that creepy man made me! I had no choice! He made me do it! I don't want to hurt anyone!"

"Calm down, little one," Mercy bade her, keeping her eyes open for any tricks. There was so much noise that it was difficult to concentrate. "How do I help you? Tell me how to help you."

Behind them, to the west of the middle pyramid of Khafre, Ku'tu and the animated sphinx battled. Both now stood on their hind legs, the top of Khafre barely coming to their midsections. Fortunately, both the rainbows and black holes overhead were hundreds of meters above their heads.

"I can't stop it!" Ami told her. "My name is Ami. I am not a Black Star. I'm just Ami. And it hurts. It hurts! Please make it stop!" she pleaded.

Mercy wanted nothing to do with black holes or singularities, but she was not getting far in her questioning. And Ku'tu and her equally titanic opponent were heading in this general direction.

"I'm sorry, sweetie," Mercy said graciously, "but I think I'm going to have to knock you out to make it stop. Is that okay?" she asked. She couldn't believe she had lived so long to hear that particularly less-than-lethal question ever be uttered from her mouth.

"I don't care! Just make it stop. Make it stop! It's killing me! It's k–" *Klonk!*

Not really knowing what else to do, considering how everything had recently gone into the shitter, Mercy compelled her magicked sleeve to unfurl, grab Ami's slumping form like the stomach of a starfish – *Hah!* Mercy thought. *A starfish for the Black Star!* – and whisk her safely back into storage. Where there was actually a nice place to curl up and sleep, almost like a silken sleeping bag. So it really wasn't that bad, she thought. But staying visible in the Prime was, so she phased back out. Despite removing Ami from the casting, the black holes remained in place, not at all affected by her disconnection from them.

Overhead, a faint, barely visible rift began to form high above the artificed construction of black holes, rainbows, and entrained, resonant pyramids.

"No! Dwayne!" Beth screamed.

Beth rushed to the two figures near the prow of the broken boat. Neither moved, but it was obvious why Dwayne was still – he had been neatly bisected by the rainbow as it sheared through the boat. Beth held Dwayne's head on her lap, oblivious to her surroundings until shaken from her reverie by the roars from the black sky above her. Looking toward Maynard's still form, she crawled to him and felt for a pulse.

"No! No! DAMN IT!" Beth's head bowed over Maynard's body, and her tears struck his cheeks. As they did, a glow spread over his face, and he opened his eyes.

"Oh, man," he said. "I feel like my entire body just took a hit from that sphinx up there. And then there was a nice, cool dip in the pool. Pardon me while I pass out..."

Beth looked stunned for a moment, then cocked her head at the dead shambling past her. The pyramid of Khafre was clear. And at the top, the rainbows were beginning to coalesce clearly between each of the Great Pyramids. With a scowl, Beth rose and began moving toward the base of Khafre, first walking purposefully, then running. As she encountered the pyramid, screaming in rage, she manifested water from the nearby Nile, bending it into physical reality as a continuously replenishing wave. Then, quite literally, she rode the wave up the side of the pyramid.

Tim knelt at the top of the short structure, as if sensing the ground for miles around.

"I could do it, but there isn't enough time." he said, raising his chin to the mass of dead coming from all sides.

Leta, looking beaten and bruised, sighed. "Do what you can. I ain't done yet." Tim closed his eyes, and she stood behind him, lifting her hands over her head. "I'm gonna burn 'em *all*."

A burst of flame erupted from her hands, growing larger, and Tim felt as if he were burning beneath the summer blaze of a desert sun. His hands flat on the ground, he felt miles of sand, and far beneath that, the Earth's crust. As Tim felt the sand, clay, and limestone beneath the massive structures, he intuitively knew that he could move them. As the sweat rolled down his face, the ground began to quake, and millions of tons of earth shifted.

Meanwhile, the growing fireball above Leta reached a critical mass and exploded outward, washing over the thousands of enemies that walked, crawled, and leapt for the pair.

Reaching the top of Khafre, Beth slowed, her hands on her knees as her manifested wave dissipated. She was now before the red-haired woman wreathed in living rainbows. Panting and exhausted, she looked at her closely. Mary floated gracefully above the apex, but the strain was evident on her face.

"You're too late," Mary said. "The binding is complete." Something in her eyes spoke of sadness, and this was the ultimate irony to Beth.

"I don't care about the binding. Or Petrus. Or any of it." With hateful effort, Beth forced herself to stand up straight. She stared hard at Mary. "You killed my boyfriend."

"Oh, that's it, then?" Mary looked dumbfounded. "The end of existence is at hand, we are trying to right a cosmic wrong, and you are pissed off because your *boyfriend's dead*? Look around. There are millions of corpses on this plateau."

Beth shook her head, incredulous. "Corpses that your Black Pope animated! How does necromancy even *begin* to right a wrong? You know what? *Fuck you.* There is no way you get the moral high ground here. Murderer!" Beth pointed her finger accusingly at Mary, her arm stiff and unyielding.

Mary looked amused and skeptical. "I'm the Talisman. I bend and bind all energy like it's nothing. What exactly is it that you think you're going to do to me with your stupid water power? Cry me a river?"

Shaking her head, Mary held up her hands, trying to weave a ward between her and the blonde girl beneath her. But she was so weary from the binding. And so thirsty she could barely think. She watched the backs of her hands, wondering why they looked so withered. And when she touched her cheek, she could feel the skin, dry and papery. Abruptly, she ceased to float in the air, and went to her knees before the young girl. She looked up at a face devoid of mercy. Then, everything went black, and she rolled down the side of Khafre, as dried and desiccated as the mummies she had once studied.

"You can't bend and bind hate, bitch..."

Beth watched her tumble, a grim satisfaction on her face.

She looked up at the myriad lights weaving above her, playing subtly around the infinite blackness of the multiple singularities. So pretty.

And then the first tremor hit.

Behind her, a sound like the exhaust end of a Saturn V rocket erupted, and Beth saw Ku'tu getting a face full of the sphinx's fire breath. In sheer rage, Ku'tu went low, clipping into the sphinx.

Both titans fell into the western side of Khafre, crunching into its face, causing another low-scale earthquake, as thousands of tons of displaced blocks fell to the plain.

Beth made her way down the side of the tilted pyramid, sliding and tumbling while the ground still shivered and shook from the impact of the behemoths on the other side. She staggered back to where Maynard lay. She was nearly exhausted. As she dropped to her knees, she checked his pulse to be sure it was strong, then placed a hand on his forehead.

"Skin against skin, blood and bone, you're all by yourself but you're not alone," she whispered.

Squinting through one eye, Maynard replied with a smile, "Nothing wrong with me..."

"Then get up, ya slacker!" she said. "One down, but we gotta move."

"HEY!"

Beth looked up to see a pair of figures running toward them. "Tim! Leta! You're okay!"

"Where's... Oh no." Leta looked down at Dwayne's body. "Fuck."

"Come on," Tim said. "Help me with this. We have to get the body back to the Luxor. Vir'gil said he could bring people back to life."

Beth helped Maynard to his feet, while Leta and Tim wrapped Dwayne's body in a canvas from the nearby boat wreckage.

To their southwest, the towering forms of Ku'tu and the animated Great Sphinx of Giza tumbled together in a massive wrecking ball. They destroyed the enclosure walls of the Pyramid of Menkaure, coming to a stop at the base of the smallest of the three great pyramids.

Enraged and in pain from magickal fire from the sphinx, which had melted through her formerly impregnable draconic skin in several places, Ku'tu finally gave into the beast within her. Summoning her energy for one last blast – an all or nothing gambit, for she was now close to total exhaustion – she reached out toward the sphinx, batting down its feeble attempts to ward itself from her mighty grasp. With a quickness belying her massive frame, she brought the sphinx in dangerously close to her own face, staring into its shark like, lifeless eyes.

Then, Ku'tu let fly with her most massive blast, unleashing hell upon the hapless sphinx. Her phlogiston breath, now finally unleashed directly in fatal proximity, impacted the glossy black face of the artificed sphinx. The scouring gout caused the face of the sphinx to glow white hot, then beyond mere heat as it reached the stage of atomic fusion. Petrus' boast notwithstanding, not even Maweth's supreme armor could endure such an assault. The sphinx's head melted completely, devoured by the ultimate fire.

Still enraged, and still spewing a steady stream of phlogiston, Ku'tu hefted the massive form of the now headless sphinx high over her head. Then, she cleanly body slammed it into the Pyramid of Menkaure, eliciting another massive, localized quake. Flexing her arms before her, cloaking her massive wings around all but her face, she continued to pour impossible amounts of phlogiston upon the ruined form of the sphinx, and the now-doomed Pyramid of Menkaure itself.

For many millennia Menkaure had stood, practically immune to the predations of both man and nature. Yet, on this day, the smallest of the three great pyramids of Giza met its match in the form of Ku'tu, the Queen-Consort of Zon T'Danu, Overlord of Aal – and the mightiest dragon of all.

Mercy phased in, near Ku'tu's head. She pointed toward Khafre. "Stomp that effing effer into the ground, baby!"

"NYAAARRR!" Ku'tu cheered, moving toward Khafre. Then, in the tongue of the Fae, she told Mercy, "I don't think I can breathe again. Beyond drained at this point."

"Then just fucking stomp it like an ant bed," Mercy replied. "Or, if you'd rather, stomp it like maybe you used to stomp human skyscrapers on your world."

"NYAAARRR!" Ku'tu agreed, picking up her pace. Flapping her wings, she lowered her shoulder, gathering speed, a hurricane force of wind scouring the dust of centuries around her.

Phasing ahead of her, Mercy appeared near Beth. "Get down, now!"

Realizing that there was no way to protect everyone from Ku'tu's pyramid destruction in time, Mercy summoned Shunya. She held it overhead, cutting into the local spacetime and establishing a portal to the Null over their heads. It was just large enough to cover them as they huddled up together. Mercy strained and held the portal for nearly a full minute as Ku'tu raged against the titanic pyramid. Mercy dropped to one knee, exhausted, as the last stone fell through.

As the last echo of destruction faded, they heard Ku'tu's massive voice boom, "It's gone, but nothing happened. The ritual is complete!"

"Damn it!" Mercy exploded, whipping Shunya once widdershins over her head, banishing the portal.

There, above them atop the Great Pyramid of Khufu, Petrus Romanus, the Black Pope, held his blasphemous paschal staff high. He appeared to be enraptured, his eyes flickering open and shut like a strobe light. Above them all, the black holes yet remained, as did their binding rainbows.

Beyond that, a bizarre strangeness loomed. A great hall was in sight, filled with tier after endless tier of chrome like spheres, meticulous in their order and arrangement. The very sight of it caused the mind to question its sanity, as if one were literally peeking behind the eldritch curtains of Reality itself. It was not meant for the eyes of those of this world. Yet, impossibly, Petrus and his two slaves had managed to rip asunder the veil 'twixt Here and There, for all the world to see.

Though it loomed above them, they knew that they dared not gaze too long at it.

"Ku'tu?" Mercy inquired loudly.

"Yes?"

"Let's give it a shot. I'm going to open a portal above him and try to assassinate him on the way down. You try to bull rush and get his attention."

"Done."

Mercy looked over the group. "I'm not going to ask anyone else to come. You've all come far enough. Be ready to run at all possible speed once I do this."

"But we can–" Beth objected.

"No, you can't," Mercy said. "You've done your part, and you did it well. Now it's time for you to run away, so you can fight another day. You and your friends are the future of Earth. When the Horde comes, kick their nasty asses. Farewell, and thanks."

Ku'tu began an immediate charge toward the Great Pyramid of Khufu. Mercy phased into the Null and rapidly moved beyond the top of the pyramidion, above which Petrus hovered, levitating in ecstasy.

Though she knew she couldn't afford another draconic breath, Ku'tu knew that slamming into the top of the pyramidion with a megaton of force would definitely get the thrice-damned prelate's attention.

As she barreled toward Khufu, half-flying, half-running, the Black Pope's eyes suddenly flickered open. With no outward sign of power, Ku'tu's forward momentum was immediately checked, and she was sent flying back hundreds of meters, slamming into the last remnants of Khafre. Unconscious, she instantly reverted to her tiny Fae form, and was lost in the dust arising from the impact.

As Mercy arrived above where Petrus hovered, his head suddenly turned up. His darkling eyes locked on hers. She was somehow not shocked by his being able to see her, even though she was in the Null.

Still believing she was faster than he could ever be, Mercy flicked Shunya, opening a portal over his head. As she fell from the air above his head, she directed Shunya down with both hands, aiming for the top of his head. However, her blade impacted instead with an invisible field above him, and threatened to jerk from her grasp. Black sparks erupted like a tiny geyser from the place of the cut. Her boots struck the field a fraction of a second later, and a numbness spread rapidly up her legs. Comically, she momentarily ran in place, mere feet above his head. Then, striking madly at the field, she slid slowly down its apparently hemispherical face.

Her body tingled, and her arms felt numb, yet still she continued to cut. She quickly discerned the faint outline of his field, which covered almost all of the top of the pyramidion. Gathering herself, she sprinted back up to the top of the field above him, then cut down toward his head. But she might as well have been moving in thick molasses, for the aura drained her entire waveform like some starving singularity.

Petrus easily parried her attack with a swift movement of his paschal staff, allowing the energy feedback from the Hatefang to course through the staff. The force was like that of a dozen tasers tagging her simultaneously. Stunned for but a second, she slid awkwardly down the field, falling almost to where it intersected the pyramidion. By instinct alone, she adjusted her mass down to virtually nil, which arrested most of her motion.

"Void!" Mercy bolted up immediately, screaming at the sky. "Now would be a great time for you to–ˮ

"Silence!" Petrus commanded her. He stared fiercely at her. "Look around you, you ingrate! Servitor of Lucifer! You and your febrile, impotent companions have achieved nothing! The Master Warp to the ZeroTime has manifested! Helel!" he screamed, booming, raging at the sky overhead. "Helel! I call you and your insane master out! Face me! Face me, or I'll command the Dragon to destroy your pathetic plane and damn all of you to the Void!"

Silence, and its dread master, Indifference, greeted Petrus.

"I command you, in the name of the Dragon, to hear my command!"

Again, silence. Save for Mercy's mocking laughter.

This infuriated Petrus. "You mock me? *Me*?" he asked, unbelieving. "I, and only I, have dared to confront those who would destroy us! Only I have dared! What have you done, pathetic faeric?"

"I've distracted you long enough for this..."

As Petrus frowned, puzzled, the night sky above burned brightly, as a tiny yet fierce light bloomed at the horizon. It flashed toward him at an angle just below the edge of the black hole above him. After a mere second of time, the force of an orbital reentry impacted into the seemingly indestructible sphere of energy around the Black Pope. Improbably, there was no normal distribution of earth-shattering force from the impact, which instead was almost totally absorbed by the sphere of protection around him. 'Almost' being the operative word.

For there had been a single iota too much energy for the sphere to absorb. Nothing more than the scream of a butterfly. Yet, this single iota had been enough to provide the millisecond of vulnerability necessary for Void to annul the sphere and penetrate it.

The flight and the subsequent impact with its abrupt deceleration from orbital-relative velocity to virtually nil had taken its toll on Void. Stunned, momentum arrested, he fell gracelessly through the breached field, sprawling awkwardly on the floor of polished black stone atop the pyramidion. Hatred burning, Void could do nothing but stare heavily at the Black Pope. Yet, still, Petrus was foolish enough not to end him then and there.

"What?" Petrus shouted even as the sphere of protection blinked back on. He stared for a moment, amazed at the figure on his hands and knees before him. "There was no way possible for you to breach my shield. I know this, because Maweth himself taught me how to weave it to ward you." He said this, hovering back a few paces from the intruder.

Petrus appraised what he saw. "I have no earthly idea why Maweth feared you so, VoidSpawn. You should have heard him when you appeared. He was whimpering like a beaten dog, in fear of his life. And from whom? You? You're nothing more than an aberration. You could have joined us and saved this world from those who would destroy it. But you chose poorly and sided with Lucifer. As such, you and your companions have earned damnation. Once I have bent Helel and the One Above to my will, I will grant you and your companions your due."

"They aren't even listening to you, feeb!" Mercy called out, slowly levitating up. "You're too small for them to even notice."

"Oh, so you have some life in you yet, eh, faerie?" Petrus taunted her, raising his paschal staff above his head in a two-handed grip. In a trice, it assumed its true eight-foot-long form. Its true form. Hatefang.

Mercy taunted him right back, waving Shunya around like a conductor's wand. "Lower that shield of yours and I'll put you down like the combat slob you truly are, boy-buggerer!"

His ego would not allow that to pass. He had just achieved something no other on Earth, in its entire history, had achieved. And he had made it look easy. This salty trollop with her effete, ineffective blade was no match for the Hatefang. It was thus that Petrus allowed his sphere of protective warding to fall.

"That's PRIDE fucking with you, Pete!" Mercy taunted him, Shunya coming around into an unusual defensive pose that none of Petrus' soul slaves had revealed to him. "The same kind of pride that makes you think you can just snuff all the souls on Earth, just so you can stroke your own ego and talk to God. How can you save the world by killing everyone on it? Ever stop to think how insane that is? How insane *you* are?"

Snarling, Petrus flew at Mercy and cut with the Hatefang. Mercy, however, simply waited for the blow, easily parrying it aside with a casual flick of her wrist. Sparks of spacetime flew, even as tiny pinwheels of rainbow lights flitted wildly about them. Overextended, Petrus fought to regain his balance, still hovering a few feet above the pyramidion.

"Bitch!" Petrus sneered. Regaining his balance, he shouted loudly, "You are nothing! Nothing!" Moving with more grace this time, he reared back with the mighty Hatefang, holding it high overhead as he prepared for a devastating cut.

This time, as he swung down with all his might, Mercy did not move. Instead, she phased, becoming immaterial. And in her place was Void. Petrus had no time to react as Void caught the cut from Hatefang between the palms of his hands. This time, there were no flying pinwheels filled with rainbows. Instead, there was nothing but Petrus Romanus, Hatefang, and a very angry looking Void, who immediately launched a devastating kick into his groin.

Petrus fell unceremoniously to the pyramidion below him, sliding down its side until he came to the edge of the top of the natural pyramid itself, some fifty feet below.

"Mercy?" Void asked her, still holding Hatefang in his grasp. Casually, he flipped it, catching it in two hands by its pommel. Curiously, its typical display of triple helix DNA runes was dismally quiet. "You have to leave now. Please go. Gather the others and get out of here."

Mercy shook her head. "Not gonna happen, Void. We've got him right where we want him. We have the upper hand."

"No, we do not," Void explained. "The only way to kill him now that he's done all this shit – tapping into the Dragon here, blending his personal power into it –" he said, pointing Hatefang at the pyramidion, "we have only one option. That's for me to run him through with this thing, impaling him into his own place of power, which will sever the connection here with the resonant death sequence. And, hopefully, hide us from the prying eyes of the ZeroTime before anyone up there notices."

"You believe Helel when he said that no time passes up there during a sim? You actually believe that?"

Void nodded. "Yes. But, even so, we can't take that chance. It's time for you to go, Mercy. See you in the next world, and don't be late..."

"Void!" she called out. But, somehow, the sphere of protection had returned, this time issuing forth from the focus of Hatefang, which Void now held. "Void! No! You can't do this! Stop it!" she screamed, hacking at the sphere with Shunya, to no avail. "Stop it!"

Implacable, Void descended to the prostrate form of Petrus Romanus, violently hauling him to his feet.

"Mercy! Milady!" Ku'tu pleaded. She was her tiny form again, bloodied and missing part of a wing. But she was yet strong beyond mortal ken, and she hauled Mercy away through the air as quickly as her little mangled wings would allow.

Mercy watched in horror as Void flew up to the top of the pyramidion. Petrus screamed, squirming helplessly in his adamant grasp. Ku'tu picked up speed, crossing the Giza Plateau as fast as she could to rejoin the group. Transfixed, Mercy witnessed Void plunge Hatefang deep into Petrus' chest. Petrus Romanus, the Black Pope, screamed in total agony. His writhing form lit from head to toe with baneful black light; an alien, otherworldly death sentence of the soul.

Mercy saw no more details, due to the angle, as Ku'tu flew them both back down to the group. However, the entire sky above the top of Khufu now appeared to be burning with an eldritch black fire, whose alien hunger bit deeply both into the pyramid and what binds Reality together.

The *thrum-thrum-thrum* reached its final crescendo, delivering its final promise to all with whom it had achieved resonance.

A brilliant white flash, like ground zero in a nuclear explosion, moved in seeming slow motion toward them. They screamed in silence, unable – and at least in one case, unwilling – to escape their fate.

eVo.144.000.mOd.112.sCe23 | YEAR ZERO | EARTH | UNITED STATES | NEVADA | LAS VEGAS

A THICK CLOUD OF DUST and billowing sand followed the group as they emerged from nowhere into the cool marble interior of the middle of the hotel. Several of the group immediately fell, their hands clutching at their ears and eyes. The others stood blinking and looked at their surroundings, wondering how they had escaped.

A crowd was waiting, with Vir'gil and Mhyrranda in front. The pair stepped forward, with Mhyrranda waving forward several designated medics from the waiting group.

As the medics handed out water and began tending the survivors' myriad wounds, Mhyrranda approached Mercy and a very confused Ami. The Japanese girl looked frightened, but stood quietly, watching the Fae for cues.

"You did it!" Mhyrranda beamed. "You saved the world! We watched it through Aal Ball." Careful with her words, she added in a lowered voice, "I'm very sorry about Void. He was amazing."

Mercy looked at Mhyrranda blankly for several seconds, her Fae expression unreadable. She then turned without a word to the others, who had now gathered around Dwayne's body, where it lay upon the canvas. Beth was kneeling beside it, crying softly as she gently stroked Dwayne's face. Maynard was speaking quietly to Vir'gil, the Entheogenic Lord shaking his head sadly.

"I fear I cannot do anything for him in this state. He must be made whole first." Bending over the body, Vir'gil reached down with a multitude of leafy branches, tendrils slowly sliding along the halves of his torso where Dwayne had been bisected. As the tendrils drew taut, the body slowly reformed, fibrous strands left behind to bind the two halves.

Beth looked up into Vir'gil's slowly undulating leafy shade, asking incredulously, "You mean you can bring him back to life after being cut in half?"

"As long as there is a fragment left of the body that can be regenerated, I can return the *Ka* to its vessel. That is to say, so long as the spirit has not yet gone on. In time, I can teach this to you, too – for you have the waters of life flowing through you."

"And Void? What do we have to do to resurrect him?"

Vir'gil's canopy stopped moving abruptly as he regarded the young woman. "Why, nothing. The blast in Giza atomized everything within many miles. There is literally nothing left of his essence to recover. I'm sorry, but he knew he was going to his death."

"He's not dead! He can't be!" Mercy shouted. As all eyes went to the Fae, she continued. "He is my syzygy, I would know if he were dead. I feel nothing." Her eyes blazed as she stared defiantly at the assembled group. Maynard moved slowly toward her, all too aware of the deadly potential in the woman.

"You feel nothing wrong, or you feel nothing *there*?" Maynard asked carefully.

Mercy's eyes closed as she reached out beyond her physical awareness. She searched for his presence, searching for something, anything that would indicate he was still living.

"It's not fair!" she wailed, her hands clenched into fists, which she raised above her head. "Chthon! You bitch! I hate you! You took him away! I've waited 13,000 years. I did everything you asked me to do. And now, you finally give him to me, then you just take him away! Why? WHY?"

With a gasp Mercy fell to her knees, her features growing pointy and chaotic as she began to cry. Slowly, silently, she willed herself to fade away from sight. She focused on clarity and calm, now that everyone wasn't staring at her, and her features returned to her control. Upon simple reflection, there was more to this than anyone knew. Vir'gil had said that both Maynard and Void would die, and they did. But Maynard was now alive. Dwayne would live, too, she knew from experience. Death wasn't always death, she knew. Sometimes it meant change. So why not Void, too? Something – *someone*, she corrected herself instantly – had returned them safely here, to Las Vegas, and it hadn't been her, or anyone else. She promised herself that she would not rest until she knew why. And who. Thus, in supernatural silence, she left the group to go retrieve Aal Ball.

"There you are, young former human. Welcome back to Las Vegas," remarked Vir'gil, as Dwayne's eyes blinked open. Looking around, he jerked wildly until he was crushed in a hug by Beth.

"Ow! Easy there," Dwayne cried. Looking around at the gathered crowd, he asked, "What happened? Did we win?"

"Yes, we won! I'll tell you all about it soon enough." Beth smiled, leaning forward to kiss a confused and very embarrassed Dwayne on the lips, while Tim and Leta smiled at each other.

. . .

"So that's it, then? The resonance was broken?" Mhyrranda looked questioningly at Maynard over the bar as she poured another drink for the two of them. "I can still feel the Luxor humming..."

"Well," Maynard said, sipping his whiskey. "The Giza pyramids are gone, and the worldwide feedback is over. Petrus' plan failed, even though he opened the ZeroTime temporarily. But the rest of the primal sources are still active, waiting to be tapped."

"And Petrus?" Mhyrranda sipped her drink and eyed Maynard.

"Like Cory – I mean, Void; Cory was his name from... from before – just gone. The amount of power in that blast took out everything for miles. The Nile river was diverted, and there is now a lake where the plateau of Giza used to be. Nothing could have survived that blast." Maynard tossed back the drink and pushed the glass forward for another.

"But what happened at the end? How did the rest of you wind up back here instead of being consumed?" Mhyrranda twisted a lock of hair around her finger, and shook her head.

Maynard paused for a long moment, regarding the redhead. "I have no clue. If I were a betting man," he continued, glancing around the vast interior, quiet in the absence of the sound of people and slot machines, "my money would be on Lucifer. Who knows? Maybe he had a failsafe routine that pulled us out at the last possible moment."

"So what now? Are we all going to keep dying until the clock runs out? Because if that's the case, I'm dragging you off to bed and going out with a bang."

"I think we stopped the countdown when we overrode the resonance," Maynard said. "But, you know, just to be on the safe side, maybe..."

"Maybe nothing, fool." Mercy strode through the door, followed by Ami, Vir'gil and Aal Ball. "Aal Ball, show them."

Aal Ball hopped up on the bar, spreading out into the shape of a large video monitor, nearly spilling the glasses of whiskey in the process. "Aal Ball!" the construct bleated, as a still image of the Great Pyramid formed. The cyclopean structure was backlit by a blood red moon, askew black holes, and the beginning of a massive explosion at its top.

"What are we looking at, exactly?" Mhyrranda asked, finishing her drink.

Mercy raised an eyebrow, pointing to the top of the main pyramid. "Look here. The pyramidion of the great pyramid." Her black fingernail indicated an oddly shaped blackness.

"Well, I'll be damned," Maynard said.

"What? What is it?" Mhyrranda looked from one to the other.

Maynard smiled, sensing where this was leading. "That's the pyramidion itself. The locus and focus of its primal power."

Mercy looked pleased. "And take a close look now. Aal Ball, forward a few seconds and zoom in on that spot."

"Son of a... Is that what I think it is?" Mhyrranda exclaimed.

The screen grew impossibly bright, causing everyone to shade their eyes against the incredible explosion. Slowly, digital frame by digital frame, the replay advanced, stopping at a precise and quite singular frame. It had to be the last one before the Great Pyramid of Khufu's total destruction. Almost imperceptible, faintly imposed upon the volume of disintegrating blackness that was formerly the pyramidion, was a winged serpentine shape. It coiled around an egg with nine constantly morphing chakras superimposed on its surface.

"Void is One with the Dragon," Maynard confirmed, a tear of hope in his eye.

EPILOGUE 1

Denny came in on I-20, and the smoke was still boiling out of parts of West Atlanta. Further off, near downtown, he saw search lights crisscrossing the sky. Following the lights, he eventually took the McDaniel exit, and turned right on Northside Drive. As he approached the stadium, the atmosphere seemed festive at first, with scores of bonfires. But there were an awful lot of people with guns, and some of them seemed angry. The nearby neighborhoods seemed untouched by fire so far, but this had to be the weirdest tailgate party Denny had ever seen.

Near the entrance to the stadium, where the lights were, a crowd of people were gathered around another large bonfire by the base of a silver avian statue. *Probably a falcon,* Denny figured.

Denny pulled up and got out, striding toward the group. *Might as well look confident. I hope they don't shoot me...*

Moving closer to the figures in the firelight, he froze for a half-step. *Are those... gorillas? Holy shit, the world just got even weirder.*

Considering the four gorillas, it was almost natural to miss the two people next to them. A very large man approached him with an arm extended. It was only after the man stood towering over him that Denny registered just how large he was – he had to be eight feet tall. His skin was a glistening black, and he was bald with wire rim glasses.

With a very soft voice that didn't come close to matching his size, the man said, "Hey. Are you the man who does runes? We thought you'd be along soon. Or at least, that's what Lucy here said. I'm Peaches, and this is Lucy," Peaches greeted him, extending a troll-sized hand.

The diminutive woman next to Peaches had pale skin, fiery red hair, and golden eyes that looked burnished in the firelight. She nodded and smiled enigmatically.

"Pleased to meet you," she said quietly.

Denny shook Peaches' hand and smiled back at the woman. "Hi – I'm Denny. And I've been dreaming about this place. It's like an unfolded origami pyramid, isn't it?" he said, admiring its unusual construction.

"Precisely," Peaches replied.

Denny smiled, returning his gaze to the giant. "Peaches, huh? A nickname from before?"

Peaches smiled winningly, spreading his arms and indicating his frame. "Yeah, I know. Before the sigil, I was a grad student at Morehouse College, five foot eight and rail thin. Now I'm putting out fires and relighting Atlanta."

Denny smiled back at the man's lilting voice, and wondered if Peaches didn't have his own form of persuasion.

"And forwarding the evolution of a species. Don't forget that," said one of the gorillas, who had approached the group silently. "Hello, my name is M'Tumba."

Denny stared at the gorilla, and grinned. "No shit."

M'Tumba made a decent approximation of a smirk, held out a leathery hand, and answered: "You humans have such interesting names."

"You realize, don't you..." Peaches interjected, "that if we use those runes to power this eight-sided monster, we are creating a Hekatek battery with every bit of potential as a pyramid? Oh yes, I've been looking up my share of mystical lore while we waited for you to show up. A nexus like this will bring light and power to a large part of the Southeastern United States, not to mention having the capacity to exchange matter with another location on the grid of ley lines."

"I guess that's the plan, then," Denny replied, smiling.

"All I know is people are starting to expect us to make things happen, and this will get some of them off my back. Let's do this!" Peaches finished, ready to roll.

For the next hour, Denny took cans of spray paint and applied the outlines of runes on every vertical surface he could reach. Passing cans to several bystanders, including gorillas, Denny taught each one a rune, and had them repeat it around the stadium's exterior.

When he was satisfied, Denny joined Lucy and the crowd of apes following Peaches to the main power switch. One last rune on the panel, and the wiring began to hum softly. The sound grew louder and a sense of vibrations, almost musical in their complexity, filled the room.

From outside, from every area surrounding the stadium, cheers went up as a bright light shot from the apex of the structure. The beam originated, not from within, but directly from the iris in the roof. It shot straight up, and was visible from miles outside the city. Streetlights came on. In buildings that were unburnt and were just without power, lights began to glow.

Lucy smiled in satisfaction as the crowd celebrated. No one saw the fires glowing in her hooded eyes.

EPILOGUE 2

EVO.144.000.MOD.1123.sCe1 | YEAR ZERO | EARTH | UNITED STATES | NEW YORK | LAKE PLACID | MCKENZIE MOUNTAIN WILDERNESS | THE ZEFF BROTHERS BUNKER

Throughout the hours and days that followed the End of the World, Vida prayed for instruction, though none had come. The voice of the One Above was gone, and Vida spent the rest of her time cleaning the bunker and taking care of Abraham and Ada. The children were terrified at first, but eventually they calmed – an eerie sort of calm, as if they understood more than Vida about the fate of the world.

Other than the noisome piles of gooey clothing, and two corpses who died of gunshot wounds during the End, the bunker was remarkably tidy. Every manual and automated process functioned well, a testament to the money used to build the haven. Of the dozen people who had initially come to the Lake Placid bunker, Vida and the children were the only survivors. Vida recycled the clothes and goo, and buried the two dead men in the small park in the center of the complex, beneath the sod and trees that were planted less than a year ago.

There was remarkably little information available, and of the signals Vida could coax from the communication center, only one was in a language she could understand. A few people had survived and maintained their location in a place called Cheyenne Mountain. The images from the screen were dark, and Vida could barely make out faces (if they could be called that) from the other end of the signal. It was as if the people in the faraway bunker had the lights off because they didn't want their trollish visages to offend. They shared information with Vida about the End from what that they had observed, and from the government channels that had been functioning at the time.

The steadily increasing death rate over the past week seemed to have tapered and stopped for some unknown reason. The current estimate was that 99% of the world had perished, and a large amount of that had been due to conflict, and random – often self-inflicted – violence. World-wide communication was in shambles, and no government had survived. People were recovering power, although anything nuclear seemed to be nonfunctional.

In almost every reported contact, humanity had changed in ways both obvious and sublime. The existence of aliens in conjunction with such a devastating weapon was puzzling. Some said it was the aliens who had fired first, while others maintained that it was in response to humanity's unprovoked strike. A rumor commonly floated was that this was all a planned step in the evolution of humanity, and that the sigil in the sky had actually triggered it. Flora and fauna had changed as well, and monstrous things walked, crawled, flew, and swam the face of the Earth. Several flights of what could only be called dragons had been seen over mountain ranges around the world.

"Miss Vida," Abe asked sweetly, "when are we going to see the pyramid in Lost Vegas?" He and Ada stood on either side of the woman's chair, holding her arms.

"Now Abraham, Ada, what have I told you about that place?" Vida tousled the boy's sandy brown curls.

Ada looked up into Vida's eyes, a serious concern in her own. "That it's a bad place, a sinful place, run by the dream witch Mhyrranda and her wicked psycho-pants?"

"That's right, mija. Mhyrranda and her sycophants are followers of Lucifer, the Father of Lies. We must never have anything to do with them. That's why we will *not* be going to Las Vegas, Abraham."

Abraham's frown was comical. "But I want to see the pyramid, Miss Vida! I'm not afraid of the wicked people!"

"We must avoid the corruption and danger and wait for another sign from God, Abraham. Now children," she continued, "let's not talk about this anymore."

The twins looked at each other before looking sadly at their nanny. Ada shook her head. She knew she had to tell her, even if she really didn't want to. She looked down at her shoes, then back up at her nanny.

"It's not over, Miss Vida," Ada shuddered. "*He* is still out there..."

EPILOGUE 3

eVo.144.000.mOd.1123.sCe2 | YEAR ONE | EARTH | MYSTERY BABYLON

IN THE FIRST MINUTE after midnight, under the baleful blind stare of the new moon, soft, fervent chanting reached its crescendo, then abruptly ceased.

Thirteen figures adorned in purple and crimson robes of finest silk, their hands linked, encircled a raised bier comprised of living bloodstone. It had been soulforged specifically for this ceremony from the innocent tears and blood of the unborn. It rested precisely at the center of the twisted ruins of the Black Tabernacle, which had been destroyed and had lain dormant since the physical death of Petrus Romanus.

He had sacrificed himself to save the world. Now, they would do the same for him.

As the final echoes of their soulsong skittered over the ruined horizon of Mystery Babylon, which once was called Rome by the mortals, the Coven of the Resurrection concluded their potent charm:

"Quia gloria eius... moriendum est..." chanted the coven, their charm complete.

For the span of a single heartbeat, nothing stirred.

Then, one of them lurched forward drunkenly, straining against the iron grasp of the two nearest, bending awkwardly at the waist. Widdershins it spread around the circle, the sensation of something darker than mere physical death, something that was eager to feast upon their souls. Bright soul's light erupted aurically about them, temporarily banishing the darkness. Something darker than even the new moon night, however, manifested from the center of the bier. It stabbed forward like a darting vampire squid, snatching the gleaming souls like the prey they truly were and returning them to the center of the bloodstone bier.

In the fleeting moment of a final thought, all the adepts of the Coven of the Resurrection knew what it was to have their immortal souls ripped from them, then greedily devoured.

As the empty robes fell silently to the ground, the Black Tabernacle pulsed once. Its fearful white light was outlined and bound by crisp, negative black light flashing from within its twisted frame. For a split-second, a ghostly image appeared atop the bier, lying in repose.

Then, the Black Tabernacle began faintly to pulsate. The white versus black light show danced about its slagged framework in resonant entrainment with the soft *thrum-thrum-thrum* that issued forth from its epicenter. Slowly, as the intensity and frequency increased, the image of a man, supine upon the bloodstone bier, translated into this world of flesh. Torn and filthy were his papal robes. Broken was his body, without life, just as it had been at the moment of his supreme sacrifice.

The Black Tabernacle's driven, pulsating lights dimmed to a low simmer, even as the *thrum-thrum-thrum* abated.

Electric blue sparks crackled as Petrus Romanus, the resurrected Black Pope, opened his eyes.

"Venite..."

SOUNDTRACK – A sample of what we were listening to while we wrote The Lightbringer's Sigil. For a complete soundtrack, please visit our website at https://anshadar.com/

"The Stage" by Avenged Sevenfold © The Stage Media Company Limited

"Aquarius" by The 5th Dimension © Sony/ATV Music Publishing

"I Speak Astronomy" by Jinjer © Napalm Records Handels GmbH

"People = Shit" by Slipknot © Sony/ATV Music Publishing LLC

"Bloody Kisses (A Death in the Family)" by Type O Negative © The All Blacks B.V.

"Spirit In The Sky" by Norman Greenbaum (p) 1969 Eric Records

"That's The Way Of The World" by Earth, Wind & Fire © Embassy Music Corporation

"Bring Me To Life" by Evanescence © BMI

"Veteran of the Psychic Wars" by Blue Oyster Cult © Sony/ATV Music Publishing LLC

"Forty Six And Two" by Tool © BMG Rights Management US LLC

"Through Glass" by Stone Sour © EMI April Music Inc

"Through the Never" by Metallica © Blackened Recordings

"Roads to Madness" by Queensryche © BMI

"Zombie" by Cranberries © Warner-Tamerlane Publishing Corp.

"Take Me Down" by The Pretty Reckless © Pretty Reckless Music / BMI

"Sirius/Eye In The Sky" by Alan Parsons Project © BMI

"More Human Than Human" by White Zombie © Psychohead Music

Dave Newton & Todd King

DAVE AND TODD MET AT NASA, and bonded over shared experiences – as in roleplaying game design, gaming, and MMOs. When Todd brought up the idea of writing again, Dave mentioned that he had some ideas percolating. These ideas meshed well with the ideas Todd had, and the two decided it had to happen. There was a story to be told, and the more they worked on it, the bigger it became, until the scope was cosmic. The two of them formed Anshadar, LLC to create the new world of EarthZero, wherein they and others will explore the boundaries of magick, morphogenetics, hekatek, and Simulation Theory.

Dave lives in Colorado with his wife and two daughters. He's discovered he doesn't hate the snow. He listens to music, is a DJ for a pirate radio station in his spare time, and is a prolific reader. He has written and co-written a variety or roleplaying games and fiction, including The Mythus FRPG, Rapture: the Second Coming, Twisted Bedtime Stories and Quest! Roleplaying for Kids.

Todd has served as a contractor for various federal agencies, including DoD, MDA, and NASA, producing multiple intellectual properties in disparate realms, including Chaotic Systems, Cryptography, Logistics, and Nanotechnology. Previously, he mutated from lead guitarist to vocalist, playing in several bands in the southern heavy metal scene, opening for acts as diverse as Lynyrd Skynyrd and Pantera. He created the SenZar role-playing game, which sold in 14 countries, and has virally influenced certain Void themes in both the current tabletop and computer genres.

Dedication

WE WOULD LIKE TO DEDICATE this book to those who came before, and those who will come after, a list too long to leave here; From the scientists, philosophers, spiritual leaders, artists and musicians who have shaped our lives, to the readers and creators who will read this, and hopefully come away entertained and inspired. And somewhere, in the infinite number of universes, to those who appear in this work - we hope we got it right. But most importantly, we dedicate this book to two people who influenced and touched our lives, and whose creative spirits inspire us still: Gary Gygax and Stan Lee. Thank you, gentlemen—you are missed.

Anshadar, LLC is pleased to present this first novel in the EarthZero Evolution series: The Lightbringer's Sigil. Stay tuned as we give you more science fiction, fantasy, and horror.

We are just getting started!

Quest! Roleplaying for Kids
The Lightbringer's Sigil
The Anshadar Effect (coming soon)
The Death Horde (coming soon)

www.ingramcontent.com/pod-product-compliance
Lightning Source LLC
Chambersburg PA
CBHW070538030726
47505CB00001B/75